LUTHOR HUSS

CHRIS WRAIGHT

BLACK LIBRARY

Dedicated, with love, to Hannah.

A BLACK LIBRARY PUBLICATION

First published in Great Britain in 2012 by
The Black Library,
Games Workshop Ltd.,
Willow Road, Nottingham,
NG7 2WS, UK.

10 9 8 7 6 5 4 3 2 1

Cover illustration by Cheoljoo Lee.

UK ISBN: 978 1 84970 130 3
US ISBN: 978 1 84970 131 0

See the Black Library on the internet at
www.blacklibrary.com

Find out more about Games Workshop
and the world of Warhammer at
www.games-workshop.com

Printed and bound in the UK by CPI Group (UK) Ltd, Croydon, CR0 4YY

This is a dark age, a bloody age, an age of daemons
and of sorcery. It is an age of battle and death, and of the
world's ending. Amidst all of the fire, flame and fury
it is a time, too, of mighty heroes, of bold deeds
and great courage.

At the heart of the Old World sprawls the Empire, the
largest and most powerful of the human realms. Known for
its engineers, sorcerers, traders and soldiers, it is
a land of great mountains, mighty rivers, dark forests
and vast cities. And from his throne in Altdorf reigns
the Emperor Karl Franz, sacred descendant of the
founder of these lands, Sigmar, and wielder
of his magical warhammer.

But these are far from civilised times. Across the
length and breadth of the Old World, from the knightly
palaces of Bretonnia to ice-bound Kislev in the far north,
come rumblings of war. In the towering Worlds Edge
Mountains, the orc tribes are gathering for another assault.
Bandits and renegades harry the wild southern lands of
the Border Princes. There are rumours of rat-things, the
skaven, emerging from the sewers and swamps across the
land. And from the northern wildernesses there is the
ever-present threat of Chaos, of daemons and beastmen
corrupted by the foul powers of the Dark Gods.
As the time of battle draws ever nearer,
the Empire needs heroes
like never before.

PROLOGUE

RICKARD SCHLECHT COULD not sleep.

The days passed in a fog, dull-coloured and blurred at the edges. The sun would rise, grey and thin through black branches, and he would walk. For miles he would walk, stumbling against rocks and roots, no longer noticing the blood in his old boots.

At night he would collapse, curled up against the bole of a tree, shivering as the wind cut at him. His mind would wander, turning down the dark paths of the forest as if it had left his body and become a spectre of madness.

His eyes never shut. They stayed stretched wide, staring out at the dark. He saw the animals, their eyes glowing like mirrors in the moonlight, before they flickered away and loped off into the endless, formless night.

At times, he would forget where he was. He would forget his name, his past, all that had happened at Goeringen.

That was the closest he came to sleeping. For a few, blessed moments, he could forget.

Then he'd come back round, stomach lurching, heart hammering, hands grasping at the leaf matter.

His jaw would snap up, and memory would flood back.

7

He couldn't forget who he was. He couldn't forget what had happened.

He could not sleep.

BEFORE, JUST WEEKS before, the world had been different.

Reisen had been a poor, isolated place, but Rickard Schlecht had made a decent enough life for himself there. The long summer had been waning, ushering in a brief time of plenty before the coming cold season, and he'd still entertained hopes that Erika would do more than just look at him with her half-approving, half-mocking smiles. He'd eaten like all the others, worked like all the others, slept like all the others.

But even then, just before everything changed, he would dream, and those dreams were dark. On the morning when it happened, it was screaming that woke Rickard from his dark dreams.

He started then, rubbing at his eyes. He pushed himself up, shoving his heavy blanket from the straw mat of bedding. Then he clambered to his feet, sweaty from night-terrors. He had only slept fitfully, a few hours before the dawn, kept conscious by a nebulous dread that had no obvious origin. Harsh, cold light bled from under the door. He rubbed his fingers across his eyes again, trying to scrub the residue of slumber away.

He had dreamed of... what? It was hard to remember.

Rickard stumbled outside, letting the door to his hovel slam shut behind him. The glare of early dawn lit up the village street, making his eyes water and his head throb.

Everything hardened into sharp relief: the dirty wattle of the walls, greasy puddles in the beaten mud, stalks of old thatch that jutted from the eaves like tufts of unruly hair. A cockerel crowed somewhere on the other side of the village, but the noise was strangled and strange.

More screams cut through the air, over and over, shrill shrieks of horrified misery. A woman's screams, bloated with disbelief. Rickard stumbled towards the sound.

Other villagers had been woken by it. A crowd of them converged on a mean dwelling just inside Reisen's thick wooden gates. Rickard knew it, just like he knew all the dwellings in the village. The woman who lived there was called Klara. She had given birth only a few months ago after two years of trying to conceive, and they had said that Shallya had blessed her at last.

Now she crouched on the ground, a filthy dress hanging from her skinny shoulders, wailing and rocking. There was something in her arms, something heavy and wrapped in strips of cloth.

Gerhardt was there, wearing his stupid headman's breeches and cloak and trying to impose himself on the situation. A sparse crowd had formed around the woman, curious and prying.

Rickard found himself standing next to Erika. He suddenly noticed how bad his headache was. Erika looked terrible – as bad as he felt – and shivered in the morning chill like the rest of them.

'What's going on?' he asked, grimacing as his thick, parched lips moved.

Erika nodded over to the woman's house.

'Look at that,' she said.

In front of an open doorway was a long pole, about six feet tall and lodged in the mud. Feathers were stuck to it, and tufts of what looked like horsehair, and clusters of…

Skulls. Very small skulls.

Rickard stared at them, blinking stupidly. Grey light reflected from the blood on the wood.

The woman's screaming became painful. He winced, and began to walk away, pushing past Erika.

She grabbed his wrist, pulling him back.

'The gates were locked,' she said, her mouth tight. 'They were locked *all night*.'

Rickard tried to shake her off. His head was hammering. Gods, he needed to sleep.

'So it's some joke,' he snapped.

She wouldn't let go. Erika kept her fingers clamped tight around his wrist. He'd forgotten how strong she was when she wanted something.

'No joke,' she said, forcing him to turn round and face the scene.

The woman was still rocking. As she moved, her dress fell away from her arms, exposing the bundle at her breast.

Rickard saw what was there and the night-terror came rushing back, as vivid as it had been during his dreams.

I saw this.

Klara's child did not cry. A swollen tongue lolled from its open mouth, laced with lines of yellow saliva. Two empty eye sockets stared upwards, bloody and hollow. Two chubby arms ended in hooves. Below the waist, things got messier.

Rickard stared. He forgot his headache as his gorge rose.

I saw them do this.

'The forest,' he murmured, suddenly transfixed by the warped child.

'What?' asked Erika.

'The forest.'

Erika shook her head in disgust.

'Is that all you can say? The poor bitch. She waited so long.'

Rickard began to shake. He saw the goat-creature again, the thing that had stalked through his dreams, grinning.

It has been here. It came through the walls.

'We have to leave,' he said.

Erika began to laugh at him. He shook off her grip and grabbed her by the arms. His fingers dug into her flesh, and she stopped laughing. Her dark eyes looked up at his, and he saw the fear engraved in her fleshy features.

'Now,' said Rickard. 'We have to leave now.' Even through his thick head and churning insides, he knew exactly what was going on.

The goat-creature. I saw it. I saw it change the child.

'All of us, out of the village,' he said. 'Before the dark comes again. We have to leave.'

He could feel himself repeat the words. He knew how stupid he sounded. He knew he wasn't an articulate man – hell, even old Gerhardt could spit the words out better than him.

Erika didn't laugh like she usually did. She said nothing, but just looked scared. All of them looked scared.

Only the woman screamed. She choked up sobs through those screams, rocking back and forth, clutching the mutant child with desperate hands.

'They will come for it,' said Rickard, turning away, feeling the nausea swill around in his stomach as he moved. 'They will come back. Oh Morr, they will come back.'

Erika's lip stared to tremble. She looked at the malformed child, and then back at him.

'Where can we go?' she asked, pathetically.

Rickard didn't know the answer to that. He felt stupid and absurd even in the heat of his conviction.

'Anywhere,' he said, as if that helped. 'Anywhere but here.'

THEY LISTENED TO him. Unbelievably, they did what he told them. Rickard didn't even know why he was ordering them around, but the sight of the child had made them all too scared to think properly and Gerhardt didn't have anything sensible to say, so they listened to him.

Only Klara remained behind. She wouldn't move, and just squatted on the ground, screaming and weeping. Another woman tried to take the child from her, and got a face raked with dirty fingernails for her trouble.

By the time the rest of the village had been roused, the late summer sun was high in the sky, burning the morning mist away and dispelling some of the bite from the air. The villagers of Reisen trailed out from the gates before noon, nearly forty of them laden with bags, staring out at the trees in the distance like children peeping nervously round their mother's skirts.

'How long?' asked Gerhardt, his stubbly jowls quivering. He didn't seem to mind that Rickard was calling the shots.

Rickard shook his head irritably. He minded. He minded a lot.

'I don't know,' he said. 'A few days. Just let's get clear of those damn trees.'

'Why are you so sure?'

'Dreams. Morr knows why, but I'm dreaming all this.'

Gerhardt nodded, looking satisfied. Drakwalders placed plenty of store by night visions.

In a long, straggling column, the villagers marched up the valley and away from the fringes of the Drakwald. A few of them looked ruefully at the fields of crops, heavy and ready for harvest, but none of them stopped moving.

North of Reisen, the land rolled in a sea of hills and dales, studded with messy copses, outriders of the deep woods that lay unbroken to the south. Few settlements had been raised there despite the fertility of the land. The villagers went swiftly through the empty country, sweating under the sun.

'Do you hear that?' asked Erika, hurrying to catch up with Rickard at the head of the column.

'I hear nothing,' said Rickard.

'That's what I mean. No birds.'

Rickard stopped to listen. The countryside was green, healthy, and silent.

He started walking again. Pointing such things out didn't improve his mood.

'So where are we going?' Erika asked, trotting to keep up. Gods, she could be annoyingly needy.

'North,' he said.

'And then?'

Rickard snorted.

'Anywhere with proper walls and men with more than pitchforks and kitchen knives in their hands. There's a place up the valley; we can shelter there.'

He looked back over the rest of the villagers, and his heart sank. They were going too slowly and would be lucky to make it by nightfall.

They had to get there before nightfall.

'Goeringen,' he said, and the name of it, solid and reassuring, gave him some hope that everything would blow over quickly and they could get back to the fields before the crops rotted in them. 'The place is called Goeringen.'

* * *

THERE WAS NO welcome at Goeringen. As the sky turned deep blue and the first stars appeared in the east, the inhabitants stared at the new arrivals with curt, hostile faces. Men were still repairing the old walls, working quickly while the light remained. Fires burned in the streets within. Everyone, so it seemed, clutched a weapon.

'You can't turn us away,' said Rickard, holding his ground before the town's headman. He was weary from the march, and his lids were heavy. He needed to sleep.

The brawny, thick-necked man gazed at the Reisen refugees doubtfully. It looked like he wanted to.

'How many of you can fight?' he asked.

Rickard shrugged.

'All of us, if we need to.'

The headman smirked wryly and gestured to an old, tired house across the street.

A woman stood in front of it, her dress lit up red from the fires. She stumbled back and forth, mouth open, eyes blank. In her arms was a bundle, wrapped in dirty linen.

Rickard saw the tiny hooves hanging from the bundle, loose and waving as the woman wandered aimlessly. He saw the blood on the cloth, stained black.

His heart sank.

Here, too.

'Yes,' said the headman, grimly. 'You'll need to fight.'

HATRED, IT TURNED out, had a stench.

It stank of musk, of blood, of matted, wet fur. The smell came before anything else, thick and cloying and clogging up the air.

After that came the flies, swarming in the night like solid clots of darkness. They got into faces, under clothes, down long leather boots. Then they bit, puncturing the skin and sucking greedily like infants.

'The fires!' cried Goeringen's headman, striding up to the tall wooden gates. 'Keep them going!'

Men waited for him by the walls, all armed, all nervous. Torches flared red in their mounts along the walls. Bonfires roared in the marketplace, spitting and cracking on old, dry wood.

Rickard perched up on the top of the walls, close by the gates, staring out into the gloom. On either side of him, young men waited, poised in crabbed fear for what was coming. One had already soiled himself. Another was mumbling some prayer to some god, over and over again, stammering the words out through his silent tears.

In the village below, children were screaming. Nothing their mothers could do would silence them. Panic shimmered in the stinking air, infectious and pungent.

Rickard couldn't make much out through the smoke, but he knew that *they* were out there. He saw the goat-face again, the one that had run through his dreams, toothy and smiling. It wouldn't leave his mind.

I couldn't get far enough away.

Down below, down where the scrubland ran up to the walls, movement broke out. Shadows became fluid, running like molten metal. Rickard saw limbs, fleeting outlines, claws, skittering things. A low growling broke out, and the earth seemed to tremble.

And then, far away, drums. Dull, heavy drums, hammered out in a broken rhythm, over and over again.

Rickard looked up, blinking the smoke out of his eyes. Morrslieb hung low in the sky, yellow and gravid. In the distance, the treetops were stained with its sick light. The branches rustled, jostling like animals.

The beasts were coming. They were coming through the hidden paths, out of the deep places, out from the hidden glades where stones shone with warplight and the shadows cackled and whispered.

Rickard had been awake for too long. His fatigue made him suggestible, and he saw phantoms everywhere. He turned to his left, and the mumbling man there suddenly looked like the hunched goat-creature of his dreams. He twitched in shock, almost sticking his blade between the man's ribs.

Calm down! Concentrate!

He fingered his blunt sword, feeling sweat make the grip sticky. His heart was thumping, fast and deep. Keeping his eyes open scared him; closing them was worse. There was no escape from the drums, from the stench, from the maddening buzz of the flies.

The beasts were coming.

The trees rustled more violently. Something broke from cover, hard to the right, something rippling and sinuous. Other shapes, dark against the dark of the night, limped and scuttled up to the walls.

Behind them, the roaring started up, wet and throaty. As if orchestrated by a single mind, many pairs of eyes opened at once, lodged in the eaves of the forest like sets of jewels on black satin. Hundreds of them stared at Goeringen, and their hatred burned pale in the night.

Rickard watched, transfixed. He felt delirious from fatigue.

'Blessed Sigmar...' he muttered.

He needed to sleep. If things had been otherwise, he would have rested at Goeringen. He was in no condition to fight.

He blinked firmly, squeezing the visions from his eyes. He took up his blade, and watched the metal tremble.

Down below, the pairs of eyes slunk out into the open, solidifying into the hulking shapes of beastmen. Their drums rose to a crescendo, rattling and booming.

As the horns blared out from the forest, Rickard Schlecht gripped his weapon and tried not to go mad from fear.

His vision was blurry, and his stomach growled from emptiness. He wanted nothing more than to curl up against the stone, eyes closed, and dream the horror away.

He knew he couldn't.

The beasts had come; real this time, not in his dreams.

He couldn't forget where he was. He couldn't forget what had happened.

He could not sleep.

CHAPTER ONE

BLOOD RAN DOWN the man's chin, sparkling in the candlelight.

Lukas Eichmann watched it trickle. He took no pleasure in it, for it indicated only damage and not the certainty he'd hoped to gain.

He let out a thin sigh and stood up, flexing his broken knuckles. He let the cudgel thud back onto the tabletop.

He felt tired. His shoulders ached.

Empty.

'You want me to take him now?' asked Udo.

Eichmann didn't respond immediately. For a moment, just a moment, he wanted to remain alone with his thoughts.

'No,' he said. 'No, I'll deal with it. Clean yourself up and wait for me at the temple. Gorbach will want to see the report before dark.'

Udo grunted. His heavy, bald head nodded slightly, glistening in the candle-dark. Eichmann saw the mess of blood on the man's jerkin as he moved away, stomping out of the catacomb's narrow doorway and up the stone stairs to the cellar above.

The chamber fell silent. The dead man stayed slumped in the chair, his chest unmoving, his jaw slack.

19

Eichmann ran his expert eye over the bruises on the man's face. They were purple and yellow and black, like rain-heavy storm clouds in a winter sky. The man's lids were dry with crusted blood. His teeth lay in his lap like pearls lost from a string.

Eichmann felt no pride. He felt no savage satisfaction in the elimination of another threat to the purity of the faithful. The body before him was just a lump of gristle and bone, held together with rolls of fat, coupled to a head full of stupid, naive ideas.

He didn't even blame the man. The world was a hard place. The powers of corruption were subtle and old, whereas men like Brego Workel were simple and possessed of crude tastes.

Eichmann turned away from the corpse, absently brushing some dried body fluids from his long leather coat. His legs ached from the long hours of hunching, head low, listening to Workel's gurgling, confused confessions.

He collected his leaves of parchment together, shuffling them from where they'd fallen on the tabletop. In all likelihood, no one would read the report he would write from those notes. He would painstakingly transcribe Workel's more coherent words, annotating them with his own observations, before composing recommendations for further investigation. He would write slowly, taking care to express himself clearly. The script would be neat, the prose efficient.

Even now, twenty years after receiving his witch hunter's medallion, Eichmann still wrote the same way he had as an acolyte. So many reports had been completed since then, all as beautifully constructed as each other, all rotting gently in the archives of a dozen temples across Middenland.

And he would do it again, knowing how pointless it was. He would take the notes up to his personal chamber and break out quill, ink and sand. He would pause to collect himself, praying for guidance, before making the first marks on the rough surface.

The ritual was important. Every ritual was important. If he ever let go of the ritual then perhaps he would remember too closely how he felt when the interrogations were over. He would see the faces of those he had killed, and, perhaps, the faces of those he had failed to save.

So he would write, taking time to do it carefully, knowing no one would read the words he agonised over. He would record everything worthy of mention, taking account of Workel's background and his extenuating circumstances, weighing up whether his death had been justly merited, commending his soul to the mercy of Sigmar, and of Morr, and of any other recognised deity who might take an interest.

And, perhaps, when all that was done and Gorbach had been consulted and other duties attended to, then Eichmann might forget the long, difficult hours of questioning. He might forget the hot, sticky feel of the blood on his hands and the dying echo of the man's whimpers.

It was always possible.

Eichmann looked down at his notes, hoping to find enough there to justify the decisions he'd made. A candle guttered out, making the chamber even darker. His lips moved as he silently read.

Plenty of incriminating material had been gathered. There were names, places, and suggestions of deeper taint, and all of it would be useful.

Eichmann only paused as he came across the final word, the one that had caused him so much trouble, the one that

Workel hadn't wanted to say and for which Udo's brutal services had been, of tedious necessity, employed.

That word would require further study. Eichmann didn't recognise it. As he looked at the text, his mouth felt dry. He had trouble mouthing it.

Hylaeus.

For some reason, it made him uneasy. It shouldn't have done. It was only a word, probably a pass or codename used by someone Workel only had a hazy knowledge of.

Another candle flickered out. Eichmann stirred himself, stowing the sheaf of parchment under his arm and collecting his instruments from where he'd placed them.

Hylaeus.

He had lingered too long in that dank, dark catacomb. His tired mind was beginning to play tricks on him.

He left, closing the door behind him, climbing the stairs wearily.

Back in the catacomb, the candles burned for a little while longer, illuminating the table, the chair, the stone walls, and the face of Brego Workel.

One by one the flames went out and shadows crept across the dead man's broken features, distorting them and making it look, for a little while before the utter darkness came, like he was smiling.

MILA EICHEN HURRIED down the forest path, her hips swaying under heavy skirts. The burden of firewood on her right shoulder weighed her down, making her list to one side and walk as if she had a limp.

It was getting cold and the sun was already weak. Summer had waned quickly that year, and the heat drained from the early evening air like water running out of a tipped glass.

She didn't like collecting firewood. Nobody did. The real woodcutters went in teams and carried rusty swords at their belts. The foragers, like her, stayed close to the fringes of the woodland, never straying far from the open spaces.

Even there, picking up fallen branches and kindling, you could feel the oppressive anger of the trees. You would stoop to pick something up and then hear a sudden crack or a low creaking. Then you would turn, expecting to see some horror with twigs for fingers leaning over you, and there would be nothing. Just the deep green shadows and the brush of leaves in the wind.

Your heart would be beating by then. You would know, somehow, that the spirit of the forest had been stirred, and that it hated you, and that it hated everything the hand of man did to it.

But firewood had to be gathered. Water had to be boiled, and food had to be cooked, and so women like Mila Eichen crossed the fields and tramped through the forest marches, on their guard, taking what they could and keeping their eyes open.

She walked as fast as she could, keeping to the patches of weak sunlight on her left and averting her eyes from the shadows on her right. The wind had picked up, and the overhanging branches waved lazily, trailing against her shoulder and snagging at her clothes.

'Late, to be working.'

Mila jumped, nearly losing her grip on the firewood.

Sat down between the roots of an old oak, half-hidden under the shade of its eaves, a man in brown robes was watching her.

He was old, with a hooked nose and sunken cheeks. His hair hung in straggling locks from a balding pate, and his hands stuck out from his sleeves like claws.

'So it is,' she replied defensively, brushing her blonde hair back with her free hand and trying not to look flustered. 'That's why I'm headed back.'

The man smiled, exposing a gaptoothed grin. The teeth that remained were yellow and uneven.

'It's still light, girl. Come here and make an old man happy.'

Mila stifled an instinctive gesture of disgust.

'You shouldn't be sitting there,' she said. 'You'll make them angry.'

'Angry?'

The man shook his head wryly and reached into the grass for something.

'Superstition, girl,' he said, pulling out an old warhammer. For all his emaciation, he could hold it well enough still. The icon of the comet was visible on its old head and there were runes carved into the shaft. 'This is the real power. Stop worrying about old stories and sit down here next to me. I could teach you a lot.'

Mila started walking again. If she'd been younger and stupider, she might have been cowed by him. She knew girls that had been, and she had heard them afterwards, sobbing in the small hours of the night.

'You should be ashamed, Father,' she muttered, leaving him behind and hurrying along the path.

She heard his laughter following her. She kept going, hoping he'd stay where he was, hoping the roots of the oak would creep over his legs and pin him there, breaking his bones.

Everyone in the village knew what he was like, and everyone knew what he did. But what could you do? He was the priest. He was the representative of Sigmar, the guardian of mankind.

Mila spat on the ground, feeling her unease turn quickly into frustrated anger.

'The old goat,' she mumbled under her breath, stumbling towards home, reflecting as she did so on quite how much she hated priests. 'I hope he chokes.'

'HYLAEUS,' SAID WITCH Hunter General Ferdinand Gorbach.

'That's right,' said Eichmann.

'Means nothing to me.'

'A shame. I hoped it might.'

Eichmann sat stiffly in his seat, his fingers steepled before him. His severe, angular face was set rigid, as always. His report lay on the large oak desk in front of him, still rolled up.

On the far side of the desk was Gorbach, his superior officer in the Middenheim temple. The chambers were his, and they were as cold, old and obscure as their owner. The veins in his bulbous nose were broken and his hands shook as they moved. Only his eyes, set deep under protruding feathered eyebrows, gave away the extent of the leathery old intelligence within.

'You have enough to make further enquiries?' Gorbach asked, leaving the report untouched in front of him.

'I do,' said Eichmann. 'The man Workel gave me other names: Arlich, Menningen. Some, like Karl Bohfels, were already under observation. I'd like to move now, before they notice his disappearance.'

Gorbach pursed his cracked lips. His arthritic fingers trembled as he reached for a silver dish at his side.

'And what, exactly, do you suspect?' he asked, pulling a wizened grape from the bowl.

'Worship of unholy powers. The type is unclear to me, but there's been traffic in proscribed articles. Workel had vials of blood in his lodgings – chicken, I think – and texts instructing on their use.'

'Small stuff, Lukas.'

'Indeed,' said Eichmann. 'But I would not see it grow.'

Gorbach popped the grape into his mouth and chewed slowly.

'You still have that man in your retinue?'

'Rafe Udo, yes.'

'I do not like him.'

'No one likes him. That's the point.'

Gorbach swallowed. The movement looked painful. With some effort, the old man sat forwards in his chair, resting his hands on the desk.

'Listen to me,' he said, fixing those dour eyes on Eichmann. 'These are difficult days. The Ar-Ulric is watching everything, and there are people here who would use any excuse to undermine us. This isn't Altdorf – you'll have to go carefully.'

Eichmann remained unmoving.

'I always go carefully,' he said.

'You, yes. Just keep the leash on your dog. I can't afford to have trouble, not if this leads to anyone with a decent name.'

'So is that the problem?' asked Eichmann, speaking coldly. 'Where this might lead?'

Gorbach gave him a weary look.

'If we need to cut throats, we'll cut throats. But *quietly*.'

Eichmann bowed.

'I understand,' he said. 'So I have your sanction to pursue?'

'Of course. You always do.'

Gorbach looked at Eichmann intently then. For a moment, his age-mottled features softened a little.

'How much rest have you had lately?'

Eichmann hesitated.

'I… enough,' he said.

'Get some more. You look terrible. Your eyes are hollow and your hair is going white. That shouldn't be happening, not at your age.'

'I feel fine.'

'You don't look it,' said Gorbach. 'I'm serious, man – relax a little. Delegate to your acolytes. Perhaps you don't need to spend quite so long on these reports. I mean, they're beautiful things, but we're not loremasters. If there's something troubling you, something in particular, then you should tell me.'

Eichmann, just for a second, lost his composure. Possible replies flitted through his mind, as if deeply buried and longing for release. He hadn't expected this, not from Gorbach.

I have seen terrible things.

I have done terrible things.

When I sleep, I see faces. And I rarely sleep.

But he said none of that. The iron mask of assurance, the mask he'd worn for twenty years, barely flickered.

'That's good advice, sir,' he said. 'If anything occurs to me, I'll be sure to come to you.'

Gorbach shook his head resignedly.

'See that you do,' he said, and reached for another grape. 'And I wish you luck with this. Go carefully, and take no chances.'

Eichmann rose from his chair and stood stiffly to attention.

'Thank you, sir. But, really, there is no luck – it is all in Sigmar's will, or it is not. So your wishes, though well intentioned, are irrelevant.'

Gorbach rolled his eyes.

'Of course,' he said. 'You're right, Eichmann. As always, you're right. Now get out of my office and leave me alone.'

THE FIRE ROARED, and Mila danced around it.

The village was not a large one and the space at its centre could only accommodate a modest blaze, but they made the best of it. Arms linked, the inhabitants of Helgag whirled around it, laughing and slurring in a warm fug of alcohol and roasted meat. Above them, the stars were out, clear and sharp.

Everyone was there. The men rolled around, stomachs tight and swollen. The women spun on their ankles, letting the hems of their dresses fly out. Children, wide-eyed from excitement and lack of sleep, chewed on scraps of warm meat and chased each other around the walls of the houses, yelling like pups.

Mittherbst, the equal-day of the waning year, was an excuse for revelling, and it was always taken enthusiastically.

Mila withdrew from the dance at last, her chest heaving and her skin shining with sweat. She staggered over to a bench where rows of jugs lay, half-empty.

She sat heavily, and the wood flexed under her ample rump. She took a jug up, and the beer went down her throat smoothly.

Over by the fire, the dance continued. It was a wild thing, all flailing limbs and thrown-back heads. The dancers threw black shadows across the ground. Mila watched them all, still panting, reeling from beer and exertion.

'He's over there, girl.'

Another woman sat next to Mila, and the bench groaned beneath two sets of buttocks.

They could have been sisters, those two. Both were

big-boned, smooth-fleshed women in their late teens. Their hair was in plaits, Mila's ash-blonde, the other earth-brown. They had the quick eyes, ready smiles and flushed cheeks of invincible youth.

'I saw him,' said Mila, frowning unconvincingly. 'Let him dance.'

The other woman laughed and slapped her affectionately.

'He won't do a thing, the dumb ox,' she said, pouring herself a drink. 'You'll have to do it for him.'

'Enough, Margrit – why are you so obsessed about this? You could do with a man yourself.'

'Only because I love you, you fat cow, and want you to be happy. Go and dance with him!'

Mila shook her head, smiling, but didn't take her eyes off the man.

Hans, old Gerhard's son, careered past. Sure, his lips were too big, and his breath wasn't the freshest, and he clumped around the bonfire like a milking cow swaying to the stool, but he was sweet and didn't strut around like he saw every girl in the village as a chunk of property.

Mila reckoned he'd work half-decently and wouldn't drink himself to death, beat her up or try to sell the children into serfdom, which made him a pretty good catch by the standards of Helgag. And so she reckoned she could learn to ignore those floppy, drooling lips; maybe even find them appealing, in time.

She watched him, her eyes glittering from the firelight, smiling, dreaming of things that, for now, were only on the cusp of being realised.

'And where's Father Reilach?' asked Margrit, swaying in time to the beat of the stamping feet and Pieter's flea-bitten regimental drum.

At the mention of the old priest, Mila snorted derisively. 'Don't know,' she said. 'Don't care.'

Margrit's eyebrow raised.

'He's not here? The gates have closed for the night.'

'And?' Mila rounded on Margrit and poked a pudgy finger in her face. 'I saw him on the way back from the woods, the dirty old dog. I don't care if he's stuck out there, howling on his own and having his flesh pulled from his bones by wood-sprites. I'd be glad of it. By Morr and Sigmar and Taal, I hope that happens.'

Margrit laughed and pushed Mila's hand out of her face.

'So what's he done to you?'

'Stop talking about him,' she said, scowling. 'You make the beer sour.'

Margrit laughed again and put her arm around Mila.

'Enough, then. Tell me more about Hans, and how you're going to trip him up and drag him off into the straw and have sixteen screaming babies.'

And Mila laughed then, a clear, immature sound that merged with the laughs of others. Half the village was laughing, or drinking, or swaying along to the dull thud of the drum.

So it was that no one noticed, right out at the edge of Helgag where the houses ran out and the stockade reared up, the gates creaking open, pushed by two sets of emaciated hands.

So it was that no one noticed long fingers grip the wood, wrapped in scraps of grey flesh, and no one noticed the ranks of eyes in the dark beyond, silent, moving slowly.

They just danced, laughing and calling out as if the world held no terrors and the warm flames would last forever.

CHAPTER TWO

BOTH MOONS HUNG over Middenheim, glaring over a red sky. The fires of Mittherbst burned on every street corner, broken by the silhouettes of dancing figures. Over the figures reared the Temple of Ulric, vast and black in the night.

Eichmann regarded the revellers coolly. He was dressed in the long leather coat favoured by his peers and kept the wide brim of his hat low over his eyes. Two flintlock pistols nestled at his waist, each one inscribed with passages from Sigmarite scripture and still glistening with drops of holy water.

'Why do they do it?' he asked.

'Sir?' asked Udo, looking bleary-eyed and half-awake.

'Why do they fill their bodies with such filth? They'll drink until dawn, making themselves ill and wasting the following day's labour. Every festival is the same. I do not understand it.'

Udo rubbed his face. His pug-nosed features reddened as his leather-gloved hands massaged the flesh.

'Everyone likes a drink, sir,' he said, cracking his knuckles and flexing his arms.

'I don't.'

'Most people, then.'

31

Udo stood taller than his master, and much broader. His head was bald and latticed with old scars like fine lacework. A long iron maul hung from his waist, tucked next to a broad-bladed dirk. His nose had been broken more than once, and one eye didn't open fully, giving him a perpetually sceptical expression.

'They'll damn themselves,' muttered Eichmann, turning away from the bonfires and walking down one of the darker streets. 'This place is ripe for damnation.'

Udo followed him with his rolling, brawler's gait.

'That it is,' he agreed. 'Just like everywhere else.'

The two men passed empty buildings, tall and gloomy in the night. Everything in Middenheim pressed close to everything else. Brick walls were surmounted with wattle-and-daub extensions, which were topped with wooden outgrowths and crowned with teetering towers and copper domes. The lintels of the houses peered over the narrow alleys, cutting out the light of the moons and drenching the mud, straw and cobbles in deep shadow. Some streets never saw sunlight even in the height of the day; at night, they were pits of gloom.

Away from the raucous bonfires the shrieks of the revellers became dim and muffled. Eichmann began to move more fluidly, as if simply being near such behaviour put him on edge.

'So I'm wondering, sir,' said Udo. 'Could this not have waited until the festival was over?'

'Feel like you're missing out?'

Udo tried not to think about the White Bull and the cheap beer in the barrels there.

Perhaps for the best; he'd left all that behind.

'Not at all,' he said, not wholly convincingly. 'This is what I live for.'

'I find that reassuring,' said Eichmann.

The witch hunter stopped walking and squatted down beside a heavy iron drain cover. He pulled out a jangling ring of keys and began sorting through them.

Udo looked at the cover uncertainly.

'Really?' he asked. 'Down there?'

Eichmann nodded.

'Afraid so. This leads to the cellars under Bohfels's house.'

Udo exhaled resignedly.

'Always the cellars.'

'I know. You'd think they'd realise this whole place is built on tunnels.'

Eichmann slotted a key into the lock and opened it with a grating twist. He grasped the edge of the cover with both hands and hauled upwards. It stayed where it was.

'A little stiff, sir?'

Udo bent down and gripped the edge of the cover. With a grunt, he pulled it clear. The stench was foul, and his face creased in disgust.

'Thank you,' said Eichmann, swinging his legs into the gap. It was narrow, but just wide enough for a man to slip through. 'Follow me down.'

Eichmann plunged knee-deep into a slowly moving stream of watery filth. The stink of it rose up his nostrils, making him gag. He waded forwards, ignoring the muck as it swilled over the top of his high boots.

Udo landed behind him with a crash, throwing up a deluge of slops, scraps and night soil.

'Blood of Sigmar,' he spat, taking his maul up in his favoured left hand and holding his nose with the right. 'You never get used to it.'

Eichmann took an iron casket lantern from his belt. He sparked a flint, and pale light wavered into existence. He took a moment to adjust a complicated-looking set of lenses, after which the lantern threw its beams out across the walls of the drain.

Ahead of them, a river of murky brown slime ran away into the dark, foamy and rancid. The roof of the tunnel curved over, just above head height and lined with greasy bricks.

The walls were broken at irregular intervals by stone pillars. Runes had been carved into them, and the angular marks were worn and ancient-looking.

Udo sniffed.

'Dwarfs,' he said, making it sound like an expletive.

'A long time ago,' said Eichmann, striding off through the river of sewage and holding the lantern high. 'Now it's just you, me and – when we get far enough down – a few filthy heretics.'

Udo followed the witch hunter, treading heavily and wincing against the smell.

'Can't wait,' he said, swinging the maul purposefully.

MILA LAUGHED WHEN the first screams broke out, thinking they were part of the festivities. She kept laughing, clutching her sides, until the first invaders broke into the open and bodies started to fall to the earth.

For a few heartbeats longer, she stood swaying, trying to make sense of what was going on. The world was spinning already, rocked by the moving light of the fire and her substantial intake of coarse beer.

Father Reilach stumbled into the circle of firelight. He had changed. His old face had become even more skull-like, and the skin had broken where it was stretched too tight. Strings of black blood, dried and scabby, laced his bleached flesh like tattoos. He walked strangely, as if his knee-joints had calcified solid. His ruined head swept back and forth, searching for something.

'Make an old man happy,' he croaked, and his voice was as cold as Morr's cowl. 'Make an old man happy. Make an old man happy.'

Mila froze. The priest's unseeing eyes locked on her. He opened his mouth in a wide grin, and the skin at his mouth-edges ripped apart.

'Come here, girl, and make an old man happy.'

He stumbled towards her, arms out. Behind him, more limping figures emerged into the firelight, shuffling and muttering. Their skin was dull grey and patchy. Raw bone glistened in the flame-light, powder-white and as dry as saltpetre.

Mila screamed. She turned tail, running from the shambling horde with all the speed she could muster. Inebriation was suddenly replaced by a cold, sharp terror.

All around her, men and women did the same. No one stood up to the creeping mass of shambling half-men. The air, which had been swollen with life and joy, instantly took on a sickening tang. Raw fear flickered in the firelight, resonating from the walls of the houses and rising from the packed earth below.

Mila careered around the walls of old Pieter's hovel, hardly noticing which direction she was going in. Her heart beat in her ribcage like a small animal scrabbling to get out.

Then she remembered Margrit.

Mila skidded to a halt. From somewhere, fresh flames had broken out. Everything in Helgag had descended into a wavering, shaking patchwork of red and black shadows, punctuated by shouts and cries of pure terror.

'Margrit!' she screamed into the night. 'Margrit, girl! Where are you?'

More shrieks rang out from the way she'd come. Some

were women's voices, pulsating with horror. Others were men's, just as high-pitched as the women's and equally warped by terror. She'd never heard men scream before, not like that, and it froze her blood as much as the sight of the walking dead.

Mila barged her way into Pieter's house. The toothless old fool had once been in the regiments and everyone knew he kept his precious sword somewhere in there.

'Shallya preserve me, this is madness,' Mila muttered as she started rooting hurriedly through piles of filthy clothing. From outside, she could hear the cries coming closer.

It was dark in the hovel, nearly pitch-dark. She began to panic.

I have to get out.

As she pushed aside the heavy wooden frame of a crude cot, her fingers connected with something metallic.

I have to get out! Leave it!

She grabbed the hilt, and pulled the long blade free. It snagged on something, and she cursed again.

Leave it!

Fingers, cold and hard, grabbed her shoulder.

She screamed again, jumping from the touch, and the sword came free. Blindly, animated by panic, she swung it round.

The blade, still in its old wound-leather scabbard, thumped heavily against the shoulder of the creature that had grabbed her, and the grip of the fingers released. She swung it again, and again, bludgeoning whatever had followed her into the hovel.

The hovel's rickety door banged open again in the fire-hot wind, throwing angry light across the scene. Mila saw Father Reilach's devastated face, no more than two feet away from hers, still grinning manically.

'Make an old man happy,' he hissed, losing more teeth from his dry mouth as he dragged himself towards her. 'Come here, girl, and make an old man happy.'

'Damn you!' screamed Mila, somehow managing to draw the blade at last and get it up into position.

She had no idea how to use it. She gripped the long hilt with both hands and swung it like a labourer with a scythe, heavy and clumsy.

The steel raked across the old man's body, but Reilach seemed to feel no pain. He kept coming at her, limping through gashes that would have felled a living man. Mila retreated as far as the cramped interior would allow, swiping and slashing. She saw the priest's hand come off at the wrist, but still he came. She managed to stab him deeply in his leading leg, but he merely limped more heavily.

Then the wall was at her back, cutting off any further retreat. Father Reilach shuffled towards her, his grasping hand outstretched, still babbling in his dry, choked voice.

'Mercy of Sigmar!' cried Mila, half out of the fear that still raged within her, half out of fury that the foul old lecher was still after her even in death. 'Curse your soul, you bastard, curse your *rotten soul!*'

She put everything into her final swipe, knowing it would be the last chance she got. Hauling the blade back round, leaning forwards into it like she did when pummelling heavy laundry against the rocks of the river, she swung.

The blade connected just under the chin and passed clean through. Reilach's head spun bloodlessly away, landing on the ground with a hard thud. His body toppled forwards, still clutching at her.

Off-balance, Mila could do nothing to stop it. The cold, dead torso of the priest landed heavily on her, pinning her against the wall before slipping, slowly, down her body.

Horrified, Mila shoved it away. The sick, charnel house stench of the necrotic flesh stuck in her nostrils. As she brandished the sword against it, she saw how the metal shook in her grip.

I have to get out!

Mila ran for the hovel's doorway. She burst out of it, right into a whole gang of limping, shambling invaders. They turned their flesh-tattered heads towards her as she blundered into them. Then they reached out with their bony hands.

Away in the distance, another woman screamed, louder than the rest. Mila knew that voice, and for a moment her horror nearly choked her.

'Margrit!' she screamed in turn, whirling the sword around her in clumsy loops.

She waded into the press of non-living, hammering them back, bereft of any plan other than an ill-defined sense of needing to get closer to where Margrit's voice came from.

Two more undead went down under her poorly aimed blows, toppling over stiffly as she chopped the legs out from under them. Even then they just kept crawling, dragging themselves along with their hands, desperate to get to her.

There were dozens more. They lurched out of the shadows, faces blank in the shifting light, bones protruding and jaws sagging.

It was then that Mila knew she was going to die. There were no villagers left in sight. Perhaps some of them had got out, perhaps none had. It didn't much matter by then: any that remained inside the walls stood little chance against the sudden swarm of otherworldly killers.

'Margrit!' she shouted again, swinging the sword as hard as she could, knocking aside any attackers that got close enough to lash at her with their fingernails.

She would find her. At the least, she would fight her way to her friend, and they would die together, as close in death as they had been life.

Stubborn old mare. That's what Margrit had always called her.

Damn right.

Crying out loud until her voice cracked, hurling her rusty blade around with feverish abandon, Mila waded back to where the bonfire still burned, and, for the first time ever, the light of battle-frenzy shone in her eyes.

'STAND BACK,' WHISPERED Eichmann, making a few final adjustments to the device in his palm. 'This is new. I'm not sure how well it works.'

'Could we not, say, test these things before we use them?' asked Udo.

'No. This one is worth more than your annual stipend.'

'I don't explode in your face.'

'I've always been glad of it.'

Eichmann finished his adjustments and withdrew from the device, stepping backwards carefully through the slime.

It was small, about the size of a man's fist, roughly spherical, bound with copper bands and studded with rivets. Eichmann had lodged it in some loose brickwork in the sewer wall. As he edged away, he unravelled a long line of twisted fuse-twine.

'Right, then,' he said, settling into position. 'Now we just–'

There was a fizzing pop, then the wall exploded.

Eichmann was hurled back against the far side of the drain. Broken bricks sailed through the air, crashing into pillars and splashing into the pool of stinking sewage. One of them slammed into the stonework just by his head, blinding him for a moment with a cloud of dust.

Udo waded out of the shadows, shaking his head mournfully.

'What did I say?' he muttered, making for the ragged hole in the sewer wall Eichmann's device had opened up, maul in hand.

'A minor defect with the detonator,' said Eichmann, hauling himself to his feet and pulling a flintlock from its holster. His vision was a little blurry, not helped by the loss of his lantern, but he managed to cock the pistol's hammer smoothly enough. 'In all important respects, though, very satisfactory.'

Light poured from the breach in the sewer wall. The gaping hole opened out into a small chamber beyond, lit by smoking torches. The explosion had blown most of the rubble inwards, and a fine mist of brick-dust swam lazily upwards.

'It did get things started,' admitted Udo, clambering through the breach.

Groaning broke out from the floor of the chamber. Men, their outlines hazy in the clouds of dust, were slowly swaying back to their feet. One of them reeled straight into Udo. A swift, expert jab with the maul floored him again, and the man dropped like a stone.

'Careful,' said Eichmann, following his henchman into the chamber and calmly sweeping his pistol over the interior. 'I want him able to talk.'

The room stank nearly as badly as the sewer. A long table ran down most of its length, covered in pelts and

animal skulls. More skulls had been hung on the walls.
Torches burned between them, staining the walls and
ceiling with a skin of black soot.

Six men were inside, all dressed in the shabby hose
and jerkin of Middenheim's minor merchant class.
Beside the man Udo had downed, one other lay face-
down on the stone floor in a gently expanding puddle
of blood. That left four, all in various stages of recovery
from the explosion.

One of them, young-looking and wide-eyed, made a
bolt for the narrow stairs at the rear of the chamber.
Eichmann drew up his pistol, closed one eye, and fired.
The man's right knee blew open and he collapsed in a
heap, screaming wildly.

Another, as brave as he was foolish, grabbed something from the table and rushed at Udo. The henchman
waited for him to get in close. He swayed out of the way
of what looked like an erratically thrust kitchen knife
before punching the maul heavily into the man's face.

The man spun backwards. His face had been driven
in, and his strangled cries only rang out for a few seconds before choking off in a fit of bloody gurgling.

'Udo, did you hear me?' asked Eichmann irritably,
reaching for his second pistol.

'Unavoidable, sir,' replied Udo, though his voice gave
away his satisfaction. 'Self-defence.'

The henchman strode up to another half-stunned figure, a balding man with a sagging paunch and terrified
eyes. The man made a half-hearted effort to scramble
away, but Udo caught him by the collar and swung him
hard into the wall. He followed that up with a single,
heavy punch to the man's face, crunching his nose into
a bloody pulp. The man, his body limp and eyes glassy,
slid down the bricks.

Eichmann approached the lone standing occupant, a bearded man with a moth-eaten goatskin shawl draped over scrawny shoulders. His thin, toothy face was tight with shock and confusion.

'Name,' Eichmann demanded, pointing the pistol barrel directly at the man's forehead.

The man looked shakily at the gun as if he didn't know what it was. Then Udo lumbered into his eyeline, blunt and monstrous, and he seemed to muster up some clarity.

'B-Bohfels,' he stammered. 'Karl Bohfels. Sirs, this was just–'

Eichmann silenced him with a backhanded swipe from the gun-hand. Bohfels staggered away from the blow, tottering a few steps before collapsing.

Udo cracked his knuckles in approval.

'Easy enough,' he said, gazing around at the damage they'd done. 'What now?'

Eichmann looked at the table. Feathers and bones were strewn across it, interspersed with vials of dark liquid and a few grubby rolls of cheap parchment.

'We'll take Bohfels in,' he said grimly. 'And I want samples of those… whatever they are.'

Udo picked up a bird's skull covered in red stains.

'I'm sure he'll be happy to tell us,' he said, turning it between his leather-clad fingers.

A ragged gasp of pain broke out from the rear of the chamber. Eichmann and Udo both turned towards it. The man with the shot knee had started moving again. He'd managed to crawl two steps closer to the closed door at the top of the stairwell and was trying to get further.

Eichmann gave him a pitying look.

'A poor effort,' he said.

Udo smiled wolfishly.

'So what about these other ones?' he asked. 'What are we going to do with them?'

Eichmann re-holstered his pistol. He felt deflated, and the stink of the sewer was getting to him at last. Udo's dog-like enthusiasm for such work was always wearying.

What is it doing to me, spending so much time with such human filth?

'The usual,' said Eichmann, drawing out his rapier with a smooth hiss. 'But stop grinning about it, for the love of Sigmar, and let's make it quick.'

MILA HADN'T STOPPED screaming inside, but her parched throat could utter nothing but broken gasps.

She'd stayed on her feet, hammering away with Pieter's sword, holding back ranks of living dead. She'd broken their bones and prised their fingers from her limbs, but still they'd kept coming. She'd crushed their fragile skulls and disembowelled them with heavy, twisting lunges of the blade, but still, endlessly and with neither fear nor weariness, they'd kept coming.

She'd made it back to the site of the bonfire, right in the centre of the village, just in time to see Margrit dragged down to the earth by a gang of claw-handed assailants. The girl had fought on for a while, throwing a few of them off her, lashing out and screaming the whole time. Margrit was like all daughters of Helgag – tough as tanned hide and strong from the grind of endless labour – and hadn't gone down easily.

But they'd got her in the end. Once she'd lost her footing, they could go for her throat. Mila had watched, still a dozen yards away, as they'd got their gaping jaws in place and had bit down.

Then they'd come for her.

No one else was left. Ever since she'd hacked and shoved her way back to the bonfire, Mila had known she was alone.

There she stood, her back to the fire, watching the space before her fill with more of the undead. They jabbered at her, and their eyes glowed.

I don't want to die. Not yet, not like this.

The undead hung back, chattering in near-silent, deathly voices. Mila stood before them, panting heavily, holding the sword as straight as she could manage, waiting for the first one to move.

'Come for me, then,' she growled, speaking out to stop her mind locking in panic. 'Who's first?'

They didn't respond. The chattering whispers grew a little louder.

'Come on!' roared Mila, swinging the sword back and forth. 'Come and–'

She never finished. The horde of undead warriors suddenly broke, folding in on itself as if something huge had impacted on it. Their whispers became thin howls of rage. The skeletons and corpses turned away from her, consumed by something far more pressing within their ranks.

For a moment, Mila couldn't make anything out. The dull red of the fire was dying fast, staining the walls of the hovels in shadow. She stayed where she was, looking around her in a kind of stupor, unsure what to do.

Could she make use of this? Could she get out of Helgag? Or should she stay close to the light? She felt her own breathing, hot and deep, and the sweat on the palms of her hands making the sword-grip sticky.

Then, finally, she saw him.

For the first time, alone in Helgag, half-deranged with fear and fatigue, she saw him.

Days later, when the last of the fires had finished burning and the ashes had cooled, she would remember many things about that moment. She would recall the way the flames glinted from the curved plates of his armour like cascades of rubies. She would remember his eerie silence in battle, more complete and more unnerving than the undead themselves. She would remember how his mournful face reared up out of the dark, fixed in an expression of frigid disdain, his bare forehead bound with rolls of scripture and shining with sweat.

At the time, though, still locked in a vice of her exhaustion, she was only struck by one thing.

The way he moved.

He carried a huge warhammer, golden-headed, spiked and heavy. It swung in perfect arcs, cleaving chests, bursting open skulls, crunching through skittering thickets of stick-thin limbs. Mighty arms, each the girth of a lesser man's thigh, propelled the weapon with efficient, murderous grace. A long red cloak swirled in his wake, wrapping him in a skirling halo of crimson.

Everything was in motion. He was like a whirlwind of steel and gold, spinning and striking his way through the heart of the horde. It was all so perfectly, so flawlessly balanced. Every blow found its mark, driving apart the knots of screaming horrors and fracturing their eerie unity. He was like a reaper in high summer, raging and circling, and they broke against him in futile fury.

Mila, her own struggles forgotten for an instant, watched it all unfold, her jaw slack and her hands loose.

They no longer looked invincible. In the face of that man's onslaught, the walking dead looked suddenly fragile. The armoured figure waded through their midst, smiting down any that got close enough to feel the bite of the warhammer.

His expression remained downcast. His thin mouth remained fixed in an unbending snarl of disapproval. He uttered no war-cry, though it looked like he was constantly whispering something to himself.

His dark eyes snapped up, just for a moment, from the slaughter, and he saw her. He fought over to her position, throwing corpses in either direction as he hacked a path through the horde.

'Daughter, are you alone?' he asked, knocking aside the grasping arms of dogged pursuers before coming alongside her and whirling around to face the rest.

Mila knew that, in the respect that he intended, she was entirely alone – all the others in Helgag must surely have died or long since fled.

But, for all that, she couldn't answer his question in the way he'd expected. Her fear seemed to have shrunk away from her, to be replaced by a strange, burning sensation in her breast.

Her sword felt light in her hands and she brandished it eagerly, looking for more targets. Her face rose, no longer disfigured by screaming, but calm and purposeful.

Hope, that most dangerous of emotions, had returned.

'Not any more,' she said, and took up the fight again.

CHAPTER THREE

Eichmann's personal chambers were expensive; he'd seen
to that. The furniture in them was of rare quality. Sub-
dued landscapes and still lives by Brach and Tollenberg
hung over the panelled walls, not the gaudily heroic
horrors that lined the plaster of the Grafs' households.

For all Middenheim's importance, its people were a
savage lot. Lukas Eichmann, an Altdorfer by breeding if
not birth, wasn't. Even now, so many years after coming
north, he retained the eye for quality he'd always been
proud of. It was, he supposed, something to hold on to.

The chair was a Loppenstadtler. No more than a hundred years old, and worked on by the master himself.
Heavy, dark wood, painstakingly carved into austere
symmetry. Some minor princes would have given their
fingers to have owned such a piece, and discerning rich
men might have paid good money just to sit in it.

Karl Bohfels, by contrast, looked like he would have
given everything he owned to get out of it. He wasn't
physically restrained; his fear kept him locked in place.
His knuckles gripped the arms. He looked like he
wanted to be sick, though from what Eichmann had
been told by Udo he'd already vomited up everything
he was likely to.

Eichmann leaned back against his desk – a late period Haupf-Kochel – and rested his hands on the very expensive tooled leather top. He pursed his lips and regarded his subject.

Bohfels looked odd. It wasn't the fact that the man was almost incontinent with terror, nor was it the lurid bruising from Udo's enthusiastic pre-interrogation session. He couldn't put his finger on it, but the man had a strange air.

Eichmann said nothing for a long time. His Zettler timepiece tocked gently in the background. Noon sunlight angled through glass windows onto a deep-pile rug woven, so he believed, in El Haikk. The two of them were alone, facing one another across a scene of well-chosen luxury. In another situation, the tableau would have been calmly companionable.

Bohfels sat there the whole time, shaking, his skin as grey as wood pigeon feathers.

Eventually, Eichmann cleared his throat.

'Do you know how many lives I have ended?' he asked.

Bohfels looked frantic for a moment, as if the question might be some kind of trick, then resorted to shaking his head rapidly.

Eichmann grunted.

'No guess? Actually, I'm not sure myself. It must be hundreds. Perhaps a thousand, if all the decrees with my name on it are to be counted. That's a lot of death, Herr Bohfels. It's a lot to have on one's conscience.'

Bohfels looked like he was struggling to think of something to say in reply. Presumably, speaking was painful to him: his swollen cheeks and blood-caked lips spoke of Udo's patient handiwork, down in the rooms below, past the cellars where the locks were heavy and no sounds escaped.

Eichmann shook his head and withdrew his hands from the desktop, clasping them before him.

'Imagine that, Herr Bohfels,' he said. 'To have killed so many men that one can no longer count them. In other times, that would make me some kind of monster. In the Empire of Karl Franz, it makes me a protected asset. What a world we find ourselves in.'

Bohfels managed to cough out something, but the words were indistinct. He tried again, moving his jaw painfully.

'Go on,' said Eichmann encouragingly.

'Are you. Going. To kill. Me?'

'Yes, you should expect that. Perhaps there is something you can do to redeem yourself, though right now I can't think what that might be.'

Bohfels began to weep gently. His lean chest rose and fell as suppressed sobs broke out.

Eichmann let impatience flicker across his austere face.

'Now then. You have been accorded some privilege – I can just as easily ask my colleague to take over this interrogation. Would you prefer that?'

Bohfels got himself under control, though his face remained a mask of misery.

'N-no, lord,' he said.

'Very well.'

Eichmann reached over behind him and withdrew a sheet of parchment with Udo's clumsy scrawl all over it.

'How did you fall into corruption, Herr Bohfels?' Eichmann asked, reading over the henchman's summary of his work as he spoke.

'Loyal subject,' said Bohfels thickly. 'Loyal to Emperor.'

'You were engaged in proscribed rites. Who showed them to you? Was it a man named Workel? Brego Workel?'

Bohfels looked genuinely nonplussed.

'Loyal subject,' he said again. 'Blessing of Sigmar.'

Eichmann ran a weary hand through his close-cropped hair. He needed some sleep. Perhaps he should have let Udo hammer out all the information.

'You were found in possession of certain objects. They are used to summon spirits. Harmful spirits.'

'Sigmar,' insisted Bohfels, nodding as if the name itself confirmed his innocence. 'Way to Sigmar.'

'I don't think you're taking this seriously,' said Eichmann, one eyebrow raising. 'Perhaps I will summon my associate.'

'No!' barked Bohfels, his bruised lips breaking into something like fluency through pure terror. 'Truth! Love of Sigmar, truth. We used charms to clear path. To Sigmar-in-Forest.'

'What do you mean?'

'Sigmar-in-Forest. Lord under trees. He would come. Clean up.'

'There is no such name. You speak heresy.'

Bohfels shook his head urgently.

'I saw him. Sigmar-in-Forest. Lord under trees. Light. Good.'

'You have been deluded.'

'Light. Good.'

Eichmann paused, thinking carefully. There was nothing in Udo's notes about this. That in itself was no surprise: brutal methods of interrogation were notoriously patchy, whatever their exponents might claim for them.

'What other names do you know?' he asked.

Bohfels's eyes glinted then, as if the prospect of survival had suddenly become a little brighter.

'Woodsman. Shepherd. Sigmar-in-Forest. Lord under trees. We worship. We make path.'

'And what of Hylaeus?'

Bohfels's expression broadened into a painful smile, like that of a man recognising a long-lost relative.

'You know! You know! Hylaeus come before Sigmar! Yes, His priest.'

'No, I don't know. Tell me about him.'

'Hylaeus come first. Show way to Sigmar. Hylaeus gatekeeper.'

Eichmann put the parchment back on the desk and scratched the back of his neck. Talk of gatekeepers and priests was very familiar: every cult from Middenheim to Marienburg used the same language. For beings of infinite guile and subtlety, the Ruinous Powers certainly had a limited palette of ideas. Perhaps that was because they knew that mortals would fall for them, over and over again.

'So where is the gatekeeper?'

Bohfels stopped talking then. His fear suddenly returned, as if he'd remembered, too late, some need for secrecy. His broken face contorted, torn between rival fears. He looked pleadingly at Eichmann, then away, then back again.

'I never ask a question twice, Herr Bohfels,' said Eichmann. He spoke quietly, but the threat under the words was blade-sharp. 'Take as long as you want.'

Bohfels looked miserable. His hands clenched and unclenched rapidly. He shot a desperate glance over to the window, several feet away. The sky outside the glass was unbroken blue.

'If I tell you,' blurted Bohfels, still stumbling clumsily over his words, 'will I be spared?'

'Answer the question.'

His tears started again. They ran like pearls over the man's bloodshot cheeks. Bohfels slumped in the chair.

One hand still gripped the arm, and his fingernails dug into the veneer.

Eichmann pushed himself from the desk and flexed his fingers. He drew a pistol from the holster at his belt and cocked the hammer.

'South,' said Bohfels, weakly. 'Drakwald.'

'The Drakwald is a big place.'

'Don't know more.'

Eichmann aimed the pistol at the man's right leg.

'I don't! We were never told!'

Eichmann closed one eye, calmly pointing the ornate barrel further up the man's thigh, wondering if he risked damaging the chair.

'Four Towers! That's all I know! Four Towers, hilltop. Close Middenheim. South! You can find.'

Eichmann paused. Bohfels had the look of truth in his terrified eyes. After years of such work, Eichmann generally knew when a subject had told him everything he knew.

He uncocked the pistol.

'Not very specific, Herr Bohfels,' he said.

'Told you everything! Everything I know!'

'Yes, I believe you have.'

Eichmann turned away. He walked around to the far side of his desk and sat down at it. To his right, a long velvet cord hung down from a brass ring set in the ceiling. He pulled it, and a low chime sounded.

Bohfels never stopped shaking.

'W-what now, sir?' he asked.

'The interview is concluded,' said Eichmann, drawing out a fresh sheet of parchment and reaching for quill and knife.

Bohfels's terror switched to confusion.

'Then... Then, I go?'

'Yes.'

Still he didn't move. He sat in place, shivering, mouth hanging open.

The door to Eichmann's chamber opened and Udo walked in, ducking under the frame. At the sight of the henchman, Bohfels recoiled, squirming in the chair as if he wanted to merge into the wood.

'Udo,' said Eichmann, starting to write. 'Escort Herr Bohfels from here and see him home. I judge him to have been misled, believing his undertakings to be connected in some way with the official teachings of the Church. He will be instructed to perform penance at the local temple for two months; Father Neumann will, I'm sure, be able to oblige.'

As Eichmann spoke, a disbelieving, desperate look slowly crossed Bohfels's face. The man never stopped trembling, but his hands relaxed slightly.

Udo nodded brusquely.

'Very good, sir,' he said, approaching the desk. 'Anything else?'

Eichmann finished writing and handed Udo the sheet of parchment.

'This is the letter of authorisation for Neumann. Take care that you give it to him.'

Udo looked at the script, reading carefully.

'I'll see to it, sir.'

Eichmann turned to Bohfels.

'You have been lucky,' he said. 'I am in a benign mood. This is your chance to start again, Herr Bohfels – do not waste it.'

Still incredulous, Bohfels didn't move. He stayed clamped to the arms of the chair. He avoided looking at Udo.

Eichmann couldn't blame him for that. Most people avoided looking at Udo.

'Though, of course, if you choose to stay here, I may discover more questions to ask.'

That seemed to break the spell. Bohfels dragged himself to his feet, staggering as he swayed up on bent knees. He didn't pull himself properly straight – it seemed something had damaged his spine quite profoundly.

'Th-thank you,' he stammered, bowing and wringing his bruised hands. 'Bless you, sir. Thank you.'

'The Church is not without its merciful aspect.'

Bohfels shuffled out of the chamber, flinching as he passed Udo. The henchman followed him out, letting his boots fall heavily on the floorboards, before closing the door behind them.

Eichmann, alone again, leaned back. He propped his elbows on the arms of the chair and pressed his fingers together.

For a long time, he didn't make another move. The clock kept up its steady, metallic ticking.

Many moments passed before he stirred again. Even then, only his lips moved, mouthing three soundless words.

What is Hylaeus?

MILA AWOKE TO a world of stifling, blunt pain. Her limbs were stiff and throbbing. Her head felt stuffed with sackcloth and her lips were swollen.

She lifted her chin a little, and the pain got worse. Steeling herself, she opened her eyes, and the world rushed back in.

She remembered fighting for so long that her arms had screamed in pain. She remembered the priest, and the endless tide of bony hands. She remembered him laying into the living dead, as silent as they were, as deadly as they were, crushing any who came close.

She didn't remember much beyond that. Perhaps she'd passed out before he'd had a chance to finish the job. In any case, she was still alive, so he must have done.

She was laying on a grassy bank overlooking Helgag's stockade walls. The sun was not far past its zenith, though a screen of grey cloud prevented it doing much to warm her.

She shivered, and pulled the strings of her bodice tighter. Every movement she made sent fresh spikes of pain into her temples. Slowly, gingerly, she pushed herself into a sitting position.

Helgag had gone. The few remaining walls were blackened and smoking. What was inside them smelled like a giant tallow candle left to burn down to the base. Even now, dark lines of smog rose up into the pale sky, twisting like plumb lines.

Mila couldn't see much of what remained within the crumbling stockade. Here and there, she could make out teetering columns of brickwork. The squat spire of the chapel still stood, though it was the colour of charcoal. Through gaps in the walls, she could see the outlines of other things: curved, thin shapes, strewn across the ground and broken into jagged splinters.

She looked away. She could still taste sour beer in her mouth. She belched, feeling the clutch of nausea close at hand, and her head throbbed worse.

'Awake, then,' came a deep voice from behind her.

Mila swung round, clutching at her bodice, suddenly aware of how exposed she was.

The man, the warrior priest, loomed over her. His warhammer was still in his left hand. His right hand clutched a bundle of dry kindling.

The events of the night tumbled back into her mind

all at once, making her stomach lurch from the memory of it.

So. You were real.

The priest looked different in the clear light of day. His armour was heavy. His cloak hung down heavily from his broad shoulders, stained and travel-worn. He still wore the leather band around his forehead, marked with iron studs and crowned with a square bundle of tight-packed scriptures.

His skin was leathery, grimy and heavily tanned, the skin of a man who spent little time indoors. The eyes, though, were the same as she remembered them: intense, dark, locked under a low ridge of forehead, as deep and mournful as a hunting dog's.

'Who are you?' asked Mila.

'You need to eat,' he said.

He squatted down beside her, letting the kindling drop to the ground. He pulled a gourd from his belt, unbuckled it and passed it to her.

Mila took it and drank greedily. The water tasted of leather, but it went down well enough.

She passed it back, wiping her mouth.

'Got any food?' she asked.

The priest rebuckled the gourd and got back to his feet.

'Sigmar provides,' he said, and made to walk back down to the ruins of the village.

'Sigmar *provides?*' she blurted, suddenly angry. As her wits returned, so did her consciousness of what had happened. 'How can you *say* that?'

The priest looked down on her. His expression never changed. It seemed locked in a permanent state of disappointment.

'Even in your grief, do not blaspheme,' he warned.

Mila pulled herself to her feet. She felt dizzy, her vision blurred, but she stayed up.

'They're all *dead*,' she spat. 'All of them. They didn't deserve it. Even Father Reilach didn't deserve it. If Sigmar were here now, with His damned magic hammer and all His saints, I'd tell Him that–'

The huge gauntlet slapped across her mouth. It stayed there, pinching her mouth painfully.

'Beware, daughter,' said the priest. 'I silence heresy. Do not utter words that would damn you.'

Mila froze, shocked, before a flush of fresh anger surged up within her. She struggled against the grip, managing to wrench her jaw free of the priest's fingers. Then she stared at him, eyes wide, outraged and flushed red.

'You… *dare*…' she said. 'Who *are* you?'

The priest's face never changed. No surprise, no anger, no amusement, just a stone-carved expression of calm disapproval. It was the face of a man for whom the world would never be good enough – it would never be pious enough, never strong enough, never wise enough. Even in the midst of her shocked indignation, Mila could see the infinite, otherworldly strength of will in that face. Beside that, her protests were as futile as a raging, petulant fishwife's.

'Unsanctified corpses are still in the village,' the priest said. 'I have much work before I can leave. Help me if you wish, but I warn you – do not curse again.'

With that, he picked up the kindling and strode off down the bank, hammer swinging heavily. Mila watched him go, open-mouthed.

She stood immobile for some time, debating what to do. Half of her wanted nothing more than to storm off, leave the strange, sanctimonious cleric to his own devices and make her own way out of trouble.

She almost turned away. She stood still for some time, her resolve strengthening, steeling herself to walk away, on up the valley.

Conflicting emotions welled up within her. The memories of the night slowly clarified again, bringing with them a tide of grief, dampening the fire of her spirit.

Margrit. Hans. Pieter.

Helgag was all she'd ever known. All it had taken to extinguish it was one night. A single, horrific night, bursting out from nowhere to consume everything in a rush of screaming and murder.

Mila watched as the priest picked his way back through the broken gates. His body, encased in plates of steel and draped in crimson, moved with an unshakeable confidence. She'd seen him fight. It was hard to imagine anything troubling him, let alone putting him in danger.

That was worth something. It was, at least, something to cling on to.

Head shaking, disgusted at her own weakness, Mila limped down the bank towards him, back towards the ruins of her home.

'*Don't curse again,*' she muttered, mimicking the man's speech bitterly. 'Gods above, you damned priest, I'll say what I want, do what I want, and I'll give you something to curse about before I'm done.'

RAFE UDO WAS happy in his work.

He knew how lucky he was. Rarely did the requirements of a profession match up so perfectly with a man's inclinations. He'd never found that in his former life. Captain Oeler had never understood his unique needs, despite the man's long service in the regiment and knowledge of fighting men. That had been a difficult relationship, one that had caused them both serious problems before its inevitable end.

Things had changed. Udo's life was still filled with violence, though it was of a more directed kind. Most of it was entirely necessary even as it was pleasurable, and that fact alone was sufficient to provoke another hooked smile across Udo's slabbed, scarred face.

He liked violence. It was pure, it was exciting, and he was good at it. Happiness, it seemed to Rafe Udo, lay largely in finding one's niche in life.

The same could not be said for Karl Bohfels, whose time alive was drawing inexorably to its brutal close.

The little man wasn't entirely stupid. His unexpected reprieve had made him cautious, just as it should have done. He'd promised to report to Father Neumann at the temple and had limped meekly homewards under Udo's stewardship, flinching and bowing the whole way. He had, it seemed, been genuinely keen to make the most of his reprieve.

But he hadn't been able to help himself. It was just too hard. He'd gone back, all the way across town to the rich quarter, hugging the shadows, moving with what he no doubt thought was excessive caution and stealth.

Perhaps Bohfels knew just how much danger he was in. Certainly he must have known the nature of those he'd been dealing with and their generally unforgiving demeanor. Or maybe he simply wanted to make contact with them again, to reassure them that he hadn't given away any information during the interrogation and that he remained steadfastly loyal to the cause.

In either case, it was a poor choice, though entirely predictable and another vindication of Eichmann's knowledge of human nature. Udo shadowed Bohfels expertly the whole way, blending into the crowds as he always did despite his size, stroking the maul that still nestled under unfamiliar, anonymous clothes.

He wore a dirty cloak and a woollen hood over his head that itched and smelled bad. Even the stench and the discomfort didn't dampen his mood much.

A few dozen yards up ahead, Bohfels paused before a large, ornate townhouse, six storeys high and covered in a gauche layer of gold leaf on the woodwork. The daub walls were cleaner than most, though a tidemark of brown damp ran along the lowest level.

The road in front of it was sparsely dotted with passers-by. Udo walked on, keeping his gait aimless, coming within a few yards of Bohfels before moving further up the street.

An old man was selling fruit from a cart at the end of the road. Udo went up to him and picked out a rotten-looking apple, turning it in his big hands, moving smoothly to get a view of Bohfels and the house.

'Are you buying that?' asked the cart's owner, a foul-breathed, skeletal figure with weeping boils all over his chin.

'Just taking a look,' said Udo, looking at Bohfels the whole time.

Back down the street, Bohfels banged on a brass knocker in the shape of a lion's head and waited for what seemed like a long time. The door, a huge slab of oak, remained bolted.

'If you spoil it,' said the old man, 'you'll have to buy it.'

'If you say another word,' said Udo, still looking at Bohfels and smiling politely, 'I'll push it down your palsied throat and choke you with it.'

The door opened. Udo couldn't see who was on the

other side, but Bohfels went in, looking around him before stepping over the threshold.

Udo turned to the old man, who was looking at him with a mix of outrage and wariness. He threw the apple back onto the cart.

'Rancid,' he said, reaching into his wallet and withdrawing a few schillings. He tossed one at the old man, who managed to catch it in greedy, scabrous hands. 'Just like you. Who lives there?'

'Klaus von Hessler,' replied the old man, scowling as he slipped the coin into his dirty grey jerkin.

Udo tossed him another one.

'There's a tavern over there,' he said, nodding towards a tumbledown building on the far side of the street with low eaves and grimy windows. 'I feel the need to wet my throat. The man who entered von Hessler's house is a friend of mine. When he comes out – if he comes out – I want you to come and get me. Quickly. Two more schillings if you can manage it before my friend gets aw… leaves.'

Udo started to walk towards the tavern.

'Don't you want your apple?' cried the old man after him.

'Have it on me,' said Udo, stowing the wallet at his belt. 'I'm not hungry.'

An hour later, the old man burst through the doorway of The Hound, swung his skinny head from side to side searching for Udo, then spotted him through the dinge and stink. He hobbled up to Udo's table. By the time he got there, the henchmen was already on his feet.

'He's–'

'Good,' said Udo, wiping his mouth, putting the empty tankard down and making for the door. 'Well done.'

'My money!' cried the old man, scurrying after him.

'On the table,' said Udo without looking back, breaking out into the street and striding out towards von Hessler's house.

It didn't take him long to catch sight of Bohfels. The man was going quickly too, hurrying like a thief with his loot, weaving through the jostling throng of Middenheimers ahead of him.

Udo matched pace, dropping in behind Bohfels and pulling the woollen hood over his head.

The two of them weaved through the streets, Bohfels moving erratically, Udo moving smoothly like a shark amid shoals of lesser fish.

Bohfels was heading back to his lodgings. Udo upped the pace. In a few moments he was right behind Bohfels, and the two of them walked in step for a while. Udo kept an eye out, watching for those quiet, narrow alleys that were the staple of his work.

One came up soon enough, and he grabbed Bohfels's collar and hauled him into the shadows. His free hand slapped over the struggling man's mouth, stifling the shouts before they began.

Bohfels knew what was going on immediately. Despite his wounds, he thrashed around like an eel out of water.

Udo dragged him further away from the street. The alley was almost deserted. At the far end, a trio of hunched beggars shuffled away rather than risk being dragged into trouble. From somewhere high up, a shutter slammed closed.

Udo crunched Bohfels into the nearside brick wall, hearing the man's skull crack satisfyingly. Bohfels reeled, losing his footing, and slid down into the filth of the alley floor.

Udo withdrew his maul and patted it affectionately.

'How stupid do you think we are, man?' he asked, pushing his hood back to reveal his identity.

Even in his dazed state, Bohfels recognised Udo instantly. He started to scrabble backwards through the dirt.

Udo crouched down, grabbing his collar with his free hand and hauling him back.

'There's no mercy for you,' he said, smiling. 'My master may look softer than I am, but he knows what he's doing.'

Bohfels stared at him stupidly.

'I… tell them–'

'–nothing?' said Udo, pulling a length of dirty bandage from his jerkin. 'I know. Look, I don't care what you said to von Hessler. We just wanted to know who was handling this thing.'

He jammed the bandage into Bohfels's mouth and wound it around the man's head.

'You led us to him nicely. Think on that when your soul comes before your foul gods. You did our work for us, and I don't think they like that.'

Bohfels tried to scream then, but nothing more than muffled yelps escaped the tight bandaging. Shuffling like a crab, he did his best to push himself back along the alley towards the street.

Udo smiled again. In moods like this, he could barely stop smiling.

'Struggle, by all means,' he said, thudding the head of the maul into his palm in preparation. 'This can be as messy as you make it, and the messier it is, the more I like it.'

CHAPTER FOUR

THE LONG DAY waned in what had once been Helgag. The priest spent hours blessing and cremating the human bodies, giving all of them the full rites of passing before committing them to flame. The bodies of the undead were also burned, though the priest recited litanies of damnation and dissolution over their smouldering remains.

When all that was done, he piled wood up against the remaining structures. He took glowing embers from the pyres and pushed them up against the dry kindling. It didn't take long for the flames to catch. Fed by the dry wind of the dying summer, Helgag began to burn a second time. The fire raged furiously, as if stoked by some vengeful power of its own, just as the sun began its long descent into the west and the sky darkened.

Mila watched the destruction take place with a sullen scowl on her heavy features. She didn't assist the priest, and he didn't ask her to. Fatigue had fallen heavily on her since waking up, and so she sat on her own during it all, brooding and hugging her knees.

The night came, bringing memory of evil with it. Though the fires raged brightly she still saw skeletal faces in every flickering shadow. She didn't dare close her eyes, but just sat on the bank above the village, jaw resting on her bunched fists, watching the flames leap up high into the starlit sky.

'Why did they come?' she asked at last.

The priest, who had been standing close by, seemed to have been expecting the question.

'I cannot tell you, daughter,' he said.

Mila smiled bitterly.

'I never met a priest who didn't want to preach.'

'What kind of answer did you expect?'

'That sin brought this doom down on us. That, if we'd been more pious and less happy, then the dead would have gone somewhere else. That Sigmar protects the righteous and punishes the corrupt. That's what I expect from you.'

The priest sat down next to her, and his heavy body sank down into the turf. His face and hands were black with soot. For the first time, he looked tired.

'But that wouldn't be true, would it?' he said. His voice was soft. 'I never speak falsehood, daughter. You should know that.'

'So why do they tell us such things?'

The priest shrugged.

'Some of my brothers are ignorant. Some are scared. It is an easy thing, to make the way of the world a response to what we do, to who we are. It makes sense of it.'

Mila frowned, giving the priest a hard look as she did so. He sounded nothing like old Father Reilach. He sounded nothing like any man she'd ever known.

'I hate that,' she said.

'So do I,' he said.

They said nothing for a while, and the flames soared up high, wavering and consuming. Trails of sparks floated down in the wake of the fire, carried by the wind and spinning into the dark.

'You have strength, daughter,' said the priest eventually. 'When I saw how many assailed your village, I didn't expect to find any alive.'

Mila didn't feel particularly strong. She felt nauseous, fragile and sluggish, and the compliment did little more than highlight that.

'And so you were just passing by, when this happened to you?' she asked, though the question sounded more accusatory than she'd intended.

'No,' replied the priest. 'Not just passing by.'

He seemed to think that had answered the question. Mila shook her head ruefully, too tired and sick to pursue the matter.

'You don't talk much, do you?' she observed. 'Your sermons must be a real inspiration.'

The corners of his mouth flickered then, as if the ghost of the shade of a smile had briefly tweaked at the hard flesh before vanishing into embarrassed oblivion.

'I've been told they are,' he said. There was no arrogance in the statement, which was uttered in the same way a man might report his height. 'But there's a time for it. Until it comes, I don't use words wastefully.'

'I can see that.'

The priest leaned forwards, staring at the pyre he had built during the day and watching it eat up the last of Helgag. The leather under his armour creaked as he moved.

'I can't tell you why death came to your village, daughter, because I do not know. I've seen a thousand villages, some pious, some as rotten as warpstone. Some prosper, some are destroyed. There's no pattern to it.'

As he spoke, his features relaxed a little. The hard edge to his mouth remained, though, as did the doleful cast of his dark eyes.

'I was once told what you have been told. For many years I believed that misfortune fell on the corrupt and the corrupt alone. Unlearning that lesson was hard. I'm mortal, like you. My faith is not infinite, and I walked dark paths on the day that truth became apparent.'

Mila listened carefully, watching the way the man's eyes reflected the light of the fires.

'But faith remains, even when understanding fails. In the end, that is all we have, and it is enough. I still believe that, despite everything I've seen. Perhaps you will too, when your grief has subsided.'

He turned to her.

'What is your name, daughter?'

'Mila,' she replied. 'Mila, daughter of Anja. And now you've asked me mine, you can't not tell me yours.'

The priest inclined his head in a gesture that, in another man, might have indicated amusement.

'My name, for what it's worth to you, is Luthor Huss, a servant of Sigmar.'

'You act like no servant of Sigmar I've ever met.'

'I've heard that said.'

'And what now, Father? Now that you've burned my home down and given me no words of comfort, what will you do?'

'The day's been long,' he said. The hardness returned to his weathered features quickly. 'I'll pray, and I'll sleep. Then I'll decide.'

He shot her a look of admonishment.

'I recommend you do the same,' he said. 'It may be too late for you to learn manners, but there's always hope, perhaps slight, for wisdom.'

* * *

THE CANDLES IN Gorbach's chamber flickered as he snorted. The old man slumped back in his seat, shaking his head.

'No, absolutely not,' he said. 'To be honest, I can't believe you asked.'

Eichmann watched him wearily, sat, as before, facing him across the oak writing desk. It was late, and he was tired. He rolled his shoulders gently, feeling the tense, pinched muscles protest.

'This is heresy,' he said. 'It points to him.'

Gorbach raised a jutting eyebrow.

'Heresy, Lukas? You have a few feathers, some dead bodies and a word no one understands. You have nothing.'

'I've burned men for less.'

'I have too, but you'll not touch von Hessler.'

Eichmann stared directly at Gorbach, and his expression was flinty.

'I can end this,' he said.

'No you can't. Not this way.'

Gorbach shook his jowly head, and irritation marked every movement.

'Do you listen to anything I tell you?' he muttered. 'We're weak here. Every day those damned Ulricans whisper poison into the Graf's ear, and he's starting to listen to it. They'll tolerate us clearing up the filth in the gutters, but we can't just go around kicking doors in. I mean, do you even know who this man is?'

Eichmann looked offended to be asked.

'He is Klaus von Hessler,' he said, seeing the words he'd already written on the official report scan across his mind. 'He is father to Alicia von Hessler, betrothed to Heinrich von Ariannon, Preceptor of the Knights Panther in Middenheim and Graf Todbringer's military aide. He is spouse to Lucia von Hessler, niece of the late Reiner Aldrech and sole heiress of the residual Drakwald bloodline. He is Master of the Middenheim Chamber of Worthies and Chancellor of the Society of Ulric. He is choleric in temper and erratic in judgement, wealthy even by the standards of a man with his connections, and carries a slight limp in his right leg after wounds sustained during the relief of Terzberg. He enjoys tournaments, hunting and infidelity, and he dislikes music, wine and Sigmarites.'

Despite himself, Gorbach's lips twitched in a smile.

'Thorough, as ever,' he said. 'Though you've made my case for me.'

'I have not. A heretic is a heretic – I can show a trail from him to Bohfels, to Workel, and no doubt to others we have under observation. Time is pressing – he must know we're close on his heels, and if we act now, this whole thing will be uncovered.'

'*What* thing?'

'Whatever cult he's inspired in the city. Whatever is driving men like Workel to engage in these blasphemies. They're all expecting something to happen, those poor fools.'

'My friend, everyone is expecting something to happen,' said Gorbach. 'Everyone is expecting comets to fall from the sky and the rivers to foam with blood. There are a thousand cults in Middenheim, and when our work is done here there will be a thousand more springing up. They will all, without exception, be fervently expecting something to happen.'

Gorbach gave Eichmann a weary, almost paternal look.

'Heresy isn't a one-off plague, Lukas. It can't be excised and forgotten. It's like the weeds of the earth, ever springing up, and we must choose which ones to pull up and which ones to leave lest we drive ourselves mad. This is one to leave.'

Eichmann sat stock-still, shoulders rigid, face set in stark disappointment.

'And that's your ruling? Your final ruling?'

'It is.'

Gorbach sighed, parting his hands expansively as if appealing for reason from a crowd.

'I've said it before, Lukas. You're tired. You need to sleep. When you're rested, you'll see the sense in this. I'll read your report and I'll ensure messages are passed, through discreet channels, to the Ulricans. They can well look after their own. I told you before that this isn't Altdorf, and it still isn't.'

Eichmann didn't move. He stared at the floor. In the candlelight, his angular face looked old and haggard.

I've been doing this too long.

'You'll read my report?' he asked.

'With interest,' said Gorbach. 'As always.'

Eichmann nodded.

'Then this matter is concluded.'

Gorbach looked relieved.

'It is. Move on to something else. Do not go after von Hessler – is that clear? Look at me, and tell me you understand the importance of this.'

Eichmann took a long time to raise his gaze to Gorbach's level. When he did so, pools of shadow hung under his tired eyes.

'Of course,' he said. 'I understand completely.'

WHEN MILA AWOKE on the second day, Huss had gone.

She threw off her blanket and lurched to her feet, sweeping her gaze across the narrow valley. Below her,

Helgag's huge pile of ashes sent pale grey smoke curling into the air.

She stomped down the slope towards the ruins, working some flexibility back into her night-stiff limbs. It soon became clear that he wasn't there. She walked all around the broken-down walls, feeling the residual heat of the smouldering wreckage against her skin.

Then she walked back up the slope, becoming more concerned as she began to consider her situation. At the summit of the ridge she gained a better view of the surrounding land. To the south lay the distant Drakwald, glowering and dark. To the north the land was broken and rolling, studded with straggling offshoots of the eternal forest. Mist still lay in the crooks of the valleys, shifting and milk-white. The sky was blank with cloud cover.

Mila stood, alone, feeling despair creep up within her. She had no idea where to go. Everything she knew, her whole world of life and work, had been destroyed. While the priest had been with her the threat of the undead had seemed diminished. Now her fear rose up in her throat again, the choking fear of being alone again in a world where such horrors walked the night.

Her heart began to beat more quickly. She clutched the hilt of Pieter's sword, still scabbarded and hanging at her belt.

'You *bast*–' she started, before noticing the movement.

Far away, against the northern horizon, the skyline was briefly broken. Almost too small to be made out, a dark shape flitted between the edges of two silhouetted copses, moving swiftly and confidently. It seemed, for a moment, as if the weak sun glinted from armour plates. Then the shape disappeared.

He was miles away already. He must have gone swiftly.

He was fitter than her, and certainly stronger. Catching him would be next to impossible, and in any case he clearly had no time for her. Just like the rest of them, all those who wore the badge of the Heldenhammer, he obviously cared little for those he professed to serve.

'You bastard,' she said again, spitting the words out. 'You damned... *bastard*.'

She took a deep breath and pulled the blanket around her plump shoulders like a cloak.

She felt like crying. She could have coped, perhaps, with having no hope, but to have had it restored and taken away again, that was hard.

'Bastard,' she mumbled again, though her lower lip trembled.

The wind blew in cold from the west, ruffling the crowns of the trees and making the ash of Helgag billow. It sounded like the whispering of a hundred voices.

'No,' she said then.

She jutted her chin out.

'No,' she said out loud.

Almost slipping on the dew-slick grass, she began to walk. She went down the far side of the slope quickly, heading north, away from the ruins, her jaw set in a clench of indignation.

'Not good enough,' she said, repeating it like a mantra.

Her arms pumped as she went, picking up rhythm as she got into her stride. Somewhere deep inside her, she knew it was hopeless. She had no chance of catching him. Nothing remained out in the wilds but death.

She knew that.

She kept walking.

AFTER AN HOUR her limbs began to ache. The chill of the night had made her joints stiff and sharp pain ran up her calves as she strode across the uneven ground.

The earth was packed hard after the hot summer. Her shoes – the cheap, wrapped leather type worn by peasants throughout the Empire – gave her little protection. After another hour she could feel the sides of her feet begin to blister.

She kept going, head down, scowling the whole time.

Mila went north, moving as fast as her solid frame would let her. She trudged up a long, winding valley, stumbling over rocks buried in the grasses. The sun rose higher in the east, warming the grey air and making her sweat. Her throat began to burn and her head started to throb.

She kept going. There was no sign of Huss, so she headed in the direction of her last sighting of him. She deviated as little as possible from that line, even if it meant scrambling straight through briars or wading through streams.

With every step her anger grew. She pushed back her hair from her face and felt the heat of her flushed cheeks on her fingers. While stooping for a drink at a stream she caught a broken reflection of her face – mud-streaked, marked with blood and bruises.

She kept going. Her stomach began to growl, and she had no food. Her thighs burned from the endless ascents. The sword weighed heavily at her waist, tangling with her legs, more an irritation than anything useful. She considered throwing it away, freeing herself of the drag.

She didn't, because Pieter had been a good enough man and his blade was the last relic she had of Helgag. It felt wrong to leave it behind, especially since the bastard priest had burned everything else.

She kept going. She hauled herself up the slopes and

staggered down the inclines, stumbling where the earth broke up and limping where the paths became choked with stones. Helgag's fields soon disappeared, replaced by a wasteland of scrub, straggling gorse and twisted, wind-hunched trees. No villages broke the monotony of that hard landscape, though there were occasional ruins on the horizon – half-demolished stone huts, or rotten skeletons of old wooden buildings.

Perhaps those places had shared the fate of Helgag, or perhaps they had been deserted for a thousand years. Mila realised then how impoverished her knowledge of the world beyond her home was. Even if there had been other towns somewhere within walking distance she wouldn't have known which way to go to find them, or what they were called.

The sun began to sink towards the west. The days were shortening and the wind was becoming chill. She hoisted the blanket back up on her shoulders, shivering as the muck-sweat on her flesh cooled her down.

Her ankle went then, turning on some half-buried stone, and she slipped to her knees. Sharp blades of pain shot up her leg.

'Morr's eyes!' she swore.

Her voice was thin against the whine of the wind. Cursing, she clambered back to her feet. Her ankle bloomed with pain, as if someone had knocked it sideways with a mallet. She limped onwards, feeling her latent fearfulness growing with every awkward step.

Night would not be far away. She was already tired, and her fatigue would only get worse. She closed her eyes for a second, only to open them when visions of massed death's heads crowded in.

'Damn you, priest,' she swore again, clenching her fists.

She stopped walking, shivering with pent-up rage and anxiety.

'*Damn you!*' she shouted, letting her head fall back and giving vent to her anger.

The cry drained away into the empty sky. In the distance, crows cawed.

She stood, shaking, knowing well just what her odds of survival were once the sun went down. She placed her left hand on the hilt of the sword, but the touch of the metal gave her no comfort.

I could lie down here. I could wait for them to come. It would be easier than struggling. After all, what is there left? Where, exactly, am I trying to get to?

She started to limp onwards again. Light-headed, shivery from cold and exhaustion, she dragged herself through the undergrowth, ignoring the snags of the thorns on her hem and the icy wash of the breeze against her flesh.

On and on, head down, labouring with each step, teeth gritted into a tight grin of determination, her mind began to cycle through visions of her own death.

As she dragged herself up another long, sharp incline, her breath went ragged. The light sank out of the sky. She realised the moisture running down her cheeks was tears, but did nothing to stop them.

A shadow fell over her.

Gingerly, not daring to summon back the hope that had been so painful, Mila looked up.

There he was, at the summit of the rise, his cloak rippling in the wind. He looked annoyed.

'I travel alone,' said Huss.

His face hadn't changed much, but, deep down, Mila thought she caught the mark of a wary, reluctant admiration on his features.

She spat on the ground and placed her bunched fists firmly on her hips.

'No you don't,' she said, her voice shaking still, but pinned with tenacity. 'Not any more.'

'SO LET ME get this straight,' said Udo, holding the lantern high and looking along the rows of books in the library. 'Gorbach told you not to go after von Hessler.'

'In a manner of speaking,' said Eichmann, seated, rifling through the sheaves of parchment on the narrow writing desk in front of him. The library was small and cramped. Every spare space, so it seemed, was crammed with mouldering old volumes.

'And you're ignoring him?'

'I never ignore what Gorbach says,' said Eichmann. 'Hierarchy is important, as I've often told you.'

'So you have. That's why I'm confused.'

Eichmann didn't look up, but carried on rummaging amid leaves of parchment. They were strewn all across the tabletop, some tied up with twine, others falling loose like autumn leaves on a forest floor.

Night had long since fallen, and the dank library was lit only with candles. Shelves lined the walls, each stuffed tightly with more bundles of parchment. The ceiling, vaulted like a chapel, was low and claustrophobic.

'Gorbach doesn't want a fuss made in Middenheim,' said Eichmann. 'I can understand that. But, as you may remember, Bohfels wasn't talking about Middenheim when he was with us. He was talking about the Drakwald. That got me thinking.'

He turned the pages, one at a time, glancing down rows of tiny, crabbed writing. Some of the script was faded, and all of it was hard to read by the soft glow of the candles. Eichmann narrowed his eyes, feeling the onset of a headache breaking out.

A few yards away, the library's lone guard moaned softly, rocking his head blearily back and half-opening his eyes. He was still crumpled against the doorframe, hands trussed securely, though the gag had slipped from his mouth. Udo strode over to him, withdrew the maul, and gave the man a vicious swipe. There was a wet crack, and the guard's head flopped against his chest.

Eichmann frowned.

'I hope you didn't kill him.'

Udo looked him over cursorily.

'Probably not.' He walked back to Eichmann, holding the lantern higher. 'But I'm still not following you.'

Eichmann's finger traced down a long list of names. The parchment was dry and flaky, and fragments of it followed his fingertip.

'Four Towers. That's what Bohfels said. We could spend our lifetime scouring the Drakwald for four towers and never come close to them. But someone in Middenheim knows where they are.'

Eichmann licked his finger and turned the page, squinting at the dense lines of script.

'If I were running an association that I wished to keep secret, I would locate it firmly in a place where I had total control. I would especially do so if I were the kind of man with extensive estates located in quiet corners of the Empire, out of sight and far from meddling templars.'

Udo looked down at the writing without displaying any comprehension of it. Though he had learned much over his varied and fortunate life, reading had never seemed useful enough to master, and even his association with Eichmann had done little to change that opinion.

'Like von Hessler,' he said, catching up at last.

Eichmann nodded.

'Very good. The location will not be listed openly, perhaps, but there's always a scrap of information somewhere if you look hard enough. Middenheimers, as I discovered soon after I was posted here, are surprisingly keen on recording their business transactions in triplicate. Possibly something to do with the climate.'

A look of benign understanding passed across Udo's heavy features, swiftly followed by a worried frown.

'He won't have left written records behind.'

Eichmann paused, betraying only the slightest hint of irritation.

'No, Udo, he will not. That is why we're not in the archives of Klaus von Hessler, and why, in strict point of law, we have contravened no order issued by my esteemed master in the temple. If you'd paid attention to the heraldry over the gate of this building, you'd know that we're in the archives of Louis Streicher, emeritus doctor of law for the Aldrech family.'

Udo looked thoroughly bemused then.

'I was busy at the time,' he muttered, remembering the heads he'd quietly knocked together in order to breach the lower levels of the sprawling mansion. 'And, to be honest, I'm starting to get lost with all these names.'

Eichmann didn't reply.

'Ah, but this is interesting,' he said, screwing his eyes up at an obscure scrawl halfway down the current sheet of parchment. 'A little more light, Udo, if you please.'

Udo leaned closer, letting the lantern's beams shine onto the crumbling parchment.

'Yes,' said Eichmann. 'Interesting.'

Eichmann took a knife from his belt and cut the parchment lengthways, extracting a strip from what appeared to be some sort of ledger. Names had been written in columns alongside figures and official stamps.

He brandished the strip at Udo, and there was a rare look of triumph on his face.

'Vierturmeburg! Couldn't get clearer than that, eh? Four Towers. Let us see: believed ruined, nominal value, lost to the Drakwald centuries ago. Legal title passed from the last elector count, Konrad Aldrech, through primogeniture, settling in the hands of the beautiful and eligible Lucia Aldrech in the year 2510, after which no records are made.'

Satisfied, Eichmann rolled up the strip of parchment and stowed it in an inside pocket of his leather coat. He got up from the desk and retrieved his hat, pulling it firmly onto his head and adjusting the brim.

'That's it, Udo. That's where we're headed. You should be pleased – there'll be plenty of opportunity to crush some skulls, and, as long as we're out of the city, there'll be no one to stop you.'

Eichmann started to walk out of the chamber, back the way they'd come. Udo followed him, kicking aside discarded piles of parchment as he went.

'Sounds like fun,' he said, truthfully enough. 'But what does this have to do with von Hessler?'

Eichmann turned for a moment before ducking under the doorway. He fixed Udo with a mildly exasperated look.

'I told you, Udo: Lucia Aldrech. Vierturmeburg belongs to her.'

Udo continued to look blank.

'And for the last ten years,' Eichmann said, speaking slowly, 'Fraulein Lucia Aldrech has been Frau Lucia von Hessler, which means, under the law and all common practice, that it belongs to him.'

Eichmann's eyes glinted in the candlelight. He looked and felt more enthusiastic about his work than he had for days.

'That's where he's been working,' he said. 'That, my violent and most useful friend, is where the secrets are.'

CHAPTER FIVE

FOOD HELPED HER mood, but only fractionally. She hadn't realised quite how famished she'd become. Huss was better prepared for a life in the wilds, and carried strips of dried meat, stone-hard loaves of brown bread, even wrinkled pieces of fruit. He'd handed pieces to her, one by one, watching impassively as she'd wolfed them down. Then he'd sat patiently as her stomach gripes had got the better of her, bending her double in embarrassed agony.

After that, they'd started walking again. Huss made no concessions to her weakened state but strode out just as always, hammer swinging in his right hand.

They went north, always north. On their left hand the Drakwald brooded, clogging the far horizon with its messy thatch of darkness. In every other direction the bleak wasteland stretched as far as the eye could see, a land of moors, thorns and tangled undergrowth.

'You would've left me,' Mila complained as she limped along, glaring at Huss in accusation. 'You would've left me to die back there. I mean, what was the point of fighting your way through all those undead, just to leave me behind? I don't understand you.'

Huss's features stayed impassive.

'No, you don't.'

'So why not tell me what you're doing out here? Why not, eh? I'm getting a little tired of dragging things out of you.'

Huss glanced at her, raising an eyebrow.

'You talk this way to all your betters?' he asked.

Mila scowled.

'Maybe not,' she said, 'but don't ask me to apologise. You turn up, drag me out of there, then wander off as if nothing much had happened. Well, it had. It happened to me. And I'm not some piece-of-shit serf you can just ignore. I won't let you. I won't stand for it.'

Despite himself, Huss let a smile flicker across his stern mouth.

'Don't smile at me!' cried Mila, waving her finger. 'Don't mock me, and don't talk down to me. I've spent my whole life being talked down to by men like you. Back then, I had something to lose, so I kept my mouth shut. Now I don't, so I won't be taking it.'

Huss stopped walking. He sighed, and gazed down at her.

He was taller than her by over a foot. His shoulders were at the level of her head, crowned with plates of armour. Everything about him radiated menace, a palpable sense of controlled violence that bled from his heavy frame, seeping over the tarnished breastplate and down to the armoured gauntlets that gripped the golden warhammer. He looked utterly immovable, like an old oak of the deep woods, fused to the earth by ancient and unbreakable bonds.

Mila glared back up at him. Her clothes, dirty and ripped, hung awkwardly from her short, stocky frame. Her lower lip stuck out childishly and her tangled hair had somehow managed to resolve itself into a chaotic mass of knots and snags.

'How long do you expect to last, travelling with me?' asked Huss. As ever, his deep voice was quiet. 'Do you have any idea where I go? What I do?'

For the first time in a while, Mila didn't have a ready answer. She just maintained her glare.

'Those creatures,' said Huss. 'The ones that destroyed your home, they're not unique. They come out of the Drakwald, striking across the settled lands. More emerge with every month. Something is driving them out of the forest, and they are terrible. They never waver. They keep on coming, consumed by their hate, blind to all but the prospect of a second, merciful oblivion.'

As he spoke, Huss's expression changed. He looked weary.

'I oppose them. Few can stand against them, so I do. I seek them out. I pray for guidance, following the inspiration given by grace. There's no rest, no respite. I've visited a dozen villages like yours since the midsummer. In some, resistance is mustered and the plague vanquished; in others, I come too late. There is never enough time.'

As he spoke, Mila felt her anger softening. Her frown relaxed, smoothing over the tight, clenched lines on her forehead.

'That is what I wished to spare you, daughter,' he said. 'I can't take you to any kind of safety, only more of what you faced back there. If you insist on coming with me, that's what you'll have to endure.'

Mila swallowed thickly. For the first time, she realised how much of her rage had been fuelled by fear. She felt ashamed.

'You should've said something, then,' she muttered, unable to look directly at him. 'What did you expect me to think, waking up on my own?'

Huss sighed.

'I expected you to head east, away from the forest. There's a town, Morzenburg, less than a day's walk along the Meusel. It didn't occur to me that you wouldn't know that.'

Mila blushed, feeling suddenly stupid, uncouth and ungrateful. All her energy, fuelled by her sense of injustice, seemed to drain away.

'Well, I didn't,' she said sullenly.

Huss shrugged, and started to walk again.

'There we are, then,' he said. 'Stuck with one another.'

Mila hurried to catch up with him. Her feet were still horribly painful and her muscles ached. The decision to follow Huss north now looked like a bad one.

'So where are we going?' she asked, limping along in his wake.

'The next Helgag,' he replied, not turning round. 'Try to keep up.'

THE SUN SHONE across Middenheim. The light was cold and harsh, throwing the towers and parapets of the massive city into sharp relief. A chill wind blew from the north, chasing out the last heat of the summer and ushering in the season of change.

Eichmann breathed it in, enjoying the taste of the air. After so long stuck in the seamy, grimy warren of houses, it felt pure.

City of Ulric, he thought, looking out over the vista. *God of wolves, war and winter.*

He sat astride his horse, the reins loose in his hands, and gazed long at the scene before him.

His entourage had ridden almost a mile from Middenheim's great gates and now occupied a ridge along the east-heading forest road. Away from the tight-wound streets it was possible to appreciate the true scale of the city. Ringed by vertiginous cliffs of pale grey, its walls reared up into the cold sky. Gigantic causeways extended up from the Fauschlag massif, arched and draped with long, heavy banners. Above those man-made ridges of stone were piled the blunt ramparts, soaring ever higher, each one stained with the scars of old wars. Pennants rippled from towers far above, proud and streaming, bearing the devices of noble families and the white wolf emblem of the city itself.

It looked invulnerable. Even as a son of the Reikland, Eichmann could appreciate why Middenlanders were proud of their heritage. The immense armoured profile of the city embodied everything they placed value in: defiance, solidity, intimidation.

Such things stirred his heart, too. Every so often, it felt good to be lifted out of the blood and murk of his profession and appreciate the heights mankind could achieve when the mood took him.

Eichmann was not, by nature, a cynical man. He had once gazed at the pale towers of Altdorf from a similar distance and wondered at their majesty. Back then, just a raw youth fresh from the backwaters of the province, he had been filled with a fiery zeal. Everything was hopeful. Everything his superiors had told him had made sense. The destiny of mankind – to tame the forest, to quell the whisperings of heresy, to forge ahead in progress and piety – seemed to be on the cusp of realisation.

It was only later, much later, that his simple faith had withered. The world was not only full of glistening towers and mountains; it also contained minds of disease and malice, and silent plots unravelling in the gloom, and dimly-lit chambers in the basements of nondescript buildings where no one went by accident, lined with shackles and with old bloodstains on the long tables.

He still believed. Somewhere, deep down, he retained the hard kernel of faith that had driven him in the early days. Much of his work had become habit, a repetition of old procedures that insulated him from the worst consequences of what his profession made him do, but the gestures weren't entirely empty. Like an old treasure, discarded in a dusty attic and covered in strands of webs, Eichmann kept that early belief alive.

His medallion, the badge of his office, hung under his shirt, cold against his scarred flesh. Every so often he would take it out and look at it, reminded of the way he'd felt when he'd first been given it. The rest of the time it remained lodged against his heart, a thin sliver of imperishable metal tucked next to the skin.

It had become something of a fetish, a charm to hold on to, a repository for all that old optimism. Even witch hunters weren't immune to a little superstition, after all.

Udo blocked his view then, breaking Eichmann's concentration. The burly henchman rode in front of him aimlessly, hacking up a gobbet of spittle and sending it spinning to the earth beneath. Then he kicked his horse further up the slope, picking his nose as he went.

Eichmann turned away from the view of Middenheim and prodded his own steed into a walk. Behind him came the rest of his entourage: thirty men-at-arms clad in steel breastplates and carrying two-handed broadswords.

Behind them came Gustav Daecher, one of the woodsmen he'd taken on for the journey into the Drakwald, his unshaven face part-hidden under a grey hood. The man's favoured crossbow was strapped to his back. Next to him was his strange-looking companion, Anselm Gartner, drooping in the saddle as his horse made its way up the track. His aquiline nose dragged his whole face down, as if it wanted to break off and start over with someone else.

After those two trundled the baggage caravans, four of them, and eight spare horses shackled in lines. At the very rear rode ten more men-at-arms, all carrying themselves with a calm, professional aura of watchfulness.

They were good men. Eichmann knew them all, by their records if not in person. Even in an Ulrican dominated city like Middenheim, the temple could always lay its hands on capable swords, and they were no hired dogs of war but career soldiers sworn to the service of the Cult and trained by ex-regimental men like Udo.

Eichmann looked up at the road ahead. Already the trees were creeping closer to the edges of the track, running roots over the earth like strands of gnarled hair. The branches hung low from the eaves, snagging against the men's shoulders as they went.

Under those eaves was the deep, green heart of the forest. In the midday sunlight, glimpses of it looked idyllic. Patches of mossy clearing were illuminated by slanting shafts. The trees were still thick with dark green leaves, yet to turn amber as the autumn wind bit harder. The turf was still rich, glowing with health and life.

Eichmann regarded it coolly.

I saw him. Sigmar-in-Forest. Lord under trees. Light. Good.

There was nothing good in the deep forest. The forest was the residual realm of old powers, pre-dating man and loathing him with an undying passion. Those who were seduced by the beauty of it in the daylight were the ones who lived to regret their folly when the moons were up and the shadows crept across the deeps.

'How many days before we get there, sir?' asked Udo,

riding just ahead of him, still excavating something resilient from his left nostril.

'I don't know,' said Eichmann, goading his horse to keep his place in the cavalcade. 'Streicher's records weren't exact. But I have a good idea, and Bohfels said it wasn't far.'

Udo nodded, finally removing whatever had been lodged in his nasal cavity. He regarded it sagely for a moment, then put it in his mouth.

'And Gorbach?' he asked, chewing.

'As happy as I've ever seen him. He likes me being out of the city.'

Udo looked around, glowering at the trees.

'Well, I don't,' he said. 'Never have. It's unnatural.'

Eichmann, for once, couldn't disagree.

'That it is,' he said, remembering the look of terror on Workel's face as he described what he'd been part of. Ahead of them, the road wound to the right, running down the ridge and into the shadow of the valley beyond. 'And just wait until it gets dark.'

FROM OUTSIDE THE walls, the next Helgag looked just like the old one – burned out, deserted, stinking from scorched human fat. In the dying light its broken stockade resembled a row of tombstones. Smoke still rose from some of the empty houses.

Mila looked at the place for a long time. It was terrifyingly similar. So much so, in fact, that for a while she wondered if they hadn't looped round by mistake and headed back the way they'd come.

'What now?' she said, her voice sounding small and insignificant.

Huss walked towards the tumbled arch of the gates.

'Safer inside than out,' he said.

Inside, everything was a mess. The earth was churned up, as if someone had run a plough through the spaces between hovels. The corpse of a carthorse lay just inside the gates, its stomach pulled open and buzzing with flies. Bloodstains, long and brown, ran across the dirty white of the walls.

It was silent. In the far distance, away where the treeline crept up from the Drakwald, the quiet chitter of birds could just be made out. Within the village, within the walls that had contained the killing, there was nothing.

'We shouldn't be here,' murmured Mila, gazing at the marks of destruction all around her. 'This is no place for the living.'

Huss didn't reply. He kept walking, keeping his hammer held two-handed, staying watchful. He headed for the heart of the settlement – the open space at the centre where the marketplace would be, and, if the village had one, the priest's chapel.

Mila stayed close to him. Dread had closed its hand over her heart again. She drew her sword, but its notched weight in her hands failed to improve her mood. Her hands shook no matter how tightly she gripped the hilt.

They went past hovels with doors hanging at crazy angles. Inside the cheap, blotched walls the few pieces of rickety furniture had all been smashed. Broken planks of wood were everywhere, as if the defenders had resorted to making them into weapons when all else had failed.

The defenders.

Where are they?

'There are no bodies here,' she said, speaking her thoughts out loud.

Huss nodded grimly.

'The dead take their own with them,' he said.

Mila shivered, remembering the way the eyeless faces had grinned at her at Helgag. It was hard to keep those visions out of her mind; they just kept creeping back in, like a nagging remembrance of a nightmare.

Eventually they emerged into the central space at the heart of the village. There wasn't much to look at – just a rough circle of packed earth surrounded by broken wattle huts. A blunt stone pillar three feet high had once stood in the centre, but it had been cracked and toppled.

On the far side of the opening was the only stone building in the village: a rough chapel crowned with an unimpressive spire of cracked stone. The windows had been glass, but all were smashed.

Huss walked over to it. The doorway had been driven in and only slivers of wood remained, standing up from the frame like spikes.

In front of the doorway lay a small wooden figurine, discarded on the ground. Huss stooped to retrieve it, brushing the dust from it. It was a crude representation of Sigmar. The hammer in its hand was little more than a square block. The head had been ripped off, and was nowhere to be seen.

Huss looked wounded. For an instant, his eyes closed, as if he were wincing against some inner pain. Mila found that reprehensible.

Real people have died here. It's just an idol.

'We'll make camp here,' Huss said. 'The walls will be some protection. Despite everything, this ground is still sacred, and they fear that.'

Mila looked over her shoulder nervously. The empty village stretched away, silent and miserable.

'You think they'll come back?'

Huss shrugged.

'Maybe.'

He strode across the chapel's threshold, ducking under the lintel, and she followed him in.

The chapel was no more than twenty yards long. It smelled foul, like diseased, long-unwashed bodies. A short nave led up to a wooden altar at the far end, over which had once hung a tapestry. A few scraps of that remained, though most of it had been ripped into tatters by vengeful claws. Hack-marks covered the surface of the altar but the structure remained intact. The windows were narrow and high up the walls, and they only let in faint illumination from the fading daylight.

Mila felt desolate.

'Shall I get firewood?' she asked, desperate to fill the aching silence with something.

Huss shook his head.

'We'll barricade the door. A fire would attract them.'

He started to walk towards the altar when a scratching noise suddenly broke out. It stopped just as suddenly.

Mila froze. Her heart started to thump rapidly.

'What in–'

Huss silenced her with a gesture. He nodded at the altar, the only structure in the room big enough to hide something.

He edged towards it, warhammer poised, treading silently.

Mila couldn't follow him. She remained frozen, weighed down with a heavy, heart-stopping horror. Everything from Helgag came rushing back.

Make an old man happy. Make an old man–

Huss reached the altar. He lifted the head of the hammer, ready to plunge it down.

'No!'

Mila hadn't meant to cry out – something wrenched the sound up from her lungs.

A spidery mass of limbs scuttled out from behind the altar. Distracted by her cry, the priest swung at it and missed.

The creature darted at Mila, scrabbling across the stone floor, eyes wide and staring, grey flesh stretched tight over bone, fingers outstretched.

She screamed, stumbling away from the staring, terrible eyes. She somehow got her sword up between her and it, but knew it would be no good – her arms had no strength in them.

Its mouth stretched open, revealing rotten gums and yellow teeth. Something terrible escaped from its mouth – a cat-like yowl, scraped out across vocal cords that had once been human.

Then it stopped dead. Its feet whipped out as Huss, grabbing it by the collar, dragged it back. He hauled his warhammer into position with one hand and lifted the wretch up before him with the other, careless of its kicking legs and raking fingers.

It hung, flailing, for a moment.

Huss's eyes narrowed.

'You are not dead,' he said.

The scrawny figure continued to struggle, yelping and whining like an animal. Huss's grip didn't relent. Eventually, the strange figure gave up and went slack in the priest's grasp. Its eyes stayed wild, though. They were bloodshot and bulbous, as if it had forgotten how to close them.

'What are you?' asked Huss.

Mila crept closer, keeping her blade raised. She stared at the scrawny figure, and her fear turned into grisly fascination.

It – he – was a man, or something close to one. His clothes were ripped into tatters, exposing a grille of skin-tight ribs beneath. His cheeks were hollow. His skin was almost yellow, and there were long scratches all over him. Those wounds hadn't healed, and the scabs were flecked with pus and new blood. He stank of sickness.

'What are you?' said Huss again. His voice had lost some of its edge, and he looked curious more than angry.

The man had difficulty speaking. He licked his dry lips with a thick tongue and swallowed painfully.

'Schlecht, I was,' he croaked. 'Rickard Schlecht.'

A dry, cracking cough made his body shake. When he recovered, his eyes had lost their deranged stare. They looked almost childlike.

'For… love of saints,' he rasped awkwardly. 'Kill me.'

HUSS DIDN'T KILL him. He put him down gently. He looked for a long time into the ruined man's eyes. Schlecht looked back at him, unable to glance away, quivering with sickness and fear.

Then the warrior priest unstrapped the bag of supplies from his back and tossed them to Mila.

'Give him food,' he said. 'Find out what you can. I'll check for more survivors.'

He strode out of the chapel, moving with his methodical, almost mechanical, gait.

Mila looked at the man. He avoided her eyes and huddled into a ball. He still looked like a spider.

She rummaged through the bag and found two old crab apples, dry and woody. Gingerly, she shuffled up to him and offered him one of them.

He looked at it like it had fallen down from Morrslieb.

'Not hungry?' she asked. 'You look pretty hungry.'

She took a bite of the other one, trying to encourage him.

'See?' she said, wincing as she chewed on the powdery, bitter flesh. 'Good. You should have some.'

Schlecht said nothing. His hands, clasped around his knees, twitched incessantly. He couldn't keep still, and his eyes flickered back and forth between Mila and the chapel doorway.

'Are you from here?' Mila asked, speaking as gently as she could, though the tone didn't come easily to her. 'What's this place called?'

Still no response. Schlecht began to rock back and forth on his haunches.

'Try to eat something.' She offered the apple again. 'It might help.'

Schlecht looked at the wrinkled apple for a moment, distracted by it. One hand unclasped from the other. His fingers, cracked dry and laced with scabs, reached out for it, shaking like a spider's web in the breeze.

Then, suddenly, he stopped. He snatched his hand back and began to shake again.

'Do you hear that?' Schlecht asked. His voice was strange, as if he wasn't speaking on his own behalf, but mimicking the speech of someone else.

'What do you mean?' asked Mila, not liking the tremor in his voice at all. 'I don't hear anything.'

'That's what I mean,' said Schlecht. He spoke in a stretched falsetto, as if imitating a woman's voice. It was an eerie, unsettling sound. 'No birds.'

As soon as he said it, Mila knew he was right. The dusk chorus, audible as they'd entered the village, had gone.

A moment later, Huss was back, breathing heavily as if he'd been running.

'Prepare yourselves,' he said, turning to face back the way he'd come. There was a note of savagery in his voice, hard and unyielding, just as it had been in Helgag.

'They're here.'

CHAPTER SIX

THE GEISTRICH WAYSTATION was as ugly and decrepit as every other waystation on the route south from Middenheim. It hadn't been built for aesthetics, just for survival. According to the marshal's logs back in the city, Geistrich had been razed eighteen times over the last three hundred years. That wasn't bad for a Drakwald outpost. Many were destroyed every few years, only to be rebuilt when the last of their inhuman attackers had slunk back into the trees.

The assailants varied. Sometimes they would be swarms of hooded goblins, on the rampage from the dark heart of their forest realms. More often they would be beastmen, those warped mockeries of humanity, roused by some random sniff of blood or mustered by a hooded intelligence atop one of the hidden bray stones. Rumours ran wild that rats the size of men had swept along the forest road in the past, though few believed them.

In truth, it didn't matter which breed of horror came out of the woods – the Drakwald was perilous beyond measure and home to many bizarre and uncharted varieties of nightmare. There was no victory against such foes short of felling every tree from Middenheim to Marienburg, a task far beyond the resources of an overstretched and war-weary Empire. All that could be accomplished was an endless stalemate. Towns were walled in and ceaselessly guarded. Major roads were garrisoned and patrolled. Punitive crusades were launched from time to time, blunting the capacity of the inhumans to rise up and attack but never extinguishing it.

The waystations were just a part of that creaking, incomplete system, standing in isolated defiance at regular intervals along the main arteries of trade. Ostensibly taverns and hostelries much like those found across more civilised parts of the Empire, Drakwald waystations resembled nothing more than miniature castles, replete with turrets, five foot thick walls and racks of defensive ballistae. All of them had a standing garrison of several hundred men and a supporting complement of servants and hangers-on many times larger. They were small towns in themselves, fortified bastions lodged deep in the heart of hostile territory, forever watchful, forever on edge.

It was an explosive concoction, thought Eichmann, as he sipped the foul mixture of water and small beer before him. Fighting men, cooped up for months on end in a tight, claustrophobic space, fuelled with ale and bonus schillings and threatened with imminent destruction at any moment.

It was a wonder the waystations lasted as long as they did. It was a wonder they didn't destroy themselves. Perhaps some did – though that, of course, would never be reported back in the city.

'I am trying to remember,' said the woodsman Gartner, tipping his tankard to one side and watching a trail of sediment ripple down the exposed pewter, 'worse beer.'

The four of them – Eichmann, Gartner, Daecher and

Udo – sat around a long table in one of the waystation's four drinking pits. The whole place stank of stale sweat, clouded alcohol, urine, rotten straw and mouldering meat. The ceiling was low and hung with heavy black beams. Tallow candles burned softly in iron mounts along the daubed walls, leaking trails of soot along the dirt-coloured surfaces.

Daecher said nothing, staring gloomily into his tankard. Udo gave Gartner a knowledgeable look.

'This is nothing,' he said, mustering a gobbet of phlegm with an expert intake of breath before spitting it onto the filthy floor. 'You've been to Ostland? Their beer has maggots in it.'

'Enjoy that, did you?' asked Daecher, still staring at his filmy drink.

'As it happens,' said Udo, musingly, 'it wasn't that bad. It filled your belly.'

Gartner's long nose wrinkled in disapproval.

'Are you joking, Udo? Is that one of your jokes from the good old days in the regiment?'

'No joke,' Udo said, taking another long swig. The rust-brown liquid left a trail down his bulky chin. 'It'll keep you marching all day, a belly full of maggots. Good for the guts, too.'

'Horns of Taal,' muttered Daecher.

'Indeed,' said Eichmann, wearying of the chatter. 'This place is hellish enough without your reminiscences, Udo – thank your fates this is our only night here.'

Daecher looked up. His dark, stubbled face was as sour as the beer.

'So, what's the plan?' he asked. 'The men have been briefed?'

'They have,' said Eichmann. 'To the extent they're entitled to be.'

Gartner put his drink down.

'What have you told them?' he asked. 'Have they been into the Drakwald before?'

Eichmann placed his calloused hands together on the tabletop.

'They've dealt with cults. They know what to expect, and they won't run from it. Most of them were with me when we broke up Bosch's coven two years ago, and there were some… troubling scenes. They dealt with that, and I trust them.'

Daecher looked unconvinced.

'I'm sure you do,' he said. 'Most of the time, I would too. But this isn't Middenheim, witch hunter, this is the Drakwald.'

'Yes, I'm aware of that.'

'Are you, though? Do you really know what you're getting into?'

Gartner chipped in.

'It's easy to listen to the stories, sir,' he said. 'You'll hear lots of old wives' tales about the forest. All that stuff about the cries in the night, the disappearing infants, the witches' candles flickering under the two moons. You'll hear all of that.'

'And it'd be true,' said Daecher, curling his mouth into a grim smile.

Eichmann took another sip of his watered-down beer and instantly regretted it. He could feel his stomach mustering to rebel, and knew then it would be a long night.

'So tell me,' he said, licking his lips distastefully. 'That's why I hired you. What stories should we believe?'

Daecher looked at Gartner, and a wry smile passed between the two of them.

'Best just to go home and forget about it,' Daecher said flatly. 'But, seeing as you're determined to go in, there are things you can do to edge up your chances of staying alive.'

Gartner nodded. 'March only by day, and only when the sun's fully up. Stick to the wide paths and never leave them. If we have to cut our way through, we go slowly, hacking down everything that could possibly grow again, right down to the roots.'

'At night, light fires,' said Daecher. The two of them spoke in turn, like an old married couple completing each other's sentences. 'There's no point in trying to lay low – we'll have to burn a lot of wood, keeping the light and heat up.'

'The forest hates fire, but it also fears it,' said Gartner. 'And we'll see the beasts coming a little sooner.'

'Anyone breaking ranks, even for a moment, is a dead man,' said Daecher.

'The men know that,' said Udo, impatiently. 'They aren't stupid.'

'You sure?' asked Gartner, looking slightly smug. 'Are you sure that one of them might not decide to take a leak on his own, just off the path, meaning to catch up with the others as soon as he's done?'

'Or one of them might listen to the voices,' agreed Daecher. They were warming to their theme. 'They're hard not to listen to. Imagine it – night after night, whispering in your ear. *Come into the trees. It's just me and my sisters. Come into the trees with us.*'

Gartner grinned.

'Oh, those voices,' he said. 'Only at night, mind, when you're half-asleep and jumping at every shadow, that's when they get at you.'

Eichmann stiffened. He didn't doubt the truth of what they were saying, but disapproved of the relish they took in it all.

'Your warnings are noted,' he said. 'I'll speak to the men. They're Middenheimers – they know all about the forest.'

'No, they don't.' Gartner's thin voice was serious. 'They might know about the woods around their villages where the worst they'll see is a half-starved wolf or an old hermit muttering spells. I'll say it again, just so you never forget it: this is the Drakwald.'

'It's worse than it used to be,' said Daecher ruefully. 'Something's got the place roused up. Whole villages have been stripped of the living, out east of here, just a few days' march away on the marginal land south of Eisenach.'

'Peasants,' sniffed Udo. 'Not fighting men.'

'You have no idea,' Gartner said firmly, putting his drink down and looking at Udo and Eichmann earnestly. 'The dead are abroad, coming out when the moons are full. The beastmen, too. They're stirring in the deep places, right in the heart of it all.'

'Beastmen,' said Eichmann, nodding. 'That's what this is about. Bohfels's totems were shamanic, as were the others.'

'So it's the herds,' said Daecher, shaking his head. 'I hope your men are up to it.'

Udo lost his patience then.

'Morr's *eyes*,' he swore, clanging his tankard on the table. 'I trained them myself, and they've fought beastmen before. We all have.'

Gartner leaned forwards, fixing the henchman with a bleak stare.

'Sure you have,' he said. 'You've fought beastmen out in the open, when they've attacked the places where men live. You've not seen them as they truly are, sunk into their natural state. I've seen things that would send a fighting man mad. Unless you've seen a muster in full sway, red under the light of Morrslieb, you've never – *never* – known fear. The noise of it – every bellow sticks in your heart. They dance around the herdstones, crushing the skulls of men beneath their hooves, rutting and drooling. They get drunk on it, the spirit of violence, and it sends them mad.'

'They *own* the deep wood,' said Daecher. 'Everything in it is scared of them, and they're right to be. If we stumble on warherd spoor, then we get back here, and we do it running. You could have four times as many men as you have and it wouldn't help you in there. I'm serious, witch hunter. Don't get ideas about the manifest destiny of mankind to tame the woods or anything like that – when we're under the trees, if they get our scent, then we get the nine hells out of there.'

'Listen to him,' said Gartner, nodding in agreement. 'I love the holy Lord Sigmar and I pray at His temple three times every feast day, but I've seen Templars rush in with their holy water and never come back. It's no good trusting to faith, sir. Not alone. That'll kill you.'

At that, Eichmann smiled wryly. As he did so, the scars on his battered face flexed across the tired skin.

'Oh, you don't have to tell me that, woodsman,' he said. 'I know all about it.'

THE DEAD LIMPED out of the gathering dark, dragging themselves along on broken limbs and grinning with skeletal jaws. Some wore scraps of clothing still; others were little more than skin and bones with cords of leathery sinew wrapped round their limb joints. Some whispered as they came, mouthing pieces of nonsense to themselves, over and over again; others were silent, stalking out of the shadows like translucent shades.

Before them came the terror. It seeped up out of the ground in a wave, rolling ahead of them, grabbing at Mila's heart and squeezing it closed.

She was not a fighter. She had never been a fighter. An overwhelming urge to capitulate rose up within her. Her bravado at Helgag was hard to remember now, and all she wanted to do was lie down and get it over with.

Perhaps death wouldn't be so bad. If it was over quickly, perhaps she could forget the fear.

'I'll hold the door,' said Huss. He was as immovable as ever. 'Stay behind me. Watch the windows.'

Mila whirled round. There were eight windows along the length of the nave, four on each side. Three still had broken glass in them; the rest were open to the elements. The windows were high up the walls – higher than she could have reached easily – but she knew that wouldn't stop them.

Schlecht started to rock on his haunches again. A low wailing spilled from his lips.

Mila, fighting against the panicked twist in her stomach, grabbed his shoulder. She recoiled when her fingers closed on it – there was almost no flesh on the bone, and it felt as fragile as duck's egg.

'Can you fight?' she asked, urgently. 'Do you have a weapon?'

He didn't even look at her. He just kept rocking, mumbling something incoherent. His eyes were out of focus.

Disgusted, Mila let him be. She stood alone in the centre of the nave, sword in hand, turning around slowly, looking from one window to the next, watching for the first of them to arrive.

'Do not fear,' she whispered to herself. 'Do not fear. Do not fear.'

They got to the doors. Huss's massive body blocked

her view, but she heard them run at him. She heard the thud of their feet on the earth, and the dry hiss of their anger, and the sweep of their borrowed blades.

Then she heard the whistle of the hammerhead, and the crack and crunch of bones being impacted. Huss never spoke. He just got to work, swinging his hammer with steady, expert strokes. He moved fluidly, stepping back to draw them on before charging forwards and scattering them.

There were plenty waiting, whole ranks of them, limping into range and grinning the whole time, looking for the gap in his defences. He slammed the hammer into them, handling the golden weapon as if it were weightless, switching it back quickly, adjusting its course to cause optimal damage before drawing it round for the next stroke.

She heard the first scratching noise at one of the windows and spun round to face it. A long, thin finger extended over the sill, probing for purchase. Another followed it, then another, until a bony hand gripped the stone.

Mila raced over to it, getting her blade clumsily into position and jabbing it up. The metal bit clean through the dry flesh and clanged from the sill. There was a shrill cry and something fell heavily to the ground outside the wall. Severed fingers dropped to the floor before her.

She swung around, just in time to see another hand come through a window on the far side of the nave. It was already gripping the stone, ready to pull its owner up after it and into the chapel.

Mila shot a despairing glance over at Schlecht. There were too many windows to guard on her own. The man hadn't moved. His eyes were still blank, and he was still mumbling and wailing to himself.

She ran over to the far wall and hacked at the extending arm coming through the gap in the stone. She severed it again and heard a heavy crunch as the body on the far side of the wall fell back to earth.

By then two more hands were creeping their way inside the chapel, one on either side of the building. She heard an echoing crash further down the nave as one of the remaining panes of glass was broken.

Even as she ran back across the nave to cut off the next incursion, she felt despair gnawing at her.

Too many. Too many. They'll get in, they'll get us, and then we will be made like them.

She swung the sword wildly at an extended forearm, missing her target. Another hand reached up after that one.

She hacked out, again and again. Her movements were frantic and ill-aimed, but they did just enough to cut through the paper-dry flesh.

Gods, this is impossible. We'll die here, trapped like rats in a sack.

Then she was running again, panting already, her hands sticky with sweat and her heart hammering away. They were going to get in.

Too many. Too many.

One of them thrust its shoulders through a window over on the wall she'd just run from and began to haul its torso through the gap.

Mila hurried back, reaching it just as the grey-skinned undead dropped down to the floor inside the wall. She lashed the blade across, cutting clean through its scrawny neck. The skull cracked to the stone and rolled away into the dust.

By then more were coming in, clambering through the windows and tumbling into the chapel. At least three were already down.

Mila moved with a desperate energy, slashing out with her sword, hacking at them before they could recover their feet.

She managed to dispatch a few more, getting to them as they were still unstable on their spindly legs. Even as she cut into them, though, more got into the chapel, pouring in through the windows whenever she was busy elsewhere. Three more wriggled through the windows, then six, then ten.

Mila retreated to the centre of the nave, backing up slowly, standing over Schlecht's whimpering body and keeping the undead at bay with ragged sweeps of her sword.

'I can't hold them!' she screamed, finally letting the terror bubble up in her throat.

One of the advancing undead got a cold hand through her defences then, grasping at her shoulder. She screamed, jerking round and jabbing at the extended arm. It came off at the elbow, clattering onto the floor, but its owner kept coming for her. It took three more swipes for the head to fall, by which time several more cadavers were advancing on her.

Mila grabbed Schlecht by the collar and hauled him away from them. He weighed almost nothing. Together they stumbled towards the doorway where Huss still fought.

Sensing victory, the undead pressed closer. Their eyes shone with a pale fire and their empty smiles grew wider.

We will take you, they hissed like reeds in a cold wind. *We will take you, and make you ours.*

Mila fought on, feeling her arms grow heavier with every stroke. There were dozens of them in the chapel now, staggering towards her, arms outstretched and fingers twitching. They didn't rush at her, just lurched onwards like drunkards, grinning and whispering the whole time.

'Damn you!' she screamed, close to tears. The aura of terror they exuded was overwhelming. 'Leave me alone! Leave me *alone!*'

Another claw got through, raking at her flank. Long fingers crept under her guard and gripped her skirts, digging in to her thigh like slivers of freezing iron.

She spun round, punching the blade down through the unliving flesh, but more fingers clamped onto her back. She went into a frenzy, lashing back and forth, letting the blade whirl around, chopping through the growing thicket of hands that grabbed at her.

Then they wrenched the sword from her grip, tugging it away with six half-cleaved fingers, whispering words of horror all the while.

Mila watched it go, pulled away into the mass of grey flesh, and knew it was over. She punched out at the nearest zombie, recoiling as her hand crunched into the brittle sack of bones. She felt cold hands close on her ankles, tight as iron bonds. Something wrapped around her waist, and she lost her balance. The world tilted, and she went down. A face loomed over hers, stinking of death and with its jaws wide open. She saw rows of teeth swoop down to her neck and screwed her eyes closed, tensing up for the final bite.

Then there was a rush of air, and something heavy swept over her. The grip on her limbs released, and she opened her eyes.

Huss had come among them. He moved just as he had done before, sweeping the hammer around him like a halo. The golden head smashed into the undead, lifting them clean from the ground and hurling them against the walls. He spun on the balls of his feet, swaying back and forth, working the heavy weapon with perfect, mesmerising poise.

They came at him, all of them, ignoring Mila now, focused on the real threat within their ranks. Dozens were in the chapel by then, thronging the narrow nave and pushing past one another to get at the priest.

Schlecht huddled close by her, cradling his head, weeping like a child. Mila shuffled over to him, trying to keep them both close to Huss, the only one of them still on his feet and fighting.

The warrior priest was immense. Watching him, cowering beside the drooling Schlecht, Mila suddenly remembered how he had been in Helgag. Nothing seemed to touch him. He was too fast for them, and far too strong. The hammer flew back and forth, obliterating anything it came into contact with. Huss swung round in circles, in perpetual motion, as silent as they were, crushing and smashing, tearing up the hissing ranks of undead and sending their broken bodies cartwheeling through the air.

They rushed at him, and he destroyed them. They scraped at his face with their curved talons, and he swatted the skeletal arms away. They lunged at his legs, snapping with emaciated jaws, and he crushed them beneath his boots. They swarmed at him like a cloud of locusts and the warhammer cut through them like a plough churning up the earth. They were smashed apart, cracked open, ground into clouds of sighing, impotent dust.

Mila looked on, feeling her jaw go slack. Schlecht still mumbled to himself, lost in a world of misery. As she watched the warrior priest, she slowly felt the vice of fear fall away from her.

They cannot hurt him. He is death to them.

The baleful assurance of the undead was beginning to break. They advanced on Huss more slowly, fearful of the sweeping warhammer. No fresh reinforcements came through the open doorway or windows. Those that remained in the chapel still attacked, though the light in their eyes seemed a little dimmer and their movements were halting.

He has broken them.

Even Schlecht stopped snivelling then, just long enough to look up and see the carnage caused by Huss. His bloodshot eyes widened, and his shuddering eased a little.

Mila couldn't stop shaking. Even if she could have reached her sword, she knew she'd not be able to wield it. Her heart still hammered in her chest, and her skin ran with sweat.

But she knew then that she would live to see the dawn. As Huss crashed and thumped his way through the remaining undead, she knew she would see another day.

She watched the warrior priest, her eyes shining.

Who are you?

Just as at Helgag, he was like a vision sent by some higher power, an avatar of invincibility thrust into a decaying world. Even amid her fear and shock, she could appreciate the full, gaunt majesty of the man before her.

By all the saints, she thought, huddled up beside the broken figure of Schlecht, hunched on the dirty floor of a ruined chapel in the heart of a devastated land.

Who are you?

CHAPTER SEVEN

ADSO THEISS BENT his back against the wind, pulling his robes tight around his old body. The chill air ran straight across the northern plains, all the way from Kislev with nothing to stop it but the low peaks running north-west up to the Sea of Claws.

He shuddered, feeling his joints ache as he struggled up the slope to the temple. A storm was coming and the air was thick with it. The sky hung above him like curdled milk, blotched and streaked with angry black cloud.

Winter was coming. All the auguries foretold that it would be a harsh one, despite the auspicious coronation of the young Karl Franz a few months earlier.

Theiss didn't know how many winters he had left. Perhaps another decade of them, or perhaps this would be his last.

His temple stood on the crest of the rise, defiant against the howling wind. The windows were dark despite the growing dusk.

Hirsch, you lazy dog. The candles should have been lit an hour ago.

Theiss felt his knuckles go raw. Gripped by shivering, he made his way up the long meandering path to the temple walls.

They looked less than secure against the growing force of the wind. Some of the outbuildings, the ones no longer used even by the acolytes, had fallen into disrepair. One of the steep roofs had fallen in and tiles littered the mud at the base of the walls. Even the central chapel, the heart of the little community, was patched up with rotting brickwork and propped with veined grey wooden struts.

The place is falling apart. Blood of Sigmar, it's getting worse.

Theiss made it to the ramshackle gates and rapped on the iron door knocker. As he did so, the door swung open. The lock was broken.

Pathetic. Truly pathetic.

He staggered over the threshold, shaking himself like an old dog. The entrance hall before him was deserted, and the firepit in the centre of the room was cold and clogged with ash.

Muttering, Theiss stalked across the hall, through the open doorway on the far side and along the cloister passage.

He found them in the refectory. The fire had been banked up there, throwing hot light across the cramped space. Hirsch and the others were lying on the tables, laughing and talking in slurred voices.

Theiss slammed the door behind him and they all jumped. One of them, Aldrich, nearly rolled off the table and onto the floor. Kassel belched loudly, and looked mortified.

Hirsch's ratty face went white with shock.

'Master–' he began, scrabbling to hide the earthenware flagon he'd been drinking from.

'Don't,' said Theiss, fixing him with a stony look. The long hike had drained him. He was cold, irritable and hungry. 'Just don't.'

He sat down heavily at one of the tables. The heat of the fire was almost painful against his frozen flesh. He lifted up his hands and looked at them.

They look like claws. Gods, this place is killing me.

'Get out,' he said, not looking at any of them. In the morning, he knew, the crushing sense of disappointment would make him more than angry with them. He'd rage against their fecklessness and ignorance then. They had been given so much and still refused to learn. Spoiled, stupid children, the lot of them.

Not now. For now, his only priority was to get warm, to get his old blood moving through his sluggish veins. He could smell meat roasting from somewhere and it made his stomach gurgle.

'Light the candles in the chapel,' he said, still not looking at any of the acolytes. 'Put out the votary articles according to the Eisal rites. Kneel before them until you sober up, then pray that I wake up less angry than I should do and that the rod of discipline has grown softer while I've been away.'

'We didn't expect–'

'I can see that, Hirsch.' Theiss fixed the young man with a cold stare. 'I came back early. Judgement falls on the ready and the unready.'

Hirsch looked down. He had the decency at least to be ashamed. One by one, they all shuffled out of the refectory and across the cloister yard to the chapel. Aldrich lurched along with them, clutching his fat stomach and looking like he wanted to be sick.

When the last of them had gone Theiss hobbled over to the fire, sat down and stretched his long legs in front of it. His sodden robes steamed. The twin-tailed comet medallion hanging from his neck glinted in the red light.

Theiss held it up and gazed at it for a moment. The metal was still winter-cold.

I was proud to wear this once. So proud, I thought my heart would burst from it.

He let it fall, and looked around the dirty refectory despairingly. Spilled beer had sunk into the wooden tabletops, staining it and making the place reek.

This is a temple. For the sake of Sigmar, this is a temple.

Theiss closed his eyes. The heat from the fire eased the ache in his flesh, but did nothing to shift the black depression in his stomach.

Something has to change.

THE STORM DID not lift. It swept over the black land bringing hammering rain with it. Thunder growled in its wake, and lightning flickered along the northern horizon, ice-white and raking.

The rain did not let up. Even when the last of the thunder had muttered away into the west, the rain still fell. It bounced from the tiles of the roofs and cascaded into the open square of the cloister. It sank into the churned up mud, swilling around and making everything greasy and foul. Old refuse was dislodged and floated across the surface, scummy and foaming. The chapel roof began to leak and columns of water ran in, pooling by the altar and running down the squat nave in streams.

Theiss drove the acolytes hard. From dawn, when their heads were most fragile, until well after the grey noon, he goaded them endlessly. He shouted orders at them, pitching his voice high and making them wince. They shot him looks of pure murder, but did as he told them. They mopped up the water in the chapel and threw it out into the yard, getting soaked and frozen in the process.

Hirsch was the worst. He slumped from duty to duty, a sullen look in his eyes. The others were little better, but had less spirit.

Sleep had done little to restore Theiss's bodily state. He felt the first stirrings of a chill in his bones, one that would bring fever if he wasn't careful. He should have rested by the fire and asked the cooks to bring him something hot and meaty, but there was too much to do. There was always too much to do. The temple was falling down around his ears and he had neither the energy nor the help needed to remedy it.

He stalked around the cloister moodily, watching the rain run down from the colonnade. It was there that he first heard the rapping on the main door. It might have been going on for some time, but the clatter of the rain and the banging of the acolytes as they rearranged everything in the chapel made it hard to hear.

Theiss limped down through the entrance hall, clutching at his staff.

'Who seeks entrance to the temple of Sigmar?' he cried, leaving the door closed. It was probably some damn fool trader, lost out on the moors and seeking lodgings until the storm passed over. Theiss would open up, of course, but that didn't mean he had to be happy about it.

No answer came. The knocker was rapped again, hard and deep. Whoever it was doing it had powerful hands.

Theiss shook his head irritably and wrenched the door open.

Before him stood a boy child, perhaps twelve winters, shivering in the rain. He was skinny, clad only in breeches and a soaked shirt. His thick, full hair looked like it had melted and part-merged with his head. Water tumbled over him, draining from his slender shoulders in rivulets.

'What do you want, child?' asked Theiss, looking down at him grimly. A potential thief perhaps, or maybe an orphan with a bottomless stomach and a head full of lice.

'To learn,' said the child.

The voice was uncommonly deep for a boy's, and he hurled the words out as if they were a challenge.

'What? You want to study here? No room! I have eight boys already and struggle to keep them fed. Go away. Go to Kemringen. Go to the seminary.'

'No.'

The boy's voice was solid with conviction. He stood there, drenched to the bone, shaking like he would die of the cold, defiant and insolent.

Theiss looked into the boy's eyes. They were deep brown, those eyes, almost all pupil. They were sad, animalistic eyes.

'No,' the boy said again. 'I will learn here.'

For a moment, Theiss didn't know what to say. He was tempted to laugh, to blurt out a bitter snort of derision.

For some reason, he didn't. The dismissive retort, the sarcastic remark, somehow they didn't spill from his lips like they usually did. He found himself lost in those eyes. They drew him in, two points of dark brown amid the wall of rain, immovable, unshakeable.

That boy wasn't going anywhere.

Theiss shook his head again, unsure what had come over him.

'Come in, then,' he said, opening the door wider. 'Until the rain abates – then, on your way. I won't have scavengers and pickpockets in the temple.'

The boy walked over the threshold confidently. His

expression was strange and serious. He stood in the entrance hall, dripping and shivering.

'Just until the rain stops,' said Theiss, but there was no certainty left in his voice. 'Then, on your way.'

'YOU'RE NOT TIRED?' asked Theiss.

The boy shook his head. The cool morning breeze ruffled his brown hair. A line of sweat ran down his temple, but otherwise he looked capable of working until the End Times. His strength was incredible.

'Even so. Come down for a moment – we'll start again later.'

The boy climbed down from the roof. As he came down the rickety ladder the rotten wood flexed under his feet. His hod was empty of the tiles he'd carried up, all of which now hung sturdily from the repaired roof.

He jumped down, landing in the mud at the ladder's base, and glared at Theiss.

'What now?' he demanded.

His energy seemed inexhaustible.

Theiss laughed. The crabbed, meagre sound struggled to escape his wizened old gullet. It had been a long time since he'd laughed.

'Rest, for a little while,' he said. 'I'm not a slavemaster, boy.'

Theiss hobbled across the courtyard and back to his private chambers. Puddles still sat in the mud, but the air smelled fresher in the wake of the storm.

'Come,' he said. 'We need to talk.'

The boy walked along behind him, striding confidently, just as he always did.

A week. It had taken him just that long to become indispensible. He carried water, he ran errands, he worked tirelessly. At that rate the outbuildings would be repaired before the full grip of the winter swept down from the north and made leaving the huddle of the walls difficult.

Theiss unlocked the door to his chambers and ushered the boy inside.

There wasn't much to look at: a few wooden, flaking icons of Sigmar, saints and old Emperors hung from the walls; the *Book of Devotions*; a mouldering copy of Saint Agnes's *Lives*; some copper bowls and trinkets sat on a chest. Only one chair stood against the wall – a high-backed wooden seat with a loose leg.

Two doors led out from the chamber on the far side. One gave access to the nave of the chapel; the other one was rarely opened.

Theiss eased himself down into the single seat, feeling his joints creak.

'I don't know where you came from, boy,' he said, 'but this can't go on.'

The child stood facing him, arms loose at his sides, glaring moodily.

'You haven't even told me your name. How can I do anything with you when I don't know your name? Come on, lad. Open up.'

The boy stared defiantly back. In the days since his arrival at the temple, his face had filled out. He'd eaten as if he'd been starving for weeks, and his cheeks, which had been pale and concave, were now ruddy and smooth.

He said nothing.

'You want to stay here,' said Theiss. 'Perhaps you can. But I must know your name.'

For the first time since his arrival, the boy looked doubtful.

'I don't have one,' he said.

Theiss laughed again.

'Of course you do.'

The boy's face creased into a scowl.

'No name.'

Theiss looked deep into those brown eyes. There was no lie in them. The boy looked angry, confused perhaps, but he had no deceit in him.

Theiss frowned.

What could take the name from a child?

He sat back in the chair, feeling the hard wood against his spine.

'You do have a name,' he said. 'All Sigmar's children have a name. Perhaps something has happened to make you forget yours. Perhaps there is a reason you can't tell me.'

He thought for a moment.

'Get the book from that chest,' he said, motioning towards the copy of *Lives*. The boy retrieved it, and handed it to Theiss, who opened it.

'These are the stories of great heroes of the Church,' he said, flicking absently from one to the next. 'Magnus the Pious, Alberich of Wurtbad, Helena the Chaste. They're all here. Tell me when to stop looking.'

'Now,' said the boy immediately.

Theiss stopped turning the pages. The text had been printed in Nuln and the type was narrow Imperial Gothic. On the verso was a short account of the life of Aldrecht Luthor, burgomeister of Rechtstadt. He had died defending his people against an incursion of beastmen – heroically, so the record stated. On the recto was that of Bohrs Huss, the pious and otherworldly prelate of pre-secession Marienburg.

'So there we go,' said Theiss, satisfied. 'Huss. Luthor Huss. Not very memorable perhaps, but it'll do. I'll tell the others to call you that.'

The boy didn't seem interested in that. He was fascinated, though, by the close-ranked lines of type on the page. He leaned forwards, peering at the text.

'You like this?' asked Theiss, turning the book so the boy could see more. 'You know what this is, lad?'

The child now called Luthor nodded.

'Power,' he said.

Theiss laughed again.

'Oh yes.'

He watched the child's serious eyes scan along the printed characters. No understanding was there, but intelligence was.

He could learn. Unlike the others, the lazy unwanted third or fourth sons who he'd been forced to educate, this one could learn.

'Very well, Luthor Huss,' said Theiss, feeling enthusiastic about something for the first time in years and liking the sensation. 'I'll teach you. Maybe that's why you came here. I suppose, the world being what it is, we'll find out soon enough.'

THEISS WASN'T ALWAYS there. Huss didn't like that. His appetite for learning was as relentless as his capacity to work. He would demand more lessons, sulking furiously when denied them. Every spare moment was spent hunched over books, mouthing the words as he gradually made sense of them. After a month at the temple he was reading primers designed for acolytes older than him. After two months he had progressed to the catechisms.

After a year he had read the entirety of the *Life of Sigmar* and had begun to wrestle with Uwe Mordecai's dense and difficult *Thoughts on the Nature of Faith*. He surpassed his fellow acolytes in everything, and they hated him for it – Hirsch in particular, who had no aptitude for anything but drinking and sleeping.

When Theiss went away, so did Huss's protection from them.

'Why do you have to go?' Huss would demand, scowling the whole time.

And Theiss would laugh.

'I have duties, boy. There are people who need a priest. Who do you think will bless their crops, marry them, bury them? The real world is out there, the world of flesh and misery. They need us – never forget that.'

He would depart then, hobbling out across the moors, grey robes billowing against the icy wind. Huss would watch him from the gates until he disappeared from view, as if by willing him to return, he would.

Then the jackals would close in, leering and slapping their fists into the cups of their hands.

After the beatings that followed, Huss would lie awake long into the night, feeling his bruised skin ache, listening to the sounds of carousing from the refectory.

He never made a sound, even while the boots were flying in. He maintained eye contact for as long as he could, glaring at them, facing down the laughs and taunts. By the time Theiss came back, the bruises had always faded.

If the old man suspected anything about what happened during his absences, he said nothing. The world was a hard place, and a man had to learn to stick up for himself.

Sigmar blesses those who fight. That was in the scriptures.

One day, Huss read it for himself. He sat alone after that, brooding on it, turning the words over in his mind.

* * *

ANOTHER YEAR. A cold, hungry one. Famine swept across the north of the Empire, driving many into the embrace of Morr and forcing more to seek refuge further south. Theiss was abroad often, ministering to those who had the will to remain behind. His skin, already dry and creased, weathered further. The flesh on his fingers sunk to the bone and the lines of care under his eyes deepened.

Huss grew stronger as his master grew weaker. A solid diet of boiled meat and hard work broadened his chest and filled out his arms. The childish petulance faded, replaced by a grim-faced, determined piety. He woke before dawn each day and knelt in silent prayer until the sun rose.

That single-mindedness worried Theiss, who had no desire to raise up a zealot.

'The faith of our fathers is for living, Huss,' he would say. 'Nothing is holier than tilling the land or tending a hearth. Sigmar, while a man, did these things.'

Huss listened patiently but did not change. His life became a cycle of study, labour, prayer and fasting.

On one mist-drenched dawn in early Sommerzeit, after the worst of the bad weather had passed over and the land was recovering some of its health, Theiss went out again. He had been preoccupied for weeks, as if the travails of the earth had sunk into his blood. He didn't tell Huss he was leaving but just set out as the sun came up, limping along, head down staring at the stony earth.

So it was that Hirsch and Kassel found Huss alone in the chapel, kneeling before the copper votary articles, head bowed against his chest.

'Praying hard, boy?' asked Hirsch, gazing at Huss with undisguised loathing.

Huss turned slowly, looking at them with his uncanny, unbroken stare.

Hirsch had grown fat in the two years since Huss's arrival. His skin had the pallor of an alcoholic, with sallow cheeks and a bloodshot nose. Every feature on that face was hard, pinched and meagre, and his eyes glistened shrewishly.

Huss got to his feet.

'Praying for the old goat to come back,' said Kassel, flexing his fingers. 'Praying for someone to save his arse.'

Hirsch nodded, walking slowly towards Huss.

'Reckon that's right,' he said. 'Reckon he likes hiding behind the old man's skirts. Wonder why? What do the two of them get up to, do you think?'

'I don't want to think about that. Some sickness. Something filthy. The old man's as rotten as a week-old corpse.'

Huss waited for them to arrive. He felt his body loosen. He had been praying for almost an hour and his soul was at peace. The arrival of the acolytes did nothing to change that. There was no fear this time, no trepidation.

'No more of this,' said Huss calmly, as if to himself.

Hirsch laughed. It was a forced laugh; a joyless, cynical sound.

'No more of what?' he asked. 'Don't like the truth?'

'Don't talk to me like that,' said Kassel to Huss, and didn't smile. 'You *runt*, creeping around in his shadow. I'll break your face, give you something to pray about.'

By then the two of them stood over Huss. Though the boy had put on weight, he was over a foot shorter than them and not nearly as heavy. He looked up at them with the same expression he used with everyone.

Fearless.

'This will never happen again,' he said quietly.

That seemed to set them off. Hirsch let fly with his right fist, just as he'd done a dozen times before, aiming it at Huss's head. Kassel cocked his own, itching to pile in.

Huss swayed away from the blows, moving smoothly and without hurry. He swung his own fist back, punching deep into Hirsch's stomach.

The acolyte winced, staggering backwards. For a moment, pain vied with shock on his astonished features.

Then Kassel hit Huss. The boy reeled. The two of them traded a flurry of punches, fast and vicious. Hirsch barrelled back into the fight, and the three of them fell into a messy, artless brawl.

For a moment, Huss held them. Ignoring the blows to his face and chest, he stayed on his feet, jabbing out, holding his hands high. He retreated slowly, grunting as the hits went in but never losing his eerie composure.

It couldn't last. The acolytes were older, stronger, and there were two of them. They hammered away carelessly, getting in each other's way, fighting with chaotic, brutal ferocity.

They hated him. They hated his quiet, serious manner. They hated the fact that he showed up their studied boorishness. His very presence in the temple was an affront to them. They couldn't remove him, and so they made his life a series of petty, painful episodes.

Huss ducked under a swipe from Hirsch and Kassel's fist cracked into his forehead. He lurched back, feeling the blood pound in his head. Another fist came in at his torso, slamming into his ribcage and winding him.

Huss dropped to one knee. He knew that if he went down fully it would be over. Just as so often in the past, they'd lay into him with their boots, sating their need to inflict pain to ease their own.

Huss lurched forwards, dodging the incoming kicks, scuttling across the floor of the nave like an insect. They came after him, robes flapping.

Panting, feeling a sharp pain growing in his bruised head, Huss made it to the doorway leading to Theiss's chambers.

'He's not in there!' taunted Kassel as Huss crashed through into the room beyond. 'He can't save you!'

They followed him in, snatching at his robes, trying to catch up and haul him back into the chapel.

Huss whirled round, looking for the way back out to the courtyard. He picked the wrong door, wrenching open the one he'd never seen opened. Inside was a shallow cupboard lined with wooden shelves. Books lay on most of them, battered and well thumbed.

Below them was a warhammer, four feet long in the shaft, heavily made with a dull iron hammerhead, wound with strips of leather and engraved with runes of destruction. A thick layer of dust covered the top of it.

Huss seized it. It felt far lighter in his hands than it should have done. He spun round, gripping the weapon two-handed.

Hirsch's momentum carried him too close. Huss swung the weapon instinctively, feeling the heavy killing-edge pull him off-balance. The hammer crunched into Hirch's stomach, throwing the acolyte back across the chamber. Hirsch reached out for Theiss's writing table as he fell, dragging papers down with him.

Kassel stopped dead, wide-eyed.

Huss recovered his balance, pulling the hammerhead back up, preparing to swing again. His hands gripped the shaft loosely, expertly, as if it had been made for him.

For a moment, Kassel and Huss stood facing one another, breathing heavily, neither one of them moving. Hirsch groaned on the floor, clutching his stomach.

Eventually, Kassel gave way. He retreated to his fallen friend, stooping to drag him away from further harm.

Huss stood over both of them, feet apart, warhammer poised. His cheeks were flushed and his heart beat heavily in his chest.

'This will never happen again,' said Huss, just as before, but this time the words resonated from the narrow walls of the chamber with the absolute certainty, underwritten by the holy weapon of Sigmar and in the presence of his image, that it would not.

CHAPTER EIGHT

DAECHER RODE AT the front of the convoy with Udo. Neither man liked the other, which was why Eichmann had placed them there. In the time they spent not talking to one another they'd be keeping a better watch.

Behind them rode the vanguard of men-at-arms: twenty men, looking around them with stiff faces in an attempt to hide their nerves. Then came Eichmann and Gartner, riding ahead of the baggage and the rearguard.

After a morning of steady progress the waystation had fallen far behind them. They'd gone several miles down the forest road before turning north-east, driving down a long track into the heart of the woods. The trees had closed in quickly, choking the verges of the track and rearing above their heads on either side. Soon the convoy found itself passing down a deep ravine, and the twin masses of foliage towered over them.

The last of the summer covering was still on the trees, and layer upon layer of leaves rustled in the breeze. Before long the views ahead were truncated, blocked off by thick coverings of brushing, twisting branches. The light of the sun grew greyer as the canopy closed off much of the sky. A deep musk hung in the air, the wet smell of crushed leaf-matter and ancient, undisturbed soil.

The trail wound into the east, looping over ridges and plunging down into briar-choked defiles. The convoy went slowly as the horses picked their way through the overgrown track and the baggage wains got trapped in the rutted earth. After leaving the forest road for the less well-trodden paths, their progress slowed to a near-crawl.

None of that particularly bothered Eichmann. The map he'd obtained was frustratingly inexact, but after cross-referencing all the written authorities he'd been able to find he had little doubt they were heading in the right direction.

Deep down, despite everything, he'd known he would be guided. Eichmann had been in the service of the Church long enough to have witnessed the hand of Sigmar in everything he did. The little nudges, the subtle signs, they were always there.

So he would arrive at Four Towers. He would uncover the nature of von Hessler's corruption, which would lead him deeper into whatever foul ministry was gestating in Middenheim. And then, as always, he would move to cut out the infection. The body would be cleansed, and he would wield the instruments.

Once all that was done, he would move on to the next heresy. There would always be another one – another scholar dabbling in necromantic arts, another damsel seduced by sibilant whispers, another knight tempted into bloodlust and given over to the frenzy of killing.

Endless. The tide of heresy was endless. It washed at the walls of humanity, those fragile bulwarks erected over millennia, gnawing and eroding, sinking and staining.

Against that, Eichmann's faith survived, but it no longer gave him any satisfaction. He knew it had become a dry, famished thing; a remnant of something to hold on to, even as it reminded him how far the world around him had fallen into decay. With every year, the memory of the white towers of Altdorf faded a little further, and the medallion around his neck felt a little colder.

There were those, he had heard, who left the service of the Temple with their sanity intact and with a cheerful heart. He had heard that. Perhaps, he speculated from time to time, such stories were even reliable.

'You don't sleep much, witch hunter,' said Gartner, riding beside him.

Eichmann turned to him, surprised from his thoughts.

'Your pardon, if I offended you,' said Gartner. His tone was friendly enough. 'I have trouble with it myself. I saw you last night, walking out in the courtyard of the waystation.'

'Did you, now?' said Eichmann. It wasn't something he particularly wished to talk about, especially not with a man he barely knew.

'Like I said,' said Gartner, shrugging. 'No offence intended.'

'None taken. Perhaps you'll ask me now why I don't sleep.'

'Perhaps I won't. I sense you don't wish to discuss it.'

'Then what about you? What's your reason?'

Gartner smiled ruefully.

'We all have one. I hate those places. They're cages, stuffed with men just like – if you'll permit me – your companion over there. Brutes and murderers.'

'Don't talk like that about Udo. He has hidden depths.'

'Very well hidden. But you take my meaning – the waystations are pits of filth. If the forest ever claimed them back, I wouldn't mourn it.'

Eichmann raised an eyebrow.

'That talk is heresy, woodsman.'

'I know you feel the same,' said Gartner calmly. 'Or I wouldn't have said it.'

'I don't, as it happens,' said Eichmann. 'They are bastions of humanity in the wasteland. The men who guard them are heroes.'

Gartner looked at Eichmann for a long time then, and his gaze was searching.

'You're an interesting man, witch hunter,' he said. 'I think of myself as a reasonable judge of character, but I really can't work you out.'

Eichmann was about to reply when a piercing scream broke out at the rearguard of the caravan.

The witch hunter instantly pulled his horse around and kicked it into a trot. As he did so, he pulled out a pistol, loaded and primed to fire. Gartner rode back along the far side of the convoy, drawing his shortsword. Shouting, coarse and hurried, rose up from the men further back.

When Eichmann arrived the rearguard was in disarray. Several of the horses had gone wild, rearing up and foaming at the mouth. Two men had been thrown from their mounts. One of them lay face-down, unmoving.

'What happened?' demanded Eichmann, riding straight up to a bucking stallion, grabbing it by the reins and hauling it back.

One of the guards, a stocky, thick-necked man with a long scar across his pug-nosed face, looked at him with fear and incredulity in his eyes.

'Meunig, sir,' he said, the words catching in his throat. 'He's... gone.'

Gartner rode to the very rear of the convoy. One of the

horses had run free, riderless and with an empty saddle. The beast wasn't one of the spares; its flanks were hung with rolled up clothing, a helm, a sword and ammunition bags for a pistol. Gartner seized the loose reins and pulled the animal back towards the others.

'I warned you all!' he shouted, looking angry. 'Stay together! No one to break formation!'

'He didn't,' protested the stocky man-at-arms, looking confused and hesitant. 'I was talking to him just a moment ago. He was less than a yard away from me. I could've reached over and–'

Another scream broke out, strangled and terrified, seemingly from a long way away. It went on for some time, before breaking down into a final, echoing sob of pure terror and anguish.

Eichmann looked up at the trees on either side of them. The cover was thick and tangled.

The rest of the men looked at it the same way. Some of them had drawn weapons, but none looked sure what to use them on. Gartner looked out into the shadow of the branches gloomily.

'What took him?' he asked.

The man-at-arms shook his head.

'I swear it – he was just *there*,' he insisted, pointing a couple of yards back up the track.

Nothing remained but the man's horse. The remainder of the rearguard had managed to restore some semblance of order. One of the fallen men had got up. The other still hadn't moved.

'No one saw anything?' asked Eichmann, looking at them all in turn.

The faces of the men were pale. One by one, they shook their heads. Some looked ashamed; others looked nervous and jumpy.

Eichmann spat on the ground and turned to face Gartner.

'What could have done this?' he asked, clicking the hammer of his pistol back into the safety position. He felt angry, but had no target for his anger.

The woodsman shrugged.

'If no one saw anything...' he said, then trailed off.

Eichmann looked back up at the sea of trees, rising away from him in steeply banked ranks. The leaves still rustled, furrowed by the wind, but the sound now seemed sinister and mocking. The branches were pressing in close, throttling out the light, reaching over them with gnarled, swaying fingers.

For an instant, he thought he saw something in the deep green haze, the merest outline of something in the mottled shadows. A tremor passed across his heart, as cold as any he had known.

'Get back in formation,' he said grimly, turning away from the sight. 'Ride close, and keep your eyes open. And steel yourselves – this is just the beginning.'

MILA WATCHED HIM sleep. She hadn't seen him sleep since she'd first encountered him, though, surely, he must have done at some point. Huss was only human. Almost certainly, he was only human.

His huge chest rose and fell under its breastplate. He lay on his back on the chapel floor, head on the stone. His mouth was open, drawing in huge, deep breaths before expelling them again. Even in such a deep sleep, movement played across his body. His right hand twitched, as if trying to grasp the shaft of a weapon. Every so often he would grimace, giving away the painful content of his dreams.

Mila watched him for a long time, fascinated. For a

man who looked so invincible when on his feet, it was strangely humbling to see him laid low. The morning sun slanted through the broken windows, reflecting from the dull metal of his armour. She had never been into one of the massive, sprawling cathedrals of the Empire with their ranks of statues and rows of tombs, but her mental image of those sacred places corresponded exactly with how Huss looked to her then.

A living saint.

The ruined door to the chapel banged open, and Schlecht limped in. He looked around himself nervously, as if the undead might still be inside somewhere, hiding as he had been.

The bodies of the dead had all been burned, just as they had been before in Helgag. Huss and Mila had seen to that, finishing their arduous labour only as the first rays of the sun had come up. Once again, Huss had killed all of them, though by the end he'd been almost collapsing from exhaustion. All that remained of the corpses was the faint odour of decay on the earth.

'Find anything?' she asked.

Schlecht shook his head, then crept towards her. He squatted some distance away, twitching and wringing his hands obsessively.

'We'll wait till he wakes up, then,' said Mila. 'But we need more food. You, in particular. Gods, you're a skinny man.'

She didn't like to look at Schlecht for too long. It came as no surprise to her that she'd mistaken him for one of the undead when he'd first emerged. His skin was as pale as sour cream and running with sores. His lips were swollen and had pulled away from his teeth, which were the butter-yellow of Morrslieb. His eyes remained staring the whole time, as if his face had been fixed into a static expression of fright and could never relax from it. What hair remained on his head was straggling and dry. His clothes amounted to little more than scraps of dirty cloth. He reeked.

He liked to look at her, though. Not in a disinterested, disapproving way like Huss, and not in the lecherous, covetous way that Reilach had. He looked at her as if she were a figment of some half-recalled memory. His bloodshot eyes followed her around, staring out from his shrivelled face like frog's eyes.

Mila exhaled impatiently. She didn't like him looking at her any more than she liked looking at him. That was why she'd sent him to look for food, knowing full well that there'd be nothing worth eating left in the ruins outside.

'I know you can talk,' she snapped. 'I heard you speak. So don't pretend you can't.'

Schlecht kept looking at her, his mouth hanging open. Saliva, thick and viscous, collected on his lower lip.

'I don't know what happened to you,' she said, shuffling round to face him. 'Perhaps, if you told me, I might be able to help.'

The lower lip trembled a little.

'My village was destroyed,' she said. 'It was just like this – almost exactly like this. I was the only one that got out. Is that what happened to you? Did the dead come there, too?'

Schlecht swallowed. His adam's apple bobbed down and up his scrawny chicken's neck. He said nothing, and just kept staring.

Mila gave up.

'Forget it, then,' she said, clambering to her knees. Her body was stiff and aching, a product of two brutal fights and days of trekking across the wilderness.

She brushed down her skirts, which were as filthy and stinking as everything else. A few yards away, Pieter's sword lay where it had fallen from the desiccated hands of its usurpers. She hadn't touched it since the undead had snatched it away, fearful that some taint of theirs would have lingered. Perhaps now was the time to clean it properly. It seemed likely, after all, that she'd need it again.

'Not the dead.'

Schlecht's voice was horrible, like she would imagine a crow's would sound if a crow could talk. Everything about it was scraped, parched, ripped.

Mila stared at Schlecht, not really understanding what he'd said.

'Not the dead,' he repeated, shaping the words slowly. It looked like enunciation was hard on his broken lips. 'The beasts.'

Mila knelt back down.

'What do you mean?' she asked.

'The beasts. I saw them. I dreamed them. Goat-face. Through the walls. Goeringen.'

'Is that where we are?'

Schlecht shook his head impatiently.

'Goeringen. Days away. They burned it. I do not sleep. I dream, when awake. I see goat-face. They hunt me. I do not sleep.'

Mila frowned, trying to make sense of what the man was saying.

'Where are the beasts?'

'Beasts are coming. After the dead. More coming. No escape.'

'Are they coming here? Where is this place?'

Schlecht swallowed again, and his eyes watered painfully.

'Don't know. Been awake a long time. Can't… *see*…'

As if released by some codeword, his face suddenly crumpled into an expression of deep, deep agony. A tear ran down his wrinkled cheek. His hands began to shake uncontrollably.

Stirred by a capacity for pity she didn't know she had, Mila swept herself up and went over to him, stooping low and wrapping her broad arms around his shivering shoulders.

'I'm sorry,' she said, ignoring the stench rising from his suppurating flesh. 'I'm so sorry. I didn't mean to–'

Schlecht grabbed her then, scratching at her flesh through her clothes, clutching at her with surprising, desperate strength. He broke into sobs – great, shuddering weeps that shook his fragile ribcage and made his cramped limbs tremble.

Taken aback, Mila remained stiff and rigid. Schlecht hung on to her like a terrified infant, howling out his huge, long-suppressed horror.

Once the shock of it had subsided, Mila relaxed her arms, letting the man within them weep, absorbing the canker of his pain. His misery seemed bottomless, like a shaft into an open soul that went on and down into the underworld.

Moving gingerly, going gently, she reached up to cradle the back of his head.

'Get it out,' she murmured, rocking him like she might have rocked a child. 'Get it out. Whatever happened, it's over now.'

And as that lie passed her lips, for just a moment, for as long as the casual falsehood lingered in the air, it felt like it truly was.

* * *

HUSS AWOKE A long time after noon. After his eyes had opened he lay still for a while, blinking and staring at the chapel roof.

Mila looked up from the fire she'd built up with broken pieces of wood, withdrawing the little pail of boiling water she'd been holding over the heat on the end of a long stick.

Huss stirred himself, dragging his heavy body up on to his elbows. He looked at her blearily.

'You made a fire,' he said.

Mila nodded.

'You disapprove?'

Huss thought for a moment, then shook his head.

'No. Good idea.'

Mila poured some of the boiling water into a chipped wooden cup and placed the pail on the floor next to the fire. She got up and brought the cup to Huss.

The warrior priest dragged himself into a sitting position and took it in both hands.

'My thanks, daughter,' he said, with feeling. 'You've been busy.'

Mila went back to sit by the meagre blaze.

'Rickard helped me,' she said. 'He found a few useful things. I think it's best for him to keep busy.'

'The sick man?'

'He's called Rickard.'

Huss took a slurp of the water, jerking his lips back as he scalded them.

'He spoke to you?' he asked.

'A little. Something happened to his village, just like it happened to mine. I think it's driven him mad.'

Huss swirled the water in the cup, watching the steam rise from it.

'So many,' he said. 'I do not understand it.'

'Don't understand what?'

Huss looked up at her as if he'd been speaking to himself and she'd interrupted him. For a minute, Mila thought he would retreat back into his thoughts, shutting her out as he usually did.

Then, seemingly, he reconsidered.

'I don't understand these attacks. I don't understand why there are so many of them, so often, night after night. It worries me.'

Mila laughed.

'It *worries* you? I didn't think anything worried you.'

Again, the hesitation before he opened up.

'Plenty worries me, daughter,' he said.

'My name, too,' she said. 'It's Mila.'

'Maybe this isn't enough. That's what worries me.'

Huss sighed deeply, and took another sip of his drink.

'There's a town within a few days of here,' he said. 'Eisenach. If they grow bolder, they'll get there sooner or later. A thousand souls live in Eisenach.'

At the mention of the word *town*, Mila felt a sudden spike of anxiety. Everything she'd ever heard about towns made her nervous. In her mind, they were vast places, teeming with corruption, noise and peril. Not like a village, where you knew everyone and everyone knew you.

Had known, at any rate.

'So,' she said, not wanting to think about that, 'is that where we're headed now?'

Huss paused.

'I'll pray for guidance,' he said. 'But I think so. The tide of corruption is growing, though the cause is a mystery to me. A stand must be made.'

Mila shot him a warning look.

'You're not going off on your own again? I won't stand

for that, not after the last time. You know that I'll follow you, even if it cripples me, and when I catch you up–'

Huss held his huge hands up in mock surrender. Once again, an elusive smile crept across his thin, austere lips. The effect on his face was remarkable. It was as if every muscle on that heavy, sepulchral visage protested against levity, dragging it back down into the habitual jaw-jutting, brow-furrowed countenance he wore when wielding the warhammer. But for a moment at least the smile lingered, breaking open the mask of granite just a little, like firelight peeping around the cracks in a locked door.

'I understand, daughter,' he said. 'I have accepted my fate. Some forces of nature are too strong to be fought.'

'And Rickard?' she asked, pressing him further.

'He can make it?'

Mila nodded.

'If we get some food into him. His mind may never recover, and he smells pretty bad, but – how would you put it? – he's still a son of Sigmar.'

Huss drained the cup of water.

'That he is,' he said, wiping his mouth and giving her, for the first time, a look that came close to approval.

CHAPTER NINE

EICHMANN RODE INTO the clearing as the light of the sun began to bleed out of the sky. The rows of trees ahead withdrew a little, exposing a wide circle of mossy grass. One ancient oak remained in the very centre, huge and knotted. Its grey branches flared out from the trunk, running across the clearing at little more than head height. It cast a long shadow.

Daecher was there, standing next to Udo. Neither of them said much. They were looking at the corpse hanging up in the canopy.

Eichmann drew alongside Udo, following his gaze.

'It's Meunig?' he asked, peering up at the gently spinning figure.

'It's Meunig,' said Udo, grimly.

The corpse hung twenty feet up, far into the swaying foliage of the oak's crown. Blood dripped down from it, splattering on the leaves and running in trickles to the earth below.

The corpse had no skin. Flayed muscle glistened in the gathering dusk, speckled with blood and sinew. Markings could be made out on the exposed flesh, angular like runes, carved into the body and welling with clotted blood.

143

'Can we cut him down?' asked Eichmann, screwing his eyes up to see how the corpse had been fixed. He felt nauseous, and swallowed heavily.

Udo squinted at the twisting cadaver.

'Gods alone know how they got it up there,' he said. 'Would those branches bear another man's weight?'

'I don't–'

Suddenly, the corpse twitched. A strangled, gargling noise broke from its lips. The sound was utterly horrific, a stomach-wrenching bleat of pure agony. What remained of its limbs broke into frantic, spasmodic jerks.

'Holy Sigmar,' swore Udo. 'He's *alive.*'

Eichmann drew his pistol and cocked the hammer.

He was too slow. Daecher had already drawn his crossbow, and a bolt whistled from the mechanism, spinning up through the leaves before thudding into Meunig's chest.

The man shuddered, jolted, then slumped still.

Eichmann turned to face Daecher. The woodsman looked as sour-faced and calm as ever.

'You might want to move back, sir,' Daecher said, grunting with effort as he loaded another quarrel into the crossbow and pulled the whipcord string tight.

He took aim carefully, moving the bow to match the swaying of the oak, and let fly again. The bolt shot true, severing the thick knot tying Meunig's noose to the tree. The body slid and crashed down through the branches before landing in a bloody heap on the turf.

The head rolled to face Eichmann. It had no eyes. What features remained on the ruined face were twisted into a mask of pure anguish.

Gartner came alongside the others. He looked down at the wet mound of broken flesh.

'Good shot,' he said.

'This man will be buried,' said Eichmann, clicking the hammer on his pistol back into place.

'We don't have long,' said Gartner, looking up at the sky. 'We have to get the fires lit before we lose the sun.'

Eichmann nodded.

'I need three men. The rest can start chopping firewood.'

He looked out the ring of trees surrounding the clearing.

'Tell them to cause as much damage as they can,' he said, and real hatred shot through his speech. 'They can hack as many of those damn trees as they like.'

AN HOUR LATER, and the light had gone. Long shadows crept along the grass from the treeline, inching out from the dark hollows and snaking over the uneven ground.

The men made camp on the far side of the oak, out of sight of where Meunig's body had been hung. Four huge fires were lit around the edge of it, roaring and crackling as the green wood burned. The timber had been slick with sap and hard to get going; Eichmann had been forced to use sprinklings of blackpowder to get the blazes started, though the timber burned well enough once the raw heat had caught.

All of the men huddled within the wavering light of the furnaces, their faces tight. Some stared out into the night, glaring at the gloom as if they could face it down. Others turned their faces away, perhaps trying to forget just how far into the forest they had already come.

Udo remained standing for a long time. His bald head loomed up against the firelight defiantly, locked in a belligerent stare that would have been at home in any Empire tavern's fist-fight.

Udo didn't suffer from trepidation. He caused it, and appreciated its uses, but only on a strictly rational level. At no point did he ever give the impression he really understood what it was.

Daecher and Gartner were similarly phlegmatic. Once the fires had been lit, Daecher spent his time cleaning the crossbow mechanism and wiping slivers of gore from his retrieved quarrel. Gartner sat quietly, his head inclined slightly to one side, listening.

Eichmann watched them all, saying nothing. He had a hard time admitting it to himself, but Meunig's death had affected him. He'd seen a hundred corpses in his time, some of them carved open on the tables of confession, but the random nature of the man's disappearance and return had unsettled him.

He could still see Meunig's sightless eyes, hollow and black. When he closed his own eyes, they stared back at him in the bloody dark.

'What are you listening for?' he said to Gartner, keeping his voice low.

'The sound of the wood. Anything unnatural. Anything out of place.'

Eichmann listened for himself. The dusk chorus ran through the trees, light and echoing. The breeze hadn't dropped, and the leaves still shifted against one another. The sound was endless, like the soft crash of waves against the shore. After a while, it started to prey on his nerves.

'And can you hear anything?' he asked.

Gartner shook his head.

'Not yet,' he said. 'But it'll be a long night.'

Eichmann turned away, looking out beyond the fires. The flames threw everything into a wavering, shifting mass of shadows. He could see between the trunks of the nearest trees, deep into the clefts where the brambles coiled.

For a moment, he thought he caught a glimpse of a face grinning back at him, horned and bearded. He blinked, and the vision disappeared. A trick of the flickering light.

'How close are we?' asked Gartner.

Eichmann turned away from the forest.

'Vierturmeburg is a day's march,' he said. 'Assuming the way remains clear for us.'

Gartner grunted.

'Indeed.'

Daecher kept scraping – *scrtch, scrtch, scrtch* – at the mechanism of his crossbow. The noise was irritating, and Eichmann had to restrain himself from snapping at the man.

This place is getting to me. I should be stronger than this.

'Does the word "Hylaeus" mean anything to you, Gartner?' asked Eichmann, forcing himself to stay focused on the task at hand.

The woodsman thought for a moment, then shook his head.

'Should it?'

Eichmann shrugged.

'It's come up a few times. A codeword, perhaps, or maybe the name of a person. Or maybe nothing.'

'That's your business, then,' said Gartner. 'I'll stick to what I know.'

'The forest.'

'Aye.'

Eichmann ran his hands through his hair, feeling his lids growing heavy and his body listless.

'How do you live, spending so much time here?' he said. 'This place is foul. I sense malice in everything around me. The air stinks with it. It hates us.'

'It does,' agreed Gartner. 'It loathes us. There are creatures in here with no names in the languages of men. They never leave the wood, and they resent our intrusion. They cannot be bargained with, and their spite is infinite.'

He let slip a low, gruff laugh.

'But give that to me any time, rather than Middenheim,' he said. 'How many times has a man smiled to your face, wishing only to bury his dagger in your back? There's no pretence here. If you learn where the danger is, you can negotiate the woods. And there's beauty here, too, if you know where to look.'

He looked at Eichmann, and his expression became serious.

'This is where we came from, witch hunter,' he said. 'This is our ancient home. We fled from it, terrified of what lay in the shadows, but it haunts our dreams still. When I leave the forest, I still see it in my sleep. It never leaves you, once it has clawed its way into your soul. Never.'

Eichmann returned the man's gaze steadily, not liking the way he was talking.

'A man's soul should have room for nothing but the veneration of Sigmar,' he said. 'One day these trees will be gone, cleansed by fire and axe. Mankind will rule here, just as mankind will rule everywhere.'

As he said those words, the trees brushed together more violently, murmuring and clashing in the breeze.

Gartner raised a sceptical eyebrow.

'You truly believe that?' he asked, smiling a little. 'You have more faith than I thought, witch hunter. Perhaps you have more faith than you realise.'

Eichmann started to reply. He knew what he wanted

to say, but the words stuck in his throat; he suddenly felt no conviction in them. It was as if the oppressive hostility in the dank air had sapped the will from him.

He saw Meunig's face every time he blinked.

'Faith is all we have,' he said, but the words sounded empty under the shadow of the trees.

As EVER, HE did not sleep.

Eichmann lay on his back, surrounded by the snoring forms of his men. They were little more than dark mounds on the earth, framed by the fires. Beyond them, the sentries stood to attention. They were in teams of two, rotated regularly. None of them strayed beyond the pools of light, and they threw wood onto the flames regularly, keeping them burning strongly.

Udo had fallen asleep as soon as his head had hit the ground, in the way warriors did. He snored like a steam tank, untroubled and blissful. Even Daecher and Gartner had drifted off in the end, eventually satisfied that nothing sinister was in close proximity. Both men kept their weapons close, though; Daecher's hand rested lightly on his crossbow and Gartner's sword was by his side.

Knowing there would be little chance of him getting any rest, Eichmann lay flat, watching the stars above him. They came out, one by one, as the last of the sunlight sank into black.

He had always relished looking at the stars. They were clean, unsullied, sailing far above the filth and misery of the mortal world. Watching them, it was easy to believe that purity was attainable and that the endless striving against corruption was not, as it sometimes seemed, doomed to failure.

The stars gave him little comfort that night. Eichmann

could feel his heart drumming in his chest. He couldn't relax. The noises of the nearby trees set his teeth on edge. Whenever a twig snapped or a bird called, sweat broke out across his forehead. He tried pushing his cloak up against his ears, but the sounds were only partly muffled.

Perhaps his nerve had gone. He'd seen it happen to others. Old Dietmar had lost it almost overnight. One week he'd been hunting cultists in the catacombs, his eyes brimming with fire. The next, he'd gone, gibbering and shuddering in his draughty old house, terrified of being alone, terrified of his visitors.

They'd found him a few weeks later, hanging from the rafters, naked as the day he'd been born, his whole body covered in writing; one word, endlessly repeated in black ink.

Fear. Fear. Fear. Fear.

Perhaps that was the fate that awaited him too. Perhaps, when one lost one's faith, that was the reward.

I have not lost my faith. I have just learned that it has limits. I still believe.

Eichmann stared at the stars, feeling his shallow breaths push against the blanket. His bones felt cold, as if the chill of the earth had risen into them.

I still believe.

The fires continued to burn, luminous and writhing in the dark. He heard the low murmur of sleeping men, and felt his own fatigue sink over him like a cloud.

Perhaps he would sleep. Perhaps, despite the cloying sense of evil that hung in the night, his physical exhaustion would tip him over the edge.

He felt himself sliding away.

Then something cracked, close to the edge of the camp, and he started. His neck muscles felt swollen and stiff, and he had difficulty lifting his head.

The flames swayed and flexed. All around them, bodies lay on the earth like corpses. The men seemed very deeply asleep, the way that only children fall.

Eichmann looked for the outlines of the sentries, and saw none.

That was odd. They had been there, just a moment ago.

He tried to lift his head again, and felt something resist him. It felt as if a series of weights, as clammy and cold as fish, had been lowered onto his body without him noticing.

He began to panic. He saw Meunig's eyes again, glinting at him in the dark.

Should he cry out?

He tried, and found that his mouth wouldn't move. He struggled, straining at the heavy bonds laid down on his flesh.

I still believe.

He felt himself writhing against an invisible hold. His body remained static, trapped by some malign power, locked down to the earth and pushed into it.

Then he saw it.

He shouted out, but no sound escaped his unmoving lips. He stretched to grasp his pistol, but his hand didn't move.

Out of the shadows came the beast.

Taller than a man, misshapen, stalking awkwardly on backwards-jointed legs, it grinned at him from a face like a goat's. It clutched at a long scythe, and coils of pale green smoke ran down its hide. Its teeth glinted in the starlight, and they were square and notched.

It crept closer, silently, walking with eerie, looping movements. It kept smiling as it came – a deranged, half-human smile on an animal's face.

Eichmann tried to scream, and nothing came out. He saw the beast step carefully over the sleeping bundles, barely brushing them with its cloven hooves. He saw its long fingers creep up the shaft of the scythe and its shaggy hide shake in the strange breeze.

Gartner! Udo!

The beast came up to him, breathing deeply. Its shoulders were hunched and bulbous. Eichmann stared up at it, eyes open in terror, his heart pumping, still unable to move.

Sigmar!

The beast gazed at him, grinning the whole while. Firelight reflected strangely from its hide. Bones and totems hung from its scraggy ribs, rattling softly as it moved. A pendant with a crow's skull swung from its neck. It smelled like an old, rotting corpse.

It stooped close, and the terrible half-man, half-goat face swooped low over his.

For the love of Sigmar!

Eichmann tried to screw his eyes shut, but couldn't. He stared into the eyes of the monster and saw his own reflection in them. The creature's breath washed over him, rancid and meaty.

I still believe!

The creature looked at him for a long time, examining him, leering inanely. Then it withdrew, pulling itself up to its full height. It pulled the scythe round, ready to plunge it down. As it did so, its mouth opened. A long tongue rolled out, as black as nightshade.

Eichmann wrestled frantically with whatever force held him in place. He felt it give a little, and raged against the deadening effect. His right leg moved a fraction, dragging itself up as if through tar.

Not yet! I can fight this!

Then the scythe came down, whooshing through the air, right at his neck.

Eichmann felt the edge bite into his flesh, and...

...STARTED AWAKE, BOLT upright, flailing like a madman.

'No!' he roared, erupting from the ground in a tangle of limbs.

He stared around him, shivering and bathed in sweat.

Mist rolled across the campsite. The grey light of dawn made everything drab and cold. Men were moving, rolling up their blankets and packing supplies into saddlebags. They turned to stare at him. Some laughed before they realised who they were laughing at, after which they hastily stopped.

Eichmann stared back at them, panting heavily. His heart was still hammering like a forgemaster's. The grinning face of the goat-man stayed in his mind for a moment, lingering like a mirage before dissolving away.

'Sir?' asked Udo, walking up to him with concern on his brutish face. 'Are you all right?'

Eichmann's pulse began to return to normal. His hands still trembled, but embarrassment took over from terror.

He felt cold. His whole body was drenched, and the chill morning air froze him.

'Why didn't you wake me?' he asked, his voice thick.

'I thought you could use the rest. Want a swig of something?'

Eichmann, still shaking, reached down and pulled his cloak around his shoulders. Around him, the men returned to their tasks. They kept their eyes low, not meeting his gaze. The fires still smouldered, though they had burned down to little more than piles of ash.

'No,' said Eichmann, feeling fragile and nauseous. 'No, I'll be fine.'

He smiled weakly at Udo.

'Just a bad dream,' he said, wrapping the cloak tighter and trying to stop himself shaking.

Udo gave him a hard stare, as if unwilling to take his word for it. Then, eventually, he gave a curt nod.

'Fair enough,' he said, turning back to whatever it was he'd been doing. 'If I ever had dreams, I reckon this place would give me bad ones.'

Then Eichmann stood alone again, feeling his breathing slowly relax. He needed some food. He needed to get back on his horse with a gun in his hand and get back to the task at hand.

Just a bad dream.

He started to collect his things, pulling the sodden blanket up from the dewy earth, moving numbly.

Just a bad dream.

Eichmann saw Gartner lead his horse over from where the baggage wains stood, and gave him a casual wave. He even managed something of a smile.

It was only as he bent down to retrieve his pistol that he saw the leather twine pendant crumpled next to it, half-masking the crushed crow's skull beneath, lodged among his belongings like a mockery.

CHAPTER TEN

BY THE STANDARDS of the northern Drakwald, if by no others, Eisenach was a big place. It stood right in the centre of the long hinterland, dividing the straggling edges of the eastern flank of the forest with the open moors and dales that ran up to the craggy massif of the Middle Mountains. The land was open and drab, exposed to the winds that howled down from the high peaks and beaten by rain from the west. The few trees that grew in that place were hunched over like old women, and their branches stretched out like grasping arms.

Perhaps the landscape had once been less devastated. Perhaps once the fields had swayed with crops and the roads had been maintained and used. No longer, though. Signs of violence and destruction littered the landscape. Corpses of animals rotted in the fields, and isolated farmsteads stood empty, their vacant windows gaping like pits.

Eisenach itself had not been spared. As Huss, Schlecht and Mila approached the town, they saw the burn marks on the walls and the earth before them churned up by the frantic tread of hundreds of feet. The banners of the Empire still flew from the turrets and the outlines

155

of men were visible on the low ramparts, but the place looked ravaged.

They walked up to the town gates as the sun hit its zenith. Huss looked as calm and focused as ever. Schlecht still had a hunted look in his eyes, but the worst of his mania seemed to have subsided during the long trek. He limped along in Mila's wake, staying as close to her as he dared, snatching glances at her from time to time with wide, fascinated eyes.

Mila tensed up as the town drew closer. The high walls intimidated her. They were far taller and broader than any she had seen before.

She remembered hearing tales about the great cities of the Empire – Altdorf where the Emperor sat on his throne of gold to dispense justice, Talabheim where the giants had carved out the hollow earth for men to dwell in, Middenheim where Old Father Ulric had forged his hammer on the backs of the mountains. Her vision of such places had always been hazy, but Eisenach looked nearly as vast and imposing as she imagined they did.

She hung back, letting Huss stride out before her, trying to hide her growing sense of trepidation with a studiously blank expression. The entrance to the town was blocked by two heavy, iron-braced oak doors, each twenty feet high and barred with rough-hewn beams. A smaller door had been cut into the one on the right, and this stood half-open. A group of men lounged around it, some leaning against the walls on either side, some out in the open with weapons on display.

Mila didn't like the look of any of them. Most were wearing breastplates and open-faced helmets, and several had long halberds in their hands. As she got closer she peered at them as surreptitiously as she was able. They had unshaven, sunken-cheeked, suspicious faces.

One of the men was drinking from a pewter tankard, and the air around them all was heavy with the smell of stale alcohol.

As Huss walked up to the gates, one of the guards, a pot-bellied man with a bushy grey beard and a long broadsword by his side, blocked his path.

'Greetings,' he said, though his voice had no welcome in it. He stared suspiciously at Huss, and even more suspiciously at Schlecht. 'What business have you here, Father?'

Huss towered over the man, just like he towered over everyone.

'When did a priest last need to state his business?' he asked. 'You know what my business is.'

The man looked over at Schlecht again, then at Mila, then back up at Huss.

'I know what it used to be,' he said, 'but things have been strange around here for a long time. I'd begun to wonder whether we'd seen the last of your kind.'

'You have no men of the Church here?' asked Huss.

The man shook his head.

'Dead, or left,' he said. 'Just like anyone with any-where better to go.'

'Then who ministers to you?'

The man laughed, but the sound was severe and desolate.

'Ministers to us?' He turned to his companions, none of whom were smiling. 'Not much call for that here, priest.'

Huss shot him a disapproving look, the one Mila was so used to seeing directed at her.

'I do not like to hear that,' he said. 'A town needs a priest. The people must have leadership. Discipline. Hope.'

The man looked at Huss sourly, as if he were the victim of some cruel joke.

'Hope?' he said, and didn't laugh. 'Where are you from, Father, with your two beggars in tow, coming out of the wasteland as if you'd never seen a dead man walking? A long way, I'd bet, or you'd not have used that word. If you knew of Eisenach and what happens here, you'd never dare to say it. It'd choke on your lips.'

Huss regarded the man coolly.

'Where can I find your headman?' he asked.

The bearded man shrugged.

'The big house, as you'd expect. Don't look for much welcome from him, though: Father Alexei was the one that persuaded him to stay. Seeing as how things turned out, I'd guess he's not too happy with that decision.'

'Your priest's counsel was sound. To stay and hold the walls is the headman's duty, given by the Lord Sigmar.'

'The Lord Sigmar be damn–'

Mila winced as she watched Huss's gauntlet lash out, fast as a snake. The clenched fist cracked into the man's face, sending him clattering back and falling heavily on his arse.

The rest of the men started into alertness, drawing weapons and edging into a semicircle around the warrior priest. Huss swept his mordant gaze across them and they shrank back, none willing to make the first move.

Mila rolled her eyes. At times, the warrior priest's unbreakable piety was just embarrassing.

'Do not curse again,' said Huss, as softly as ever.

The bearded man looked up him, half-stunned, blood running down his whiskers in thick lines. He started to reply, but the words didn't seem to come. He stared at the priest stupidly, his eyes dull with shock.

Huss turned to Mila, his face locked in impatient disdain.

'Come,' he said. 'We have work to do.'

EISENACH'S STREETS WERE narrow and winding, clogged with refuse and glassy with old puddles. The houses were mostly mean dwellings with single storeys and wooden slat roofs. Nearer the centre the buildings became a little grander, with overhanging gables and steep-pitched roofs hung with tiles.

The people looked at the three of them suspiciously as they passed. The Eisenachers were shabbily dressed for the most part, with hunted expressions on their narrow faces. They hung back as Huss approached them, pressing their backs against the dirty walls and lowering their eyes. A few of them looked briefly hopeful as he came among them, and Mila saw an old couple make the sign of the comet against their breasts as he passed, but most of them shared the expression the bearded man had worn – sullen, bitter, betrayed.

Mila had once seen her sister's child give his mother the same look when she'd been sick for many days and had been unable to look after him. It was an infantile reaction, one that spoke of weakness and misplaced entitlement.

They are like children, these people. Gods, I was wrong to fear them.

Huss ignored them all and strode down the filthy streets, letting his heavy boots splash up the muck on to his cloak. His mood had descended into anger during the brief walk through the town, and his jaw was clenched tight with it.

Perhaps, thought Mila, he couldn't stand weakness.

No, that wasn't it. He could tolerate some forms of

weakness, since he let Schlecht tag along with them. She couldn't quite put her finger on what it was he hated so much. Lack of resolve, perhaps, or maybe dishonesty.

In any event, it made him exhausting to be with. Any deviation from the purity of purpose he possessed seemed to generate a surly, driving rage in him, and one out of all proportion to the crimes that provoked it.

Mila found this irritating. Huss was a master warrior, capable of tearing aside undead horrors with the same casual abandon with which a lesser man might swat away a biting insect. Not all men were built in the same image. Other men feared the dark, and they were right to, since they had no weapons with which to combat it. It was all very well preaching severe morality from a shell of ancient armour and with a mighty warhammer to wield; most peasants of the Drakwald margins had no such luxuries.

Huss wouldn't be deflected, though. He ploughed across the straw-covered marketplace in the middle of the town, an irregular square surrounded by a jumble of dilapidated merchant houses. Chickens ran across his path, squawking and screeching. A group of children playing in the mud took one look at him and fled, terrified.

The headman's house stood on the far side, if what the guard at the gates had said about it being the biggest were true. The structure was brick-built and slightly cleaner than the others. Some of the windows had glass in them, and crude figures had been carved into wooden beams on the eaves of the overhanging second storey. A high chimney, tottering above the tiled roof and supported by wooden struts, belched out dark woodsmoke.

As Huss got close to the house, a jaundice-faced guard clambered to his feet, fumbling for his halberd.

'Get back,' said Huss, glaring at him.

The voice, as ever, was soft, but the tone of absolute, utter threat was so potent that the guard actually did it. By the time he'd recovered his poise, Huss had kicked the door open and was climbing the unsteady staircase up to the next floor.

Mila gave the guard an apologetic shrug as she hurried past him. Schlecht scuttled behind, anxious not to be left alone.

The interior of the house looked like a palace. Fires burned in stone fireplaces. Tapestries, some of them pale with age, hung over the wide mantelpieces. The floor was polished wood, as were the stairs. Mila looked around her furtively as she struggled to match pace with Huss, catching mere snatches of what seemed to her to be riches beyond the dreams of Ranald.

Huss didn't pause to enjoy the scenery. He reached a double doorway on the first landing and strode towards it. A man dressed in the patched and grimy robes of a loremaster moved to prevent him, saw the look on his face, and retreated hastily.

Huss shoved the doors open and burst into the room beyond. Mila and Schlecht followed him, swept along in his shadow.

The room was even finer than the entrance hall. A fire crackled away in a huge, pillared fireplace. Paintings hung from the walls. Mila had to struggle hard not to stare at those – the realism of the faces in the portraits both amazed and unsettled her.

In the centre of the room was a desk. Behind the desk sat a portly man with a quill in hand, surrounded by piles of parchment. His hair was flecked with grey and his jowly face was heavily lined. Alone among the inhabitants of Eisenach, he didn't quail under Huss's gaze.

'It's more usual to make an appointment,' he said dryly, looking up from heavy-lidded eyes.

Huss stood before him, though Mila could still sense the slow burn of anger within him.

'You are the ruler of this place?' Huss asked.

The man bowed.

'For as long as it survives,' he said.

'In its current state, that will not be long.'

'So you have eyes.'

Huss's countenance darkened.

'Not many men live to mock me, headman,' he warned.

The man raised a weary eyebrow.

'Mock you, priest?' He pushed his chair back from the desk and stood. He was short; beside Huss, almost comically so. 'I'm not mocking you. Why would I do that?'

Mila looked closely at the headman. Heavy bags hung under his bloodshot eyes. Every movement he made came with an accompanying tremble, betraying his extreme fatigue.

'Perhaps you're used to men fearing you,' the headman said, looking at Huss dispassionately. 'A month ago I'd have feared you too, but I've seen things since then. I've seen the dead rise from the earth and rip the hearts from the chests of the living. I've seen newly-dead infants clamber out of the ground, gurgling with the savour of blood.'

As he spoke, his casual drawl sank into articulate bitterness.

'I've marshalled the defence of these walls for twenty days and twenty nights, watching as men I've known from childhood died at the hands of things I'd thought confined to nightmares. I've watched priests like you chant litanies of destruction, only for them to fail. I've seen homeless wretches from the land around us crawl into Eisenach every day, all with tales of horror, all looking for some kind of refuge. But the dead follow them. There's no refuge. They'll break through. Perhaps tonight, perhaps in another month.'

His pudgy hand clenched into a fist, then opened uselessly again.

'You've chosen the wrong town to take shelter in, priest,' he said. 'Eisenach is no sanctuary for you. The people won't listen to your prayers here. They believe, as I do, that no one will answer them.'

Mila sucked through her teeth then, looking nervously between Huss and the headman, fearing that those comments might count as the kind of heresy the warrior priest liked to punish directly.

Huss, though, remained silent. Slowly, he turned away from the headman and walked over to a window set in the far wall. He wrenched it open, giving him a view back over the town.

Down in the streets, men and women moved around listlessly, their limbs heavy and sluggish. Sentries walked along the ramparts, heads low. From somewhere out in the mass of ramshackle dwellings, a woman was screaming, over and over. A pall of despair hung over the dishevelled town like a thunderhead preparing to discharge.

Huss crossed his huge arms and watched it all. His eyes glittered under his low brows, intent and pitying. For some time, he didn't move. No one broke the silence.

'What's your name, headman?' he asked at last.

'Loeb Treicher.'

'Will the dead come tonight, Loeb Treicher?'

'They come every night.'

Huss turned back from the window.

Even in such a simple movement, Mila could see that his gait had changed, and she recognised the febrile energy that consumed him during his eerie battle-focus. For a moment, she thought he might strike Treicher, and her heart began to beat faster.

'I am now the master of this town,' Huss announced, as if that were an unarguable fact of creation. 'I will raise its men and women to fight, and you will give me every assistance.'

Treicher started to interject, but Huss spoke over him.

'This is what will happen,' he said. 'The dead will come and I shall stand against them. I shall smite them with the holy fervour of the blessed. I shall make their sluggish minds fear the name "Eisenach" even when all other fears have no sway over them.'

Huss's voice had a strength to it that Mila had never heard before. In the heat of battle he had always spoken quietly; now, his words reverberated around the room like the low growl of artillery.

Your sermons must be a real inspiration.

'I shall lead your people,' he said. 'I will show them the folly of despair and the glory of faith. I will demonstrate the infinite power of the Lord of Mankind. The dead will come, and I will crush them. The defiled will come, and I will destroy them. The corrupted will march, and I will break their wills and scatter their foul bones across the bare earth.'

Huss started to walk towards Treicher. The headman backed away from him, finally seeming to realise what manner of man he'd let into his inner sanctum. Huss appeared to have grown, to have thrown off a long-worn cloak of diffidence and revealed his true self.

Mila couldn't help but smile to herself, thrilled by the

transformation. Huss looked then as he had done in the chapel with the sunlight shining on his armour, clad in the raiment of the warrior heroes of old.

The living saint. The servant of Sigmar.

'You will fight with me, Treicher,' Huss said, and his voice rang with grinding, fervent conviction. 'All the men of Eisenach will fight with me. The dead shall come to this place, looking for a town poisoned by fear, and will find instead a town of burning zeal, steeled by faith, made strong by the inexhaustible spirit of man. You and I will stand on the ramparts, proud against the coming of the night, summoning the courage of our fathers and bringing a second death to the slaves of fallen gods.'

Huss drew closer, dominating the cowering Treicher, declaiming all the while.

'We will show them the path of valour. We will expose the lie that there is no answer to the prayers of the faithful, and demonstrate with our body, mind and soul that there is but one liege-lord for mankind, one master of our destiny and one hope for the redemption of us all, and that is the Lord Sigmar Heldenhammer, the Blessed, the Mighty, the Undefeated.'

By then Huss was looming over Treicher, who had shrunk back against the side of the desk and was looking terrified.

'And you will do all of this, just as I command,' warned Huss, jabbing his armoured fist into the headman's chest and pinning him to the wood, 'or I will kill you myself, Loeb Treicher, and feed your worthless, faithless corpse to the monsters I have come here to destroy.'

BY DUSK, EISENACH was a place transformed. Huge fires were lit, anticipating the coming dark. The streets were cleared of refuse and piles of replacement weapons were dragged out into the open from their caches, ready to be cleaned and repaired by teams of workmen.

Huge vats of cooking oil were taken from the tavern kitchens and hauled onto the ramparts, where they boiled away furiously. Hasty repairs were made to the battered gates, which were further reinforced by lengths of wood hacked out of Treicher's expensive doors and interior panelling.

The banners flying listlessly over the town were taken down and cleaned. An old Imperial standard was found from somewhere, bearing the white wolf device mounted over the griffon of Karl Franz. Huss ordered a flagpole cut from one of the few trees still standing outside the town walls. The restored standard was fixed to the headman's chimney, the highest point in Eisenach.

There was something infectious about the warrior priest's energy. He strode back and forth ceaselessly, eyes blazing, rousing the dispirited citizens of the town with both words and deeds. He drove the fighting men out of the taverns and bawdy houses and forced them to stand in detachment order while he harangued them. By the time he was done, even the hardiest of them looked willing to take a place on the walls rather than endure more of it.

Those were the men who still had their weapons in their hands and possessed something like the will to fight. In the slums, the places where Treicher's writ barely ran, those who had lost everything huddled in dirt-caked misery. Refugees from devastated villages crouched in the foul-smelling shadows, squatting amid rotting scraps and pools of standing water, resigned to a death that seemed little worse to them than the life they'd inherited.

'Come,' said Huss to Mila, his movements still animated with that inexhaustible zeal. 'I wish you to see something.'

The two of them, with Schlecht silently in tow as always, made their way through the swamp of muddy streets into the slum quarter, running the gauntlet of suspicious, ignorant looks as they went.

Mila didn't like to make eye contact with the people there. They looked much like Schlecht had looked when they'd come across him – ragged clothes hanging from skeletal frames, sunken cheeks, sore-ridden flesh, brittle tufts of matted hair. The stares they gave were hostile and hunted. They were the dregs, the human refuse of a town that had learned to give in to its fear.

As Huss strode through their miserable kingdom, he called out to them.

'To me, sons and daughters! Forget your pain! Forget your despair! A new power is among you! To me!'

Amazingly, some of them followed him. Only a few came at first, creeping warily out of the gloom of their hovels as if unwilling to believe that anything could alter the inevitability of their squalor.

Once the first of them had limped into the open, though, a few more followed, staring at Huss all the while with suspicious eyes. Then others came, hobbling on calloused feet or leaning heavily on the shoulders of others.

'Why are we doing this?' whispered Mila to Huss. She had to trot beside him to keep up. 'These people can hardly stand. They're sick.'

Huss smiled.

'Watch them, daughter,' he said. 'Do not judge them.'

Mila almost laughed out loud when he said that. Ever since she'd met Huss, he'd done nothing but judge her.

He seemed to spend his entire life in a state of judgement, as if that attitude had become the entire reason for his existence.

She said nothing, though. When he was in such a mood, she knew better than to argue the point.

They arrived at a narrow opening between the ranks of hovels. The space was little more than a wide slick of mud and straw, dotted with discarded vegetable peelings and animal droppings. As Huss turned to face the crowd that had emerged in his wake, a half-starved pig with a grille of ribs along its skinny flank shuffled out of his path, grunting with irritation.

Huss clambered onto a mound of accumulated refuse, uncaring of the way his boots sank deep into the filth. As he reached the summit, he stooped to pick up a handful of the stinking matter.

Huss held it high, showing it to the assembled crowd. Mila looked around carefully. There must have been a hundred of the wretches clustered around her, all sick and rheumy. More arrived even as she watched, slinking out of their dens of desperation and illness with curiosity written on their emaciated faces.

'This is what you have become!' cried Huss, showing them the rotting garbage in his armoured fist. 'You are the filth. You are the rubbish. You are the slime and disease that this town wishes to forget. You are where the sins of humanity have come to squat.'

Mila rolled her eyes. Some of the refugees were standing very close to her, and they smelled almost as bad as Schlecht did. There were a lot of them, and it didn't look like it would take much to make them angry.

'Do you have no *shame*?' roared Huss, crushing the slime between his fingers and letting it slop to the ground. 'Did you never aspire to more than this? Or have your souls and dreams become as shrivelled as your bodies?'

There was a low murmur of discontent among the crowd. One man, a rat-faced, gap-toothed wretch with a long scar across his eyes and a messy, stubbled chin, started to mutter to himself angrily.

'This is what they have made you into!' cried Huss, undeterred. 'You have let them. You have let them drive you into this stinking pit, never lifting your hands against them, letting them tell you that you deserve it, that your station can never be any better than this.'

That got their attention. More people were arriving at the rear of the crowd all the time, shuffling into place and looking up at the massive armoured warrior priest who had come into their midst.

Mila swallowed nervously. There was no getting out now. All exits from the grimy space were blocked. She stared studiously ahead of her, hoping Huss knew what he was doing.

'You are wrong,' said Huss. 'They are wrong. You can be so much more than this. You can be *angels* of destruction. You can be the deliverers of Sigmar's holy justice. You can be His finest servants, the purest of them all, the most devastating and the most potent.'

By then the crowd were hanging on his words and following his every move with their tired eyes.

'Do you disbelieve me?' Huss asked, staring at them all, one by one. 'Do you think I've come to trick you, just like so many have done before? Do you think I ask for what little money you have, offering nothing in return?'

Huss laughed. That made Mila start; she'd never seen him laugh before.

'I ask for *more* than that! I ask for your *souls*. I ask you to give them to me, to hold them up and let me mould them anew. I ask you to give *yourselves*, to surrender what meagre will you have left and deliver it for the cause of the coming test.'

He drew the warhammer from his back and brandished it. It cut through the foetid air as he hoisted it aloft, ushering in a fleeting breath of fresh clarity.

Is it glowing? Am I going mad, or is that gold light coming from it?

Despite herself, Mila felt her spirits rising. Huss looked magnificent. It didn't matter that he stood knee-deep in dung and slime – he was magnificent.

'You can rise above this!' Huss roared, and his mighty voice echoed around the yard. 'You can fight with the fervour of the Lord Sigmar himself. You can be His chosen, the instruments of His will. It was for *you* that He bled, and for *you* that He fought. *You* are those for whom He forged this Empire. *You* are the inheritors of His mantle.'

The murmuring in the crowd grew in volume. They were not angry now. They were excited. Mila saw the same gap-toothed man clench his fists, gazing up at Huss with something like rapture.

'Sigmar blesses those who *fight*,' roared Huss, pointing the hammer at each of them in turn. Though it might have been a trick of the fading sunlight, it did indeed look like the runes on the hammerhead were shining with gold. 'Rise up, and forget your despair! Rise up, and forget your sickness! Rise up, and become *great!*'

The crowed pressed forwards, agitated.

'Will you follow me?' asked Huss, glaring at them.

Yes!

The reply was weak, scattered across the crowd, fractured and disparate.

'Will you follow me?' asked Huss again, his voice growing stronger.

Yes!

This time it was louder. Men stood up straight, uncurving hunched spines and pushing their shoulders back. Women lost their look of haggard care and started to smile again.

'Will you *follow me*?' asked Huss, and the echo of his challenge rang around the enclosed space like the report of a gunnery line.

Yes!

The crowd roared its acclamation, surging towards Huss like the breaking tide, reaching out to him with desperate hands.

Huss gazed down at them beneficently, sweeping the huge hammer through the air in glittering curves.

'Rise up, for the Empire!' he cried.

For the Empire!

Mila realised then she was shouting alongside all of them, caught up in the mood of sudden frenzy without realising.

'Rise up, for Karl Franz!'

For Karl Franz!

She shouted as hard as she could, reaching out like the others, consumed with a sudden desire to fight, to prove herself, to become Chosen.

The hammer rose into the dusk, an outline of defiance against the fading light.

'Rise up, for Sigmar!'

For Sigmar!

The bellow of the crowd was deafening. They punched their fists, stamped their feet, cried aloud.

They were no longer a crowd of the dispossessed. They were an army.

Mila, feeling tears start in her eyes, turned round to look at them, overcome by the rapid transformation Huss had wrought.

Beside her was Rickard Schlecht, the man who had lost everything, who had wept in her arms like a child, whose hope and life had been destroyed at Goeringen by the evil that now marched on Eisenach.

His eyes were alive with the shimmer of tears. His arms were outstretched, reaching towards Huss as if the priest were an avatar of the Heldenhammer himself. His scrawny chest was pushed out, as bold and brave as any knight of the Emperor's.

'For Sigmar!' he was crying, shaking with emotion, weeping with the fervour of a man reborn.

CHAPTER ELEVEN

THE LIGHT OVER the Drakwald was failing again. The days seemed shorter than they should have done, as if the sunlight was squeezed out of the sky by the grasping trees and sucked up by the dank, thirsty earth under them.

Eichmann pulled on the reins and his horse came to a standstill. Around him, his men did the same. Gartner, as ever, was closest to hand, and nudged his steed to Eichmann's side. Udo clumsily tried to follow him but made little headway along the cramped, rutted track.

It might have been Eichmann's imagination, but the henchman seemed to have become jealous of the attention he paid to Gartner's advice. If true, that was slightly absurd, but also strangely appropriate. Udo was a strange character: both brutal and innocent at once. Perhaps that was the key to him – a feral child, locked in the massive body of a witch hunter's man-at-arms.

'That's it,' said Eichmann, squinting at the western horizon.

'You're sure?' asked Gartner.

'What else could it be?'

The sun was sinking quickly towards the outline of

trees in the west. It looked like a giant, bulbous ball of blood, barred by spears of black cloud.

The horizon was broken by a jagged silhouette. Four huge towers, half-ruined and laced with holes, jutted up into the sky. Two of them still seemed vaguely Imperial in outline – heavily built, square-edged and crowned with toothy lines of battlements. Two others had half-collapsed and looked more like spikes of stone rearing up from the tangle of trees. Eichmann had an unsettling vision of massive twin rib-bones, and reprimanded himself. His imagination was beginning to run as wild as the land.

'We should make camp here,' said Gartner, staring at the ruins dubiously.

'No, we get there tonight.'

Gartner gave him an incredulous look.

'You're mad. We should wait for daylight.'

'No.' Eichmann's tone was final, and the severity of it shocked even him.

Am I scared? Scared to sleep again before this sickness is uncovered?

'It's less than a mile away,' Eichmann said, running his gaze over the broken shadows against the sky. 'We can be there before the last of the light fades.'

'We can't.'

Eichmann turned to face Gartner and his eyes flashed darkly.

'Do not forget yourself,' he snapped.

Gartner glared back at him. He looked deeply unhappy, both at the order and at Eichman's tone. For a moment, Eichmann thought he would defy him. He steeled himself, ready to reach for his pistol if necessary.

Grudgingly, the woodsman backed down. He shot a glace over at Daecher, who was some way behind and out of earshot.

'I do this under protest, witch hunter,' he muttered.

Eichmann nodded. He took up the reins again, ready to kick his horse into movement.

'I'll be sure to include that in my report,' he said.

Gartner shot him a sardonic look.

'Yes,' he said. 'I'd heard you were keen on those.'

CLOSE UP, THE castle loomed massively in the night, black against the shroud of stars. Its towers stretched far beyond the wavering canopy, spiked and broken. The wind swirled tightly around them, as if drawn in by the stone itself.

'Stay close,' whispered Eichmann, checking his pistols for the twelfth time.

He stood at the base of the round motte that led up to the gates. Aside from the moan of the wind and the ceaseless rustle of the trees, the castle was silent. No bodies moved on the battlements and no banners hung from the half-ruined walls.

Udo cracked his knuckles noisily and let out an acrid belch.

'Better,' he said, looking satisfied. His eyes had the glint in them that they always did before battle.

Twenty of the men-at-arms crouched alongside, as did Gartner and Daecher. The rest stood guard over the baggage wains, which had been left down the slope of the hill as far away from the looming tree-cover as possible.

Eichmann started to move, keeping his body low, looking up at the approaching walls the whole time. He didn't carry a torch – none of them did. They went by the light of the stars, keeping to the scarce shadows, going as stealthily as they could. All the men had short swords drawn except Daecher, who carried his crossbow as always, and Udo, who had his maul in one hand and a dagger in the other.

Gartner crept alongside Eichmann, looking both irritated and nervous. His long nose protruded into the darkness like a snout.

'Sense anything?' asked Eichmann.

Gartner shook his head.

The gates drew nearer. Trails of moss and lichen covered the surface, thick with old fronds. The air was heavy with the fungal smell of decay. The wooden gate itself had long rotted away, and the stone arch, half-collapsed, stood open to the elements.

Beyond the arch was an open courtyard, overgrown with brambles and grasses, cast in shadow from the high walls.

Gartner halted. He cocked his head, looking like a tracker dog on a scent.

Eichmann held his hand up and the men waited, pausing on the threshold of the castle as if waiting for an invitation to enter.

'What is it?' hissed Eichmann.

Gartner stayed listening, his eyes narrow.

'Can you not hear it?' he asked at last.

As soon as he spoke, Eichmann did. From somewhere up ahead there was a soft beating, like a heart's, low and muffled.

Eichmann listened to it intently. The beats reverberated from the stone, just on the edge of hearing, as diffuse as mist.

'So we're not alone,' he said. 'That's good.'

They crept in under the arch. The courtyard beyond was studded with huge lumps of fallen stone and covered in grass and briars. In the faint starlight it looked like a graveyard. The heavy outer walls soared away on all sides, broken open with gaping holes.

Eichmann felt his heart start to beat in time with the low rhythm of the drum. He forced his muscles to relax. His neck ached from tension and his movements, normally loose and composed, were tight.

He was on-edge, tense, jumpy.

I need to sleep. I need to rest. I need to forget all this.

Something flashed across an open patch of sky, a dark shape, right on the edge of vision.

'Down!' he whispered.

As one, the men crouched down into cover, looking up warily, keeping their swords poised. The four towers rose high over them, one at each corner of the ruined keep ahead.

'Sir?' Udo was looking at him questioningly.

'I saw something,' said Eichmann, running his eyes across the starlit courtyard, seeing sinister shapes in every pile of masonry or broken section of wall.

Udo looked out and up, clearly sceptical. He sniffed noisily.

'I see nothing,' he said. 'I smell plenty.'

Eichmann could sense the men's impatience. They didn't like skulking in the shadows. Only Gartner was keen to hang back. The woodsman squatted in the shadow of a huge headless statue of a knight, looking like he'd rather be anywhere else.

'Down below,' he whispered. 'It's coming from below us.'

Eichmann looked across to the far side of the courtyard. The broken-up flagstones continued for a while. After that was another arch and what looked like stairs running steeply down. Beyond the stairway was the bulk of the main keep, colossal and drab.

Gartner was right. The soft drumming came from in there.

'Very well,' Eichmann said, getting ready to move again. He tried, and failed, to shake the rictus of cold dread that had dogged him since Middenheim. 'Down it is.'

UDO DIDN'T GO stealthily. Unlike those born in the forest he didn't have the capacity to creep forwards like a cat, treading carefully on soft leather shoes and leaving every leaf untouched. He walked into the dark as he always did, stomping on iron-capped boots, relishing what was coming with all his soul.

He wasn't entirely immune to the crushing atmosphere of the forest. The noises got to him just like they did to everyone else, and the frustration of being surrounded by presences he couldn't fight made him short-tempered.

Unlike the others, though, the fug of threat didn't beat him down. It made him keener to fight; to break out into the healthy, heart-cleansing application of force that brushed away the cobwebs and kept him sleeping soundly. The longer he went without action, the worse his mood became.

But that was all right, as action was close now. He could feel it in his muscle-wrapped body. His left fist clenched the handle of his maul and his right fist clasped his dagger, both wrapped tight with expectation.

Udo knew his limitations. He knew he'd never make a decent soldier – he'd tried that, and failed badly. He'd liked the fighting part, but those episodes came too infrequently to keep his relentless appetites sated. In the long gaps between battles, he'd had to drown his instincts in beer, which had proved a bad strategy. He'd fought with his own side, provoking brawls with his comrades when there was no real enemy to square up to. They'd hated him, and he'd despised them. An uncertain future of drunkenness and dishonourable discharge waited for him, dooming him to an early, futile death.

But then Eichmann had come. Udo could still remember the day the witch hunter had arrived at the barracks, appraising the men of Oeler's regiment for recruits to the Church. Udo had assumed he wouldn't get picked. He'd assumed, as the others around him must have done too, that his far-from-glittering service record would have counted against him. He'd assumed that the Templars of Sigmar would have been after more pious, more controlled servants.

All of that had been wrong. Eichmann had looked at him for a long time, peering into his eyes, calmly appraising him. It was the first time that Udo had felt seriously ill at ease. It was as if Eichmann had dragged his heart up out of his chest and started dissecting it before his own eyes.

That had been uncomfortable. He'd not known whether to take a swing at Eichmann or just back away. The uncertainty itself had been sickening – in every other situation, before or since, he'd known exactly what he'd wanted to do, and had never regretted a decision once he'd made it.

'This one,' Eichmann had said then. The way he'd spoken, it was as if the recruitment had been waiting to happen since the beginning of time.

This one.

The words still echoed in Udo's mind. Every so often, on the rare occasions when he grew frustrated or impatient with Eichmann's moodiness or torpor, Udo would remember how those words had made him feel.

Those words were why his loyalty to Eichmann was

beyond reproach. They were why, in his blunt, brutish way, Udo had stayed devoted to him for so many years. The devotion was unshakeable now, like the loyalty a child has to his father.

He had been chosen. In a real sense, he had been saved.

This one.

Ahead of him, the starlight ghosted the edges of the stone with faint lines of silver. Udo lowered his head, peering down the long stairway. The steps were cracked and dented, as if a millwheel of spears had been run up and down it.

At the base of the stairway was another overgrown yard. On the far side of that was the facing wall of the castle keep. An open doorway gazed back at him blankly, looking like a rectangle onto the abyss. The quiet, booming noise of the drum came through that gap. Still almost too soft to hear, it was picking up in pace.

When the first beast broke from the shadows it was as if a piece of the masonry had detached from its place, grown limbs and launched itself at him.

Udo saw it early and spun his dagger into a throwing position. The beast leapt out from the left, swerving around a shattered stone column.

A crossbow bolt shot out, slicing past Udo's shoulder and burying itself into the patch of darkness. The beast let slip a choking, barking cry of pain. From behind him, Udo could hear the *thunk-click* as Daecher quickly reloaded.

Then more of the creatures emerged, leaping down from the walls and crouching down like huge, malevolent toads. They were skinny and ugly, all misshaped limbs and bony outgrowths. Their faces were long and bestial, crowned with horn-stubs and scraps of hair. Their eyes flashed in the dark like a cat's, and they moved with a clumsy, lurching gait.

Udo spun on the ball of his right foot, picking his target and hurling the dagger. It flew through the air, glittering as it spun, before thumping into flesh. Even before the creature had fallen Udo had drawn another dagger from its sheath and was looking for a fresh target.

Eichmann's pistol cracked out, briefly flashing bright white across the scene. It exposed more than a dozen of the beastmen, bounding over the stones on backwards-jointed legs, kicking up their hooves as they came.

Ungors. Corrupted foundlings. Filth.

Udo grinned, recognising the nature of his foes, and ran to meet them.

The first one careered into his path, swinging a cleaver in its clenched fist. Udo ducked down low and thrust himself upwards. His helmet clanged into the beast-man's chin, throwing it back. As it staggered away Udo lashed out with his maul, feeling it connect and dig deep. Black, stinking blood splattered across his face. He laughed through it.

Then another ungor was on him, barking a hate-filled, guttural challenge. Udo spun back round, thrusting out his dagger-hand. The blade cut into the beastman's midriff, tearing straight through the tough hide. The ungor roared at him, wrenching away from the blade and bringing an iron mace down on Udo's shoulder.

By then Udo had moved again, whirling out of contact and getting into position for the maul. He swept it up diagonally, feeling the heavy head of it come across and crunch into the ungor's temple, cracking open the bone and biting through the soft pulp beneath.

The beastman fell away, yowling. Beyond it, more

of them loped across the courtyard towards him. Eichmann's pistol fired again, felling one of the bigger creatures. Udo heard the swish of another quarrel flying out, then the clash of metal as the swordsmen got in among the enemy.

'Blood of Sigmar,' said Udo, still smiling, picking his next victim with an expert eye. 'I *love* this.'

EICHMANN STRODE TOWARDS the open doorway, stowing his second pistol in its holster and drawing his rapier from its scabbard.

The ungors sickened him more than they worried him. It was still possible to make out remnants of humanity in their bestial faces, albeit of a cheapened, mutated sort. They were creatures of raw spite, as wiry and malicious as any of their greater kin but more capable of being broken when the odds were against them.

One of the mutants clattered towards him, bounding across the flagstones on cloven hooves. It ducked under an ill-aimed slice from a swordsman before charging straight at Eichmann, bucking and leaping as it came.

Eichmann waited calmly, judging pace and speed, before flashing out with the rapier in a single, precision movement.

The ungor stopped dead. It glared at Eichmann for a moment, surprise scored across its goat-like face, before sliding to the ground. As it crumpled, its innards spilled out of its chest, carved open as cleanly as a surgeon's incision.

Eichmann stepped over the corpse and carried on walking.

'Can you handle these, Udo?' he called out.

The henchman was busy several yards away, gouging the eyes from a shrieking beastman.

'Glad to, sir,' came the enthusiastic reply.

More ungors raced towards the witch hunter. Eichmann reached into his coat and withdrew a collection of small spiked spheres. He threw them ahead of him like a fisherman casting a net, and they tumbled and bounced across the stone.

'What are you–?' began Gartner, just as the first of them went off.

The explosions cracked out, bursting out like a volley of cannonade detonations. The ungors were thrown from their feet, clutching their eyes and screaming. A dozen of them went down, bloodied and covered in fizzing, burning powders. One of them clawed its way out of the varicoloured mist, and its skin was running clear of its bones like curdled milk. It looked up at Eichmann for an agonised moment, reaching out with a shaking claw, before its eyes popped messily and dribbled down semi-liquid cheeks.

'Watch yourself,' said Eichmann to Gartner, turning to the rest of the men and giving a rapid series of battle-signals. 'The bounce is unpredictable.'

Twelve of the swordsmen broke away from combat and joined up with Eichmann as he strode through the dissipating clouds of dust towards the doorway. The rest stayed with Udo, moving into a defensive formation and covering their rear.

Daecher and Gartner hurried to keep up with the witch hunter, holding their mouths as they ran through the steaming stench of dissolving ungors.

'What *is* that stuff?' asked Gartner as he followed Eichmann under the doorway.

Eichmann didn't answer. He broke into a jog, speeding up as his eyes adjusted to the gloom under the keep gate. Though dark, it wasn't entirely pitch black at the far end. The stone was picked out with a faint sheen of blood-red. The further he went, the more the glow intensified.

Red. It had to be red.

His men were close to him. He could hear the thud of their boots on the ground and the clink of their armour as they ran. He hadn't seen any of them fall yet, and that reassured him; Udo had trained them well, and they were holding their nerve.

The corridor leading in from the gateway ended in another flight of stairs heading steeply down. The red glow was coming from its base. It moved like firelight, flickering and ebbing. The sound of drums was stronger, booming up at him like the rhythm of the heart of the world.

Eichmann paused at the top of the stairs, flanked by his men. He withdrew a small rosewood box from his belt and flicked it open.

Gartner watched him, fascinated.

'Close your eyes and cover them,' ordered Eichmann, adjusting a copper dial inside the box. From below, where the stairs ended, strange noises were beginning to filter up. 'Do it now.'

He clicked the box shut just as the first ungors began to lope up the steps. He threw it down the stairwell and it bounced and spun, letting off sparks as it ricocheted among the stamping hooves. As it hit the bottom it popped open. Eichmann recoiled, clamping his hands over his eyes. Just in time, Gartner and Daecher did the same.

The box blew up in a single, brilliant blaze of white light. The hard clap of the explosion ricocheted from the walls. Even behind his closed lids Eichmann could feel the piercing pressure of it against his eyes. The inferno lasted for a few heartbeats, raging wildly like all the fires of heaven, before finally flickering out.

Eichmann opened his eyes and adjusted the brim of his hat.

'Follow me,' he said coolly, watching ungors writhing in agony at the base of the stairs. All around him his men were recovering themselves.

Gartner blinked heavily, his eyes watering. Eichmann smiled at him.

'Close them too slow?' he asked, striding down the stairs.

'You're enjoying this,' muttered the woodsman, wiping his eyes and following him down. Eichmann's smile faded.

'You have no idea,' he said.

At the bottom of the stairs was a wide chamber. It had been carved deep into the ground and was studded with a forest of squat stone pillars. Perhaps once it had been some sort of crypt or archive. Iron brackets hung from the pillars, the kind that held burning torches, though no flames burned in them now.

The chamber extended back for a long way, perhaps fifty yards, and the far end of it was lost in a haze of red. The sound of drumming boomed out through the churning clouds of dusty smoke, vibrating along the stone floor and making the layers of dust tremble.

The walls were lined with filth, glistening and viscid. The air was sickening, suffused with a heavy aroma of decay that hung amid the miasma. Flies buzzed angrily, disturbed from their vomitous feeding. Bleached animal skulls hung from twisting iron chains, their eye sockets like pools of oil. Bones lay across the floor in messy piles. The chanting and the drumming had stopped, replaced by a pain-drenched groaning from both human and non-human throats.

Bodies of ungors lay on the ground, twitching feebly. Blood ran from their eyes in dark lines. Among the beastmen were men and women, also blinded, as naked as infants and covered in rough daubs of filthy brown sludge. Some of them wore bone pendants around their necks or had scraps of pelt hanging from their shoulders. Shapes had been cut deep into their grey flesh, crusted with old scabs.

'Spread out,' ordered Eichmann, trying to make out what was hidden in the rolling red clouds at the end of the chamber.

His men fanned out across the crypt. Eichmann drew another rosewood device from his belt – his last. The stench ahead of him was very strange. Aside from the stink of sweat, filth and blood, other subtle aromas hung in the air. Some kind of crude incense, perhaps.

Ahead of him, something was stirring. A huge shadow began to emerge from the fiery mist. Three ungors stumbled into view ahead of it, dazzled by the explosion but still on their feet. They limped out into the open, swinging their weapons sightlessly.

Eichmann threw the second box out in front of him, right into the path of the shadow.

'Cover your eyes!' he shouted as the device opened up.

A second crack echoed out, and the box detonated. A blaze of white light snapped out, briefly exposing the chamber in stark relief. Eichmann felt the fiery intensity of it even from behind his gloved hand.

'Holy mother of Sigmar!' he heard Gartner swear.

'Trust in faith,' warned Eichmann, uncovering his face and checking the deployment of his men. His boots dragged on the sticky floor, trailing long lines of slime behind them.

Gartner was still next to him, shaking his head, holding his sword before him with both hands.

'*Don't* do that again,' he hissed, staring into the murk ahead.

'Calm yourself.'

The shadow clarified out of the gloom. It emerged into the open, as blind as the ungors but very much alive.

Twice the height of a man, three times as broad, clad in a thick, shaggy hide and crowned with two pairs of twisted horns, the beast came into view. Four hooves thudded against the stone, treading heavily. Massive arms clutched at a long, leaf-bladed spear. Human heads, drained of fluid and as wrinkled as prunes, hung from its flanks as trophies. A heavy, rust-studded chain ran around its bunched-muscle torso.

Its long face, bearded and lined like an old man's, ran with blood from unseeing eyes. A tatty wreath of dried leaves hung, lopsided, from its bald forehead and long brown stains streaked from the corners of its loose-lipped mouth.

A fug of alcohol preceded it, mixing with the cocktail of reeks in the claustrophobic chamber. The creature stank of vinegary wine-fumes, mixed with the unholy stench of man and beast.

'Centigor,' said Gartner, spitting the word out.

Eichmann felt his heart sink.

In the wake of the huge monster came more ungors and humans, staggering from the cloud of fire and clutching their eyes. Some looked as if they could still see, and they all hefted crude weapons in trembling hands. The humans were in a terrible state – bleeding from hundreds of small wounds and reeling as if heavily drugged – but still they came on.

Eichmann braced himself.

'Stand firm,' he ordered, seeing the taut expressions on his men's faces. 'We are men, masters of the world. We shall prevail.'

The centigor recovered itself first. Its huge head lifted, still sightless, and let slip an echoing, throaty roar. Its massive arms flung back, stretched in a gesture of raw belligerence. Its forelegs stamped and pawed at the ground, grinding furrows in the slime-covered stone. Sheets of sweat cascaded from its stinking flanks.

The ungors around it shrieked with rage, given strength by the huge presence in their midst.

Then the centigor lowered its head, took up the spear in two hands, and charged.

CHAPTER TWELVE

Treicher had predicted correctly. Night fell, and the dead came.

Their advance had no order to it, just a ragged sweep of stumbling bodies emerging out of the darkness and dragging themselves up to the walls. They came out of the west, massing up to the gates, whispering to themselves, caressing their weapons with dry, fleshless fingers. Empty banners swayed above them, dirty white and devoid of any emblem.

Mila stood on the walls, clutching at the sword she'd carried with her since Helgag. The effect of Huss's speech had not entirely drained away, but it was hard to maintain her sense of defiance in the face of the enemy.

There must have been thousands of them – rank after rank of chattering corpses, walking in stilted rows, eating up the ruined land and treading down what was left of the shattered crops beneath their feet. They leered up into the night just as they had done before, their faces bleached white from the exposed bone.

Mila realised then why Eisenach had been driven so far into despair. The bands of undead she had encountered before were mere fragments of a far greater host. The horde before her was greater than any gathering

189

she'd seen, living or dead. It seemed to extend forever, filling the land from right to left with a blanket of endlessly marching bodies. In the dark of the night it looked like a whole swarm of pale-backed insects, advancing methodically in near-silence.

Treicher had taken his place on the ramparts overlooking the gate. He was surrounded by his bodyguard, about two dozen heavily armoured swordsmen. Mila stood fifty yards along the walls to the left, flanked by men with halberds. Every inch of rampart above Eisenach was occupied by defenders, all staring out into the dark with tense, nervous faces.

At first the halberdiers on her section of wall hadn't wanted her anywhere near them. Women were unlucky in war, apparently. After she'd punched the first of them full in the face and turned on the second, fist cocked, they'd adopted a modified position.

The man on her left was called Erich. The one on her right with the black eye and split lip was called Dieter. Both of them wore open-faced sallet helms and had breastplates over their jerkins. The metal on their armour was dented and thin, and Erich's had a long crack running from the base of it which flexed as he moved.

Like everyone else, the men had an air of grim anticipation on their faces.

'So here they come again,' said Erich, gripping his halberd with sweaty hands.

'Where's your priest now?' asked Dieter, doing the same.

Mila concentrated on the approaching enemy. She hadn't seen Huss for a while, not since he'd led his crowd of dispossessed back into the slums with promises to show them the light of salvation.

She hadn't seen him since he'd sent her away, like she were an errant child too simple to understand the complexities of what he, the servant of Sigmar, was doing.

Even now, you cannot bring yourself to trust another.

'He'll be here,' she said, keeping the irritation out of her voice.

The first undead reached the walls. They crept along at their own pace, marching steadily, neither speeding up nor slowing down. When they came up against the stone they began to climb. Bony hands extended upwards, clutching at the masonry like claws and dragging scrawny bodies up after them.

A trumpet blared out from Treicher's command position. Men leaned over the edge of the parapet and began to pelt the attackers with rocks. Where their aim was good, the skulls and sinews of the skeletal climbers shattered, pitching them back to earth with faint, high-pitched shrieks. Other missiles fell harmlessly, whistling past the front rank of climbers and crashing to the ground. Soon a hail of rocks was cascading down the sheer walls, cracking bones and ripping through dry flesh before thumping into the mud below.

Many undead were knocked back by that storm. Others hung on, doggedly crawling higher even as their companions were broken into pieces around them. None of the attackers slowed their pace – they advanced remorselessly, one handhold at a time, creeping ever closer.

A second trumpet blast issued from the gatehouse. Cauldrons of boiling oil, still fizzing from the fires that had been heating them, were tipped over the edge. The liquid sluiced down onto the mass of climbers, clinging and scalding. A mortal army would have broken under that deluge, screaming in agony. The undead just kept on coming, drenched and slippery but still clambering over one another to reach the summit of the stonework.

Their work done, the pourers of oil stood back from the edge. In their place came archers. Each one nocked and drew a long arrow with a swathe of wet rags tied around the point. Flames were applied, flaring up as they caught on the combustible mixture. The archers leaned over the edge, aiming their darts where the oil had been thrown. They loosed their arrows in a massed flurry, and the darts spun down into the dark like a cloud of sparks from a bonfire.

As soon as the arrows hit, vivid flames roared into life in a series of crackling, rolling explosions. Even the undead caught in that inferno screamed then – a piercing, thin wail that set the defenders' teeth on edge. Thrashing around, the burning corpses crashed down to the earth or blundered back away from the walls, spreading more flame and confusion as they staggered.

By then the walls of Eisenach were completely surrounded. More oil-fires flared up, throwing leaping shadows up against the walls. Thick columns of black smoke began to churn, obscuring the view and making the air sour and choking. Through all of that, more undead clambered inexorably over the thickets of twisted, broken bones on the ground, heedless of the death throes of their comrades and fixated only on the walls and the living souls inside them.

A third trumpet blast rang out across the defensive lines, and the archers withdrew. They were replaced on the edge of the ramparts by men armed with halberds, swords and axes. Those newcomers were immediately greeted by the sight of those few undead who'd somehow managed to claw their way to the top of the walls through the rains of stone and fire. The parapets rang like blacksmiths' anvils as the foremost climbers were cut down and sent cartwheeling through the air to crash down into the growing mass of bones below.

The fires had blunted the first attacks, but not halted them. More undead crawled through the raging furnace to reach the base of the walls and started climbing. With every warrior dispatched by the defenders from the summit another two started to climb up from the bottom.

The undead climbed slowly, patiently seeking out handholds in the stone, looking up with pale green eyes, smiling absently the whole time as if anticipating the taste of blood. Some had once been men, wearing fragments of their old armour over their wasted frames. Others had been women, or even children, still clad in scraps of cheap woollen shifts and clutching at moth-eaten dolls as they crept ever higher. Whatever various expressions they had worn in life had been replaced by the same horrific, blank grin.

The first of the undead emerged close to Erich. A long forearm poked up, wavering in the air and scrabbling for purchase on the top of the wall. Erich waited for it to extend fully before hacking across sharply with his halberd blade. The arm severed at the elbow, dislodging the climber and sending it tumbling.

Then another one emerged, grasping on to the lip of the parapet and clutching tight. Mila jabbed down with her sword-edge. In her eagerness she missed the target and the blade clanged against the stone. Another hand appeared next to the first. Grey-skinned fingers clamped tight, ready to drag their owner up and over the edge.

Dieter intervened, slicing his halberd edge expertly across from the other side, breaking the climber's wrists. The attacker sailed back down to the earth, leaving two dismembered hands clutching the edge.

'I had it,' snapped Mila, glaring at Dieter furiously.

'Just making sure,' he said, already back at work with another arrival.

By then more arms were feeling their way over the edge. All along the wall, swordsmen busied themselves slicing at the grasping hands and punching the undead back down to earth.

Mila looked up, just for a moment, out across the slowly moving sea of bodies. Smoke continued to drift across the besieged town, making her throat dry and itchy. Sounds of combat rang out across the walls – the sharp scrape and clang of metal weapons interposed with screams and shouts of the human defenders.

Through all of it, the dead kept coming. There seemed no end to them.

'Where *are* you?' she breathed, looking in vain across the walls for Huss.

'Right here, darling,' said Erich, laughing, wielding his halberd with a calm, resigned discipline, but looking nothing, nothing at all, like a warrior priest.

RICKARD SCHLECHT WAS in pain. He was in more pain than he had been since the horror at Goeringen. His flesh throbbed, scored by the burning implements. It felt as if his muscles were turning to mush, bubbling and steaming and dripping out through his pores. He'd learned how to scream again, and the movement of it wrenched his jaws.

It was fantastic. After so long in a state of half-life, he was alive again. His nerves burned with the savage, joyful agony of it. It cauterised him, sealing up the gaping wounds of memory. Part of him wanted to sing, just like the others were doing, but his jaw ached too much for that yet.

Around him stood the other brothers and sisters of the Faithful. They had all changed. Their skin wept, not with pus and sickness, but with blood from the damage they'd inflicted on themselves. Some of them were chanting, swaying on their sore-riddled legs and mumbling words they hadn't heard before that day as if they'd learned them from childhood. They all had the comet on them, angry and red, the mark of salvation.

Schlecht had the comet too. It was what brought the pain, the marvellous, blessed pain that seared away the evil dreams. He wrinkled his forehead, feeling his flesh pucker and split. Fresh blood ran into his eyes, blinding him with a lens of red.

He laughed, even though it cracked his lips. To his surprise, he found that he was dancing. Even in his former life, he'd never danced. Erika had tried to make him many times, but he'd always found a way to refuse. It had seemed stupid; impious, even.

Now he did it without thinking. His feet just moved, keeping time with the beating drum that echoed out from the heart of the slum, shuffling along with the rest of the tide of humanity around him.

They all wore the clothes they'd worn before, but there were new rips in the rotten fabric. Their flesh had been exposed, revealing raw marks of whipcord and dragging nails. Brothers and sisters both cavorted in messy ranks, mortifying their flesh further, wielding gouges and flails, holding their heads back and laughing through the flames.

On all of them, the comet blazed, red as the setting sun.

It was hard to make out what they were singing. Schlecht wasn't really listening in any case. He heard endless cries of *Sigmar, Sigmar*, as well as other words he didn't recognise. He didn't recognise them even when they slipped from his own bleeding lips.

It was all part of the ecstasy. It was all part of the fury.

'Sons and daughters!'

It was him. He was back among them, the Father, the one who brought the pain.

The people screamed anew, reaching out to touch him, rubbing new dust into their wounds to demonstrate their fealty.

Schlecht hung back. Enough remained of his old life to keep him from screaming. He remembered the way the Father had appeared when he'd first seen him. Those melancholy eyes, sweeping across the deserted chapel – the saddest, gentlest gaze he'd ever witnessed.

Schlecht had seen the agony in the Father's soul then. He'd seen right through it, down the bitter heart of it, where old memories curled up and still resided, unassuaged and as raw as flayed flesh.

Now he saw a different side to him. It was hard to remember that first, pitiable impression, even though he knew it must still be in there somewhere.

And there had been the woman too, the one who had brought him a different kind of pain.

Where was she?

'Sons and daughters!' cried the Father. He came among them, huge and dark, striding through the throng of Faithful like some great beast of the deep emerging out of the crashing surf. 'This is your moment. This is the task for which your lives were ordained.'

The screaming reached a new pitch of intensity. Schlecht felt his comet burst into a fresh wave of pain. He stumbled in his dance, fixing his eyes on the one solid presence in their midst.

'What is noble?' asked the Father, sweeping his gaze across them.

Death!

'What is blessed?'

Death!

'What brings release?'

Death!

They called out the word louder each time. The thunder of it made the earth tremble. Schlecht called out with them, feeling the syllable resonate in his chest.

He'd never been violent. The prospect of violence had always made him sick. He could still remember how he'd felt on the walls of Goeringen, just before the beasts had come over them. He'd wanted to vomit, to pass out, anything to escape the overwhelming stink of horror.

Not now. He wanted to fight. He wanted to lose himself in fighting. The world seemed better for that.

'You have cowered behind these walls for too long,' said the Father, holding the Instrument aloft. 'Now we will leave them. We will bring death to the enemy. We will bring destruction among them. We are the true living death that will scour such evil from the world.'

Schlecht watched the Instrument wave before his eyes. In another life, he'd have called it a brand – an iron rod used to mark cattle. The twin-tailed shape at its tip glowed crimson. It was that which had scored the comet into his living flesh, eating it up and turning the skin into a bloody, agonised paste.

I venerate it.

He turned, and saw how close he was to the gates. They were opening. Beyond those doors he saw an army of death coming closer, a host of empty faces with marsh-green eyes and vacant smiles.

Then the Father came before the Faithful, casting aside the Instrument, the bringer of the comet, and taking up the Hammer. His armour and cloak were red from the fires and he moved like a river in flood, vast and supple.

'For the honour of mankind!' the Father thundered, breaking into the run that would carry him beyond the gates and out into the host of darkness.

And behind him, sweeping from the cauldron of fire like winter's maelstrom, came the Faithful, the ones he had marked, the Chosen of Sigmar. They screamed as they came, trailing blood in their wake, and their eyes were alive with the promise of death, and ruin, and the burning fury of the world's final judgement.

'THE GATES ARE open!'

Mila heard the cry from far over to her right, a panicked voice that somehow rose above the clamour of battle.

It spread quickly and soon men on either side of her had taken it up.

'The gates are open!'

Erich turned to Dieter, ignoring her and looking suddenly terrified.

'Morr's arse,' he blurted, 'they've let them in!'

From behind him, another skeletal arm reached over the lip of the parapet, clutching at his unprotected back.

Mila leaped on it, hacking down viciously with her sword, sending yet another climber down into the mass of corpses at the base of the walls.

She grabbed Erich and shoved him back into position.

'Damn you!' she shouted. 'Don't worry about the gates – worry about the walls!'

The undead were still coming up them. The stonework was covered in them – a living tapestry of gaunt limbs and gaping jaws. One withered climber pulled itself over the edge and clattered down onto the parapet.

Erich clubbed it with the butt of his halberd, sending it stumbling backwards, before swiping heavily and taking its head off. Its dislodged skull sailed down into the town below. Erich kicked the rest of the corpse over the edge before looking at Mila with desperation in his eyes. He was dog-tired.

'They've opened the gates,' he said weakly, as if that made everything they were doing on the walls pointless.

Mila finished sawing off another emerging hand before she risked a look over the edge.

Perhaps her night vision was better than Erich's, or perhaps she hadn't spent so long in despair that every new development seemed like a portent of imminent doom.

'So they have,' she said.

Men were streaming out of Eisenach. Even in the dark she could see the savage energy in their charge. They were throwing themselves at the enemy, hurling their bodies at the invader. They were like a raging river, sweeping all before them.

They were chanting. The voices were raucous, disjointed and shrieking, but they easily drowned out the pervasive low chatter of the undead around them.

Death! Death! Death!

At the head of the tide of men was a familiar figure, hauling his warhammer around in devastating, crushing arcs. The head of the hammer glimmered in the firelight, smashing aside those that stood in its way, just as it had done at Helgag, and at the unnamed village where Schlecht had hidden, and wherever else it had been wielded.

Mila watched it for a moment, spellbound. Something

about Huss's battle-rage entranced her. She knew just
how he would be fighting: tight-lipped, almost silent,
whirling into contact with that peculiar grace he always
summoned when the war-fervour fell on him. If any of
the undead got close enough they would hear the prayers
he muttered constantly, just before they died their second
death, hammered back into merciful, silent oblivion.

He was like a hero of the old legends given human
form and placed within the world of real men. The host
behind him rushed at the enemy with a zeal she'd never
seen before.

*You have shown them the way of defiance. You have made
them believe again.*

Mila was stirred by a fresh scraping at the parapet. An
undead climber pulled itself up over the edge, screaming soundlessly at her, its jaws extended grotesquely.

You have made me believe again.

She stepped back, letting it come on, readying herself
for the sword-thrust. On either side of her, Erich and
Dieter were already busy with their own battles.

Mila watched the figure clamber over the edge. She
saw the stretched-tight skin across its skull, as translucent as wet parchment. She saw the shrunken hands
grab on to the stone, squeezing it like a sponge and
sending hairline cracks snaking across it.

She saw its eyes in the gloom, pale green and glowing
like twin stars. When it saw her, it smiled widely and
licked its broken lips. It limped towards her across the
narrow ledge, arms outstretched.

Mila waited for the right moment to swing. She'd
learned to take her time, not to rush into the stroke that
risked missing and leaving her open to attack.

Just at the right moment, she flung her blade round,
dipping it a little as it angled in. It made contact just

above the shoulder where the warrior's jutting collar-bone stuck out from its protruding ribcage. The metal bit deep, parting the dry flesh and cutting halfway through the neck.

The dead warrior jerked away from the sword, still coming for her, its head hanging on by a tangle of half-severed tendons.

Summoning all her strength, Mila yanked the blade the rest of the way across, dragging it two-handed. The notched steel carved through the weak flesh, ripping the head free and sending it bouncing and rolling across the stone. As the decapitated body toppled towards her, still with arms extended, she pulled back, using the momentum of the sword-thrust to carry her round and away.

The headless corpse fell at her feet, lifeless and empty. The eerie light in its eyes died, though the grin stayed locked on its severed head.

Mila looked down at it in triumph. She knew others would already be coming to take its place, tearing up the walls like rats fleeing fire. For a moment, though, she relished her triumph. She no longer feared them.

She had stood firm, just like the rest of Eisenach, and found resolve she didn't know she had.

We are strong. The night is dark, but we have the strength to endure it.

She placed her foot on the skull of the warrior, and pressed down. The bone flexed, cracked, then shattered. The lurid grin on the corrupted face broke, dissolved into clouds of shards and dust.

'For the love of Sigmar,' she said, making the sign of the comet on her breast. Though she'd said the words many times in her life, in lifeless rote or in impious expletive, that was the first time, the very first time, she had believed in them.

You make me believe.

Then she pushed roughly past Dieter and hurried along the ramparts to the ladder leading down to the town below.

'Where are you going?' shouted Erich from behind her, struggling to hold off his latest adversary.

'The gates are open!' she shouted back, grasping Pieter's sword tightly and starting to descend, as if that answered everything.

THE ZEALOTS KEPT running, howling words of power and hatred as they came. The bulk of them surged from the gates in a single, tangled mess, falling over one another in their lust for killing. When they reached the enemy, they fell among them with astonishing savagery. They hacked with their improvised blades, kicked out with badly-shod feet, ripped with calloused fingers.

The undead reacted slowly. The first ranks of them were swept away by the sudden impact, knocked over and trampled into the blood-sodden earth. Zealots were borne down too in the confusion, crushed underfoot or driven into the waiting blades of the enemy. Like two huge rivers crashing through flimsy dams, the two armies mingled into a mess of struggling limbs and flashing metal.

Huss powered through the heart of enemy, striding at a furious pace and laying into the undead around him on either side.

'What is noble?' he roared as he went. 'What is blessed?'

The responses thundered out from the horde following him, making the air shake and the ground tremble.

Death! Death! Death!

Once the first fury of the charge had been blunted, the zealots fell in droves. The undead came at them with their eerie, near-silent brutality, and proved just as hard to kill as they had done on every occasion before. Only a decapitation or a near-complete dismemberment was enough to halt them. Even after sustaining huge wounds – having their diseased limbs ripped from their torsos or having their distended stomachs ripped open – they'd keep staggering onwards, reaching out with their long fingernails or dragging up their rusty blades.

The difference was that the zealots were just as unstoppable. Unlike the warriors of Treicher's retinue, they were completely undaunted by the foes they faced. They shrugged off near-mortal wounds, chanting wildly all the while and sprinting madly to meet the next set of blades. Even after they'd been felled, they crawled through the mud on all fours, biting at ankles and pulling apart sinews. When their cleavers and meathooks were knocked from their hands they used their fingers and teeth, just like the enemy did.

The carnage was staggering. Neither side had any conception of fear, retreat, or restraint. Eyes were gouged, throats were torn, ribs were hooked out and jaws were smashed.

One undead warrior plunged its sword clean through the midriff of a screaming zealot, twisted it round and cut him in two. The man, his upper body reduced to a glistening pile of entrails and organs, roared in gurgling defiance and managed to grab his killer by the ankle and drag it down to his level. With his last, frenzied breath, he pulled the warrior's skull from its spinal column with a dry snap. The two of them collapsed into one another, merged into a single expanding pool of gore and bone fragments.

Perhaps, left to themselves, both armies would have destroyed one another. The difference between them, though, was Huss. Wherever he went on the battlefield the zealots were roused to apoplectic levels of maniacal slaughter. They screamed his name aloud as they fought, their palsied limbs blurring as they hurled their weapons around artlessly.

He led them always. Though they charged forwards with all the speed they could muster, he was always ahead of them. His warhammer blazed with dazzling golden light, leaving long trails of afterglow hanging behind it as it swept round in its killing arcs. Huss hurled the bodies of the undead high into the night air with the impact of his blows, breaking them open and discarding what was left for his followers to mop up. He ploughed on, ever further from the gates, punching a long line of ruin through the ranks of the corrupted and cracking the unity of their advance. The attack on the walls faltered as more and more of the undead were dragged into the fight with the zealots and their indomitable warrior priest.

A lumbering figure lurched up to Huss, carrying a heavy halberd in both hands. In life the bearer must have been a big man, and scraps of old regimental dress still hung from its moon-white flesh. Its heavy jaw hung open and pale light spilled from it like a candle in a lantern. What remained of its skin was speckled with black sores and contusions. With a soundless bellow, it swung the halberd, aiming for Huss's throat.

Huss jammed the hammerhead back, blocking the incoming swipe and shattering the stave of the halberd. Before the creature could react, he plunged onwards, jerking the hammer back and sending it reeling. The horror nearly fell, but somehow managed to stay on its feet just in time for Huss to free a hand and punch it full in the face with his clenched gauntlet. Its skull cracked open, falling apart to expose a clump of desiccated brain matter. Huss kicked out, and the headless corpse thudded to the earth.

Then he whirled round, sweeping aside two more advancing undead warriors. His eyes narrowed, seeking out the next target.

'Father!'

Somehow, that voice rose above the clamour of the fighting like a clear bell. As soon as Huss heard it, his heart went cold.

His gaze swept back, over to where the sound had come from. It was hard to make much out in the fiery murk – smoke still rolled across the battlefield from the fires at the base of the walls.

For a moment, he saw nothing at all – just the close press of figures occupied in the grisly business of organised murder.

Then she emerged, hacking her way clumsily through the bodies around her. Other troops stood with her, each one pale with fear but fighting on nonetheless.

'Get back!' he roared, almost unconsciously knocking aside the clutching arms of another creature before striding towards her. 'What are you doing here? Go back!'

Mila laughed at him. Her blonde hair flew out as she worked her blade back and forth, handling it like a child might handle a length of flotsam.

'Sigmar protects!' she called out, blocking the incoming swipe of a cleaver before pushing back the undead creature who'd lashed out with it.

Huss fought his way over to her, barging between her and her adversary. He crushed its skull with a single crunch of his hammer before grabbing her and pulling her towards him. The living and dead continued to fight all around them, clamped together in a brutal, brawling action.

'Go back to Eisenach,' he hissed. His eyes flashed with anger.

Mila shrank back at that. Despite the horror and bloodshed around her, his glare seemed the only thing with the power to cow her.

'I thought–'

Huss shook her roughly. He could feel anger and fear – terrible fear – threatening to overwhelm him. She stared at him from frightened eyes, wide-eyed and shocked.

'I told you to stay on the walls,' he said.

'I know, but–'

'Go back now. You make me *angry*, child.'

Mila wrenched herself loose from his grip, tearing her bodice as she spun away. She glared at him in turn, her face streaked with hot, appalled tears.

'You said–' she blurted, choked with surprise. 'I thought–'

As she struggled to get the words out, a stick-thin undead creature swayed into her path. Huss spun away from Mila and launched himself at it.

He crashed into it, knocking it from its feet and falling to the ground on top of it. Huss butted it viciously in the face, and the scripture bound across his skull blazed with fire as it struck the unholy flesh. The creature screamed in agony. Huss leapt back to his feet, towering over the writhing horror. He raised up the hammer, two-handed, and brought it down heavily, driving the ribcage of the prone cadaver deep into the blood-soiled earth. He hit it again, then again, until nothing remained of it but slivers of cartilage floating on a puddle of gore.

Then he turned back to Mila, panting heavily. He reached out for her, but now she flinched from him.

'I will not see you harmed,' he said, his voice thick with hesitant emotion. 'Do you not understand, girl? I will *not* see you harmed.'

She stared at him, torn between shock and hurt.

'Why?' she asked, and her voice was as weak as a child's. 'You risk all these men's deaths, and not mine?'

'No more questions,' Huss said, taking up the war-hammer and brandishing it menacingly. 'You and your men – go back to the walls. Wait for me. I'll come for you – I promise. Go *now*.'

He didn't wait for her to obey him. He knew that she would. More undead were already limping in his direction, perhaps heartened by his sudden distraction. Only by keeping their attention on him would he safeguard her withdrawal.

Huss strode towards the enemy, hefting his golden hammerhead with savage relish. As always, the weapon felt light in his hands. Undead creatures stumbled at him, marching into combat with their unearthly lack of fear.

It is a sin to savour the deaths of those who were once men, he thought.

Huss broke into a run, building up the momentum that would release the killing-edge of his warhammer.

But if it preserves her, I will embrace that sin.

Huss released the pent-up force, watching with grim satisfaction as another skull was demolished by the raw power of his fury. More deaths would come, one after the other, until none were left standing to face his wrath.

By the grace of Sigmar, if it preserves her, I will savour the deaths of every one of them.

CHAPTER THIRTEEN

TWO OF EICHMANN'S men leapt up at the charging centigor, swinging their blades wildly. Neither got close
– the enraged creature lashed out with its hooves,
crunching into them with wild, slashing kicks and
knocking them bodily away. Barely slowed, it charged
onwards, swaying drunkenly as it came.

Eichmann waited for it, rapier in hand. The rest of his
men streamed out on either side of the reeling beast,
getting in among the ungors and humans and blunting
their erratic progress.

The centigor was huge, over twice the height of a man
and far heavier. Its lower half had the look of a massive destrier, but it was far shaggier and filthier than any
natural horse. Its hide swam with sweat and blood, its
long beard thrashed as it moved, its hooves were cloven
and cracked the stone flags as they fell. Though blinded
and enraged by the device, it still scythed the leaf-blade
edge through the air in the hope of catching something.

Eichmann watched it lumber towards him, judging
speed and momentum. He'd have to be precise. He felt
his leg muscles, already tired from the long march, tense
to move.

The centigor careered at him, lashing out and

bellowing as it came. Eichmann leapt, rapier in hand, just as a crossbow bolt shot out from over to his left. The quarrel thumped into the centigor's thick neck, burying itself inches deep and sending out a jet of hot, dark blood. The creature roared and bucked away.

Eichmann tried to check himself, but thudded face-first into the monster's rearing torso. He bounced off the iron-tough flesh, staggering away across the uneven floor before collapsing to his knees.

The world around him disappeared into a whirl of blood-red fire and movement. He crawled away from where he thought the monster was, somehow keeping a grip on his rapier as he scrambled across the slime-covered stone.

Something heavy slammed down by his head and he rolled away from it. A shadow, stinking and musky, passed over him and he realised he'd ended up under the centigor's legs. His vision cleared a little, exposing the hairy underbelly of the beast and the churning muscles of its hind legs.

Gagging from the stench, he scrambled to his left just as a barbed hoof stamped down. Another crossbow bolt thumped into the creature's flanks, making it rear up again in blind rage.

Eichmann scuttled out from under the hooves, only to see the beast's spear-tip plunging down after him. He darted away from it, losing his precarious footing and sprawling back across the floor. Effluent splashed across his face, making his eyes sting and his skin smart.

Attracted by the noise of his splashing, the creature powered after him, bellowing with incoherent rage. Eichmann had time to see another of his men rush up to it, only for the centigor to swat him away with a contemptuous swipe of its spear. The leaf-blade cut right through the man's midriff, ripping out his internals and strewing them across the stone in a splattered arc of vital crimson.

Though blinded and wounded, the beast was still powerful enough to kill them all. It seemed to sense the presence of those around it, and wielded its weapon scarcely less efficiently than it would have done sighted.

Eichmann got to his feet again and backed up against the wall of the chamber. He could feel hot, thick fluid running down his collar. Two squat pillars stood on either side of him. There was no way out, and no way further back.

'Blessed Sigmar,' he whispered, clutching the rapier tightly in his right hand and preparing for the impact.

The centigor came at him, head low. Its human-like face was locked in a snarl of maddened rage, and bone-white froth spilled from its ragged lips. It stabbed down towards him two-handed, searching out more flesh to impale.

Eichmann swerved away from the blade and pounced right up into the path of the creature. His left hand grabbed on to the centigor's shaggy mane and he hauled himself up as if mounting a carthorse.

The beast jerked back. It twisted round, freeing up an arm and trying to grab the witch hunter and throw him off, but Eichmann hung on, dragging himself up over the bucking shoulders and away from the huge searching fingers. His boot lodged in the looped chains under the centigor's ribcage and he pushed himself up from it.

The centigor lurched savagely, backing away and reaching for him with its human arms. Eichmann kept moving, grabbing fistfuls of hair and hauling himself further up onto the creature's back.

It bucked like an unbroken steer, roaring in outrage

and trying to wrench its torso round to face him. Keeping hold of his mount with one hand, Eichmann twisted the rapier point-down, and thrust. The blade punched into the flesh where the small of the creature's human back fused with the spine of the horse.

The centigor screamed and thrashed around even more frantically. Eichmann pushed the blade in further, twisting it deep down into the muscle.

All of a sudden, the creature's legs gave way. With a crash, it fell to the ground, its horse's hooves splayed out under it. The human half remained active, raging and lashing out, but its lower body went as limp as wet sackcloth.

Eichmann withdrew the rapier and clambered free of the wounded centigor, backing away from it warily. It tried to turn, twisting back on itself with the spear in hand, but couldn't get the whole way around. Blind and paralysed, its bellows became increasingly weak. In a final gesture of defiance it hurled the spear out. The shaft clanged harmlessly from the far wall.

Breathing heavily, Eichmann looked around across the chamber. The ungors were all dead, as were the wretched humans who had been among them. Several of Eichmann's men lay with them, but most had survived and stood watchfully with their weapons in hand. Gartner clutched at a wound to his arm and looked pale from blood-loss. Daecher, the one who'd loosed the crossbow bolts, didn't meet Eichmann's gaze.

Just too late to be useful, Udo lumbered down the stairway leading up to the surface. He was covered in a slick of blood from head to toe but still looked remorselessly cheerful.

'Need any help, sir?' he asked, looking at the carnage approvingly.

Eichmann turned back to the centigor. It had stopped roaring. Its huge arms hung weakly by its sides as it slumped into a painful-looking hunch. Its flanks were shivering, and a low, grating wheezing escaped from its ruined body. A pool of blood had spread out from under it and was gently growing.

As his breathing returned to normal and his heartbeat thudded a little less urgently in his chest, Eichmann felt his battle-energy dissipate into loathing.

The emotion was helpful. He'd come to dislike interrogating his own kind, but such distaste didn't extend to beastmen. After the hellish journey through the forest, it was time for some answers.

He sheathed his rapier and flexed his tired fingers.

'I do, Udo,' he growled. 'Get the instruments.'

IT DIDN'T BREAK as a man would break. Its strength was phenomenal and its will was near-inexhaustible. It raged against the men as they bound its arms and spat defiance at them as they brought the heated tongs and flensers.

Eichmann looked into its face the whole time. Such was his habit, a minor courtesy amid the whole sordid business of truth-finding. Some of his counterparts, for all their skill in the dark arts of interrogation, could never look into a man's eyes while they worked. They'd concentrate on what they were doing, blanking out the screams and sobs, focusing their mind on the information they were gathering to the glory of Sigmar's holy name.

Eichmann always maintained eye contact, however distressing it became. That, he had always thought, was the least he could do – it prevented the experience from becoming purely mechanical and reminded him that at all times his trade involved hurting those who, like him, were mortal creatures and in possession of mortal souls.

He would often see faces of those he hurt afterwards, especially in the dark of sleepless nights. That was the price he paid; for all that, he still did it.

We are all mortal souls.

When the centigor broke at last, its roars degenerated into a warped kind of bovine weeping. The sound was horrific, and echoed around the chamber. Its huge head, streaked with fresh blood, hung down at last. Its unseeing eyes went dull.

Eichmann came in close then, ignoring the reek of musk and agony. Though tied down and deep in the final pangs of excrucitation, the creature's head was still higher than his.

Up close, its face resembled that of a drink-addled old man. Its skin was leathery and wrinkled, scored with ancient tattoos and scars. Crude metal studs had been driven into the bone and the flesh puckered up against them. The hair of its beard was thicker and coarser than human hair and hung in snarled swirls.

When it opened its mouth to draw in huge, shuddering breaths, fangs glinted redly in the firelight. Its exhalations stank of raw meat and alcohol.

'I know you can understand me,' said Eichmann, holding the instruments in view as he spoke. 'You know the tongues of men.'

The centigor stared at him with unseeing hatred, following the noise of his speech, and said nothing.

'What has been done here?' asked Eichmann.

At that, the centigor laughed weakly. Its huge chest shuddered, and blood bubbled out of the ripped corners of its mouth.

'Sigmar-in-Forest,' it muttered, slurring the 's' sounds like a drunkard.

Its speech was slack and heavily accented. The mouth and tongue which so easily produced animal bellows had trouble forming the words of Reikspiel.

Eichmann moved in closer, resting the tip of a long spiked instrument gently against the raw flesh of the centigor's chest.

'What does that mean?' he asked.

The centigor chuckled, and its eyes rolled. It was drifting away into a haze of pain and insanity.

'He's coming. Sigmar-in-Forest.'

'Where is he coming?'

'Gallowberg,' said the centigor. 'He waits at Gallowberg.'

Eichmann narrowed his eyes.

'What is Hylaeus?'

'What?'

Eichmann shoved the spike deep into the bruised flesh. The centigor winced, too exhausted even to let slip another snort.

'What is Hylaeus?' demanded Eichmann. 'What does that mean?'

The centigor began to cough up blood. Its enormous strength was coming to an end.

'Mean nothing,' it rasped, summoning up a final look of hatred to shoot at its tormentor. 'Mean nothing.'

Eichmann saw the lie in the creature's eyes. He twisted the spike viciously, tearing up sinew and skin.

'I will burn this place,' he hissed, coming to within a hand's breadth of the creature's face. 'I will return with an army of men and I will tear down every tree within a hundred leagues. I will destroy every shrine and kill every changeling abomination that squats in the roots. I will shatter your standing stones and break your altars. The earth will be ploughed and seeded with crops. Nothing will remain.'

That seemed to wound the centigor more than anything else, and its ruined face warped with pain.

'Tell me what Hylaeus is,' said Eichmann, his voice almost a whisper over the bloodied hole where the beast's ear had been. 'Then this will be over.'

Great tears rolled down the creature's cheeks. The head lolled, heavy with pain and fatigue and drunkenness.

'You say wrong,' it muttered, barely audibly. 'Not Hylaeus.'

'Tell me how to say it.'

'Hush.'

'Don't dare to–'

The centigor lifted its head, staring blearily out at him. It could barely move its lips.

'Hush,' it said again, stumbling over the syllable. It concentrated, screwing up its brow for one last effort.

'Huss.'

'GET ANYTHING?' ASKED Udo, wrapping a long bandage around his bleeding knuckles. He sat in a corner of the main courtyard in front of the keep, not far from the stairway down to the crypt.

Eichmann came to sit by him. He collapsed onto his haunches, aching and stiff. Above the ruined towers of the castle, the eastern sky was already dark grey and lightening fast. Mist hung like cobwebs in the corners.

'I did,' he said.

Udo kept wrapping.

'And?'

'This ritual was not the only one,' said Eichmann. 'The creature told me there are many more taking place across the Drakwald. Dozens of them, perhaps hundreds.'

'For what purpose?'

'I couldn't make sense of what it said. Something about "Sigmar in the Forest". Perhaps a muster for some campaign. The beastmen are being stirred up, that's clear enough.'

Udo gave him a serious look.

'We've seen bacchanals like this before,' he said. 'They use them to imprint devotion on the humans, to enslave their wills, and to create fervour in the mutants.'

Eichmann nodded.

'This is just an outlier,' he said. 'The cells will be gathering soon.'

'To where?'

'Do you know the name "Gallowberg"?' asked Eichmann.

'No. Gartner will.'

'And "Huss"?'

Udo stopped winding the bandage and thought.

'That's a Marienburger name. I do remember...' He shook his head. 'Maybe it'll come to me.'

Eichmann rested his elbows on his drawn-up knees.

'How about you?' he asked. 'What did you find?'

Udo went back to bandaging his hand.

'Plenty of ungors, a few humans. They were all drunk, and we got some of them in the middle of, er, activities. That's why they were so easy to kill – they were busy when we got here.'

'Get any of them alive?'

Udo looked briefly embarrassed.

'Sorry,' he said. 'Didn't know you wanted that.'

Eichmann shook his head.

'Maybe I didn't.'

Others of his men began to emerge into the open

then, up from the stairway leading down to the underground chamber. They had grey, exhausted looks on their faces.

There would be no rest for any of them. The chamber and the bodies within it would be burned, and then the long march back to the waystation would start.

'I begin to wonder if Gorbach was right,' Eichmann said. 'There are a thousand cults in every town across the Empire. We could chase this one down and find a hundred more waiting for us at the end. It might mean nothing. Do I still have the hunger for it?'

Udo finished winding the strips of cloth, tore off the remnant and stretched his fingers out.

'I do,' he said. 'I'm enjoying myself.'

'I'm glad.'

'Seriously. This is better than Middenheim.'

'Udo, there's more to this work than knocking heads together.'

'Is there?' The big henchman hacked up a bullet of phlegm and expectorated deftly. 'With respect, sir, you spend your time agonising about what you do, writing reports that no one ever reads and memorising the Articles of Interrogation when anyone else would just do what comes naturally. I sleep at night. I have a full belly.'

He pulled his leather glove over his bandaged hand.

'We've broken up another cult and killed a bunch of heretics,' he said. 'That's a good thing. What more do you want?'

Eichmann didn't know what to say to that. No one else would have dared speak to him like that. Udo was different, of course, but it was still impertinent.

'What do I want?' he asked. 'Yes, that's a question.'

He rubbed his face with his fingers, kneading the hard

skin, trying to make his thoughts sharper. The exhaustion he'd felt for so long was growing within him, piling up like leaves in an autumn gale.

'We could go back to Middenheim,' he said. 'We've proof of von Hessler's heresy, and that'd be something.'

Udo laughed.

'You don't want to do that.'

'No, I don't.'

Eichmann looked up, out at the long silhouettes of the four towers, stark against the cold light of dawn.

'Every step we take uncovers another morsel,' he said. 'A name, a sign, a direction. We're being led.'

'That's a good thing?'

'Depends who's doing the leading.'

Gartner and Daecher, together as always, walked towards them out of the mists. The taller woodsman had painful-looking rings around his eyes and looked haggard from his injury.

'Nothing's left alive,' Gartner reported. 'A few dozen beastmen, some human cultists, and that creature. The rest of the keep's empty. Fires have been made ready – just give the order.'

Eichmann nodded absently.

'What's the Gallowberg, Gartner?' he asked, half-hoping the man wouldn't know.

'A name I haven't heard for a long time,' said Gartner, warily. 'And then in unreliable tales, most of which are nonsense and not worth listening to.'

'Humour me.'

'It'll be east of here,' said Gartner, reluctantly. 'Hard marching, back through the heart of the forest. There's a deep valley, so sheer they say that the light of the sun barely hits the ground. You'll hear stories of stones there, ancient places soaked in evil. Listen to the village wives and they'll make the sign of the comet when you mention it. They'll tell you what happens in that valley, and it'll be all screams in the night and changelings spawning under the gaze of witches.'

'Just like here, then,' said Eichmann.

Gartner shrugged.

'This is real,' he said. 'I have no idea if the Gallowberg is.'

'But you think so.'

'Possibly.'

Eichmann looked back at his men gathered over by the stairwell entrance. Their movements were clumsy with fatigue.

So, do I follow this? I could forget it all, go back to the city and chase after easier prey.

I'm tempted – I'll admit it.

'They all said the same thing,' mused Eichmann. 'Workel, Bohfels, the creature. Sigmar-in-Forest. And Hylaeus, or Huss, or whatever. Something about a great change coming, a saviour waiting in the dark places. This here is just the fringe of it, and von Hessler is nothing but a minor prince with a penchant for the exotic, but it leads deeper down. These cults – they're the froth on the poison's surface.'

With some effort, Eichmann pushed himself to his feet. He stretched out, feeling his spine unravel slowly, laced with dull aches.

He'd made his decision, the only one he was ever going to make.

'You don't have to come with me,' Eichmann said to Gartner. 'I hired you to take me to the castle, and you can pick up your pay at Geistrich.'

The woodsman looked at him doubtfully.

'You won't get to the Gallowberg on your own. When

these cults draw together you'll do well to get out of the Drakwald alive.'

Udo snorted.

'We've done pretty well so far,' he said.

Daecher shot him a scornful look.

'You have no–'

Eichmann held up a warning hand, ignoring both men and looking evenly at Gartner.

'You'll double your pay if you lead us to this place,' he said. 'Think on it.'

Gartner thought on it.

'No.'

'Triple, then. And a contract with the Church in Middenheim, signed by me. That's worth more than any amount of schillings.'

Gartner shook his head, smiling wearily.

'You don't have the men,' he said. 'They'll pick you off, one by one.'

Eichmann pulled the witch hunter's medallion out from his shirt.

'We can get men – as many as you like. They'll fight for money, or they'll fight to stop me burning their houses to the ground. Either way suits me fine.'

'We're miles from anywhere.'

'That can be remedied.'

Gartner laughed out loud.

'Taal's teeth, you're persistent.' He kept smiling, and it made his awkward, pale face look even more lopsided. 'But I don't think you've any idea what you're doing. I think you're stumbling blindly from one half-whisper to another.'

'It's my job to listen to whispers,' said Eichmann.

'Even if they go nowhere? Even if they drive you mad?'

Udo leapt to his feet, his hand on the shaft of his

maul. Daecher responded immediately, snapping the crossbow into place.

Eichmann rolled his eyes.

'*Enough,*' he said, glaring at both of them until they stood down, before turning back to Gartner.

'Look, I don't really care what you think of me, woodsman,' he said, 'but I will go to the Gallowberg, and I will find out what's drawing these cults together. If you won't guide me there then I'll find someone who will and they'll get the benefit of the Church's largesse in your place. But this is nothing to do with money – this is all about duty, something I thought you took seriously. Perhaps I was wrong about that.'

Eichmann's voice carried more conviction then than it usually did, and Gartner looked briefly taken aback by it. The woodsman shot a glance at Daecher, who offered nothing in return.

An uneasy silence passed between them before Gartner finally shook his head again.

'You don't have enough men,' he repeated.

'So what do you recommend?' asked Eichmann.

'Break from the forest out east – there's a big place within a few days' march that'll have a garrison. Reinforce, resupply, and then head back into the woods for the Gallowberg. It'll be hard – the beasts will be on your scent now and you'll have trouble raising men if the plagues of undeath have got this far north.'

'That can all be addressed,' said Eichmann. 'What is this town, and how do we get there?'

'The town's called Eisenach,' said Gartner resignedly, looking like a man who'd made a decision he'd live to regret, 'and don't worry – you've convinced me. I'll take you there myself.'

* * *

something to the others, something that they clearly
found annoying – perhaps remonstrating with them for
not going quickly enough, or too quickly, or some other
failing.

As Huss watched her, she stumbled on something,
ipping over some half-buried pile of limbs or bones.
e half-believed he heard her curses ring out across the
d of desolation.

ou're safe.

s thin lips twitched at the corners. Like the sun creep-
ver the horizon, the smile that only she brought to
s suddenly threatened to break out again.

*have you become so precious to me? What power rests
ou that gives me hope? Are you as she was before? Is
ted even to ask?*

here was a commotion behind him. Huss
und, bringing the hammer up reflexively and
ack into the tight expression of command.

ood before him, scrawny and stinking. His
e same grey as the dawn and covered in
es. Most of his teeth had rotted away and
othes were covered in bloodstains where
m his bony figure. The sign of the comet
forehead into a bloody mess.

ing like a child on its birth-festival. For
didn't recognise him, but then realisa-

t shouted, still lost in his world of
a severed head in one hand, clasped
air. The marsh-light that had once
eye sockets had long died away.
e shrieked. 'The fire! The comet!

THE SUN CAME up, and victory came with it. Huss strode
through the breaking sea of the enemy, carving them
apart like the prow of a galleon. They still limped up
to him, clutching at his robes, scratching at his armour-
plate, and so they died.

Fatigue had no hold on him. He had no idea how long
he'd been fighting – hours, at least. He still moved as
he'd taught himself to, fast and heavy, using the weight
of the hammerhead to swing himself round. The enemy
were too slow and too weak. Their numbers were no
advantage to them once the night faded and the hopes
of living men rekindled.

In his wake came the Faithful. They still screamed like
a whole host of maddened children. They still ran at the
undead with no fear, ripping them apart with their own
fingers and gnawing at the rancid flesh on the bones.
Their eyes stared wide and their jaws hung open, lost in
paroxysms of ecstasy and boundless anger.

The Faithful had swept all before them, stumbling
over their own tattered robes to get at the enemy. Huss
hadn't been able to tell how many had answered his
call – many hundreds, certainly. Less than half of them
remained alive. Their fury hadn't made them impervious to harm; quite the opposite. They'd sprinted into
impossible positions with all the fervour of the zealot,
charging into ranks of waiting blades as if they were
wheat to be shoved aside. Even when they were cut
open and dying they still crawled onwards, scraping at
the soil in their desperation to get at the foe.

So they had died; but they had also killed.

The two armies had resembled one another – each
without tactics or formations, just amorphous masses
of bodies scrambling to get into close combat. Neither
held back nor let forces remain in reserve, and each

had forgotten any notions they might once have had of restraint, manoeuvres or positions.

Huss prayed as he fought, near silently. The words spilled from his mouth as effortlessly as his hammer arced through the clearing air.

Guard the souls of those whom I slay. They were once mortal flesh and precious to You. Let them find peace in death, as all Your children aspire to find peace in death. Break the bonds that compel them to walk in the realm of the living, as is forbidden by the laws that You set down and ceaselessly guard.

Huss brought the hammerhead down in a mighty plunge, crushing the bare skull of a wasted warrior and breaking open its ribcage. Before its companions could shamble closer, he'd hauled it up again, ready to swing it across in the broad curve that would slam them aside in turn.

Animate Your Faithful with the fire that restores. Let them kill in Your name before they find their end in this world. And for those who stumble, remember their sacrifice for the immortal glory of mankind. Remember them as You remember those whom all others forget.

The undead never ran. They stayed fighting in the approaches to Eisenach even after the morning light had crept over the devastated fields. They still killed, even at the end, bringing down the reckless who charged at them with fire in their eyes.

Remember them.

Huss stayed at the forefront of the final attack, bludgeoning his way up a long, broken strand towards a ridge of burned and broken trees overlooking the town. As he strode, his boots sank deep into the churned earth. Sweat poured down his neck, flying out in a glittering spray as the hammer swung.

It was only when he'd crested the rise, breaking back of what resistance remained, that he allowed self to rest at last. On either side of him his swept onwards, many carrying wounds that wo long since felled lesser men. They still sang and savagely as they had when they'd broke gates.

Huss looked back the way he'd come. land around the town had been cleare Bodies, those of the once-living a undead, littered the black earth aro last residue of the fires still burne umns of smoke into the lifting g The walls were streaked with so but they still stood.

Some of Eisenach's men but most had descended to of soldiers moved acros watched, going slowly a corpses and splintered the hard fighting for feared the last remn

Huss watched th breathing return heavy in his ha ments, runnin

It was a w

Moving diers wer to be b ily thr head sho like all go

The stream of exclamations was barely coherent. Even as the sick man babbled his joy, others came to join him. They rushed up to Huss, arms outstretched, fingers dripping with blood.

My zealots. My creations.

'The Father! The bringer of revenge! The protector!'

They made little sense. Their powers of speech had been degraded badly by the blind fury that propelled them to acts of heroism and desperation. It was all they had left: the fury and the faith. Before he had come among them, of course, they hadn't even had that.

Huss regarded them tolerantly, satisfied at their work but unable to share in their euphoria. In time, even the zealots would calm down a little, giving in to rest and sleep. When they awoke, the worst of the frenzy would have passed.

But they would never be as they had been. For the rest of their short lives they would be weapons, instruments of the Heldenhammer's will. They would follow Huss until the ends of the earth if he let them, chanting all the while until death took them.

That was the gift he had given them – to lose the final trappings of their humanity in return for a measure of blessed forgetfulness. They no longer felt their wounds, nor wallowed in their old miseries, but instead inhabited a vivid world of pure conviction, able to achieve feats far beyond what their old selves would have contemplated.

Huss spread his hands out to them.

'You prevailed, children,' he said, moving his left hand in the sign of the comet. 'Remember this day. Remember that you always had the power to defeat the unholy. It was within you, waiting to be unlocked.'

His heavy gaze ran across the growing crowd of

supplicants, watching their red-rimmed eyes stare back at him.

'You always had the power,' Huss said again, more wearily now, but with the same conviction that had roused them back in Eisenach. 'All you needed was the freedom to believe. All you needed was to be shown the path to unlocking that freedom. In Sigmar, all things are possible.'

His voice lowered then and his eyes lost their focus, as if he were seeing images from a long time ago.

'All you needed,' he said, 'all any of us has ever needed, was faith.'

CHAPTER FOURTEEN

'WHAT IS FAITH?' he asked.

'You know what faith is,' said Theiss

'I know what I read. I know what I feel. But do I feel the right things? How can a man know his soul is pure?'

Theiss looked up at Huss from his sickbed. He felt worse than he had done for weeks. His body ached from where he'd spent hours ravaged by cramping pain. He could taste blood on his tongue and his hands trembled when he lifted them.

What was worse, Huss was tiring to be around. The acolyte never wanted to know the things a young man ought to want to know. He had no interest in women or beer or food. That was to his credit, of course, but it became wearying all the same. The youth's brown-eyed gaze was so intense, so unbroken, that simply being around him became an effort after a while.

'What do you want me to say?' asked Theiss, pulling a fur-lined shawl closer towards his throat to try to ward against the cold. 'You do everything right. You pray, you fast, you train. That's enough, lad.'

Huss didn't look convinced. His earnest face stared back at Theiss, red from where he sat by the crackling hearth. His brow was creased in consternation.

229

'I doubt, sometimes,' he said.

'Of course you do,' said Theiss. 'We all doubt.'

'You don't.'

Theiss raised an eyebrow, surprised, before snorting out a bitter laugh.

'You think that?' He shuffled to lean closer to where the boy sat, feeling his narrow hips grind against the wooden slats of the bed. 'Oh, I've doubted. Look around you. Before you came here this temple was falling into the earth, and I prayed for deliverance for years. Do you think I wanted to end my days out here, lost on a forgotten hill with the company of drunks and lechers? There were times when I thought Sigmar had deserted me. I was tempted – I could have disavowed it all.'

Huss's eyes widened slightly.

'You're shocked?' said Theiss. 'Don't be. That's your problem, lad – your standards are too high. You read the lives of the saints and want to be one yourself, but you're human, flesh and blood like I am. You'll fail, you'll doubt. None of us is any different.'

Huss shook his head.

'I won't fail,' he said.

'You will.'

'No.' Huss clenched a burly fist in frustration. 'The power of Sigmar is without limits. It gives us strength. The purer we are, the more strength we possess. Eliminate impurity, and our power will be without limits.'

Theiss narrowed his eyes. Something about the tone of Huss's voice made him uncomfortable.

'The power of a priest is a mystery, Luthor. None of us, not even the Grand Theogonist himself, knows the means by which the grace of Sigmar is bestowed, so don't ever think yourself equal to those secrets.'

'I *am* equal to them.' Huss looked defiant again. 'I've

felt the power running through my body. I've felt fire
behind my eyes, burning so hot that the pain can't be
described. There have been days when I had to leave the
temple, get out into the wilds, just so I didn't let it show
to the others. I could have killed them a dozen times,
and they deserved it many more.'

Theiss chuckled weakly.

'For the sake of my coffers, I'm glad you didn't.'

Huss scowled, and Theiss felt instantly sorry. The boy
still looked up to him with the unconditional veneration a child felt for his father, and it was easy to bruise
such devotion.

'They're jealous of you,' said Theiss, speaking seriously again. 'They see in you what a priest should be,
and it makes them hate you. They never go in the chapel
any more – I don't let them, for they get nothing from it.
You, on the other hand...'

Theiss looked fondly at him. For all that the boy
could be insufferably pious, he undoubtedly possessed
something special. In four years he'd grown so quickly.
Now on the cusp of manhood, Huss towered over every
other inhabitant of the temple community, spiritually
as well as physically.

On occasion, Theiss envied Huss's certainties. He
could no longer share them, at least not in their undi-
luted form – he'd seen too many disappointments for
that, and too much loss – but the very presence of the
young acolyte reminded him why he'd entered the
Church in the first place.

*I can remember why I studied for so long, dreamed for so
long, laboured for so long.*

'You ask me how you know when your soul is pure,'
Theiss said, letting his head fall back onto the pile
of musty furs at the head of the bed. 'Let me tell you

something you'll not find in any of your books: you'll never know. And I can't help you to know, either – only you see what goes on inside that serious head of yours. Only you know whether you're reciting the benedictions before the altar with all your heart, or whether you're mouthing the words and thinking about the milkmaid from the next valley along.'

Theiss broke into a cough. Huss remained still, unsmiling, his wide eyes shining in the firelit dark.

'I used to think that was unfair. I used to think that the Lord Sigmar might have made things a little easier for His mortal followers. Perhaps, I used to think, He might manifest himself in the world more strongly, just as the foul gods of the heathen northerners are said to do.'

As Theiss spoke, a wistful smile creased across his dry lips.

'But then I realised the truth of it. He doesn't do so, not because He can't, but because that would rob us of the thing that you fear so much: doubt. The Ruinous Powers care nothing for why a mortal might fall into their worship – they will trick, coerce and snare whoever they can, for each fallen soul makes them a little stronger. The faith of mankind is different. We're not tricked into the love of Sigmar. Our faith is no snare, nor can a man be coerced into a life of holiness. We must fight through our doubt to see the truth, just as a man must fight to crest the summit of a mountain. Take away that doubt, take away that struggle, and we'd be no better than the raving fallen who gibber at the sight of visions and cheap magick.'

Huss frowned at that, but said nothing.

'Remember it, Luthor,' said Theiss, 'when you go out into the world, armed with that fearsome faith of yours.

Others will doubt more than you. They will falter where you will endure, and they will give in to fear where you remain steadfast. Do not despise them for that. They were made to be that way, just as you were made to lead them.'

'Weakness is to be purged,' said Huss. 'It opens the door to corruption.'

'And what would you know of weakness, lad? When have you ever struggled against an obstacle so great you thought it would overwhelm you? Every day, where the winds howl and the nights are chill, men and women face up against foes far beyond their ability to fight. They know fear as you have never known it.'

Theiss hacked up a gobbet of phlegm and spat it to the floor.

'Perhaps you will find your fear one day,' he said. 'Or perhaps it will find you, and only then will you get the answer to your question. No man has faith until he's known fear – until that day, your devotion is no more worthy than the belief the sun will rise tomorrow.'

Huss looked away from Theiss, over to the fire. He didn't speak for a long time. Theiss watched him in turn, wondering if he'd spoken too harshly. He decided that he hadn't. The world was a harsh place, and it was better that Huss learned it sooner rather than later.

'So when are you going out again?' asked Huss eventually, still staring at the flames.

Theiss sighed, pushing himself down further under the scruffy layers of hide. He shivered. The cold seemed to have lodged in his bones and the very idea of heading out across the moors made him feel ill.

'I don't know,' he said. 'Soon. Why do you ask?'

Huss turned back to face him. As ever, his expression was intense.

'I'll go with you,' he said. 'You've preached about these men of the Empire, about how my duty is to lead them. It's time I started.'

THEISS RODE ON an old mule, swaying with the beast's movements as it trod down the long tracks. He would half-sleep from time to time, nodding drowsily until the beast stumbled or his cloak fell open, letting in the wind.

Winter had been hard again and spring had been slow to come. The earth was iron-hard and black, lined with frost like spiders' webs. The long grass of the moors rushed and whispered, always moving, never still.

Huss walked ahead of his teacher. He could have gone much faster had he been on his own and he chafed at the slow pace. Whereas Theiss had swaddled himself in layers of clothing, Huss wore only his rough grey acolyte's habit and a traveller's cloak.

At night, once Theiss had finally fallen into his light, mumbling sleep, Huss would wrap his heavy body in the cloak and lie for an hour or two, gazing up at the sky and silently watching the stars. Very occasionally, Huss would look at his master. Theiss's face never seemed fully relaxed, even in slumber. The old man's features twitched, and he talked to himself in low, muttering tones. Huss could never catch the words, and in any case he didn't like to listen.

When daylight came, the walking would resume again. A second mule was used for supplies and had been laden with saddlebags full of dried meat and flasks of small beer. Huss led it by a long halter, barely giving it a second glance as he walked, yanking on the rope harshly whenever it dawdled or stumbled.

Aside from the edible supplies, that mule also bore

the old warhammer from Theiss's study. During the first day out from the temple it had remained wrapped in oilskin and neither of them had mentioned it. Back in the temple precincts, Hirsch had been the one to strap it on to the mule's already heavily laden back, and he'd scowled the whole time, remembering his humiliation.

Only on the second day, in the early morning while he was still alert, had Theiss asked Huss to unwrap it.

'You've used this before,' he said, smiling shrewdly.

Huss nodded.

'Once,' he said.

'Holding it wrong, I expect.'

'No doubt.'

'You need to learn to use this weapon,' said Theiss. 'It's the weapon of a priest. I can barely lift it now, so consider it yours to use.'

Huss didn't thank him. He took it up, gazing at the old, weatherbeaten shaft and the blunt iron head. It felt heavy in his hands, heavier than when he'd used it against Hirsch and Kassel.

After that, he practised for hours at a time, swinging the warhammer while he walked. Theiss gave him advice, tutting and snapping until he got it right.

'Don't wield it as you would a blade,' Theiss would say, perched on his mule and looking critically at Huss. 'You can't draw it back quickly – it'll take you off-balance. Predict where your enemy will be before you swing. Predict, predict.'

One lesson in particular was repeated over and over.

'Your whole body must move. Everything must move. No, you're holding it like a pitchfork – lean into it. Yes, now round with the weight of it. Move back! Everything must move. Everything. Get it wrong and you'll break your wrists.'

At the end of each day's march, Huss's arms and chest would ache with a tight, stretched pain. He would look at the stars while Theiss mumbled in his troubled sleep, wrapped in his cloak, feeling his body slowly recover itself. Each night, though, his arms would ache a little less. Each night, he felt the strength in his biceps wax a little more. After a while, he missed the feel of the weapon in his hands.

After four days' travel heading into the wind they climbed down from the moors and along the long valley of the River Annig. Dry grass was replaced by scraggly gorse and wiry grey-barked trees. At the end of the valley, columns of smoke curled thinly into the white sky.

Theiss looked at the smoke grimly.

'That's the first one,' he said.

Huss followed his gaze, shading his eyes against the cold light.

'What's it called?'

'It is called Hnel, and like every settlement in this region it is a miserable pile of horseshit.'

Then Theiss looked at Huss warily.

'When you first came to the temple,' he said, 'you must have come through these valleys. Maybe even, this is where... You don't–'

'Remember?' Huss looked out at the valley floor, running his eyes across the drab landscape carefully. 'No,' he said at last. 'I don't remember this place.'

'Even now?'

Huss remained impassive.

'Even now,' he said.

'Well,' said Theiss, drawing in a weak, wheezing breath

and tugging at his old cloak. 'Maybe one day you will. Keep moving for long enough and you'll find where you came from. The world is only so big.'

Huss said nothing.

HNEL LIVED UP to Theiss's scorn. Dirty, half-rotten houses clustered around a low stone bridge over the river. The stockade walls were wooden and nearly falling down. The smoke from the fires was peaty and brown, and the paths through the houses were deep with dark mud. In the centre of the place was a rough clearing in which a rough-hewn pole had been lodged. Perhaps once it had carried an Imperial standard; now it was bare, stuck up into the cold sky like a rib.

The wind churned down the wide valley slopes, chilling everything it touched but failing to dislodge the pervasive smell of manure, slops and rancid sweat. Animals, thin and palsied, rooted around in the refuse. The people weren't much better: they stared at the priests as they rode into the village from under low, wary brows. The men were ill-shaven and rat-faced with sores around their mouths and calluses on their gnarled hands. The women were vacant-eyed and greasy-haired with drooping expressions and smocks streaked with grime.

Huss tried not to meet their eyes directly. Part of him wished to believe that these people were exceptions, and that the rest of the Empire was full of the ruddy-cheeked, rambunctious peasant-stock he'd read about in his devotional books. He found that thought hard to sustain, though. Deep down, he knew that there were a thousand Hnels across the vast northern country, each just as prone to the vices of poverty and desperation as this one.

These are Sigmar's children, he thought. *These are Sigmar's children.*

Theiss didn't seem perturbed by the sights before him. Presumably he was used to it. He rode into the central space and dismounted, sliding from the mule's back awkwardly. Breathing hard, he smoothed his robes over his bony frame.

Huss came to stand beside him, feeling bulky and extraneous, as the villagers shuffled from their hovels towards the two of them. They kept their eyes low and their hands clasped before them in supplication.

Theiss unwrapped the tools of his trade: a tin ewer, a long and threadbare stole picked out in bronze-coloured thread, a leather-bound copy of the *Catechisms and Ordinances*. His age-raddled fingers shook as he placed them beside him on a lop-sided stool used by the peasants to play games of bones on.

A man, slightly less undernourished than the others, came up to Theiss and bowed. He had a thin beard around his yellowing jowls and a ragged, unhealed scab on his right cheek.

'Father,' he said, keeping his head lowered.

'Headman,' replied Theiss, handing him the ewer.

The man hurried away to fill it with water. The others clustered in front of Theiss and Huss, rubbing up against each other, gently stinking.

'You said you wanted to see them,' said Theiss out of the corner of his mouth, busy making preparations for the rites to come. 'Get used to it, and stop gawping.'

These are Sigmar's children.

Huss clamped his mouth closed and straightened up. He felt the shaft of the hammer in his right hand and instantly regretted bringing it with him. It made him feel ostentatiously, stupidly powerful. Even without it he would have been more than a match for any of them a dozen times over.

He felt sick. Illness and decay hung like heat in the air. Merely keeping his place beside Theiss was an ordeal. The purity of the scriptures he had read in the temple seemed a long way away.

The headman stomped back from the well and returned the ewer to Theiss. The old priest straightened up stiffly and began to sanctify it, ready for the ceremonies to come.

Huss knew the words of the sanctification. He knew all the words to all the rites and could have recited them himself in far stronger tones.

But he didn't. Looking out at the throng of petty misery and deep-hammered dirt, he found his tongue lodged in his dry mouth, unable to say anything at all.

These are Sigmar's children.

THEY KEPT COMING, one after the other, limping on blistered feet, desperate for the touch of holy water on their brows and words of power whispered over them. Even the surliest, burliest brutes sloped up to the priests, eyes down, mumbling the responses when prompted and making the rough sign of the comet against their chests as they withdrew.

Theiss ministered to all of them, reading out the text of the *Ordinances* patiently, listening to their complaints, issuing suitable blessings for various ailments and urging them to remain true to the paths of faith. They nodded and mumbled and shuffled back whence they'd come, satisfied once some holy water had been dribbled across their pox-studded brows and words they didn't understand had been recited over their lice-laced heads.

Babes were brought to them to be blessed, tightly wrapped in strips of old cloth. Some slept in their mothers' arms, looking red, blotchy and hot. Others bawled and screamed as water was dripped over their faces, their fists curled tight into tiny cudgels of rage.

After the procession of blessing had ended, the dead were next. All those villagers who had died since Theiss's last visit had been laid in shallow graves just beyond the village's edge. Theiss meticulously read out death rites over each one, commending each fallen spirit to the care of Morr and issuing binding wards against necromancy and corruption.

By the time he was finished, the light was failing and the old man was clearly flagging. He turned to Huss and shot him a wry smile.

'All done,' he said. 'Hnel is safe again, and we can rest.'

Huss looked at him humourlessly.

'You need it,' he said. 'The night will be cold.'

'The headman's offered us his hospitality. Get ready to dine like the Emperor.'

They went straight from the graveyard to the headman's hovel, a low-roofed daub cottage on the outskirts of the village. Huss had to duck low to get through the doorway.

Inside, the air was thick with smoke. Something that looked like a skinned cat turned on a spit over a weak fire in the centre of the floor. Half a dozen peasants were already there, squatting in the eye-watering shadows. The headman sat cross-legged on the other side of the fire. Behind him was a heavy brown curtain, drawn across the full width of the room.

Theiss bowed, and sat down beside the fire. The headman passed him a wooden bowl filled with some kind of broth.

Huss took his place by Theiss's side. The headman looked at him suspiciously, then passed another bowl to him. Huss took it, trying to ignore the smell of fish bones and vomit coming from the steaming grey sludge inside.

'You bring your student with you,' said the headman to Theiss, scooping a handful of broth into his mouth and slurping noisily.

'I do,' said Theiss, politely sipping the foul liquid. 'I am old, and a man must have a successor.'

The headman chewed thoughtfully, and translucent juice ran down into his sparse beard.

'You aren't that old,' he said.

Theiss smiled tolerantly.

'I am, headman. A few more seasons, and then…'

He trailed off, an odd expression on his face, before sipping more of the broth.

Then, a strange noise came from behind the curtain – a strangled sob, or a cry of pain. Huss put the bowl down instantly, turning to face it.

'What's behind there?' he asked.

Something about the noise made the hairs on the back of his arm rise up. He felt tense, and the cottage interior suddenly seemed far more cramped and claustrophobic than it had before.

The headman's face went pale.

'Nothing,' he said. 'You are tired. Eat.'

The noise came out again. This time it lingered. For as long as it lasted, Huss's heartbeat picked up.

He stood clumsily, spilling the contents of his bowl.

'Sit down, lad,' ordered Theiss.

The headman jumped up from the floor, briefly interposing himself between Huss and the curtain.

'Do not go,' he said, and his eyes were wide and desperate.

Huss pushed him aside and ripped the curtain across.

On the far side was a space of a similar size to the one he'd been sitting in. Straw, mouldy and rotten, covered the floor. Dirty sheets lay in a pile in the far corner. The stench was even worse than the broth – a hot, sick smell of decay. Two women looked up at him in shock, their eyes wet from tears. Inbetween them lay a girl, no more than seventeen summers, bathed in sweat. She writhed on the straw, her blonde hair matted and glossy with moisture. Her face glowed in the gloom like an ember, red and mottled.

Theiss got up and limped over to Huss's side.

'Blackfever?' he asked the women, looking grimly over the scene.

They nodded fearfully, backing away from the looming shadow of the two priests.

Huss took a step towards the delirious girl. Something about her fascinated him. Her face, despite the ravages of the fever, was more beautiful than anything he'd ever seen. It was the face of a tortured angel.

He felt the painful fire start up behind his eyes, the sign that Sigmar's grace was working within him. His fingers itched, and he clenched his fists tightly.

'Will she live?' he asked, never taking his eyes from the face of the angel.

Theiss placed a restraining hand on his shoulder.

'It's blackfever, lad, and that's an end to it. They'd have brought her to me if there was any hope.'

The headman came to stand beside them. He gazed at the girl with a look of pure desolation on his hard face.

Fire raged behind Huss's eyes. He could feel it building up, swirling like storm clouds within his breast.

'She's not dead yet,' he said, shaking off Theiss and kneeling down on the straw.

'Do not touch her,' warned Theiss, grabbing at him again. 'The fev–'

'Do not touch me!' roared Huss, whirling round and glaring at his master. His anger was sudden and terrible, fuelled by the growing fire within him. He felt like he was burning up, as if the fever in the angel had transferred to him and driven him mad.

Theiss recoiled, startled at the acolyte's tone. Huss ignored him and turned back to the angel.

She moaned, thrashing her head back and forth. Her eyes were closed, her mouth open. He saw the beads of sweat on her lips shining like tiny pearls. Her blonde, cropped hair stuck to her forehead in lank curls and the valley where her neck met her torso was pooled with moisture.

Looking at her was like looking at some gilded icon of the saints, trampled and thrown down into a fallen world of degradation and squalor.

Huss's inner fire raged, raw and vital. He placed his hand on her forehead, and the touch was as hot and painful as grasping a flame.

From far away, he heard Theiss's voice.

'You cannot! You *must not!*'

Huss pressed his palm tightly against the girl's burning skin. It felt like the surface would break under the pressure.

Underneath it, he sensed her blood coursing. He sensed the sickness within her, fizzing and boiling like water in a cauldron.

Then, like the rush of visions in a dream, he saw her face in other times – the firm smooth skin of youth, eyes sparkling, hair whipping out in a breeze of summer. He saw her looking over her shoulder, laughing a pure, clear laugh of insubstantial happiness. Her heartbeat, strong and regular, as firm as oak roots.

And under that, deep down beyond the limits of mortal sight, he felt her soul, trembling within the crumbling temple of her body. It cowered before him like a candle flame caught in a draught, hovering on the fractured terrain between life and death.

Come back.

He didn't know how he was able to speak to her. Nothing else remained for him but the burning within him, the sacred fire that took him outside his body and into hers.

Her soul responded. She was surrounded by darkness, by an infinite space of nothingness, but still she heard him. She was afraid, and alone, but his words found their way into what remained of her being.

Come back, daughter.

She came to him. She struggled against the pull of the darkness, lashing out against the terrible gravity that propelled her downwards.

Her soul turned away from the abyss. Huss saw her again then, just as she had been before – dazzling in her beauty, vital and joyous.

Come back.

She reached out a fragile hand, feeling for his in the shadows. Slender fingers extended, searching, grasping. He tried to catch them, but there was nothing to hold on to.

She was slipping away. Panic choked him. He had gone too far – he would be dragged down with her. He went down deeper, sinking into the well of shadows.

Hold on! Remember life! Resist!

There was a final flicker of resolve before the end. She looked at him one last time, and frightened tears ran down her face.

He felt his heart would burst with grief.

Then the image faded. Her soul drifted away, lost in the shadows like a curl of smoke. The residue of it spun down into the deep dark, away and away, far out of reach.

Huss hung, motionless, over the void. His hand remained outstretched, static and impotent, pointing after her, clutching at nothing but darkness.

The fire had gone. His power had not been enough. He shivered, lost in the freezing emptiness, feeling tears of his own run down cheeks that had never felt them before.

The angel had gone.

Dimly, he heard Theiss's voice, as if from underwater. The old man was shouting, or perhaps chanting. He sounded terrified.

Huss ignored him. The only words he heard were ones that had been spoken days ago.

You'll fail, you'll doubt. None of us is any different.

I won't fail.

You will.

No. The power of Sigmar is without limits.

In that cold place, he knew the lie of that. There were always boundaries, places he could never go.

Huss held his hand up before his face, the one that had failed to catch the dying soul. He looked at the flesh there, laid thick and strong by nature, as tough as horsehide.

Why did You give me these hands?

But there was no answer, just the dim echo of the abyss and the final, chilling resonance of terrified tears.

IT TOOK THEM another day to climb up the far side of the long valley, heading north-east into the weather. The mules picked their way sulkily along the eroded tracks, bristling against the rain-heavy wind and chafing against the halter.

Theiss swayed on his mount, wrapped up tight against the cold. He was still angry and had barely spoken since leaving Hnel. Huss strode ahead of him, letting the rainwater course down his face and neck, carrying the hammer casually over his shoulder.

They only stopped moving once they had reached the summit and the whole wide plain country opened up in front of them. Under the lowering sky the vision was impressive in its brooding majesty.

'You could have died,' said Theiss eventually, shifting uncomfortably in his saddle. His tone was as sharp as it had been since the night before.

'I didn't,' replied Huss.

'If you'd been on your own, you would have.'

'I wasn't.'

Huss didn't turn to look at his master. His expression was as bleak and unmoving as it had been since leaving the headman's house. His eyes seemed to have sunk deeper into his blunt face and there were dark lines under them. He stared out at the rainclouds moodily.

'You're no priest of Morr, nor a healer,' said Theiss, shaking his head. 'You can succour the living, but you can't go chasing after souls.'

'So what's the point of us?'

'What's the point?' Theiss looked exasperated. 'We give them hope. We show them how to remain strong. We comfort them when no others will.'

Huss's belligerent expression faltered then. Behind those mournful eyes, he still looked so painfully young.

'I almost had her,' he said, his voice cracking.

Theiss's face softened a little.

'That's not your gift, lad. You were made to fight.'

Huss looked up at the sky miserably. No more tears came, but his blunt lip jutted out, trembling.

'She was an angel.'

'That she was,' said Theiss, kicking the mule forwards to get closer to him. 'A rare one too, but the world's a wide place. There are devils in it, and monsters, and spirits of the divine, and angels of mercy and grace among them.'

He got close enough to place his old hand on Huss's shoulder.

'She wasn't the only one,' he said. 'Live long enough, and you'll see that.'

CHAPTER FIFTEEN

MILA AWOKE AND felt sunlight on her face. For a while she lay still, listening to her own breathing.

The aches came afterwards. She shifted in her cot and felt her arms throb. Her legs, which had been painful ever since the long trek from Helgag, felt like shafts of lead.

She pushed herself higher up against the straw bolster. Her mouth was dry and her eyes itchy. It took her a while to remember where she was and how she'd got there – her slumber had been very deep.

She'd not dreamed, and that had been a relief. In the brief snatches of sleep she'd managed to grab while out in the wilderness with Huss, night visions had been vivid and troubling. Margrit had been in many of them, either as she had been in life or with the ravaged features of the undead. Hans had featured too, with his awkward looks and heavy gait and clumsy manner. She'd shed a tear over him more than once, whenever she'd remembered what her hopes for life had been before the coming of the plague and how they'd shrivelled away.

Even Father Reilach had been in her dreams; not as the cadaver he'd become, but as the wizened old man he'd been before. The contrast between him and Huss was almost painful. Until Huss had entered her life, Reilach had been the only example she'd had of a priest. Whenever Reilach came before her, it was as if an old life, full of futility and hypocrisy and low-slung fear, had suddenly reasserted itself. Despite the horrors stalking the wilderness during the days of flight, it had been a relief to wake up from those dreams.

Mila blinked heavily and rubbed her eyes. Her skin felt tight and grubby. The cot smelled unsavoury, something she feared was as much down to her as the previous occupant. Since arriving in Eisenach there had been precious little time to do more than march and fight, and she felt as dirty as a dog.

She needed something to drink and something to eat. She needed a wash. She needed to comb the tangles out of her hair, darn the holes in her dress and pick the lice from her clothes.

Those needs were good to have. The ordinary requirements of life seemed important again, which was surely a sign that things were getting better.

She swung her feet over the edge of the cot and dangled them over the straw floor. The room was small and uncluttered. A single glassless window let pale sunlight in, exposing cream-coloured walls of flaking daub. She'd been the hovel's only occupant during the night. Eisenach's population had sunk to half what it had been before the attacks and there were plenty of empty houses to take over for those who wanted to.

Mila found herself wondering who'd lived in the place before she'd stumbled into it, dropping from exhaustion, after the last of the fighting had petered out. No personal effects had been left on display; no clothes, devotional items, cooking utensils or linen for the cot. The rough wooden bedframe was the only thing left inside. She'd stuffed some old cloaks into it to fashion something of a mattress; after sleeping rough for so long it might as well have been made from duck-down and silk.

The fighting against the remnants of the undead had lasted until well after noon of the previous day. The warriors hadn't melted back into the shadows before the dawn – as they had before – but had held their ground to the end.

The toll in dead had been heavy before the last of them fell. The largest detachment of casualties had been among the zealots Huss had raised up. Out of hundreds of them, less than a quarter remained alive. The few survivors hadn't been daunted by that – they'd applied themselves to the long and arduous task of dragging bodies into mounds for the flames with disturbing enthusiasm.

The regular soldiers, bone-weary after the fights along the parapets, had quickly decided that the job could be left to the crazies. Mila had limped back to the town along with them, too exhausted to feel anything other than a vague sense of relief that it was over. Some half-hearted efforts had been made to clear the walls and streets of debris, but they soon trailed off into nothing as the men sloped off to their hovels or the drinking dens. Treicher had made little effort to stop them – the last Mila had seen of him, he'd been heading the same way.

She, though, had been determined to stay on her feet until Huss came back. For perhaps an hour she'd waited for him, propped up against the walls of her chosen dwelling, expecting him to come striding through the gates at any moment. Typically, though, he'd remained out in the field, working tirelessly to give the last rites to the dying and the dead.

As her eyes had shut of their own accord, she'd stumbled into the cot at last. She'd thrown herself onto the pile of old cloaks, barely noticing the smell of unwashed bodies as her face buried itself into the folds, relishing the embrace of sleep as it fell over her like a tumbling landslide.

Awake again, she had little idea of how much time had passed. Her throat was parched and an itch across her eyes wouldn't go away. She got up stiffly and walked over to the door, pushing it open heavily.

The light outside was sharp and white. A chill breeze ran down the street, spotted with drizzle. Refuse was everywhere. In the distance, over by a mean-looking house she knew was used as a drinking den, two bodies lay immobile in the gutter. Crows had perched on the roofs opposite, and they looked sleek and fat.

She stepped over the threshold into the street and almost tripped over a bag of bones at her feet. The bag shifted and a ragged head emerged from one end of it.

Schlecht looked, if such a thing were possible, even worse than usual. His forehead had been disfigured by some huge wound. The edges of it had gone yellow, and the centre of it was as black as night. His fingers, nearly as slender as quill-ends, shivered as he extended them from his baggy sleeves.

He grinned as soon as he saw her, and the movement made his hollow cheeks distort.

'Woman!' he exclaimed. 'Awake! Praise Sigmar!'

THEY WALKED TOGETHER from the hovel towards the centre of the town. The sun was near its zenith, though the pall of low cloud cast everything in shades of grey.

Smoke from huge pyres still rolled lazily into the sky, making everything smell of charred flesh.

Some men lay in the street where they'd fallen, driven to insensibility by exhaustion or inebriation. Those who remained on their feet had a bleary look in their eyes. Everything was sluggish and flat-footed, and the few citizens of the town who acknowledged her presence did so half-heartedly.

Mila had long since forgotten her fear of large settlements. The people of Eisenach were more or less the same as those she'd known in Helgag. The clothes were a little more ornate and the habits were a little different, but they'd all screamed the same way when the dead had come. Now they looked like shadows of themselves, stumbling around as if they couldn't quite believe the long nightmare had ended. Huss had given them the victory they had stopped believing in, and the shock of it was yet to fade.

'You'd think they'd be pleased,' she muttered as she stepped around a long puddle of slops in the middle of the street. 'Why aren't they pleased?'

Schlecht said nothing, trotting alongside her contentedly. Every so often he'd mumble something to himself, or make the sign of the comet, or suddenly shout out the name of Sigmar. It was all fairly random, but it seemed to make him happy. It was only after Mila had been walking next to him for a while that she noticed the truly prodigious amounts of blood on his clothing. Some patches were so steeped in it that they looked like they'd been dipped in oil.

The two of them entered Eisenach's central square and walked over to Treicher's house. It looked a good deal shabbier than it had done when they'd arrived, stripped as it was of most of its decoration and surmounted by a roughly-hewn flagpole. Men clustered around the empty front doorway, leaning against the stone and drinking from tankards.

As Mila approached, they backed away from her. Everyone in Eisenach knew who she was and who she'd come with. Treicher was with them, and waited for her to arrive. Unlike the others he seemed to have found time to have a shave and don fresh clothes. The deathly pallor had left his skin. He even looked a little less jowly than he had before, though that might just have been the light.

'I wondered when you'd emerge,' he said to her.

'What's going on?' Mila asked, glancing cautiously at the others and trying to ignore Schlecht clutching at her skirts.

'Recovery,' he said. 'Though it might've been nice if your priest was on hand to help.'

At the mention of Huss, Schlecht started growling from the back of his throat. He sounded like a lady's lapdog let loose amongst wolves, albeit a lapdog covered in gore.

'He's not here?' asked Mila.

'He's not been seen since before dawn.'

'Well, he deserves some rest, does he not?' she said, feeling suddenly uneasy.

'Rest.' Treicher smiled at her coldly. 'Yes, I daresay he does.'

He lost his smile, pushed himself from the wall and came up to her. He was not a big man, but he was still able to look down on her.

'Don't think I'm not grateful, girl,' he said, though the tone in his voice was anything but. 'But I used to govern a town of men here. They weren't perfect and we had our share of problems, but at least they knew how to follow an order and make a living for themselves. Look at what your priest has left me.'

Mila turned, following the headman's gaze. Over on the far side of the square some of the zealots had congregated. Most of those who remained conscious were still chanting something. Some of them stood silently, twitching. One woman had ripped her clothes free of her waist and was busy lashing herself over her own shoulder with a crude flail. A man sat heavily in the mud, absently spooning handfuls of it into his mouth.

'They don't listen to reason,' said Treicher. 'They can barely speak. All they want to do is kill, or sing, or whip themselves. He's poisoned their minds.'

Schlecht scowled angrily at Treicher as he spoke and his scrawny fists balled. Mila laid a hand on his shoulder gently.

She didn't like looking at the zealots any more than Treicher did, but she knew that before Huss had come they had been little better, just hidden away in the slum quarter where they could be ignored by the luckier residents.

'What do you dislike most, headman?' she asked. 'That they no longer listen to your orders, or that they exist at all?'

Treicher gave her an equivocal look.

'Like I said, it's not that I'm not grateful. I just want to know what I'm supposed to do with them, and who's going to help put this place back together. Your priest's the only one they'll listen to – if you could ask him to speak to me, just for a moment, that would help.'

At the mention of Huss, a twinge of fear passed through Mila again, just like that one she'd had before in Helgag when he'd left her alone.

'He's not *my* priest,' she said defiantly, mastering that

fear with difficulty. 'I've no idea where he is, but he'll be back here soon enough. He made a promise, and you should know that he's not the kind to break it.'

HUSS STRODE UP the long defile east of Eisenach, ignoring the dull ache in his limbs. His hammer rested over his shoulder, freshly cleansed from the blood that had caked it after the battle. It had taken an hour to prise the last of the residue from the intricate golden surface, and another hour to complete the rites of sanctification.

He had carried many warhammers in his long career, each one more powerful and ornate than the last. His current weapon was ancient and steeped in the faith of long-dead clerics, a far cry from the crude hammer he'd inherited from Theiss as a boy. It always seemed little short of sacrilegious to let the blood dry on it, so he'd worked hard before setting off again.

After that it had been walking, hour after hour, across the blasted moors and back towards the Drakwald. Eisenach, Helgag and all the other settlements had been strung out in a long line in the borderlands between the mountains and the forest. In all the long months of fighting the plague of undeath Huss had never ventured far under the eaves of the trees. No sane man did.

Now, though, the deep wood could not be ignored. The legions of the dead continued to grow, and they all came from the same source.

Huss marched heavily, hauling his massive body up a long, twisted gorge. His forehead glistened with a coat of sweat even though the wind from the north was cold. His armour, which over the years had become like a second skin to him, glittered dully under the fluttering of his cloak.

He said nothing as he went and no prayer escaped

his thin lips. Every so often he would pause, breathing hard. He would put the hammer down for a moment and lean his hands on his knees. Sweat would drop from the end of his nose.

He would linger just long enough for his breathing to return to its habitual metronomic pace. He might eat, taking out dried meat from the gourds at his waist. Whenever he remained still for too long, he would feel the knotted muscles of his body gradually tighten, waiting for the inevitable strain to be put on them again. He would feel the weight of the armour plates on his shoulders, like the heavy beam of an ox's yoke.

In those moments, he would see only her.

I should have told her why. She will not understand.

Then he would haul himself back to his feet, treading on iron-tipped boots and powering on up the slope.

She will be angry.

His head would stay low, fixed on the choked mass of rocks and rubble ahead. His eyes would remain intent, locked on the landscape as if searching it out for hidden corruption.

I've become weak. I've let her affect me.

His gauntleted fingers would clutch the handle of the hammer tightly as if for reassurance.

I should have told her why.

HE REACHED THE summit, and the land opened up before him. For a moment he stood still, panting, keeping the warhammer in his right hand. The wind moaned at him from under the grey sky, chilling his sweat-sheened skin. His cloak stretched out behind him, billowing in the surge. He narrowed his eyes, gazing out at the huge expanse of the earth as it yawned away to the horizon.

The high place he stood on was bald, scraped clean

of all but sparse strands of grass by the never-ceasing wind. A low stone pillar had been erected there, covered in moss and lichen. Skulls had once adorned each of the four faces, but the detail had long worn smooth.

To the east, to the south and to the north was forest. It was endless, like a great swirling mass of dark cloud sweeping up from a storm-wracked horizon. The trees, dark and glossy pines interspersed with spreading oaks and ash, jostled close together, choking out the light of the sun and draping the land in a cloak of shadow.

From his vantage, Huss could see for miles. The forest extended out like a discarded sheet, replete with folds, gullies and wrinkles. Deep clefts had been driven into it like wounds, as dark as old scabs. Crags jutted out above the canopy, granite-grey and jagged, but they were little more than flecks of rock against the vastness of the gently rippling foliage.

Huss breathed in deeply, tasting the air. Even from so high up, the tang of mulch and moisture marred the clean savour of the wind. There were other aromas there too – the sweetness of decaying things, the sharp musk of beast-spoor and, under it all, the deep-sunk metallic stench of ancient blood.

The smells were familiar to him, just as they would have been to anyone brave enough to pass under the shadow of the trees.

He took up the hammer, holding it two-handed before him. The gold of it shone coldly in the dull light.

As You have ever guided me.

Huss turned slowly, scanning across the wasteland, watching intently. He could feel his heartbeat slowing. After the effort of the long ascent, it fell back to its usual heavy rhythm.

Guide me now. Show me the heart of the darkness.

His lips moved soundlessly as he spoke the words.
The shaft of the hammer felt warm, as if old embers had
been left against it.

*Show me the source. Show me where the corruption is
born.*

He kept moving, back and forth, sweeping his melancholy gaze across the ancient forest. With every pass he
saw more. He saw a grove of ash that had stood since the
founding of the world, draped in grey and surrounded
by a fog of forgetfulness. He saw a ruined tower rearing
from the branches, as white as bone and graven with
strange, looping runes. He saw a flight of red-winged
birds skim across the canopy, heading north, each
with glowing eyes and hooked talons under their long
bodies.

Show me.

The hammer-shaft became warmer. The gold of the
killing-edge deepened.

Huss closed his eyes, still moving, still searching.

He heard the thud of heavy feet in the dark places, of
hooves churning the earth as they careered along the
muster-paths. He saw standing stones in hidden glades
surrounded by skulls, defiled deep by old libations. He
felt the strangling progress of new shoots against the
hoary bark of millennial growth. It was all moving,
straining, struggling.

Show me.

He saw the whole landscape in motion. Husky breath
shot out in gouts from bestial nostrils as huge things
– bull-faced, horse-faced – trampled through briars
to reach herdstones in lightless gullies. The graves of
men stirred as corpses writhed and scratched at the
loose earth. Wood-spirits uncurled within the boles of
trunks, luminous green and chuckling with malice. The

Drakwald was mustering, drawn together by the power in its heart. When that muster was complete, it would burst across the lands of men like a destroying flood.

Show me where it begins.

The forest spread out before him, first blurred, then in focus, as clear as if his earth-bound eyes had been open to see it. He saw the patches of intense darkness where the creatures of corruption were gathering. Like stray ribbons of quicksilver on an anvil, they were coalescing, pooling, coming together. Men were among them, draped in animal pelts, offering up prayers to the foul powers that raised the dead.

They came from the west, from the sewers of Ulric's city, from towns along the river, from the overrun waystations. Peasants were among them, dull-eyed and fanatical, as were noble-born men with fine robes and armour.

Always east. After the bacchanals and blood-rituals they went east, driving through the thick undergrowth with the beasts padding and growling beside them.

Living men, dead men, beastmen, spirits, wights and witches; all sucked towards the same point.

Huss screwed up his eyes further, feeling the heat of the hammer grow. For a moment, the visions came more strongly.

Then he saw her. She came before him as he had last seen her – angry, flushed, stumbling through the wastes in the company of halberdiers.

The visions faltered.

Not now!

She stood before him, as cross as she had been before, hands on her plump hips, remonstrating with him.

You know that I'll follow you, even if it cripples me, and when I catch you up–

Huss's eyes snapped open. The grey light of the real

sky flooded back in, chasing out the visions and replacing them with the hard-edged world of the senses.

Huss fell to his knees, light-headed and groggy. Fresh sweat broke out across his wind-cooled face. Blood thumped powerfully in his temples, and the palms of his hands curled up tight. He found himself breathing heavily, and let the hammer fall to the ground. It hit the earth heavily and rolled to one side.

He didn't get up for a long time. When he did, his expression was haggard. He picked up the hammer haltingly, nearly stumbling as he tried to lift it.

He looked back out at the implacable landscape. His face, so often a rigid mask of resolve, was lined with doubt. He looked over his shoulder, back along the route to Eisenach, then again towards the Drakwald.

You know that I'll follow you.

Even without farsight, the corruption hanging before him was palpable. The air reeked of it.

I oppose them. Few can stand against them, so I do. I seek them out. I pray for guidance, following the inspiration given by grace. There's no rest, no respite.

It was a while before he started walking. He stood, strangely indecisive, wrestling with the visions he'd seen. He didn't pray again, nor did he consult the scriptures he carried in scrolls at his belt.

The wind seemed to drag him back the way he'd come, back to where he knew she was. It tugged at his cloak and wrapped itself around his breastplate. He let himself rock back onto the balls of his feet, as if he could be pushed back by the breeze alone.

But then, grudgingly, grindingly, he took the first step down the far slope. Once he'd made the first one, others followed. Soon he was marching towards the first of the trees, hammer over his shoulder.

His every movement was stiff and laboured, as if, for the first time in his life, his actions were marked by a subtle flavour of resentment. His mouth remained locked in that downturned clench of disapproval, and his eyes remained steeped in the soft melancholy that he'd worn even as a child.

But still he marched, alone against the approaching sea of shadow, just as he had done since old Theiss had died.

No rest, no respite.

THE NEXT DAY was colder, and the damaged houses of Eisenach shuddered in the wind. The last fingerholds of the hot summer had long been loosened, making way for the long season of storms and shortage.

A semblance of normality returned to the town, though nothing more than that. The guards at the gate remained in uniform, but other men put their swords away. Some merchants opened up their stores again, but many others had nothing to sell. The farmers had no land left to cultivate and so stayed behind the walls, drinking away the last of their savings and muttering into their beer.

Only the zealots remained in good spirits. The absence of Huss did little to dampen their mood, and they kept up a constant round of chanting and fasting. Some of them died from wounds sustained in the fight against the undead. The bodies weren't buried, but were instead burned on pyres some distance from the city walls. The deaths brought no diminution of their ebullient mood; if anything, it seemed to strengthen it.

Food remained scarce, though, and the ruined countryside around Eisenach was incapable of making up the shortfall. The last of the animals inside the walls were slaughtered, and the screams of the herded pigs lingered long in the chill air.

Treicher did his best to restore what could be restored, but his hollow expression gave away his pessimism. Winter in the northern Empire was a hard time in any year, and Eisenach's troubles had left it perilously weak in the face of the coming hungry season.

Tempers were febrile in such an environment. A group of men swaggered down the main street one evening, spoiling for a fight with the zealots, whose endless singing and flagellation were setting everyone's nerves on edge.

They got their fight, but it didn't last long. The men soon learned that those with no hope for living fought like daemons, and were sent packing back the way they'd come leaving two of their comrades in the street behind them. Their bodies were never found, and Treicher decided not to pursue the matter. The zealots were left alone after that, and the sound of fresh hymns echoed around Eisenach with renewed fervour.

It was after that that Mila left the town and strode out across the blackened fields. Schlecht followed her, as faithful as a dog.

After it had become clear that Huss wasn't coming back, Mila's mood had been changeable. At first she'd been furious, shouting at the blank walls of her hovel and kicking out at the ramshackle cot.

Then she'd calmed down, reasoning that priests had always been disreputable and prone to using promises in devious ways. The fact that Huss had fooled her for a while was no surprise – he was a learned man, steeped in the ways of writing and rhetoric, whereas she was nothing more than a peasant with a heavy arse and a thick head.

After that came the black slough of depression, settling down on her like a thundercloud. She knew perfectly well that Huss had been totally different to every priest – or man – she'd ever known. For a short time, he'd shown her the possibility of another life, one that had had wider horizons than the mere grind of staying alive. He'd been impossibly grim and pious, to the point where she'd wanted to scream at him in frustration, but that piety had given him truly astonishing power.

Huss feared nothing, and dared everything. To be in the presence of that, just for a fleeting moment, was to witness the truth of old legends coming into being before her.

On top of that, Mila had even dared to believe that such a man had come to place her in some special category of affection. For all his preaching on the sanctity of the whole of humanity, she'd found herself believing that his concern for her safety had assumed a privileged place amid the myriad of his cares and duties.

Perhaps it had, which was why he hadn't taken her with him. Or perhaps it was a stupid delusion, based on nothing. In either case, his withdrawal was painful, and it made the world seem pale and diminished.

Mila walked quickly, striding across rutted furrows, her mouth set taut. Schlecht struggled to keep up, and was soon wheezing like an old hound.

'Where going?' he asked pitifully.

'Away,' she said. 'I need to get out of that place.'

She had no real idea which way she was heading. Her earlier promise to follow Huss wherever he went had been exposed as totally hollow – even if she knew where he'd gone, she'd have been unable to follow his trail.

After a while she felt her feet begin to ache. She reached the burned husk of an old tree, standing alone amid a wide bowl of trodden-down crops, and sat down heavily beside it.

Schlecht, grinning from relief, collapsed opposite her. He lay on his back, mouth open, his pigeon chest rising and falling deeply under his sagging robes.

'So why aren't you with the others?' asked Mila at last, noticing just how bad Schlecht's skin was getting. His spirits might have recovered but his body looked more ravaged than ever.

He raised his head to look at her, but didn't seem to have understood the question.

'The zealots,' she said. 'The other ones like you. Why don't you stay with them?'

'Others like me?'

He looked genuinely confused. Mila gave him a hard stare, not in the mood to be made fun of, but he seemed unaware of the similarities between him and the other zealots.

'I saw you in that battle,' she said. 'I saw you fight. You couldn't have done that before.'

Schlecht gave her a sidelong glance, the kind of false-shrewd look a man gives a village conjuror when he's seen through his tricks.

'There is no *before*, sister,' he said, explaining the situation carefully. 'There is only *now*. Praise for that.'

'What about your home? What about Goeringen?'

A brief flicker of recognition registered on Schlecht's face for a moment. In a flash, a tremor of pain marked itself across his features.

Then it was gone again, replaced by the fixed smile, the steady gaze, the disturbing glaze of unfractured certainty.

'My home is the earth,' he said. 'This is my home. My home is in death.'

Mila lost patience. Schlecht's thoughts were increasingly hard to follow, and if there was logic in them still it was of an elusive kind. Whatever damage had been done to him by the beasts had been compounded by battle-mania, and if that was supposed to be a cure then it was a harsh one.

'Fine,' she said, looking away from him. 'Whatever you say.'

Then Schlecht stiffened. He rolled suddenly onto all-fours and started sniffing like an animal.

Startled, Mila half-rose.

'What is it?' she asked.

Schlecht began to growl. He bounded away, stumbling onto his feet as he capered up the far side of the bowl. Mila started after him, unnerved by his sudden change of mood.

'Where are you going? Come back!'

He kept running. Just as he reached the lip of the bowl, dark figures emerged from over the edge – at least two dozen of them, all mounted on horses and clad in armour.

Schlecht didn't hesitate. He leapt up at the nearest of the horsemen, slavering and scratching. The man – a mighty figure with leather gloves and a scarred face like a murderer's – swatted him away with a swipe of his fist. Schlecht collapsed, writhing in the soil. The man drew a long maul out, kicked his horse on and reached back to swing.

'Stop!' shouted Mila, hurrying up to them as fast as she could. 'Please, don't hurt him – he's sick.'

Another man, riding at the head of the band, nodded sharply. The man with the maul grudgingly pulled his horse up and let Schlecht alone.

Mila reached the edge of the bowl, panting heavily,

and looked up at the man who'd made the gesture. He was old, and his angular face was lined and weather-beaten. A blunt chin protruded from under the brim of a wide hat that shaded his eyes and made it hard to gauge his expression. He wore a long leather coat that might have been fine once but was now covered in overlapping layers of mud and grime. He looked weary, jaded and cynical.

'Your friend should be more careful,' he said. 'Udo doesn't like wasting a chance.'

'Your pardon, sirs,' said Mila, reaching out for Schlecht and pulling him roughly away from the horsemen. 'He's not in his right mind.'

The man with the hat inclined his head slightly.

'Then make up for his transgression,' he said. 'We're headed for the town of Eisenach – is it far?'

Mila nodded, clamping her arms around Schlecht and stopping him from struggling. He seemed dazed from the blow to his head and drooled over her hands.

'It is,' she said, 'though you should know the place is half in ruins.'

The man smiled thinly, as if that was only to be expected.

'You can lead us there yourself,' he said.

Mila bristled at his tone. In times past she might have been intimidated by such a lordly manner, but after Huss few men seemed impressive.

'I'm not headed that way.'

The bald-headed man, the one who'd nearly killed Schlecht, let slip a snorting laugh. He hacked up a gobbet of phlegm and spat on the ground.

'Yes, you are,' said the man in the hat. His tone was reasonable enough, but there was an uncompromising finality in his speech.

Mila stood her ground a moment longer. She looked up at the horsemen around her, and they looked back at her with amused, disdainful faces. Any one of them would be more than a match for both Schlecht and her combined.

She brushed her hair from her face and looked up at the man in the hat as defiantly as she could.

'No, I'm not,' she said. 'Not unless you can give me some very good reason why I should do what you say.'

The man nudged his steed forwards and it stepped closer to her. Mila swallowed nervously but held her ground. As the man neared, he drew a silver medallion from his shirt and dangled it in front of her.

The face of it showed the symbol of the comet, engraved on a heavy disc of metal. When Schlecht saw it he froze.

'This is the sign of my office,' said the man, softly. 'Perhaps you know what it means. Your friend seems to.'

Mila knew perfectly well what it was, if only by reputation. There couldn't have been a soul alive in the Empire who didn't recognise the badge of a witch hunter – stories of such men were seared into the minds of children by frightened parents, desperate to avoid seeing one for real.

Her bravado melted away, and she felt her palms go clammy.

'I didn't know,' she mumbled, unable to look up at his face for fear of what she'd find there.

The man withdrew the medallion.

'Evidently,' he said calmly, tucking it back into his shirt and taking up the reins. 'But perhaps we can dispense with this foolishness now. Walk before me, and bring your monster too. He smells foul, but he's got spirit.'

He rolled his shoulders absently, and the movement exposed the lethal flintlock pistols at his belt.

'He'll need it, too,' he said. 'You all will.'

CHAPTER SIXTEEN

DOWN INTO THE gorges, the light failed quickly. Creepers hung between the overreaching branches, looped like nooses. The earth sank into a sticky swamp of clutching mud, studded with decaying leaf matter and crawling grubs, and the air became hot and sweet even as the autumn gales cooled the high moors beyond the treeline.

When the sun passed its zenith the darkness in the hollows intensified, turning slowly from leaf-green to nightshade. Bird-chatter rang from the boughs, panicky and urgent. The trunks of gnarled trees creaked, and furred creatures scurried through the roots, trembling with the coming of the dusk.

Huss paid them no attention. He strode down into the lightless gullies, tramping down the thorns and weeds and thrusting aside whipping birch twigs with both arms. He left a broken trail behind him like the wake of a galleon, all pressed-flat grass and crushed growths. Sap ran down his armoured forearms like streams of tears.

He could feel the hostility of the forest. With every step he took the hatred in the air intensified. He could almost taste it, as if spores of loathing had spun up from the mulch under his boots and clamped on to his tongue.

271

What meagre paths existed in those depths soon gave
out, replaced by tangled walls of vines and clogged pits
of thorns, forcing him to cut his way through. The warhammer was useless for such work, so he strapped it to
his back and drew out a wide-bladed hunting knife.

With the passing of the light it became hard to maintain his bearings. There were no landmarks to guide
him, just a screen of dark, snarled branches extending
in every direction.

For all that, he knew he was heading to the heart of it.
Whether by the action of divine grace or by the designs
of darker powers, he knew he would emerge into the
bowels of the Drakwald's corruption.

It was, as so much in his life had always been, a matter of trust.

He thrust aside a matted curtain of hanging growths,
stinking with rotten fruits still clinging on from the
long-departed summer. The forest thinned a little ahead
of him, allowing shafts of fading sunlight down through
the broken canopy above.

Huss cut down the last of the obstruction and clambered over a fungus-covered trunk towards the light.

As his body moved, he felt a heavy ache in his muscles. He couldn't remember the last time he'd slept
peacefully through the night. His trek in pursuit of the
undead, from one village to another, had lasted seemingly forever. For a long time he'd assumed the attacks
were random raids of a kind that had plagued the
Empire for as long as it had existed. Now it was clear just
how much he'd been wrong. Minor victories like that at
Eisenach would do little to stem their numbers – they
would keep coming, one after another, until no power
was capable of resisting them.

Any mind capable of drawing the fractious denizens

of the wood together in common cause was of a different order to the perennial threats of the Drakwald. The unity of the attackers indicated an individual at the heart of it: a master of dark magic, perhaps a necromancer, or a fallen magister, or a sorcerer from the heathen north.

In the face of that, the wisest course of action might well have been to retreat back to civilisation and seek to provoke some kind of organised resistance – a crusade against the hidden presence in the woods. Battle wizards existed in Middenheim as well as ranks uncounted of war-hardened troops, and if Huss had been a witch hunter or an army general, that's no doubt what he would have done.

But he was neither of those things. Even for an itinerant priest, he was uneasy working with the political hierarchies of Imperial cities. His uncompromising manner earned him few friends there, and he found the underhanded, subtle methods of the noble classes bewildering. The patient business of building consensus and working within the arcane rules of the Empire's overlapping jurisdictions was not his strength.

In any case, he had always worked alone. He had always gone straight to the heart of the problem, trusting to his massive physical strength and unbreakable faith. No task he had set himself had ever been too much for those qualities, and he trusted in them far more than the uncertain support of weaker souls.

In another man, that might have been arrogance. In Huss, it was merely the certainty of the true believer, as well the painful knowledge, delivered by old experience, of his own shortcomings.

He followed a long and tortuous route further down towards the gulley floor. Huge trees, some with trunks the width of peasants' cottages, reared above him, hunched over like old crones.

At the bottom of the gulley the ground levelled out. Strange boulders rose from the undergrowth. They were covered in lichen, some of which glowed with a pale phosphorescence. The open sky above him shrank into scattered patches in the overarching canopy.

Huss paused, listening carefully. He only heard his own breathing.

He looked back up the way he'd come, and saw trees piled up against the high horizon like an inquisitive crowd at an execution. The trail he'd bludgeoned through the branches seemed narrower than it should have been, as if it had half-closed in on itself already.

Huss turned back and kept going, treading warily. The loudest noises were the falls of his boots against the rock and the steady *thump, thump* of his heartbeat. The decaying aroma in the air became ever more concentrated, sticking in the back of his throat as he breathed.

The forest opened up a little further before him. The trees drew back, exposing a narrow glade. More boulders stood there, sharper than the others, filed into points like the gravestones of the heathen of Araby. The lichen glowed more fiercely, yellow in the dark like the shine of a cat's iris.

Huss slid the knife back into its sheath and unstrapped the warhammer from his back. The golden head looked dull and lifeless in the gathering murk.

The glade was no place to stop for the night – it was overlooked, dank and had no vantage of the land around. More than that, though, was the feel of the place – death had sunk into the earth there, draining down into the black soil like blood from a felled corpse. It felt as if the echo of a scream had been captured, distilled and locked into the stone and loam, resonating soundlessly even after the murdering had long finished.

Huss rounded another boulder, taking care not to touch the shimmering crust of lichen. Ahead of him he could see the glade coming to an end as the mass of trees closed up again.

Then he heard it.

He tensed instantly, keeping the warhammer high in a loose grip, ready to swing. He could feel the blood throbbing thickly through his veins, his breathing picking up, his heart rate increasing.

It came again – a whimper, or maybe a muted chuckle – over to his right, muffled amid a collection of man-high rocks.

No animal made such a call. If anything, it sounded… human. It sounded like a child.

Another whimper sobbed out from the rocks, then a choking cough, then a gurgle.

As You have ever guided me.

Huss whispered the prayer as he crept towards the noise. The eerie standing stones passed him on either side, huge and glistening in the night.

Something flitted quickly over his right shoulder, and he whirled to face it. For a moment he thought he caught sight of a ragged cloak, dark as ink, and a wrinkled face with empty eyes and a hooked nose.

Nothing was there; just a single tree, closer to the stones than the others, bent and twisted like a village hag.

Huss realised then how tightly he was gripping the warhammer and how quickly he was breathing. He forced himself to calm down, reciting elements of the liturgy over and over, taking solace in the retreat to faith.

The mutant shall be slain, and glorious will be the slaying

*of it. For the mutant is the perversion of the purity of Man,
and Man is the master of the world. Only in Man is there
salvation and freedom from the world's corruption. The forest
shall be cut, the beast shall be hunted, and the mutant shall
be slain, and glorious will be the slaying of it.*

Still mouthing the words, he turned back to the
stones.

Ahead of him, lying on the turf, was a bundle of rags.

Beyond the bundle loomed the tallest of the stones.
The top of the menhir had been carved crudely into the
shape of a bull's head, from which brown stains ran in
long streaks. Feathers, bones and lumps of glistening
flesh, still glossy from the blood that caked them, had
been laid around the bundle.

Huss felt the aura of evil magnify. The thickness at
the back of his throat curdled, and the words of faith he
had spoken to himself sounded suddenly hollow and
listless.

He crept closer to the bundle. Something inside it
moved as he approached; a jerky, writhing wriggle like a
spasm of some maggot or worm.

Huss paused, only a couple of feet away, poised to
strike down with the hammer. Despite all his efforts,
despite all his long years fighting against the serried
forces of corruption, his heart was beating like a gal-
ley's kettle drum. Something about the bundle chilled
his soul.

It twitched again, and some of the rags fell away from
it. Flesh was exposed – human flesh. A little arm, no
longer than his hand, flashed out, white against the
dark.

It whimpered again, just like an infant, choked by the
rags that lay across its mouth.

Huss took the weight of the warhammer in his right

hand and carefully extended his left hand towards the rags.

Still he hesitated. Then he pulled the rags free.

An infant's face looked up at him with sorrowful, terrified eyes. It looked half-starved and close to death. It couldn't have been more than a few months old, but the baby-fat had withered away leaving a shrivelled covering of skin behind.

As soon as it saw Huss it stopped whimpering. It lay still, gazing up at him, eyes wide.

Then it smiled.

'You will die here, priest,' it said.

Huss started, pulling his hand back.

The baby laughed, and its pointed fangs gleamed in the night. It shook the rest of its rags free and struggled to its feet. One of its legs ended in a cloven hoof; one arm was twisted backwards and had a covering of hide. It stood awkwardly before him, swaying on bent legs and grinning.

'We will drink your blood, Luthor Huss,' it said. The voice was horrific – an otherworldly mix of babyish prattle and full adult malice. 'We will drink it while you still live and vomit it up before your open eyes. We will–'

Huss swung the hammer down, crushing the fragile creature under the heavy golden killing-edge.

A pool of black gore spread out across the grass, studded with fragments of bone, skin and fur. The nightmare child's head had been crunched into oblivion, but the echo of its voice still lingered.

–strip your skin from your body and dangle it before you. We will take out your heart and give it to the lords of beasts. We will–

The hammer came down again, and again, thudding into the soft earth and driving the gore-soaked rags deeper down.

The voice died away at last. Huss took a step back, holding the hammer ready, breathing heavily.

The bull's head on the stone gazed back at him blankly.

Moving slowly, Huss turned away from the scene, retracing his steps back through the standing stones. He started to recite again, saying the words under his breath to break the chilling silence.

The forest shall be cut, the beast shall be hunted, and the mutant shall be slain, and glorious will be the slaying of it.

He kept on walking, striding out a little more firmly as he recovered his poise. The child had been an apparition, nothing more, sent to test him. He'd seen worse in the covens of village witches.

The mutant shall be slain.

He reached the edge of the glade and the unbroken forest soared up away from him, ready to receive him into its depths again.

Huss strapped the hammer to his back and took up the knife again. As he did so, his hands trembled. He clenched his fists, waiting for the tremor to subside.

Man is the master of the world.

Then, taking a last breath of sickly air, Huss plunged back into the shadow, disappearing into the sea of branches as if fading into the underworld.

THE FIRES BURNED furiously in Treicher's audience chamber – there was plenty of wood for them to consume, and the nights were getting colder.

The headman sat on his chair looking as if the gods had belatedly cursed him for some long-forgotten misdemeanour of his youth. His fingers twitched in his lap and his eyes seemed to wander around the room randomly. The siege had taken its toll, but the stream of uncompromising visitors had proved the final straw.

'So, let me see if I understand the situation,' he said. 'We've just won a battle which very nearly destroyed us. We have no reserves of food for the winter and our crops are ruined. Every village that might be able to supply us has been ransacked, and for all we know the dead will come again when their strength is recovered.'

The witch hunter nodded to all of that. For a Templar of Sigmar, the man had a surprisingly calm demeanour. He sat opposite Treicher, his long legs crossed, resting his gloved hands on his knee. With his hat taken off, his short-cropped grey hair was visible, as were the dark bags under his eyes.

'I understand that, headman,' said the witch hunter.

'And now you're asking me to make all my men available for a… what is it? An expedition into the woods chasing beastmen?'

'I'm not asking you, Herr Treicher, I'm ordering you. And you can call it a crusade, if you wish – that might make it easier for you to swallow.'

At that, Treicher's fat face oscillated rapidly between despair, fury and resignation.

'You realise you're damning us further with this?' he said. 'You realise we can't possibly survive after this?'

The man standing over the witch hunter's left shoulder – a huge figure kitted out in black with a scar-latticed bald head and a criminal's face – growled threateningly. His little eyes, sunk deep like a pig's, flashed with outrage.

The witch hunter ignored him.

'What do you think will happen if the Drakwald is left to fester?' he asked. 'They'll keep coming for you. Think of this as your last chance.'

The witch hunter uncrossed his legs and leaned forwards.

'I've been chasing this thing for months, headman,' he said. 'It started small, as such things always do, but now it's grown. Someone's been building up power here, using foolish and gullible men to foment beast-cults in cities while dredging up the dead from the wilds. They're coming together now, enacting foul rites in the deep places and crystallising in the forest even as we speak. If it's not halted here, it'll only spread. If I have to choose between the survival of Middenheim and the survival of Eisenach, then I'll not hesitate to make that choice.'

'You *have* made that choice,' said Treicher.

'So I have,' said the witch hunter.

Treicher looked miserably around him. His audience chamber, once ostentatiously arrayed with finery, was a gutted shell. His clothes were dirty and frayed. Since the heady days of the summer, things had degenerated very fast.

'You have nothing,' he said, emboldened into candour by his desperation. 'You've a name that I've never heard of and some guesses that your cults are connected to what happened here, and for all that you will drag us into a place we all know breeds only madness and death.'

The witch hunter smiled humourlessly.

'The sacrifice of your men is sanctified,' he said, 'and their souls, you may be assured, will be the souls of martyrs.'

Treicher snorted weakly, giving away what he thought of that.

'But I know more than you suspect,' continued the witch hunter. 'I know the name of the man at the heart of this. His name is Huss.'

At that, Treicher's eyes went wide with shock. He laughed

then, looking at the two men before him slyly as if he'd just discovered something incriminating about their wives.

'Huss, you say?' He chortled to himself. 'Well, that's interesting. Now I wish you'd got here earlier.'

'Why's that?'

'Because it was Huss, Luthor Huss, who saved us. He's a warrior priest – one of your kind, Templar. I'd have expected the two of you to be… well, on the same side.'

'Huss is here?' The witch hunter, just for a moment, looked totally thrown.

'Not any more. He left once he'd done his work turning half my men into fanatics.'

'So where did he go?'

'I've no idea.'

The witch hunter's amiable expression changed then, replaced by a level, frigid glare.

'Consider your words carefully, headman, and reply again.'

'It's the truth,' said Treicher. 'He left without warning. He had companions, though – they're in the town still. A peasant girl – Mika, I think – and a ragged man with some affliction, though the last time I spoke to them they were as much in the dark as I am now.'

The witch hunter motioned to his henchman, who inclined his head. The big man stalked off, and the clump of his boots echoed up from the stairwell as he thumped down towards the doors.

'This is news to me, Herr Treicher,' said the witch hunter, crossing his legs again and sitting back comfortably in his chair. 'The man's name has been bound up in this since the beginning, though I confess I don't yet understand exactly why. Perhaps he's an innocent, perhaps not. In either case, the fact he's been here confirms me in my belief that I was right to come.'

Treicher looked back at the man nervously. He had the distinct impression that giving away Huss's presence in Eisenach had not made his own position any easier.

'Stay here as long as you wish,' he said. 'My chambers are at your disposal, and I'll instruct my staff to aid you in any way they can. But will you not reconsider your talk of a crusade? Surely it can wait until things are clearer?'

The witch hunter shook his head.

'Oh, no,' he said. 'No, this does nothing but add to the need for haste. Huss has been here, and I know where he must be going. Whether he's part of this for good or ill, he'll be headed to the same place that I am and it's imperative I reach him before he gets there.'

He gave Treicher a rare look of understanding.

'Your commitment to your townsfolk does you credit,' he said. 'Were I in your position I'd argue the same way, but I've seen the quality of men here, and many have the look of killers to them. I'll take them all. I'll strip this place of every man who can carry a blade, and I'll send word for more to come after them. You'll come too, as will the girl who travelled with Huss.'

As he spoke, the witch hunter's eyes lit up, as if a long-dormant excitement in the chase was slowly being rekindled.

'We'll pierce the heart of this together, Herr Treicher,' he said. 'You may as well start sending instruction to your men now, since this Huss has a start on us and I do not propose to lose him.'

He smiled again, but this time there was more warmth to it than before.

'Try to get a few hours' sleep when you can,' he said. 'We leave at dawn.'

* * *

'WHERE GOING?' ASKED Schlecht.

'Ssh!' said Mila crossly. 'Stop asking me that, and keep your voice down.'

'I get torches.'

'No. I told you. Not until we're clear of the walls.'

'So where going?'

'Morr's arse!'

Mila whirled round, her face red with exasperation. She pulled Schlecht after her, and the two of them huddled in the shadow of the hovel where he'd been staying. Dusk had long since fallen and the town was dark and silent.

'Do you want to see Huss again?' she asked.

The man's eyes lit up.

'Then shut your mouth and *listen.*'

Mila looked over her shoulder, convinced she'd heard footsteps behind them a moment ago. The street was empty.

'The man who we guided here,' she said. 'He was a witch hunter.'

'Yes. Good man.'

'No, not a good man. Witch hunters are *bad men*. We've got to get out, go and find somewhere else.'

Schlecht looked doubtful.

'Where?'

'I don't know. But look.' She unslung a bag from her shoulder and opened it up. 'Food. Some water. Enough to keep us going for a while. We can get far away, where all this madness hasn't caught up yet. I need to clear my head of priests, and you need a healer. And a bath.'

Schlecht wrinkled his scabby nose up, still unconvinced.

'The Father-'

'Is *gone*, Rickard. If he'd wanted us to wait for him forever, he'd have said so.'

Schlecht hung back, digging his fingernails into the loose daub of the wall.

'Look,' said Mila, 'if you want to see him again, you need to do what I tell you. Remember that bald man? The one with the black gloves? He'd kill you if his master let him. We need to *go*.'

'That's sound advice.'

The voice wasn't Schlecht's. Mila spun around again, just in time to see a huge black shadow looming over her. Long arms reached out to grab her by the neck.

She would have been seized but for Schlecht. He launched himself at the shadow, screaming with wild abandon. The two of them crashed together, rolling over in the mud like pigs.

'Damn you, Rick–' she started, backing away in confusion.

The henchman managed to grab hold of Schlecht's collar. With a grunt, he hurled the skinny man away from him. Schlecht flew through the air, limbs flailing, before crunching heavily into a pile of half-hacked-up firewood.

Then the man looked up at her, and Mila remembered how to move.

She dropped her bag and ran, sprinting as hard as she could down the narrow streets. Her feet hit the uneven earth hard, kicking up splatters of dried mud behind her.

She could hear footfalls behind her almost instantly, gaining quickly. She ducked under a low-hanging tavern sign and skidded around a corner, wheezing like Schlecht did. Her pursuer seemed to miss his footing, and she heard a hard thump followed by a sputtered curse.

She didn't stop. She careered down another long street, back towards the poor quarter where Huss had roused up the refugees. The walls approached, and at the end of the street she saw the ladder leading up to the parapet. She ran towards it. As she leapt onto the rungs, she felt the whole structure flex under her weight. She scampered up it, two steps at a time, hurrying like a rat racing up a rope, expecting at any moment to feel the heavy slap of hands on her back.

She got to the top, panting raggedly and feeling dizzy. She spun round, squatted down and grabbed the head of the ladder. With a huge heave, she pushed against it. It began to swing away from the walls before something huge and heavy suddenly hit it, knocking it back.

Gritting her teeth, she pushed out, hearing the man's grunting as he climbed up it. She saw the top of his bald head emerge from the gloom – it was almost at the top.

With an almighty shove, Mila flung the head of the ladder away from her. It toppled back into the street below, and she heard it crash down amid the dust and refuse.

She collapsed back onto her haunches, her chest heaving. She needed to catch her breath, just for a minute. As she did so, she stared back at the edge of the parapet where the head of the ladder had been. It looked less smooth than it should have done – there was a black lump of something on the lip, something that looked a lot like...

A hand. Another one appeared next to it, black-gloved and bulky. Mila leapt to her feet, horrified. She hesitated for just a moment, torn between stamping on the fingers or setting off again.

The hesitation was enough. Her pursuer hauled himself over the edge with a massive heave. His ugly, pug-nosed face scowled at her for an instant before he pushed himself up further.

By then she was running again, tearing along the narrow parapet, trying to get far enough along to find another way down. The way was treacherous, still strewn with discarded weapons and refuse from the siege. She had to pick her way, edging around obstacles and keeping clear of the steep drop on her left. It was nearly pitch-dark, and she almost ran straight off the edge twice when the parapet suddenly narrowed.

The dog-like breathing was getting closer again. Something behind her crashed to the earth as the pursuing man smashed it aside, followed by the clatter of a pile of spear-shafts being knocked over. He was charging now, hurtling straight through anything in his way.

Her only chance was to find a way down before he got too close. Mila began to scan the edge as she ran, looking for the head of another ladder leading down. It was only as she saw the first one peeping up across the stone lip that her left foot plunged out into nothing.

She pitched forwards, screaming out of instinct, her heart frozen in terror. For a terrible moment there was nothing under her at all – just the yawning gulf between the wall's edge and the hard earth below.

She screwed her eyes closed, bracing for the impact that would dash her brains out and shatter her ribcage.

It never came.

Slowly, stupidly, she opened her eyes.

She was hanging from the parapet by one arm. Below her was the street-level of Eisenach, far enough away to confirm that the fall would have been fatal. To add insult, a whole sheaf of arrows had been left standing in a pen, pointing upwards – they would have gone through her like a quarrel shot through wet paper.

Mila swayed gently for a moment, taking that in. As her senses returned, a sharp pain made itself evident in her right wrist, the one she was suspended by. It felt like her hand had been nearly ripped off and her arm almost wrenched from its socket.

Gingerly, not really wanting to find out what had saved her, she looked up.

The man who'd been chasing her looked down from where he lay, face-down on the parapet surface. His arm, clamped to hers at the wrist, hung down like a plumb-line. The other one must have been wrapped around something out of view.

He looked furious.

'I'm going to pull you up now,' he grunted painfully, his bald head shiny with sweat and effort. 'And if you so much as sniff while I'm doing it, you fat bitch, I'll break every bone in your body.'

CHAPTER SEVENTEEN

DAWN BROUGHT NO relief. Huss had marched through the night, resting only briefly to eat, banishing his fear through ceaseless activity. No beast had waylaid him, and he made good ground.

As the sun rose, he arrived at the summit of a bald hill that broke through the canopy. He stood for a few moments, looking out over the wilderness of trees ahead, before sliding down against the dead trunk of an old ash near the top.

He let his eyelids droop fractionally. The weight of fatigue clutched at him, pulling him into the semi-forgotten abyss of sleep.

He resisted it, knowing the danger, reciting the litanies over and again to keep his mind alert.

I must not sleep. I must not sleep.

HE WOKE WITH the sun high in the sky and the breeze shaking the branches around him.

Starting, he reached for his warhammer, staring about him with the expectation of mutants coming at him from every direction.

He was alone. The empty forest gazed back at him from below his vantage, rustling in the wind.

Huss shook his head, and let the hammer fall.

That was stupid. You need to be stronger.

He unclipped a gourd from his belt, wrenched off the stopper and took a swig. The water tasted stale and brackish. Then he stretched out his arms, feeling the tendons ache as he extended them, and took a proper look around him.

He'd come a long way east. While down on the forest floor it had been hard to maintain his course with any kind of purpose, and he felt sure he'd been taken far out of his way by the twisting paths and undulating landscape. His destination was in any case vague – a blurred and shifting vision granted to him from a long way away. He might wander for days before coming anywhere close to it, or he might stumble across it in a matter of hours.

He re-stoppered the gourd and strapped it back in place. He opened his mouth and closed his eyes, tasting the air, feeling the rhythm of the earth below him.

Further east. Always further east.

For a second, a vision of something flickered in front of him, and he snapped his eyes open again.

It had been gold, like flax in the sun. A face had risen up, pleading and terrified.

Huss shook his head, clearing the fragmentary image from his vision and taking a deep breath down into his lungs. The empty sky extended away from him. In the far distance, right where the sea of foliage met the horizon in a haze of grey, a flock of birds was winging its way over to the south.

It looked innocent; benign, even.

So it begins again.

Hoisting his hammer onto his shoulder, he started to walk again, ever deeper, ever further, back under the all-embracing shadow of the wood.

* * *

'HOW'S THE HAND?' he asked.

Mila didn't reply. She didn't even bother to scowl at the witch hunter, since he seemed impervious to hostility. Since they'd left the town, he'd treated her as courteously as ever, but that somehow made things worse.

She could cope with hostility, even condescension – all of those things had been part of her life for as long as she could remember. It was far harder to cope with a cultured man speaking to her, so it seemed, as an equal. Huss had never done that. Even when they'd been travelling together, his tone had always been that of a father speaking to an errant or wilful child.

'You seem to think I'm your enemy, Mila,' said Eichmann. He rode his horse with an easy grace, reins held lightly in fine brown leather gloves. His wide-brimmed hat shaded his eyes, hiding the rings of darkness around them. 'I'm not sure why that is.'

Mila looked up from her precarious seat on her mule. The whole concept of sitting on top of a horse still hadn't really sunk in, and she felt uncomfortable and ludicrous. The men riding around her sat as easily as Eichmann did, staring ahead blankly or chatting to one another in low voices. They carried their weapons overtly, and the icons of the Church of Sigmar were prominent on their tabards.

Behind them stretched a long train of infantry. She could barely bring herself to turn in the saddle and look at them. Some, the zealots, marched enthusiastically, still chanting their hymns to Sigmar and relishing the coming battle. They had warmed to Eichmann almost as quickly as they had done to Huss. The other troops, the regular halberdiers and swordsmen who had defended Eisenach for weeks already, they dragged their feet as they walked in long columns, looking up at the vanguard with haunted, suspicious looks. They had no enthusiasm for what was to come, only a grim, fatalistic awareness of what resisting orders from the Church would bring them.

'If I'd known who you were when I first met you,' said Eichmann, 'I'd never had spoken to you the way I did.'

No trace of mockery was in his words. For all that, Mila couldn't bring herself to believe them. There was something unsettlingly smooth in the way he carried himself. He didn't adopt the blunt, uncompromising stance that Huss had always done – the witch hunter had the look of the city about him, a faint slipperiness, perhaps, or maybe just a weary kind of pragmatism.

'We have a long journey ahead of us,' he said. 'I'd welcome some words from you before we reach our destination, even if they're as hostile as your face.'

Mila snorted.

'Why not resort to your usual methods?' she asked. 'That way you can find out anything you want.'

Eichmann smiled. It was a wistful smile, the smile of a man who spent his whole life being reviled and feared and for whom such reactions had lost any power to affect.

'If you insist,' he said, equably. 'But I'd prefer not to. Can we not talk a while, the two of us, like decent people?'

Despite herself, Mila shivered at the casual way he took up her offer. Even in jest, she knew just what a man like him was capable of.

'What do you want to know?' she asked, cautiously.

'What your friend's up to.'

'I've already told you. I told that pig who works for you, and I told Treicher. I don't know where he's gone, or why.'

'In all your time together, he never mentioned his plans.'

'No,' said Mila. 'If he had any, I don't think he thought I'd understand them. He travelled around from place to place. He went after the undead, the beastmen, the corrupted. Towards the end, he thought they were all coming together.'

Eichmann nodded.

'He never mentioned the forest?'

'Not really. He avoided it, just like everyone else.'

'If they've got any sense,' agreed Eichmann. 'But he's headed there now.'

'How do you know?'

'I ask the questions,' he said.

Mila slumped in her saddle. Her arse ached from the constant movement and her spine felt strangely compacted.

'He left a while ago,' she said, sullenly. 'What makes you think you'll catch up with him?'

Eichmann nodded over to his left, where a long-nosed man rode at the head of the column, his head nodding with the motion of his steed.

'We have a rare guide,' he said. 'He knows routes that no others do.'

'Huss knows the land.'

'I don't doubt it, but he's alone, and the woods are perilous.' Eichmann shot Mila a warning look. 'You sound as if you'd prefer we didn't find him. Take it from me, his only hope is for us to overtake him.'

He looked ahead as he spoke, and Mila followed his gaze. On the eastern horizon was a long, low smudge of green.

'I hear great things of this man,' said Eichmann. 'But he's just one man.'

* * *

THE FIRST BEASTS emerged in the late afternoon, loping under the shadows, wheezing as they ran. They were big, with bunched-muscle shoulders and low-hanging, distended animal faces. They ran along the muster-paths in columns, thrusting aside the thick briars in their way as if they were merely reeds.

Their skin was dark red, or the stained brown of ancient leather, or the colour of a fallow deer's flank. Their eyes were without whites and glistened cruelly. A pall of musk hung over them as they came, acerbic and heavy with bestial sweat.

They carried the weapons of men, looted from old wars and roughly daubed with the blood of their former owners. Cleavers, axes, broad-bladed swords, all were held low in clenched fists, swaying in a drumbeat rhythm as the warriors jogged methodically along the green ways.

They were heavier and darker than the ungors of Vierturmeburg, with huge, curling horns that swayed as their heads swayed. They went with the swagger of seasoned fighters, stuffed full of the angry rage of bulls and stallions.

Gors, they were – beastmen in their full state, neither man nor animal, warped children of the outer dark, despisers of the hearth, the plough and the threshold.

Half a dozen of them charged down the narrow channels between the trees, packed close and jostling. Their hooves ploughed up the earth as they came, throwing clods of turf high into the air. They went confidently, coursing through their element like birds wheeling high in the firmament, unwatchful in their arrogance.

'Sigmar!'

Huss swung out from behind the trunk of a great oak, hurling the warhammer into the muzzle of the leading gor, breaking its neck and throwing it back into the bodies of its pack-members behind.

Then he crashed into the rest of them, swinging the great weapon in the familiar arcs, kicking out with his iron-shod boots and punching with the clenched gauntlet of his left hand.

He felled two more before the rest of the pack recovered. Those closest surged at him, rushing at the warrior priest with their blades whirling. Huss held his ground, meeting the oncoming steel with the shaft of the warhammer. The weapons clanged together and Huss grunted as he was forced back.

One of the gors swung at him, going in low and swiping its cleaver at his braced feet. Huss pulled out of the path of the blade before ducking back into range and plunging the hammerhead into the beast's oncoming chest. The beast roared in pain as the golden metal punched through its hide, cracking ribs and tearing through muscle.

Huss pushed on, wrenching the hammer back to meet the next incoming swipe. One gor was cracked back onto its haunches, but another pounced, sweeping a rusty sword down at Huss's shoulder. The blade impacted heavily on the priest's pauldron, knocking him back and sending radial judders down his arm.

Huss staggered, losing his foothold for a moment before restoring balance just in time to meet another incoming blade. He knocked it away with the warhammer before launching himself directly at the looming monster. His head collided with the gor's, with Huss's forehead butting the bearded chin of the beastmen.

The creature reeled back, glassy eyed. Another took its place, but by then Huss had pulled a knife out with his free hand. He thrust it expertly, weaving through the incoming gor's clumsy guard and burying the cutting edge into its stomach.

Huss spun round, wrenching out the blade as he turned and dragging it into the path of the still-stunned gor that he'd head-butted. It recovered just in time to evade the knife, but by then Huss had brought the warhammer up again in his right hand. He hurled the head of it down, whistling it through the air like a loosed arrow, and it thumped messily into the beastman's sloping cheek-bone. The golden edge passed through cleanly, shattering bone as it went and throwing the curved-moon halves up into the air in a shower of dark blood.

Huss stood still then, panting from effort, weapons in hand, surrounded by the bodies of the slain. All six gors lay on the ground, bloodied and unmoving. Leaves, disturbed from their branches by the flurry of activity, drifted earthwards lazily.

For a few heartbeats, everything remained static. Huss could feel his lungs labouring, his hands aching from exertion.

Then, from far away, a horn sounded. The noise was crude and abrasive.

Others were coming, stirred by the scent of blood on the wind.

Huss stooped to wipe the clotted gore from his knife before turning away from the scene of carnage. He strode off down the muster-path, moving strongly but without haste. He pushed his way up the slope, back into the thick undergrowth of the trackless forest. After a few more strides, he was gone, vanished into the maze of green like the memory of a shade.

The forest slumped back into silence. The broken hooves of the slain beastmen twitched and shuddered as the last of their blood ran out over the earth, sinking deep into the soil of their heartland before draining down to the roots.

EICHMANN DREW HIS horse up and looked around him warily. His men fanned out ahead of him, picking their way carefully through the dense woodland. The ceaseless cries of the zealots at his rear kept on going, just as they had done since breaking from the open ground and into the Drakwald again.

He turned to Gartner, who was gazing ahead with a doubtful expression on his face.

'The right path?' he asked.

Gartner hesitated before replying.

'Assuredly,' he said. 'But we won't be alone for long. Can you not sense it?'

Eichmann listened carefully. For a moment, all he heard was the crashing clamour of his troops as they hacked their way through undergrowth, punctuated by unintelligible cries from the zealots.

Then, under all of that, he picked out a low murmur running between the twisted trunks of the trees. It was like a far-off thunderstorm, growling away in muffled violence.

He inclined his head, trying to pick out the detail. The sound was extremely faint.

'What is that?' he asked.

Gartner smiled wryly.

'The beasts,' he said, and the nonchalant tone in his voice failed to disguise the undertow of fear there. 'Remember what I said in Geistricht, about the muster? This is your chance to see it.'

As the man spoke, Eichmann realised he'd slipped his hand to his medallion. The metal felt strangely reassuring between his fingers.

'So we're headed right for them?'

Gartner shrugged.

'Something's got their blood up,' he said. 'If we keep going, we won't be able to avoid them.' Then he paused, frowning. He dismounted and dropped down to all-fours, crouching low in the mass of leaves and sniffing like a bloodhound. He looked up again, head cocked to one side, and didn't move for a long time.

'They're moving away,' he said at last, getting back to his feet and grabbing the reins of his horse. 'At least, I think they are. If we maintain this pace, we may miss the worst of it.'

Eichmann looked back up, out into the endless rows of trees before him. In the late afternoon sunlight the forest looked placid. Beams of gold slanted down through the enclosed haze, alighting on patches of turf and mossy hillocks studded with wild flowers.

'Will engaging them take us far out of our way?' he asked.

'No, not really,' said Gartner, 'but you can't–'

'Yes, I can, Herr Gartner.' Eichmann gave him a serious look. 'We have an army with us. Not a big one, I'll grant you, but they're armed and fed, and at least half of them are itching to fight something.'

He let the medallion fall from his fingers. For a brief moment, the vision of the goat-faced scythe bearer flashed before his eyes.

'Huss is in here somewhere,' he said. 'From what I've been told of him, our best chance of finding him is following the trail of bodies.'

Gartner shot a filthy glance over at Mila, who rode some way behind, escorted by a brooding Udo. The woodsman had already been affronted by the way the girl's testimony had distorted their route, an attitude which Eichmann found wearying.

'So what are we doing here, witch hunter?' Gartner asked. 'Finding the Gallowberg, or running down this priest?'

Eichmann shrugged, kicking his horse onwards into a walk and pulling the brow of his hat lower.

'They're one and the same thing, Gartner,' he said. 'Find me one, and I'll show you the other.'

THE LIGHT WAS fading from the western sky by the time the beasts caught up with him. Huss had destroyed three more small groups of them, but with each encounter the stranglehold closed a little more tightly about him. He was soon forced to head back west, weaving his way between the outstretched spurs of the gathering warherd as it came together.

More gors arrived with every passing hour, charging up out of the heart of the woods with blazing eyes and weapons held ready. Their bands got bigger – first in groups of a dozen or so, then of many more, thundering between the gnarled trunks in trailing clouds of spoor and filth.

Huss ran down the course of a winding stream at the base of a steep-sided depression, splashing his boots in the water to dull his scent. He went steadily rather than hurriedly, jogging to preserve energy, looking out for a good place to make a stand. Soon, he knew, the warherd would close in on him and he needed a suitable location from which to defend himself.

He felt no fear. The cries and bellows of the pursuing beasts rang from the canopy, overlapping and resounding as the bands mustered, but none of it made an impression on him.

Once the real fighting had started, his earlier sense of oppression had lifted. As ever, wielding the warhammer freed up his soul, lifting his spirits and forcing his mind to focus on the pure business of killing.

Theiss's words came to mind as he ran.

You were made to fight.

So it had proved. It was the exercise of that peerless skill at arms that gave him his only true release.

Ahead of him, the ground angled steeply upwards. Tall trees cloaked either flank of the ascent but a single trail remained open in the centre, albeit clogged with decaying leaf-matter and the ubiquitous tangle of straggling thorns.

As Huss began the ascent, a bellow of triumph rang out from behind him. Four wine-red gors burst from cover less than fifty yards down the stream's course, splashing through the water with a clatter of hooves on stone. Their roars were answered from further away.

Huss picked up the pace, lengthening his stride as he thrust upwards between the lines of trees. As he neared the summit of the incline, a skinny ungor leapt out at him from the cover of the undergrowth, screaming and brandishing a long gouge in its warped hands. The priest swatted it aside contemptuously with the warhammer, hardly breaking stride as he did so.

More ungors burst out, grunting and barking in their thinned-down versions of the gors' war-cries. They lunged at him, fearful of the sweeps from the warhammer though eager to sink their claws into man-flesh.

Huss was forced to halt his ascent. He lashed out, working with both hammer and knife. The half-breeds were no match for him in combat, but the longer he was tied up with them, the nearer the gors got to him. More than a dozen had now come into the open in order to race up the stream-bed, and a chorus of bellows from further down the valley told of more to come.

Huss never spoke, matching the silence he'd displayed when fighting the undead. He snapped the spine of the closest ungor with a vicious punch from the hammer-shaft before ripping the guts out of another with the knife. A third sprang up at him from behind, hands extended and clutching a length of strangle-wire. Huss ducked low as he turned, shouldering the incoming ungor and sending it tumbling back down the slope. Then he surged forwards, kicking out at the last of them as they tried to catch him and drag him back.

By then, the bigger gors were closing quickly. From experience, Huss knew they could run for miles without tiring. Their muscles were stone-hard from a life of constant violence, and they lived for nothing more than bloodshed.

He crested the summit of the rise, finally breaking into open ground. Twin lines of trees pulled back, exposing a clearing ahead of him. Waist-high grasses extended away, waving in the breeze. On the far side of the clearing the trees rose up tall, more akin to the firs of the far north than the broadleaved natives of the Drakwald. Serrated outlines clustered up against the eastern horizon, glowing pine-green as the setting sun slanted its failing rays at them.

In the centre of the clearing was a ruined pile of stone, covered in blotches of cadaver-pale lichen and streaked with thick growths of moss and ivy. The ruin might once have stood taller and wider than a house, though now the walls were semi-collapsed. Three pillars still stood at the corners, cracked and listing. A domed roof had crowned the central chambers long ago, though only a section still remained, curved and exposed like a spine ripped from a torso.

It had been a chapel, a place of worship. What folly or

bravery had led to its being built so far from the warm centres of civilisation could only be guessed at – perhaps the land about it had once been as open as the moors to the west, only to be subsumed and broken as the Drakwald spread across the fields during dark and forgotten centuries.

Huss ran over to the chapel entrance, taking heart instantly from the building's presence. Several chambers, though doorless, still stood reasonably intact. He went through the doorway and up the old steps to the altar dais, feeling broken stones settle and flex under his tread.

The altar still survived, though open to the elements and bereft of adornment. It was long and low, carved from a single block of stone and with the mark of the comet hacked crudely in the front panel. A long crack ran across the top of it, and one corner had crumbled away into dust. Roots splayed out from the flagstones around it, pushing them up and generating spider's webs of fractures.

Huss leapt onto the altar-top, whirling around as he did so to face the enemy. For a few scant seconds, he stood alone in the broken sanctuary, surrounded by nothing but the ancient walls of the holy site. He ran his gaze across the chapel and felt a swell of pride in his chest.

Even here, the hand of Man is present.

Then the gors burst in, shoving each other in their eagerness to get at their prey. The closest of them roared in triumph, brandishing a halberd two-handed over its corrupted frame before loping up to the warrior priest. Others crashed in behind it, snorting and stamping.

Standing on the altar, warhammer and knife in hand, Huss waited for them to come to him. In the final moments before the impact, he breathed a benediction, taking a last sliver of comfort from the familiar symbols of faith around him.

Then the lead gor bounded up to him, bellowing as if its veins would burst, and the world descended once more into blood, steel and fury.

'FASTER!' ROARED EICHMANN, standing up in the saddle and flourishing his flintlock.

A roar of approval came from the zealots, and they surged forwards. The rolling mass of bodies destroyed everything they passed over. Tangled thickets of thorn and nettle were flattened by their headlong charge. They ran up steep slopes as if piles of gold waited for them at the top, and tore down the far side with equal abandon. Some unfortunates were trampled underfoot by their comrades, though that did nothing to halt the astonishing fury and speed of the flagellant army in full flow.

Eichmann had to push his horse faster just to keep up with them. Marshalling them was like trying to keep control of a wayward herd of animals. They attempted to respond to his commands with commendable fervour but had difficulty with more than the most basic instructions and were liable to charge off in entirely random directions if not given a strong lead.

Now something else had got them stirred up – as they'd torn through the trees, one of them, somewhere near the front rank, had taken up the cry of 'Father!' and it spread through the rest like summer wildfires. They sprinted with insane abandon, crying out the single word over and over again.

Udo grimaced as he tried to keep control of his jittery steed. Like the rest of the mounted troops, he'd been swept along with the headlong rush of the zealots.

'Bloody madmen,' he spat, hauling his horse's head round to avoid plunging into a deep ditch filled with knife-sharp rocks.

'Indeed,' said Eichmann, kicking his horse on through the maze of trees. 'Mad as electors, but rather splendid all the same.'

Udo grunted and shook his head. He rode with one hand on the reins and one hand clutching his precious maul, hunched ready to use it.

'The regular soldiers,' he said. 'They can't match this pace.'

Eichmann shrugged. He was enjoying the thrill of the chase. For the first time in months, he actually felt alive. The wind in his hair, the breakneck progress through the heart of the woods, the joyous shouts of the zealots, it all combined to banish the deep-set exhaustion from him.

'They'll catch up,' he said. 'Go back and join them if you want.'

Udo snatched a look over his shoulder. The rearguard of Eisenach infantry were already a few hundred yards behind them and making heavy weather of the difficult terrain. If they weren't careful, they'd lose touch entirely.

'Gartner's with them? And the girl?' Udo asked, turning back to the pursuit.

Eichmann nodded.

'The charge doesn't suit them. I thought it might appeal to you, though.'

Udo shot him a sarcastic smile.

'It's perfect.'

Eichmann laughed, just as the first of the zealots broke through into a steep-sided valley with a stream running along its base. The coomb ran northwards for perhaps half a mile, shaded at the high edges by the endless ranks of sheltering trees.

The witch hunter followed close on their tail, crashing through the dense foliage and into the open.

Ahead of him, the land was crawling with movement. Beastmen – far bigger than the meagre crop of ungors they'd encountered previously – were charging along the valley floor in a series of loose packs. Despite the hollering of the zealots, the creatures' eyes were all fixed firmly away from them – to the north. They were hunting, running with intent and focus. There must have been over a hundred of them, and from the sound of it more were arriving at a rapid rate.

Eichmann felt a spasm of excitement and nervousness run through him. This was the muster Gartner had told him of.

'Soldiers of the Empire!' he roared, spurring his horse down the slope and towards the warherd. 'You know the enemy! Kill them all!'

From the corner of his eye he saw other mounted troops kick their steeds into a gallop, raising spears and swords into position as they did so. The cavalry careered down the hillside, weaving between the tree trunks as they closed in on the enemy.

Incredibly, they weren't the first to break into combat. The zealots, all of whom had just kept on running, made it first. Their cries of frenzy drowned out everything else, even the startled bellows of the beastmen. They ripped straight into the gors, leaping into the air before crunching into the loping mutants.

Eichmann saw a zealot fling himself from the top of a boulder and smash into a group of three beastmen, taking them all down in a tumbling, tangled heap. The gors recovered quickly, ripping out his heart in a spray of blood, but the sacrifice bought time for other zealots to close in. A dozen of them raced into contact, swiping and lashing out with their improvised blades, chopping the beastmen open in a flurry of whirling steel before ploughing onwards.

Once the gors realised their danger and responded, the bloodshed really began. The creatures were far bigger and stronger than the undead warriors had been at Eisenach, and their counter-attack was furious. Bull-headed warriors lowered their horns and charged, tearing through the stomachs and torsos of the oncoming zealots and shaking their bodies open. They aimed their axes, halberds and swords with startling precision despite their lumbering appearance. Cries of aggression were soon mingled with screams of agony.

Eichmann directed his steed straight into the heart of the storm. A gor charged up to him, nostrils flared and axe poised to swing. He shot it through the forehead, stowed the pistol and drew his blade from his belt. Another gor ran up from the other side, leaping over the body of a headless zealot to get at him. Eichmann pulled his horse round expertly, exposing his rapier-hand, and flashed out with the slender blade. The sword flickered across the creature's broad face, slicing open the tough hide and popping the two eyeballs like raw eggs.

The beastman staggered back, tearing at its face for just long enough for the zealots to catch up with it. They piled in as enthusiastically as ever, punching their rusty weapons into its reeling flank and tearing strips of hide from quivering muscle.

Eichmann looked up to see Udo ride on past him, goading his horse into the rapidly forming-up ranks of beastmen. His henchman looked as boundlessly aggressive as the flagellants, and his maul whirled round his head in wild circles over his head.

'To me, you stupid bastards!' he bellowed, riding

straight through a milling knot of chanting zealots and dragging them further into the mass of the warherd ahead. 'Run straight!'

Eichmann couldn't suppress a smile at that even as he sheathed the rapier and reached for his second pistol. The beastmen were formidable fighters, but they were outnumbered badly and caught out of position. The momentum of the flagellant horde seemed to be unstoppable, even as they absorbed their usual heavy toll of casualties.

He flicked the reins and his cantering horse broke into a gallop, leaping over the thick-limbed corpse of a fallen gor before plunging straight into a fresh pack of them. Its hooves flashed out as it came among them, catching one gor full in the face and cracking the cheekbones in two.

Everything was in motion, unfolding with such speed that it was hard to make out what the shape of the battle was. Cries of rage and anguish rose up from both sides, locked in a cacophony of brutal, frenzied combat.

Eichmann pulled up again, letting his troops maintain the fury of the charge. He sat tall in the saddle, peering north, watching the course of the stream loop along the valley floor until it veered sharply to the left just before a steeply rising incline flanked with dark trees.

Despite all the fighting, the beastmen were still running towards that slope. Some had turned to face the zealots, but others, further up the valley, just kept on going. Whatever was at the summit was the thing they'd come for, and even the intervention of an army of fanatics hadn't succeeded in diverting them all. Their single-mindedness was impressive.

'Hylaeus,' Eichmann breathed, allowing a flicker of satisfaction to pass across his face. 'At last.'

Then he checked his loaded pistol, cocked the hammer and prepared to ride back into the fray.

THE LAST OF the light fell over the ruined temple, leaving only the melded shimmer of the full moons. Both Mannslieb and Morrslieb blazed away in the empty sky, and their combined beams fell on the earth in shades of ivory and yellow.

The gors still thundered up to him. Scores of them lay dead at the foot of the altar, warped and broken in a mass of limbs and protruding bone. They'd come in waves, rushing at the lone island of stone from all sides. Each time, Huss had beaten them back, sending the dead thudding to the earth and the wounded limping back to the shadows. Whenever a gap opened up in the assault, though, another bull-gor would come barrelling into the cramped space, thrusting aside its shamed or wounded counterparts as it came.

Now the warrior priest waited for the next assault. His breathing was ragged and deep, his shoulders hunched. The head of the warhammer was heavy with slops of gore and his armour was draped with scraps of hide and lengths of hair. Blood, his own blood, ran freely from two wounds across his forehead, and his left shoulder-guard had been dented. His breastplate carried a deep transverse crack, the cause of the two fractured ribs that lay under it.

Huss rotated slowly, scanning the rows of eyes that, for the moment, hung back in the gloom. The light of the moons caught in those eyes, and they glimmered like discs of corrupted silver.

The gors no longer roared aloud as they came. They snorted heavily, breathing as deeply as the warrior priest did. Many carried deep wounds, just as he did. They knew his death was just a matter of time, but for all that they still hung back from the bite of his warhammer.

Huss watched them steadily, tensed for the first sign of movement. The pain from his many wounds barely registered. All he saw was corruption, ranks of it, waiting to be cleansed.

Then, over at the low entrance to the chapel sanctuary, something new stirred. The gors shrank back at the sound of it, keeping their heads low, glancing back between Huss and the doorway. A muffled crash rang out as something heavy was dashed to the ground. Heavy treads pounded on the stone in the antechamber, making the lintel of the entrance tremble.

Huss tensed his fingers, adjusting his grip on the hammer-shaft, still waiting, still silent.

It pushed its way in, squeezing through the narrow gap and making the doorway fracture. Two huge hooves fell onto the flagstones. A vast body, wrapped in corded muscle and hung with stinking pelts, rose up before him, uncurling slowly as the monster stretched out. A huge head hung before him, kept low, weighed down by two mighty, curved bull's horns.

Its bare flesh glistened in the moonlight, mottled with fresh bloodstains. Iron rings had been driven into its flesh, from which hung drained human heads, jangling together like baubles. A panoply of misshapen armour – pauldrons, greaves, spiked roundels – clung to the creature's frame as if bolted there.

Once inside the sanctuary it rose to its full height and gazed at Huss with a bestial, contemptuous hostility. It took up its weapon, a gigantic two-headed axe, and a gout of rancid breath issued from its flared nostrils.

The other beastmen stayed out of its way, cowering around the edges of the sanctuary and watching it with wary fascination. It was far taller than they were and almost twice their girth. Whereas they were twisted fusions of forest creatures and debased men, this was another breed altogether – purer, stronger, more deeply steeped in the depths of the world's corruption.

Bloodkine, such creatures were called by men, and of all the serried horrors within the horde of the deep wood they were among the most feared.

Huss remained unmoving. He watched the creature carefully, scouring its flanks for any sign of weakness. For the first time, he felt weariness creep up his arms. He had been fighting a long time, and this monster was fresh to combat.

Then he bowed his head, banishing such thoughts from his mind and drawing deep of the reserves which had never failed him.

As You have ever guided me.

The monster bellowed, throwing back its bull's head and flinging its huge arms wide. Loose stones fell from the remnants of the roof, twisting down to earth in columns of dust.

It lumbered towards Huss, sweeping the axe up into position. It hauled the blades in a ponderous motion, trusting to its enormous strength rather than speed.

Huss waited until the last moment, his warhammer poised to parry, before leaping back. The beast's axe-head slewed round just in front of him, almost grazing the surface of his breastplate. As the metal flashed past, Huss pounced forwards, lashing out with his own weapon.

The head of it cracked into the bloodkine's shoulder with such force that any normal gor would have been thrown from its feet. The monster in front of him merely grunted, reeling back a pace or two, before surging back in to the attack.

Its axe-head glittered yellow along the leading edge.
The bloodkine hurled it down at Huss, wrenching it
through the air like a blacksmith smashing the hammer
down onto the anvil.

Huss thrust his warhammer up to block, bracing it
with both hands. The weapons collided with an echoing
clang. The force of the impact ran down Huss's extended
arms. He cried out and sank to one knee, crushed by the
enormous weight.

The bloodkine sneered, and exerted more pressure.
Huss's arms began to buckle. Sweat ran down his forehead, glistening in the moonlight, and his wrists shook.
He resisted for a moment longer, gritting his teeth in
dogged determination, before his muscles gave way.

The axe plunged down. Huss pulled back, barely keeping hold of the warhammer as he snatched himself out
of harm's way. The bloodkine's blade bit deep into the
lid of the altar, breaking open the stone. Huss managed
to maintain his position on the edge for a moment, but
then the creature pulled the axe-head free, ripping up
the altar-top further and sending Huss clattering to the
floor on the far side.

Huss leapt back to his feet, scrabbling to get the warhammer into position. The bloodkine was on him
quickly, hammering down at him with the axe. None of
the gors interfered, though they all watched the drama
unfold with rapt attention.

Huss rolled away from the impact, wincing as the
bloodkine's blade slammed into the floor beside him.
He tried to get up, to bring his own weapon to bear,
but the bloodkine kicked out with one of its massive
hooves, knocking the warhammer from his grasp and
sending it spinning across the flagstones.

Huss scrambled to his feet, hastily drawing the knife

from his belt. The bloodkine hammered the axe-head down again, and Huss had to throw himself headlong to evade it.

The monster's axe missed him by an inch and cut straight through the flagstone, shattering it and plunging deep into the earth beneath. It lodged solidly, and the bloodkine heaved on the handle, trying to haul it back up.

Seeing his chance, Huss leapt straight at the creature, knife in hand. He managed to stab up at the bloodkine's torso, piercing the flesh, before the monster swung round, hitting him with a backhand blow from its massive fists.

Huss spiralled away, his vision going red. He had a brief impression of the whole chamber spinning around him in a blurred procession. His head lurched up groggily, trying to make out where the bloodkine was.

By then the creature had left the axe standing amid the broken flagstones and had come after him. It punched down again, catching Huss clean in his upturned face. The impact was staggering – Huss collapsed to the floor and the back of his head cracked against the stone. Blood splashed across his eyes, and he felt the sharp pain of a broken nose.

Acting purely on instinct, he scrambled backwards, barely able to see a thing, feeling his consciousness begin to ebb away.

The bloodkine reached down for him, grabbing him by the collar and hoisting him into the air as if he weighed no more than a child. Huss felt his feet leave the floor and a surge of nausea and disorientation rippled through him. His hands went numb, and he dimly heard the *clink* of his knife falling to the floor.

He managed to lift up his eyes, and saw the bull-headed

monster glaring at him. Its tiny eyes blazed with a thick, intoxicated bloodlust. Though the rest of the world had disappeared into a haze of pain and confusion, Huss could still just about meet the gaze of those eyes.

He spat in the creature's face. His gobbet of spittle and blood hit it right between the eyes – and the blood-kine's head exploded.

Huss fell to the floor, hitting the ground hard as the creature suddenly let go. He looked up, bewildered, to see the beast's gigantic body topple backwards and crash into the semi-ruined altar. For a moment, it felt as if the world had been up-ended. The gors in the chamber stared at the fallen bloodkine as stupidly and with as much surprise as he did.

'For the Empire!'

The voice came from the entrance to the sanctuary. Huss swung his head around, still groggy from the beating he'd received, and saw a man with a wide-brimmed hat leap into the chamber. More men piled in behind him bearing swords, cleavers and axes. A crossbow bolt whistled across the sanctuary, thunking solidly into a beastman as it turned to meet the unexpected enemy.

The fighting was brutal, bloody, and over very quickly. The gors, taken by surprise, were cut down efficiently by the human invaders. The man with the hat fought as if possessed, slicing through the lumbering gors with precise, whip-smart rapier strokes. In his left hand he held a smoking pistol.

Once Huss caught sight of that, he slowly began to realise what had happened. As the last of the beastmen were finished off, he crawled over to where his warhammer had fallen. Grasping the handle gave him some strength back, and the dark circles swirling in front of his eyes receded a little.

He staggered to his feet, holding on to the edge of the altar for balance, and came face to face with the man whose shot had saved his life.

'You're Luthor Huss?' demanded the man, looking at him as if a long-recurring dream had suddenly stumbled into the waking world.

Huss found that he couldn't speak. His lips were split and bleeding, and his tongue seemed to have swollen from where he'd bitten down on it. Once back on his feet, his head felt light again, and it was all he could do to nod weakly.

The man stowed his weapons and ran his arm under Huss's armpit, catching him just as he began to slide back to the ground. He grunted from the sudden weight, and called one of his troops over to help him.

'Let's go,' he snapped at his men, and the soldiers began to file out of the chamber.

Huss felt himself being dragged through the doorway, and somehow managed to keep hold of his warhammer. He had a vague impression of all-consuming darkness, then moonlight flooded across the scene again.

'Were you alone?' the man asked.

Huss nodded. Pain was returning. His ribs, his arms, his face – all of them throbbed from their wounds. He could feel his body, tough as it was, start to give up on him. The cumulative effect of exhaustion and hours of fighting began to overwhelm him.

Struggling to keep his eyes open, he lifted his head.

He looked down a long valley, one he only partly remembered running along just a few hours before. A host of human troops fought amongst bands of beastmen. Some looked little better than vagrants or fanatics, and were flinging themselves at the enemy with abandon. Their cries of rage and joy were familiar to him, though he couldn't quite remember why that was.

Other troops had come among them, fighting in the solid, conventional style of the northern Empire. A square of halberdiers had taken position halfway up the far slope of the valley and was holding its ground. Cavalry units held the centre, supported by loose formations of swordsmen in the livery of Middenheim.

All of them were busy with combat. The valley was filled with the sound of battle – the cries of dying men, the sharp ring of blade against armour, the roars of hostility from charging detachments.

It was only then that he saw her, no more than fifty yards away, and his heart leapt into his mouth. The dullness, the confusion, it all melted away. His vision crystallised on her in a locus of fear and sudden hope.

She rode amid a small group of cavalry, flanked by swordsmen, her blonde hair looking silver in the starlight. She was shouting something, waving her sword around in that clumsy way of hers, just as she had done that night in Helgag.

He smiled at that, unconsciously, just as he'd always smiled when she came close to him. Amid all the filth and fear and violence, she was a rare jewel of purity.

She'd come back.

You know that I'll follow you, and when I catch you up–

He was still smiling when the beast shot out from the shadows, hidden by the curving line of boulders near the water's edge. It ran up quickly, veering past the blows of swords and spears, darting between them like a daemon's shadow.

It went straight for her, axes in both hands. She saw it coming, but it was far too strong and far too quick. She managed to get her sword up to block the first of the axes, but the second buried deep in her chest, nearly severing her head from her body.

Huss started forwards, shaking the hands from his arms, suddenly choked with horror.

'*Mila!*' he roared, and the echo of his shout drowned out all other noises, rebounding from the trees like the aftershock of cannon-fire.

She fell instantly, and the sword dropped from her hand as she slipped from her steed. The swordsmen around her closed in on the beast, cutting it down brutally.

Huss started to run down the hill, staggering towards where she'd fallen. He felt his legs give out under him, and he toppled to his knees.

Tears of rage sprang from his bloody eyes. The world reeled on its axis.

'Mila!' he cried, though the word cracked in his throat.

She looked up at him. Even from such a distance, even so grievously wounded, she somehow managed to lift her head.

Her face was scored with pain and blood ran from her open mouth. She extended a hand towards him, shaking, before it fell to the ground.

Right at the end, before her eyes went dull and her head hit the earth again, she recognised him.

Just as he had always done when laying eyes on her, she smiled.

Mila.

Huss tried to crawl towards her, but fell onto his face. He dragged himself a yard or two further before he felt hands gripping his armour, hauling him up again.

He would have fought against them, but the last of his strength was going, falling away like the soul of the angel.

Grief welled up within him, vast and overwhelming.

The battle raged on, but it had no more consequence for him than a winter storm. He let the warhammer drop from his fingers, unable to bear the weight any longer.

His head lolled, and the world spun round him. Tears mingled with the blood on his cheeks, running in pale rivulets down his battered body.

The darkness came for him, rushing up out of the forest like a phantom of the deep, all-consuming, all-powerful. It washed across him, chilling him, dousing the horror, ripping it away into terrible forgetfulness.

Huss looked up one last time, catching a glimpse of the bloodied tangle of blonde hair in the distance, discarded amid the gore and mud.

Mila.

Then the darkness took him.

CHAPTER EIGHTEEN

'WHAT IS CORRUPTION?' he asked.

'You know what corruption is,' said Theiss.

'I've read of it. I've not seen it.'

'You see it in everything around you. You see the indolence of your fellows. You see decay in the fields, sickness lurking in still water.'

'That is the world's corruption. Scripture speaks of another darkness, one from beyond the edge of creation, one that spills across the lands of living men.'

'Chaos.'

'Yes. What is this?'

'I cannot tell you. I can only show you. It will be my last lesson, but that is, perhaps, as it should be.'

'And then?'

'Yes, Luthor. After that, should you pass the test, you will be a priest.'

HUSS STOOD ON the hill overlooking the village, and the chill breeze cut through his armour. It fitted him badly. The temple only had a small armoury, the contents of which were mostly rusty and warped by time. His breastplate had once belonged to an older man with a much looser belly, and it felt slack against the leather

319

underpinning. Theiss's old hammer felt too light, as if the head of it had been hollowed out.

Huss had outgrown such things, and he knew it. The day would come when he would leave the temple and strike out for the wider world.

Theiss now rarely left his bed and stayed cooped up in his chambers for days at a time. He was too weak to minister to the people of the surrounding lands as he'd once done, too weak even to say the rituals over the altar. He'd closed up the chapel and spent hours alone in there, praying for his soul. Huss hardly saw him, and when he did the old man's face was lined with care and worry. Death was coming for him at last, and for all his wisdom, Theiss did not wait for its approach with grace.

Deprived of the use of the chapel, Huss left the temple more often than he stayed in it. The old place became strange to him, and the shelter it had once provided seemed less comforting. He criss-crossed the freezing moors instead, his warhammer lodged over his shoulder, blessing the dead and the newborn and offering wards against sickness, curses and the evil eye. He soon became inured to the grind of it, and no longer found the death of the innocents as much of a trial as he had once done.

Death, transition and suffering. That was what the life of a priest involved, and that was the burden he took on so others could master the trial of living.

Hirsch, Kassel and the others had aged too, but none of them were close to achieving what he had. To the extent he cared, Huss guessed the other acolytes would spend the rest of their lives in the temple. If they ever received holy orders, they would make no good use of them but would continue the empty life of drinking, gluttony and whoring that so many village clerics in the trackless depths of the Empire sank to when far from the eyes of those who might possibly discipline them for it.

Their hatred had become irrelevant to him. None of them any longer dared to look at him with so much as a spiteful glance. They were like the rats in the attic spaces – something to be regretted, tolerated, and despised. Theiss wouldn't give his dispensation to any of them. Even in his weakened state, the old man trusted important tasks to none but Huss. He'd said as much, right before Huss had set off.

'It's no shame, to seek another to take on this burden,' he'd said then.

'It would be a great shame, on both you and on me,' Huss had replied, looking down on the old man as he shivered under the goatskin blankets. Theiss's skin had been sickly and bulbous, and in the candlelit darkness it had made him look almost like an animal.

'Then you'll take it on yourself?' Theiss had asked, looking at once hopeful and wary.

'I prayed for guidance.'

Theiss had raised an eyebrow then, as if he'd found that disturbing.

'What did you learn?' he had asked.

'That this has been ordained,' Huss had said. 'That there is a pattern and that I'm meant to be there.'

'Don't look for a pattern in everything, lad.'

'Nonetheless.'

Theiss had looked uneasy, but had eventually nodded.

'Then the grace of Sigmar be with you, Luthor,' he had said, his voice weak. 'Do not fail in this – I wish to see you back here again before the end.'

'I will return,' Huss had said, as seriously and impassively as ever.

Six days later, after a long trek across the howling

wasteland, Huss adjusted the straps on his armour, shivering a little as the wind crept into the gaps between the plates. As well as being awkward, the breastplate was heavy. Marks of purity had been hastily placed on the metal, but some had worn away on the march across the moors.

Huss took out a small scrap of parchment and unfolded it in his palm. The inscription sat on the dull silver of his gauntlet, and the heavy gothic script seemed to weigh it down.

Huss read it slowly, mouthing the words as he scanned the lines.

In all this, recall the cardinal virtues.

Strength, to endure the storm.

Wisdom, to learn its origins.

Pride, to see its weakness.

Contempt, to slight its power.

And in obedience to these precepts, you may no longer fear the storm; for then, and in truth, you will be the storm.

Huss folded the parchment tightly on to itself. He wrapped it in a strip of leather until it resembled a lozenge the length of his little finger. Then he took up another strip of leather and bound the scripture tightly to his forehead. The material felt snug against his flesh, and he took comfort from its presence.

He looked down at the village in the valley below, and witnessed again the truth of the reports that had come to the temple three weeks ago.

No one knew where the beast had come from. Some said it had risen out of the village well, draped in slime; others that it had stalked up from the limits of the forest, over a week's march away.

What no one disputed was its power. Weismund had been a prosperous, busy place by the standards of the highlands. By the time the beast had finished its work, the village was in ruins.

Huss had seen devastation before. He'd seen habitations laid waste by the passage of warfare or famine, but nothing that had prepared him for the sight laid before his eyes then.

You speak of Chaos.

The earth itself had risen up, breaking open in great shelves of stone. Creepers had burst from the living soil like snakes, shooting out across ruined walls and roofs. Fluid, as black and viscous as oil, bubbled gently in the recesses, steaming as it cooled in the winter wind. The rocks themselves had been tortured, stretched into grotesque shapes like the distended jaws of a screaming man.

A pall hung over the whole place, sweet-smelling and sickly. Clouds roiled above the village even though the rest of the sky was clear, and they swirled in a bluff of bruise-purple, green and yellow. Strange noises echoed out from the ruins – gurgling cries, or agonised weeping, or rutting grunts of aggression.

Nothing came out of Weismund now but those cries. The few men who'd survived the coming of the beast now cowered in refuges far away, gibbering fearfully or staring, wide-eyed, out into the night.

Huss adjusted his armour, took up the warhammer, and strode down the slope. He went confidently, sinking his boots deep into the yielding turf. The sweet aroma from the village wafted over him as he approached the outskirts, growing in intensity with each step.

Things were worse inside. Flies swarmed in huge black clouds over the ripped-up bodies of the dead. The flesh of the slain had swollen and burst, leaving trails of pus and blood across stretched-tight skin. Unseeing eyes stared out from faces locked in the final clench of excruciation; clawed hands clutched at the churned-up earth in futile gestures of desperation.

The ground was covered in a slowly moving mist. It curled up against the vacant doorways of empty hovels, rolling and folding like the vapour from boiled milk. By the time Huss reached the heart of the village the mist had thickened and risen to knee-height. It was hot against his flesh, warm like heart-blood.

Strange cries followed him in. Nameless things scuttled away from him into the shadows, snuffling or barking as they went. Footfalls, heavy and hard, sounded from far off, down the winding lanes between the shattered houses, though no owner emerged at the end of them.

Huss ignored them. Only one creature deserved his attention – the one that had done this.

The bringer of ruin.

It emerged to meet him from the shattered shell of an old chapel, uncurling like a grub out of a wound. Then it waited for him, hunched double and leaning on a twisted staff.

Its spine curved up and over like the line of a longbow, breaking free of the skin and muscle below it. Its head hung low, suspended on stretched sinews and lolling drunkenly. Thick, knotted hair covered every part of it. An obscene goat-face stared out from the mass of rancid fur, crowned with four sets of spike-sharp horns. Its eyes were deep yellow pools of filmy malice. Its feet were cloven hooves, though its hands were like those of a man's. Long, dirty fingernails clutched at a crooked staff, and a ragged cloak hung loosely from its bulging shoulders.

The mist came from under that cloak. It ran down the

creature's backwards-jointed legs as if it were defecating constantly onto the ground. The stench was almost overpowering, and Huss felt his gorge rise just looking at it.

All that was foul enough, but there was something else, something indefinable, that made things worse. The beast was *wrong*. It shouldn't have existed. When it trod on the earth, the earth shrank back from it, cracking open and splitting. Grass stems withered and folded. Insects burst up from the soil spontaneously, flickering and buzzing in clouds of angry confusion.

It was neither man nor beast – it was an aberration, a pustule of corruption birthed from the dreams of Dark Gods and lodged in the world like shrapnel in a gash.

It looked at him, and in its gaze was an alien loathing.

'Brave, to come here, boy,' it said.

Its speech was the eeriest thing of all – the goat-mouth, never created to utter human words, stretched and warped as it moulded itself around the syllables. Though intelligible, the result was ineffably strange and unsettling.

'You do not belong here,' replied Huss. His voice, normally so strident, sounded weak as it pierced the miasma of corruption. 'Go back, or I will end you.'

The goat-creature didn't scoff, snarl or laugh. It just stared at him, as if it didn't fully understand the concept of retreat.

'You're a priest?' it asked, incredulous.

'I am,' said Huss.

'Not yet,' said the beast. 'Half a priest.'

Huss hefted his warhammer, judging the weight of it, watching the creature all the while. It didn't look like it could move fast. It looked like it could barely hobble more than a pace or two before falling apart under the weight of its bulbous, swaying shoulders.

'Do you know what *I* am, half-priest?' it asked.

'A changeling-spawn,' said Huss. 'An aberration.'

'Yes, yes. What else?'

'I did not–'

'I'm a priest, boy. I'm a priest of my kind. I'm like you.'

The creature's eyes narrowed, and it shuffled towards him. As it moved, its whole arched body shook. Tiny skulls, each suspended from strips of cured flesh, jangled against one another. Its clawed hand rose up, pointing at Huss.

'But I'm old too,' it said, 'as old as the bones of the world. I chewed on the flesh of men long before you were spawned in your mother's guts. You're young, half-priest, and your fat and sinew will nourish me further before you die.'

Huss suddenly felt his arms go heavy, as if weights of iron had been thrown across him. He tensed his biceps, resisting the sensation.

'Soul of the Heldenhammer...' he whispered, beginning the recitations that would carry him into action and sustain him throughout.

Then he launched himself forwards, swinging the hammerhead round to collide with the creature's elongated face.

His movements, normally so fluid, felt clumsy and slow. The hammerhead didn't draw properly, and his charge fell far short. Huss almost lost his grip on the weapon entirely and had to work not to pitch forwards onto his face.

The creature advanced on him, now mere feet away, wheezing like a burst bladder. It kept its claw pointing at him as it swayed closer, muttering some unintelligible cantrips of dark magic.

Huss gasped, and fell to one knee. It felt as if the air had suddenly grown as thick as soup. He gasped for breath, gagging on the poisonous filth on the breeze. His head dipped perilously close to the layer of swirling mist at his knees. Curls of it rose to meet him, snaking up towards his nostrils eagerly.

'Hnngh…' he grunted, dragging himself back to his feet with massive effort. His vision went cloudy and he felt his grip on consciousness loosen.

The creature hobbled up to him, spouting guttural blasphemies with every step. The earth beneath its feet began to ripple like water. Dark effluent bubbled up from the cracks in it, moulding into tentacles, hooks and fingers. Strands of matter clamped onto Huss's legs, dragging on him and pulling him back into the embrace of the soporific mist.

Huss retreated from it, still dizzy and disorientated. The ruined buildings whirled around him in a merged procession, blurring with ghostly after-images. He gritted his teeth and spoke words of faith aloud. The scripture on his forehead grew hotter and the cloying curtains of mist shrank back a little.

He stopped retreating, gathered himself and launched into a heavy hammer-thrust. His muscles screamed against the horrific pressure on them, but he managed to drive the killing-edge out with some speed and heft.

The beastman swayed back out of its path, and the crushing weight on Huss's shoulders eased a little more. Huss powered forwards, his jaw set firm against the deadening force around him, determined to exploit even the tiniest of openings. He lashed out again with the hammerhead. There was no art to the manoeuvre, just a desperate attempt to generate some momentum.

The head whistled through the clouds of mist and

cracked heavily into the beastman's flank. The creature staggered to one side, and its hooves skittered on the broken ground.

Huss drew the hammer back, ready to strike again, but that time the warhammer flew up far faster than it should have. Its heavy iron head suddenly disintegrated, shattering into a dozen pieces. Huss stared at the severed shaft for a moment, horrified, before he felt the dragging fingers of the mist coming at him again.

He pulled himself away from the beast once more, casting aside the useless hammer and fumbling for the knife at his belt. The creature limped after him, still chanting words of power.

It spat out a final curse, and the earth under Huss's feet erupted. He fell heavily onto his back. The mist layer crashed over him like the incoming tide, and the world disappeared into a haze of whiteness. Spluttering, his eyes streaming, Huss forced his head above the surface again, only to see the creature rearing over him. The beastman had drawn a weapon – a cruel, double-bladed dirk – and had it poised above his prone body as if he were a sacrificial offering.

The beast plunged the dirk down, aiming straight at Huss's heart. He rolled over heavily, fighting against the strands of semi-solid fingers that clutched at his armour. The dirk missed its aim but punched through the plate of his left arm, driving deep into his muscle.

Huss cried out. His arm felt instantly hot, as if a swarm of insects had been loosed into the wound and were stinging at the tender flesh. A fresh wave of nausea and disorientation overcame him, and his head dipped below the level of the mist.

He sank down, gagging. Everything blurred into a

muffled, echoing world of confusion. He saw a huge hunched shadow lean over him.

The dirk rammed through the crust of the mist, slicing through Huss's breastplate as if it wasn't there. The blade dug deep, puncturing his skin below his ribcage and twisting deep into his gut.

Every instinct screamed at Huss to drag himself away from that pain. It was incredible – a blazing, roaring furnace of agony. In the hazy world of his blunted senses, it felt like a fire had been kindled inside him and was thundering out of control.

For a second, he almost obeyed that primal instinct – he almost hauled his broken body out of the path of the beastman and crawled away like a bedraggled rat.

But then his clenched fist shot up, clearing the surface of the mist-sea. His gauntlet connected with the creature's jangling bone-charms. His fingers locked on to the leather cords, and he pulled down savagely.

Caught off-balance, the beastman toppled forwards, collapsing on top of him. The mist scattered, ripped into shreds by the huge creature plunging through it. Huss pulled it closer, ignoring the foul stench of the beast as it smothered him.

For a second, their faces were inches apart. The creature's old eyes gazed into his. Its breath, stinking like weeks-old putrid meat, washed over him.

Huss seized it by the throat, clamping his hands around its scrawny sinews and clasping tight. He could still feel the hot storm of pain from his wounds, and knew well enough that the monster's hands were still free to strike at him. Ignoring all that, he shoved his huge palms together, crushing the creature's neck.

The beastman struggled instantly, thrashing out with its arms and arching its warped spine. Its eyes bulged, ringed with the red of its veins, and its swollen tongue lolled out.

For Huss, everything sank into oblivion but the face before him. He barely felt the pain as the dirk whipped round a third time, driving into his torso and opening up another deep wound. He hardly felt the creature's bucking attempts to break free of his hold, and he ignored the slaps of bloody saliva that rained down from its gaping mouth.

The mist wormed its way into his lungs. The edges of his vision sank into darkness, leaving only a vague patch in the centre, concentrated on the choking face of the creature he had in his hands.

Its arteries bulged up from the surface of its skin. Blood splattered out as the vessels burst. Its attempts to breathe got weaker and weaker, descending from desperate heaves to pathetic, coughing hacks. It kept at him, stabbing again with the dirk, lacerating his face with its long claws and kicking out against him with its trailing hooves.

Huss never let go. With every last fragment of strength that remained to him, he clung on. He pressed down with his thumbs, pushing through the polyps and cords of the creature's throat, squeezing the last of the life from it.

It looked at him one final time before the end. In its bloodshot eyes there was nothing but horrified surprise; by then, the hatred had gone, replace by the chill fear of the hunter become prey.

It tried to breathe, ripping muscles open along its neck, then its limbs went rigid. Its whole body trembled, shivered, then slackened. Its chin slumped on to Huss's chest and its long tongue snaked out across his breastplate, spotted with pus and sputum.

There was a final shudder, and it fell still.

Huss kept his fingers locked in place, unable to unclamp them even if he'd wanted to. He felt the last fragments of his consciousness running out of his body like blood from his many wounds. He could sense the poison in the beast's blade coursing around his system.

His head fell back against the earth. A shadow fell across his eyes, dark and consuming.

He tried to raise his head again, and failed. Sickness reared up again, dragging him into oblivion.

He had a final image of Theiss's old, tired face.

Do not fail in this – I wish to see you back here again before the end.

And then he passed out, lost in a world of pain, poison and fatigue.

A LONG TIME passed before he awoke. He came to as the sun was going down, and deep shadows ran across his body.

The creature still lay on top of him, death-heavy and stinking. Its rotten head rested on his chest and its eyes were open, though the narrow irises were dull and opaque.

Huss lay for a long time, breathing in shallow gulps, stretched out where he'd fallen. The wound in his stomach ached badly, as did the lesser wounds in his arms and side. His throat was as dry as ash, and it hurt to swallow.

Eventually he summoned the strength to move. Going slowly, pushing against the resistance of his cramped muscles, he managed to shove the carcass of the creature to one side. It slid from his chest, collapsing limply as it rolled into the dust.

The infernal mists had long gone, though their sickly

stink remained on the stone. Weismund, or what remained of it, felt as cursed as it had done when he'd entered it.

Every breath was painful, and every movement was agony. It took Huss a long time to push himself up into a sitting position. His stomach wound opened again as he did so, and fresh blood pushed through the caked scabs. He gingerly lifted his breastplate up and saw the puffiness of the flesh around the incision.

For a while longer he just sat there, sluggish with pain, feeling his blood course thickly around his body. He managed to unstrap the breastplate and cast it to one side. He stripped the armour from his wounded arm and ripped up strands from his cloak to use as bandages, wincing every time he moved.

Once strapped up, Huss got to his feet. He felt dizzy immediately, and his empty stomach growled like a caged dog. His eyes fell on the remnants of his ruined warhammer, which lay a few feet away from him. The shaft was intact but the head was broken into several pieces.

Limping, Huss went over to it. It was as he bent down to retrieve the handle that he saw the full extent of the damage. The shards of iron from the hammerhead showed drill-marks on the underside. The weapon's runes of protection had been subtly altered, and the fault lines in the broken metal were almost completely smooth.

It had been tampered with; made to shatter.

Huss knelt in the ruins of Weismund then, staring at the pieces. Of all the wounds he'd received there, that one was the most grievous.

He didn't get up again for a long time. When he did, his face was grey and his eyes were dark. He left the hammer lying in the dust along with the broken armour plates.

Then, limping still, his face contorted with pain, Huss began the long journey home.

WHEN HE REACHED the temple, eight days later, the sun was going down. The sky in the west was the deep red of embers and barred with streaks of coal-black cloud. The last of the light lingered for a while on the edge of the world, flaming like a wound.

Huss limped up the path to the gates. He remembered the first time he'd ascended the hill towards the ramshackle collection of buildings, years ago. He'd fought through the driving rain back then, head low and fists balled. Now he hobbled like an old man, riddled with the pain of the creature's wounds, his head thick and aching.

Underneath it all was a new kind of anger. Names ran through his mind, one after the other.

Hirsch, surely. Though Kassel is almost as bad.

The fury of the betrayal burned hottest in him, worrying away at his heart like forge-hot ingots. The long journey from Weismund, each step a fresh pain in his already battered body, hadn't dimmed it. For a while he'd begun to dream that the old jealousies had been put away, and that if the acolytes would never learn to truly love him then at least they'd seen the futility of plotting against him.

Aldrich? He was always the quietest. Did I underestimate him?

For all of that, the sheer cowardliness of it all astonished him, as did the pettiness. Their grievances against him were so shallow, so mundane.

But then perhaps he'd not realised the full extent of

their resentment. Perhaps the sight of him basking in the favour of the old priest, the man they all despised for his weakness and piety, had been too much.

It must have been hard for them to kneel while he delivered the sermons in Theiss's stead. It must have been hard for them to see the old man's weapon gifted to him rather than them. Above all, it must have been hard for them to have such a reminder, all the time, of what they could and should have been.

Hirsch.

The gates of the temple neared. No lights had been lit in the outer walls, and the blunt shapes of the outbuildings were black against the darkening sky.

Huss reached the doors. He didn't bother drawing back the heavy iron knocker but kicked straight through the half-rotten wood and shoved the broken planks aside. He limped over the threshold, no weapon in his hands, his head low and his long face fixed into a tight mask of resolve.

No candles burned inside. The air was cold and still, like that of a grave. The rushes on the floor were going stale and their sharp aroma stung his nostrils. Far ahead, down the corridor and through the cloisters, he could make out some kind of noise. It was hard to pin down what it was – muffled shouting, or maybe pleas for mercy.

Then, with a sudden pang of horror, Huss recognised Theiss's voice in those cries. Right on the heels of that, he realised what his prolonged departure had meant – the old man had been on his own.

Huss picked up his pace, breathing heavily as he dragged his body through the pillars of the cloister and over to the chapel. He cursed under his breath, disgusted with his self-absorption. The target wasn't him at all – it was the priest, the master of what scant treasures the temple possessed. His own death was merely the means to that end, a way of clearing the path to the objective the acolytes truly desired.

Another locked door barred his path. He grabbed the brass handle with both hands and heaved. It resisted, flexing on its hinges, before the rotten wood around the lock splintered with a ripping crack and came away in his hands.

He threw the door open and plunged inside. The light of fires glowed across the flagstones now. They seemed to be everywhere – in braziers, in torches, in glowing iron bowls of embers. The chapel was just beyond. As he neared it, he heard Theiss's voice raised up in desperation. He'd never heard his master plead for anything before, and the sound of it stabbed at his heart.

I should have come sooner.

Huss clenched his fists, took a deep breath, and hobbled inside.

More fires had been lit within the nave. The whole place was bathed in the angry red of leaping flames and felt as hot as a bread oven. Spires of smoke boiled up from braziers, merging into a moving ceiling of darkness that ran up along the stone of the arched roof and pooled in the apexes.

Theiss knelt before the altar with his back to Huss. He was wearing robes Huss had never seen before – black, with a sheen on them like silk. Those robes rippled as the old man wrenched his body round to face the intruder, and the reflection on them was as red as polished garnet.

Huss limped towards him, looking around him as he came, trying to spy the ones Theiss had been remonstrating with.

'Master,' he rasped, his throat still painful from where he'd inhaled the miasma of the beastman. 'Are you–'

He didn't say another word. Theiss shrank away from him, his eyes dark with horror. Huss came to a standstill, swaying from exhaustion, staring at him.

'*You*,' whispered Theiss, and the word was strangled with fear.

Huss stared back at him, dumbstruck.

Theiss had changed. His deeply wrinkled skin had firmed up, tightening into a leathery expanse of youthful flesh. His rheumy eyes were intense and dark, as if the pupils had dilated across the whites. Where his old hands protruded from the sleeves of his robes, they were firm and strong.

His hair, which had been white, was dark and matted. Sideburns ran down his jowls, thick and gnarly. Even the backs of his hands were covered in a thin layer of down, as if tufts of hair would grow there too, given time.

But it was his voice that most betrayed him. It curled around the word *you* just like the beastman in Weismund had, stumbling over the syllable with muscles that were no longer comfortable with human speech.

A changeling-spawn. An aberration.

Theiss stood before him for a second longer, frozen in surprise and terror. His fingers clenched and unclenched. His dark eyes looked up at Huss. They glowed soft and deep in the warm light, just like an animal's.

'I was *dying*, lad,' he croaked. The noise was pitiable, a fragile echo of the voice he'd once had, diminished by pleading and self-pity. 'You'd never have understood.'

Huss felt the shock gradually slough from him. The scene before him crystallised, sharpening up into a vista of sickening corruption. He suddenly smelled the sickness in the flames, so different from the holy incense used in the sanctified rites. He suddenly saw the animal bones piled high on the altar, defiling the cloth beneath.

He gazed into the face of the man who had taught him the lore of the priesthood.

He gazed into the face of the man who had given him his name.

The face was no longer that of a man; it was a face of a beast.

And it was then that the final barrier broke open.

Huss *roared*, casting aside the hurts of the journey in an instant, summoning all the vast power that lay within his huge frame. He charged straight at Theiss, his fists balled in fury, his mournful face stretched into an agonised howl of outrage and betrayal.

Theiss darted away from him, leaping back over the altar in a frantic attempt to get away. He crashed through the piles of bones, scattering them across the stone floor.

Huss bounded after him. The flames in the chapel seemed to whirl higher, goading him on. He no longer saw his old master before him – he saw a filthy, corrupted shell of a man, an outrider of Chaos placed within the holiest sanctums of the Church.

Theiss scampered like a ferret, darting down from the dais and into the sanctuary beyond. His robes fluttered behind him, flaring up as trailing flames licked at them. They exposed wiry flesh beneath, already knotted into thick cords of muscle and studded with the first growths of hair. He could never have moved as fast before his transformation.

Huss thundered after him, barging aside braziers full of burning coals and ripping down the centuries-old tapestries that warded the high altar. He stretched out, grabbing at the priest's trailing robes, missing his fluttering hem by a finger's width.

Theiss swerved suddenly to one side, skirting the walls and darting back towards the nave. Huss slipped as he tried to follow, crashing into a tall candelabrum and sending it clanging to the ground. The lit candles rolled out across the floor and onto a length of fallen tapestry.

Then Huss was up again, surging after Theiss with his heavy, thudding tread. The priest flitted between pillars, making for the door at the far end. His naked feet clattered against the stone as if they were made of bone rather than flesh.

Theiss was quick, far quicker than his age-weakened body had any right to be, but Huss was still fuelled with the white-hot inferno of rage, unbridled and given full expression for the first time. He caught up with Theiss just as the priest reached the door handle. Huss grabbed the old man's shoulders in both hands, whirled him around and threw him bodily back into the chapel.

Theiss hit the ground and rolled along the central aisle, back towards the altar. He staggered back to his feet again, but by then Huss was on him. Huss grabbed the old priest by the neck, hauling him off his feet before hurling him back through the air. Theiss's scrawny body cartwheeled over on itself before crunching against the stone edge of the altar with a sickening snap. His head bounced from the stone and blood ran down from his forehead.

Theiss reached up, his hands shaking, for something to grasp on to. His fingers clamped on to the iron cage of a brazier and he pulled against it, trying to drag himself to his feet and ignoring the sizzling burns from the red-hot metal.

Huss strode up to him ominously. He watched The-iss clumsily knock over the brazier, spilling the blazing coals across the floor. By now flames were already begin-ning to flicker up from the torn-down tapestries. Brazier coals rolled over piles of rushes drenched in holy oils, and the sound of the fuel igniting was like the rush of winter wind.

Theiss stared up at Huss as he approached, his face lined with terror.

'It'll come to you too, lad!' he shrieked, frantically trying to back away from his pupil. 'You've seen what death is! You've seen the well of souls! Wait till the fear hits you – it'll come for you too!'

Huss didn't say anything. He couldn't say anything – his mouth was clamped into a frozen grimace of disdain, teeth gritted and lips pulled back. The flames leaping up from behind the altar did nothing but fuel his mood of destruction.

Huss grabbed Theiss for a third time, hauling him onto the altar-top and slamming him down, face-up. The old priest struggled, but Huss held him firmly in place.

'This would never have happened, but for your damned piety!' Theiss spat, his fear transforming into a hopeless kind of defiance. 'Nothing is ever good enough, nothing is ever holy enough!'

Huss kept his left hand pressed onto Theiss's chest while he raised the right one high above the man's face. He stared at Theiss the whole time, his eyes blazing with furious loathing.

Theiss glared back up at him, the sinews on his warped neck standing out as if they longed to burst free.

'Taste well this holy revenge, Luthor Huss,' he cried. 'It'll be the only thing you'll ever taste! No mortal will ever share this with you. None will laugh with you, none will love with you!'

His lips twisted in a bizarre fury of their own. Only his eyes told the full story – that his anger was with himself, with his weakness and with his cowardice.

'You'll be *alone*, Luthor,' he shrieked. 'You understand nothing of us. You know nothing of our temptations, for you are never tempted.'

Huss stayed his hand a moment longer. His fist hung in the air, trembling, poised to plunge down.

'A priest, oh yes,' said Theiss, looking oddly gleeful. 'But a man? A true man? *Never.*'

Theiss flung the last word out with all the accumulated venom of a whole life spent in failure. Staring down into the warped beast-creature's face, Huss saw Theiss's life spread out from end to end. He saw the hopes of youth, marred by the crushing labour and disappointment of adulthood, followed by the horror, the all-consuming horror, of his soul's extinction.

Then his fist fell, cracking into Theiss's face like a hammer falling on an anvil.

Huss lifted it up and crunched it down again, then again. More punches flew in, hard and fast. He used both hands, beating the prone body of his old master, pulverising what was left of his head and neck until the entire structure gave way. The bones shattered, the skin broke and the muscles were flattened into a bloody, stringy pulp.

Huss kept flailing. The blows became ill-aimed. The more he hit out, the less he was able to restrain himself. His pants of effort became grunts, the grunts became cries, and the cries became *howls*.

The last vestiges of control sheared away. A black rage reared up inside him and swept aside any final fragments of restraint. Huss ripped Theiss's body apart, flinging the pieces aside in great bloody swathes. Gore splattered across his face, his arms, his hands. When there was nothing left to tear into, he went after the piles of bones on the altar, throwing them aside in sweeping armfuls. The skulls flew through the air, shattering as they collided with the pillars in clouds of dust.

The fires were blazing out of control by then, raging down the aisles of the chapel and surging up towards the windows. The space got even hotter and the glass in the panes began to fracture.

Huss whirled around and lurched down the nave, smashing everything in his path. He hurled candelabra to the ground and they shattered. He dragged down the lectern and broke its eagle-headed cover into pieces.

Huss stormed into Theiss's private antechambers and tore the books down from the shelves. He didn't even see the titles of them as he flung them into the flames. He grabbed the old priest's robes and threw them into the roaring inferno, fuelling it further.

Then he stumbled back into the body of the chapel, his eyes dark and his jaw clenched in the fixed grip of mania. The glass over the altar blew apart, scattering slivers across the floor.

Only then did the main doors, the ones Theiss had been trying to reach, slam open. A blast of cool night air rushed in, followed by cries of alarm and surprise. Men broke inside, holding up their hands to ward against the ferocious heat.

Huss swept his gaze over them, and his nostrils flared. *Hirsch. Kassel. Aldrich. This doom shall encompass you, too.*

The acolytes glared at him in horror, just for a second, before turning tail and charging back out. A single

glance at the carnage inside and the bloody form of
Huss striding straight at them was all they'd needed to
see.

Huss pursued them out of the doorway and across
the yard of the cloister. The night felt astonishingly cold
after the furnace of the chapel, and the rush of frigid air
clarified his senses. He felt suddenly acute and lethal, a
sharper, more deadly variant of the all-consuming rage
he'd felt in the chapel interior.

The acolytes scattered as soon as they reached the far
side of the cloister yard. One of them went sharply left,
making for the refectory. Another darted up the winding stairs to the scriptorium, while a third ran straight
ahead, down the short corridor leading to the main
temple gates.

Huss followed that one, and his boots echoed down
the narrow way like the beating of a war-drum. The
acolyte managed to leap through the ruined doors of
the gateway before sprinting out and along the main
track across the moors. Huss barrelled after him, crashing through the remains of the doors without slowing
down.

It was only then, lit by the twin light of the moons,
that Huss saw which acolyte he'd gone after. Hirsch had
always run clumsily, impeded by his slack, ale-ruined
body. He didn't get far over the broken ground, and fell
heavily onto his face before getting more than fifty yards
from the gates.

Huss caught up with him just as the inferno in the
chapel flared up properly, smashing the remaining windows and sending tongues of vivid flame surging out
into the night. The blood-red glow rolled down the hill
after him, casting long lines of shadow.

Hirsch tried to scramble away but Huss swept him up

in one hand, wrenching him from his feet and holding him off the ground. Hirsch only had time for a single glance of utter terror before Huss smashed his bloody fist into the acolyte's startled face.

The man's head snapped back with a crunch of breaking facial bones. Huss let him fall to the earth before kicking him savagely in his distended stomach.

Hirsch cried out aloud, curling into a ball and cradling his head in his shaking hands.

'*Why?*' he squealed, his voice as high-pitched as a girl's.

Huss crouched down over him, flexing his fingers to finish the job. He pulled Hirsch's protective hands away from his face before clamping his own onto the man's neck.

'Nngh!' Hirsch gurgled through a mix of saliva and blood from his demolished nose.

Huss pressed down, relishing the last of the rattish man's life ebbing away. The icy wind swirled around him, cutting through his threadbare cloak and chilling his body.

Something in the chapel detonated then, and a vast bloom of red erupted into the sky. Raging light bled across Hirsch's panicked, choking face. His features were as pinched and unwholesome as ever. His breath stank of blood, rancid cheese and sour beer.

It was a miserable, meagre face.

It was human, and it was terrified.

Suddenly, as if ripped away by the icy wind from across the moors, Huss felt his rage blow itself out. His madness, stoked by fatigue and by the shock of Theiss's treachery, shrivelled. He looked down, down at the hands that were strangling the life out of another man.

Horrified, he snatched them back.

Hirsch hauled in a huge, shuddering breath, then coughed up a heavy gobbet of blood and phlegm. He inhaled again, shaking uncontrollably, before looking up at Huss with fear and hatred in his face.

Huss stared down at him. He could smell blood on his own arms. In amongst that blood was hair – animal hair.

A wave of nausea, as profound as that conjured up by the creature in Weismund, shuddered through him. He staggered to his feet, holding his bloody hands in front of him.

Hirsch shuffled away, shifting backwards on all-fours. His expression oscillated between bewilderment and outrage.

'Blood of Sigmar,' he cried. '*Why?*'

Huss backed away, shaking his head.

Hirsch spat a slug of blood onto the ground and half-rose, propping himself up on shaking limbs. He looked at Huss with the same quality of hatred he'd once used in the chapel antechambers, back when the acolytes had still dared to torment him.

The old man's as rotten as a week-old corpse.

They had known about Theiss. They had known long before Huss had done. Unlike him, they knew the myriad ways a man's soul could condemn itself, and they'd treated the old sinner and his rites with the contempt they had deserved.

They never go in the chapel any more – I don't let them, for they get nothing from it.

Only Huss – pious, gloomy Huss – had been too wrapped up to notice, lost in an austere world of doubt, angst and scripture.

'You've destroyed… *everything.*'

For the first time, he felt the gnawing of a terrible,

enervating doubt. He heard the boom and crash of a tower falling in on itself in the temple, and the noise of it struck at his heart.

Hirsch crept away, dragging himself across the earth on hands and knees and spitting up more blood. From the temple itself came more stragglers – cooks, servants, other acolytes. They were coughing or weeping. When they saw Huss, standing out in the fields like a statue, they averted their eyes in terror and shuffled further out into the wilds.

Huss ignored them, locked in his own private horror. It felt as if the world had dissolved underneath his feet.

He didn't know what to do. For the very first time in his life, he didn't know what to do.

You'll be alone, Luthor, for you understand nothing of mankind.

Yes, that was right – he failed to understand the weakness of others. He always would, and that would be his great weakness.

You know nothing of our temptations, for you are never tempted.

He was blind. Anyone getting close to him, anyone breaking through the outer shell of devout reserve, they would be in danger from that blindness. They would suffer, just as the temple acolytes had done, just as Theiss had done, just as the angel in Hnel had done.

He wouldn't allow it – never again. Any who got too close, any who risked seeing the emptiness, he would send them away. Such pain could never be ventured again; not for him, and not for them.

Huss looked up, into the east, and saw the soulless expanse of night howling across the moors. It beckoned to him, as if recognising a kindred spirit.

Once he started walking, he never looked back. With

his massive shoulders sloping, he limped off, feeling the pain of his injuries return even as the mania of battle finally slunk away.

A priest, oh yes, but a man? A true man?

Once he started walking, he knew he would never stop. That would be his penance, to remain alone, insulating humanity from his dreadful blindness.

Never.

CHAPTER NINETEEN

'SO WHERE IS he?' asked Gartner, sitting down heavily on a mossy bank overlooking the valley.

Udo, already seated, picked flecks of old sausage skin from his teeth with his fingernails.

'Still in the ruins,' he said.

'Have you heard anything?'

'No.'

'That doesn't bother you?'

'No.'

Gartner shook his head resignedly, and looked out over the site of the battle.

The sun was high in the sky but it didn't do much to penetrate the thick forest cover. The stream at the base of the valley ran rust-red from the blood in the soil, and its banks had been trodden into a muddy swamp of hoof-marks and boot-prints. Corpses of beastmen still lay where the creatures had fallen. In the thin light of day, they looked even more warped and corrupted than they had in the heat of combat.

Some men still stumbled around, all looking drained. The ones on their feet were the regular soldiers from Eisenach. The least weary and wounded of those had been corralled into sentry duty and stood in groups further up the slopes, watchful and sullen.

The zealots slept. Their battle-fury had been utterly consuming, and even their unnaturally stimulated bodies needed rest eventually. As the sun had come up and the last of the beastmen had been killed or driven off, they'd collapsed, falling where they'd been standing and sliding quickly into heavy, exhausted slumber. Once unconscious their ravaged faces took on a look of child-like innocence.

No more than two hundred of the fanatic warriors still lived, roughly half of those who had entered the Drakwald and less than a quarter of those, Gartner knew, who'd been mustered at Eisenach by the warrior priest. They'd performed great things, but their campaign was rapidly coming to an end – another engagement on a similar scale would finish them.

The non-zealots had done better at surviving but had proved less effective at killing beastmen. For all that, Gartner had been surprised by the Eisenachers' discipline during the battle. Perhaps after surviving for so long against the undead their backbone had been stiffened beyond what would normally have been expected. Or perhaps, knowing that their homes still lay in semi-dereliction and winter was fast approaching, they just had little enough to lose.

'This is madness,' muttered Gartner, leaning his elbows on his knees and looking out at the scene of devastation.

'We won, didn't we?' said Udo, still chewing.

Gartner gave a hollow snort of a laugh.

'That's all that matters to you?'

Udo shrugged.

'Not at all,' he said. 'I like the process. You know, the killing.'

Gartner gave him a doubtful look.

'You'd do this even if you didn't have a reason, wouldn't you?'

'Aye,' said Udo. 'If I could find a way.'

'Then I hope it's made you happy.'

'It has.' Udo grinned. 'You know, you keep telling me how terrifying the beastmen are. We've fought them twice, and beaten them twice. This place is strange – I'll admit that – but it's not the living hell you promised.'

'Not yet,' said Gartner, refusing to rise to the bait. He didn't feel like arguing with the man about things he could know nothing of.

Udo grunted, and flicked a speck of teeth-picked food from his fingers onto the ground.

'You don't think much of Eichmann either, do you?' he asked.

Gartner looked at him, surprised.

'What do you mean?'

'You think he's weak,' said Udo. 'Burned out. Compromised.'

'No I don't,' said the woodsman. 'At least, not all the time. I do think he's allowed himself to get sucked into a fool's chase, and I think he'll find nothing more than misery waiting for him at the end of it.'

'Like I said, you think he's weak.'

'No, that's not what I said.' Gartner looked up towards the hill to where the ruins stood, guarded by lonely looking sentries. 'I think he's looking for vindication. I think he's begun to doubt what he does, who he is, and he'll keep looking for something to reassure him that it's not all been for nothing. He'll keep at it, chasing down every sniff of heresy, until he finds some really monstrous, really terrifying, creature squatting at the end of it, one whose death will actually mean something.'

Udo shrugged.

'I'll tell you something,' he said. 'You and he both think too much.'

'Perhaps. Or perhaps we need something more in our lives than swinging a maul into the faces of heretics.'

'And as I keep telling him,' said Udo, 'there's really nothing better.'

'Well, you'll get your chance again soon enough.'

Gartner looked away from the ruins, and back over the valley. The stink of the beasts mingled with the growing putrescence of the corpses. If the army didn't move on soon, other creatures would latch on to that scent.

'I hope this priest turns out to be the wrong man, I really do,' said Gartner. 'I hope he's a nobody, a foolish traveller who came here looking for death. I hope this'll end here, and we'll cut our losses and limp back to Eisenach while we still can.'

His elbows slumped back onto his knees.

'I hope that, whoever he is, that man is not Luthor Huss.'

'YOU ARE LUTHOR Huss, priest of Sigmar?' asked Eichmann.

His voice was not unkind, but neither was it soft. The warrior priest had come round less than an hour ago, but the need for haste was pressing and no time could be wasted.

The two of them sat alone in the sanctuary of the ruined chapel. The bodies of the beastmen had been dragged out of it but their stench still hung heavily over the stone. Blood from the night's combat was sprayed across what remained of the walls, and the dry splatters were a muddy brown in the weak sunlight. The altar had

been ripped nearly in two by the huge monster Eichmann had killed, and one half of it listed awkwardly
on its base.

Eichmann leaned against the half that had remained
intact, his arms crossed over his chest. The warrior priest
sat opposite him, slumped against the wall. He sat heavily, his arms loose by his sides. His face wore a vacant
expression, as if he were only half-seeing the objects
around him.

Eichmann took a close look at him, scrutinising the
man as he scrutinised all his subjects. Huss had sustained a number of wounds, some of which looked
serious. His face was badly bruised and his lips were
swollen. His armour, which was of a fine make, had
been badly damaged, and his long cloak had been
ripped nearly to pieces.

The priest must have been fighting for hours before
Eichmann had arrived. The floor of the sanctuary had
been littered with the bodies of beastmen, all of them
killed from terrible, crushing warhammer wounds. If
he hadn't seen it for himself, Eichmann might not have
believed slaying on such a scale were possible.

'I ask you again,' he said, breaking his rule of never
offering a question twice. 'Are you Luthor Huss, priest
of Sigmar?'

The man's eyes flickered up to meet his. They were
mournful eyes, nearly as dark as those of the forest creatures he killed. In those eyes, among many other things,
was hatred.

'I am,' he said. His voice was low and sullen.

'Do you know who I am?' asked Eichmann.

'I see your medallion. I don't know your name.'

'I am of the Middenheim Chapter, working under the
authority of Ferdinand Gorbach, and my name is Lukas

Eichmann. I came here to find you. For a long time, I wondered whether I might have to kill you when I did. Now, after seeing what you did in Eisenach, I have no idea what to do with you. You are an enigma to me, Luthor Huss.'

The priest shot him a gaze of weary loathing.

'You have no jurisdiction over me, Templar,' he said. 'You cannot detain me, and I will not stay here to answer your questions.'

'I saved your life,' said Eichmann.

'You *killed her!*'

The change was instant. Huss's face distorted into a blazing mask of rage. He leapt to his feet in a movement of surprising fluidity and took a single stride towards Eichmann, his hands raised in tight fists.

Eichmann stared back, suppressing the urge to reach for his weapon. He maintained eye contact.

'The girl?' he asked, speaking slowly and calmly. 'I'm sorry. I didn't know she was precious to you.'

For a moment longer, the fire in Huss's eyes roared. His fists trembled, as if he were eager to use them.

Then, just as suddenly as it had arrived, the fervour drained out of him. His shoulders relaxed, and he stumbled back against the wall. His expression sank into emptiness again.

'She was not put in danger needlessly,' said Eichmann, picking his words carefully. 'She was required to identify you. If she had been left behind in the ruins of the town, she would not have been much safer.'

Huss stared at him in accusation, unmollified. The priest's gaze was hard to meet, and Eichmann found himself struggling not to look away. For all his wounds, his grief and his exhaustion, there was something terrifyingly austere and intimidating about the man.

'Why did you come?' asked Huss, bitterly.

'Like I said,' replied Eichmann. 'To find you.'

'Why?'

'Your name, or a corruption of it, is being spoken from here to Middenheim by cultists who barely remember their own. They speak of you as the herald of Sigmar-in-Forest, and mutilate themselves in rites to hasten your coming. Rituals are invoked to raise the dead, to rouse the beasts, to draw them together in an all-consuming coven of destruction. All this is being done in your name.'

'Absurd,' said Huss, shaking his head contemptuously. 'You are mistaken. Look at me – do you see signs of corruption?'

'No, none at all,' said Eichmann. 'Don't mistake me for some neophyte – I know full well how reliable the utterances of heretics and beastmen are – but consider this.'

He uncrossed his arms and placed his hands on the cool stone of the altar.

'They all said the same thing. And the last of them, a creature of darkness I killed in the Drakwald, told me you would be at the Gallowberg. That's how I found you, and that's where we are. We could be in the heart of it before nightfall. So, you see, the predictions have proved rather reliable.'

Huss listened. Despite his earlier outburst, despite his evident exhaustion and grief, he weighed up the words soberly. For a while, he said nothing, digesting the information he'd been given.

Then he let out a long, weary sigh. He looked hollowed out.

'They were trying to kill me,' he said. 'The beasts. Is that not proof enough? You have been misled – you have come here, endangering the ones I endeavoured to spare, for nothing.'

Eichmann smiled wryly.

'Perhaps they had come to kill you,' he said. 'Or perhaps they had come to take you, to deliver you the short distance to the appointed place where your destiny will be made clear. Perhaps you know what that destiny is, or perhaps you do not. You are a man of learning, Father. You know as well as I do that the ways of the enemy are subtle, and that to take the appearance of things for reality is the first of the many errors of our trade. All we have in the end, all any of us have, is faith.'

Huss glared at him, and his expression retained an element of resentful loathing. Underneath it all, though, was a profound seriousness. The priest weighed up what he was told soberly, and Eichmann found himself admiring that. During the short interrogation, he'd found himself admiring much about Huss. Unlike the dregs and filth Eichmann habitually encountered, Huss was a man worthy of his respect. In other circumstances, the two of them might even have been friends.

'So you've found what you came for,' Huss said. 'What does your faith tell you now, witch hunter? What is the next move in your game?'

Eichmann thought carefully before responding. He'd wondered what Luthor Huss would be like for a long time. Now that the man himself stood before him, belligerent and grief-stricken, he felt a splinter of doubt creep into his thinking. If the priest were a heretic, then he felt sure he'd know. For all that, there was something unsettling about the man: a certain darkness in his gaze that he'd seen before in other men, men who'd flirted with damnation or madness.

Not that such considerations made much of a

difference. The demands of the quest remained much the same as they'd ever been.

'The forest is roused against us,' Eichmann said, leaning back against the altar. 'Even if we wanted to fight our way out of it, I suspect we've come too deep. In any case, survival has never been a noble aim for a servant of Sigmar.'

He smiled again, just as wryly as before.

'So we will go to the Gallowberg,' he said. 'We will uncover the darkness at the heart of this, even if it proves the end of us. There may not be redemption for the likes of you and me, but all mysteries must unravel eventually.'

THE BEASTS CAME over the walls, slavering and wheezing. The moon burned pale, flooding the roofs with a sickly, pus-coloured sheen. From somewhere down in the streets below, women were screaming and children bawling. The air fizzed with fear, fuelled by the endless drumming from outside.

They clambered up the walls, racing across the stone as if gravity had no hold on them. They piled over the top, teeth bared in nightmarish, dagger-like rows, hacking out with their borrowed weapons.

He tried to stand firm, braced for the impact like all the others along the narrow wall-top. Though his throat was parched from terror, he kept his halberd held high, and it shook violently.

The first one came at him too fast, ducking under the attacks of others, running straight at him as if he'd been marked out from the beginning. He managed to jerk his halberd blade down, but it was too big for the narrow space and the metal edge *clanked* awkwardly from the stone edge. He saw red eyes in the dark, raging with animal hatred, and felt a heavy cudgel crack into his shoulder, hurling him from the walls.

He plummeted down, spinning into the fiery air as the walls collapsed around him. Those walls were already broken into ruin where the giant monsters crashed through them, bellowing and braying. He saw the ground rush up to meet him, faster and faster, and screwed up his eyes, tensing for the impact...

Rickard Schlecht awoke with a jerk. His eyes snapped open, and he sprang to his feet.

He stood stock-still for a moment, panting feverishly. He didn't know where he was. Goeringen? The place the Father had taken him to, with the big walls and the walking dead?

Memory was slow to come back. He remembered a man with a wide-brimmed hat and a silver medallion. He remembered a march, a long way across the moors, and then a headlong charge through dark trees. He remembered beasts, just like the ones that had come before, but now he could fight them.

He'd run, just as the others had run, loping into battle like a rampaging wolf. He'd killed, and killed again. He licked his lips, tasting dried blood on them. The taste was musty and thick – it wasn't human blood.

Something nagged at him. He felt as if something important had slipped from his mind.

He looked about him, still panting. Others of the Faithful had been woken and were already on the move. Men with heavy armour and bright swords were striding among them in orderly ranks. The army was moving again, resuming the hunt.

That made Schlecht happy. Whenever he was forced to be quiet and still, the bad dreams threatened to come back. He liked marching, and singing the holy songs, and sprinting into battle with the tang of blood making the air taste sacred.

He looked down at his feet and saw the sword that had lain next to him on the ground during his sleep. It was an old sword, in a wound-leather scabbard that had been deeply notched. There was blood on that scabbard, just as there was blood on everything.

That made him think of what he'd forgotten. There was something – someone? – missing. He frowned, picking up the sword and turning it over in the grey sunlight.

For a moment, he was on the edge of grasping it again. He began to form the image of a face, a woman's face – the features of someone who had once shown him kindness. The image was framed with gold, shimmering like corn in a summer breeze.

Like an angel.

Then one of the Faithful, a big man with bloodshot eyes, grabbed him by the shoulders.

'Praise Sigmar! We march!' the man blurted.

The man lumbered off, joining the columns of the surviving Faithful as they mustered for war.

That drove the image out of Schlecht's mind, and he found he couldn't get it back. All he could think of then was the glory of killing, and it made his mouth water. He looked down at the sword in his hands, and it suddenly seemed like nothing more than a good thing to kill with.

Schlecht grinned, and started to run. He kept the sword with him, buckling the scabbard to his belt as he went, thinking how best he might employ it.

The muster excited him. From somewhere, someone started chanting the holy canticles, and he started to join in.

He'd forgotten the dream already, and forgotten what it was that had bothered him. All that remained was the joy that came with the comet, with the gift of the Father.

Perhaps he would see that Father again. Perhaps, as they raced once more into the jaws of struggle, the Father would come among them with the golden warhammer and lead them into victory.

He hoped so. That hope was what drove him onwards, made him strong, gave him the courage to fight the beasts. Without it, he was nothing. Without it, all of them were nothing.

For Rickard Schlecht, there was no longer anything else.

The pain lessened with every stride. It remained with him, but it lessened.

Huss kept his head down as he marched, refusing to look at the human troops around him. He ignored the screaming ranks of the zealots, even though they'd rushed up to him when he'd emerged from the chapel, clamouring for his touch. The other soldiers, most of whom he'd roused into defiance on the walls of Eisenach, kept a respectful distance. Perhaps they were shocked by the state of him – his broken armour and bloodied face. If so, then he cared little. The adulation of mortal men had never been something he'd sought for its own sake. It had been a tool, a means to combat the strengths of the enemy.

He didn't know where it came from, the power to dominate men's minds and turn them into weapons. For as long as he'd pursued his lonely ministry, that had ever been his most potent gift, far more so than his strength at arms or physical endurance. Wherever he chose to exercise such power, men forgot their weaknesses and were transformed into fervent defenders of home and hearth. In the past, he'd led entire armies of zealots in battle across sorcery-blasted plains, sweeping aside the blasphemies of the corrupted in a welter of righteous hatred. The power unleashed by his oratory and example could be frightening.

It frightened him. He'd seen what the zealots turned into when the battles were over. Bereft of foes to attack, they wandered rootlessly, turning their energies towards self-harm and half-coherent mumblings. It was a terrible gift, to be given hope, and so he'd come to give it sparingly, only when it was clear no other choices remained. Those he made into fighters died quickly once their fighting was done, and such sacrifices made his soul ache.

He remembered talking to Mila, out in the wilderness north of Helgag. He'd wanted to explain that to her, as it was clear she saw him as no different to the priests who willingly sent men to die in their stead. Even from the beginning, he'd found himself wanting her approval – for her not to hold him in contempt for what he was.

Those had been secret thoughts, unworthy thoughts.

Imagine! A lord of men held in thrall by a peasant girl!

Huss remembered the childlike hurt in her eyes after she'd caught up with him for the first time, back when he'd attempted to leave her behind after Helgag. She'd not seen the agonised indecision on his face before he'd come back for her.

He almost hadn't come back. He'd almost kept walking, leaving her to whatever fate would have befallen her out in the wilds.

Before he'd returned, he'd spent time rehearsing what he'd say to her. In the end, the words had come out wrongly, just as they so often did when he was forced to speak, not of faith or sacrifice, but of how he felt.

He'd wanted to say so much. He'd wanted to say that his first sight of her in that village, with her jawline set in frightened determination and her blonde hair flying around her face, had nearly made his heart stop. He'd wanted to say that her soul had been visible to him then, blazing like a star in a field of darkness.

He'd wanted to say that her soul had been so achingly pure, so furious and so defiant, that tears had nearly started in his eyes at the sight of it. Only once before had he seen a soul of such piercing vivacity, and it had slipped away.

He'd wanted to say that she should get as far away from him as she could, because all those who stayed close to him either lost their humanity or lost their lives. He was like an apothecary's poison that saw off the disease while ravaging the body. He was dangerous, as lethal as the plague, for he always walked paths of darkness and knew well enough that mortals could not stay on such paths for long.

He'd wanted to say that he'd seen the angelic nature of her soul on that night, and that she was too precious to die in futility, and that her duty was to preserve herself and live, for her destiny could yet be a mighty one, an inspiration to thousands in the times of gathering darkness.

He'd wanted to tell her about Hnel, and what he'd seen there.

What he could never have admitted to himself then was the reason why he didn't say those things. It was not because he became inarticulate when driven to open his mind to others – though that was always true – nor because he feared telling her the truth about her nature. It was because, after so long labouring against the horror and the violence and the diseased of the earth, he'd needed her. He'd needed to be reminded that beauty in humanity endured, that it was worth fighting to protect. Without that, his austere ministry was nothing better than the brutality of those he contested.

So he had let her remain close. It had been weak. Even as he'd slain the undead in their hundreds, driving the frenzy of the Faithful into new heights of savagery, he knew he'd been weak.

Weakness was always punished. Such was the way of the world, which never changed, and which had been ordered by powers of dreadful sagacity long before the fathers of mankind had taken their first timorous steps from beneath the cover of the trees.

As Huss walked, the pain remained with him. It lessened, but it still remained. He barely noticed the light fading from the sky, nor the trunks of the trees growing larger and more twisted. He didn't see the stars come out and the shadows creep across the ground like unravelling ribbons. He didn't hear the gathering roll and murmur of drums, nor the baying of creatures stirring themselves into their battle-frenzy.

Only at the end, as the witch hunter Eichmann drew his rag-tag army into order and frantic cries rang out down the hastily arranged ranks, did he look up and see where the march had taken him.

It was journey's end. Ahead of him, masked by unnatural flames and the moonlit outlines of standing stones, was the Gallowberg.

CHAPTER TWENTY

NO TOWERS STOOD in that cursed place, despite what the whispered stories of old women said. The sides of the valley sloped steeply down, sheer as cliff-edges, enclosing the land within like the rim of a giant cauldron. The trees within the bowl were all distorted, as if giant hands had burst from the earth to rip them into new and grotesque shapes. Branches twisted around on themselves, sprouting bulbous growths that hung low and trembling, seemingly in defiance of gravity. Bushes with thorns the length of a man's forearm stifled the landscape, competing with knots of strangling ivy and bindweed. Everything had a glossy sheen to it, like the dark-green of pine needles, and it glimmered softly under the light of the moons.

Five menhirs had been erected in the centre of the cauldron. Each was over fifty feet tall, blunt and rectangular. The tallest of them was in the centre, and it dominated the land around it. Fires had been lit on the summits of the surrounding four, and they blazed furiously in virulent shades of crimson and purple.

The stone columns exuded ancient malevolence. The air moved strangely in front of them, shaking as if in a haze of heat. Old runes had been beaten into the surfaces, though the wearing years had smoothed their edges and made them impossible to read.

At the base of the pillars, the earth boiled in a quagmire of movement. Lit by many more fires, figures gyrated and writhed, dancing around the standing stones in a long, snaking procession. Humans were there, naked and daubed with blood and pigment. In a blasphemous parody of the natural order, they were driven along by gors carrying barbed flails.

Other creatures stalked in their midst. Undead mingled with the living, limping in scattered bands, their eyes glowing and mouths hanging open. In their wake came malformed beasts from far-off unlit glades – gibbering spawns with a hundred mouths and luminous tentacles, living trees that shuffled forwards with the crack and shiver of creaking bark, packs of scorpion-tailed warhounds with hunched spines and vast, dribbling maws. Spectres hung above them all, translucent and pale, wailing and swooping in lazy arcs. Huge centigors reared up to swipe at the shades as they passed over, roaring in their intoxication before plunging back into the mass of shifting flesh.

The whole place burned with a fever of adulation and expectation. Screams of living men mingled with ecstatic cries of delight. Huge monsters with hides the colour of brass ran amok, goring anything in their path before swerving back drunkenly to take their place in the dance. Skeletal creatures with black robes and skull-masks capered, flinging their skin-stripped arms wide to summon up more infernal energies. Goat-faced shamans held aloft staffs spitting with witchlight, and crackling energies snapped between them.

Above the stone columns, the sky was broken with rapidly swirling tatters of cloud. The moonlight fell in flickering shafts between them, illuminating the revels in shifting frames of sudden light and dark. Clouds of incense, thick and pungent, rolled up from huge braziers, changing through the whole spectrum of colours as they were sucked up towards the summit of the columns. Chunks of warpstone had been nailed to tree trunks in iron caskets, and the eerie rocks glowed with yellow-green light.

Eichmann stood before the sea of madness for a moment, taken aback by the scale of it. He'd read of bacchanals in the forbidden libraries of his order but had always assumed the worst tales had been exaggerated. Now, though, there could be no doubt of their existence. Even from more than two hundred yards away, perched on the southward lip of the cauldron, he could taste the foul perfume of the ceremony at the back of his throat. The air felt dense with it.

The revellers in the cauldron seemed too preoccupied with their own activities to notice the newcomers on the ridge to their south. Eichmann's forces clustered together unhindered, overlooking the debauchery. None of them said a word. None of them moved.

As he watched the spectacle, Eichmann felt paralysis creep over his limbs. The branches of the trees around him rustled in sympathy with the churning winds below. They seemed to whisper half-understood words to him, at once seductive and mocking.

He knew then that everything in that place existed to drink the blood of mortals. The beasts, the spell-summoned creatures, the living dead, the trees, even the stones beneath his feet – all of them shared in that primordial hostility.

Eichmann raised his hand to his face and saw sweat glisten from his palm. He remembered the goat-faced horror with the scythe, the one from his dreams, and instantly felt his heartbeat quicken.

The whole place was soaked in terror. Everything in the forest for miles around, it all drew its corruption from this source.

After so long on the trail of the network of cults and heretics, he had finally found the heart of it all.

Now it would kill him.

'What are your orders?'

Eichmann whirled round, startled out of his thoughts, to see Huss looking up at him calmly.

The priest had chosen to march to the Gallowberg on foot, even though he'd been offered the use of a horse. From his mounted position Eichmann towered over the man but, despite that, Huss still dominated everything in his presence. His bare head shone in the starlight, picking out the bundle of scripture bound tightly to his forehead.

Eichmann took a deep breath, forcing his mind to clarify.

'Can we – can the men – fight that?' he said, not really intending to speak his thoughts out loud. The atmosphere of intimidation was getting to him. Already he could hear murmurs of panic from his troops lined up on the ridge.

'The men can fight anything,' replied Huss, still icy calm.

Udo pushed his steed to the front rank, drawing alongside Eichmann and gazing down at the scene with undisguised relish.

'Agreed, Father,' he said, thudding the head of his maul into his palm. 'I like your attitude. This is what we came for.'

For the first time, Eichmann noticed the physical

similarity between his henchman and the warrior priest. Udo shared the same broad shoulders, coarse features and blunt expression. If Huss had been just a little shorter, a little cruder and a little less literate, they might have been brothers.

Eichmann shook his head, trying to clear the fog of fear from his mind. He knew what the source of it was, and also that it was unworthy of him to give in to it. Above all, he was a Templar of Sigmar, one of the chosen few. He'd seen horrors of all kinds in his long career and had never yet flinched from them. Even when his faith had seemed uncertain, he'd always done his duty.

And so he always would.

'Order the men to form up,' he said, and his voice became stronger as he spoke. 'Assault formations, zealots in the front ranks.'

He drew his rapier, and the steel flashed coldly in the moonlight.

'No quarter, no interrogations,' he said. 'Kill them all.'

UDO WAS THE first to move. He kicked his steed viciously, making the animal buck and kick out before lumbering into a trot, then a canter, then a charging gallop. He guided it down the steep incline, adjusting in the saddle as it leapt across obstacles and around the looming shadows of the ancient trees. The hot air rushed past him, sticky with perfume and musk. As he crouched in the saddle he pulled the maul from his belt and whirled it loosely.

'For the Empire!' he roared, feeling the first spikes of battle-lust kindle in his chest. He didn't really care for the idea of the Empire, for its electors or its laws, but the rallying cry still slipped easily enough from his lips.

The rest of the cavalry caught up with him quickly

enough, and a line of horsemen soon swept along in the fevered night, their spears and swords glittering in the tortured moonlight. Behind them came the zealots, already frothing with anticipation and falling over themselves to get at the enemy. The Eisenachers came on behind, hurriedly forming up into squares and marching down from the ridge with only half-hearted resolve.

The men would need an example if their fear were not to get the better of them. They'd need to see that the foul inhabitants of the cauldron could be killed, and that honest weapons of Imperial steel would bite through their spell-addled flesh.

That was something Udo felt he could readily provide.

The front rank of the cavalry tore across the base of the cauldron and smashed into the outer ring of cultists and beastmen. As the horses charged into the heart of the enemy, the world around them collapsed into a firelit whirl of hacking, rearing and shrieking.

Udo spurred his own mount onwards, carving deep into the reeling press of bodies. He swung the maul around in underhand arcs, enjoying the dull thuds as it repeatedly cracked into the skulls of unprepared heretics. He saw a human woman turn to face him just in time to see the maul-head smash into her surprised face. It came out the other side, dragging a cloud of shattered bone and skin with it before her body collapsed into the mud.

'Ha!' he roared, licking his lips as blood flew across his mouth.

Ahead of him, the bigger creatures were beginning to see the danger. Gors threw their flails aside and took up axes. The dance around the stones faltered, and even the ethereal spectres paused in mid-flight, staring out at the invaders with gaunt, shimmering faces.

Udo kept going, fuelling the momentum of the charge for as long as possible. He could hear the pounding of the other riders close on his heels and took heart from that, knowing that the cavalry spearhead would do its greatest damage in the first stages of the battle.

A knot of beastmen loomed up out of the flickering gloom and Udo's horse ploughed straight into them. Its hooves flew out, breaking the ribcage of one of the beasts and severing the arm of another. Udo lashed out, stooping low in the saddle to hammer down on the reeling creatures.

Then one of them, a gor with a wrinkled face and red eyes, managed to get its axe round, slicing into the horse's chest. The animal screamed and flailed out, kicking the gor away and wounding another with its scything hooves.

The wound, though, had been deep, and the horse crashed to the ground. Udo, prepared for the collapse, leapt from the saddle before the death-throes of his steed could trap him. He spun around, smashing the maul into the oncoming throat of a shaggy-faced gor before switching back to parry an incoming cleaver from another beastman warrior.

All around him, the cavalry charge was grinding to a halt as the press of bodies got denser. Udo saw men torn from their mounts by dozens of bestial hands before being ripped apart. He saw other horsemen choose their moment to dismount, lashing out with their swords as they landed.

Then the zealots arrived. The flagellants flew into contact, their eyes staring with hatred and their improvised weapons hurled around in clumsy swipes. Dozens smashed into the front ranks of the enemy and more arrived with every second.

A bulky gor with a horse-like head and a long cloak of roughly-sewn pelts strode up to him then, hefting a short-staved halberd and pawing the ground in challenge.

Udo looked at the monster quickly, sizing it up and making an instant assessment of where and how to attack it.

'Come on then,' he snarled, beckoning the creature towards him with his free hand and baring his teeth. 'Let's get this started.'

HUSS RAN, AND as he ran he felt his whole body loosen. The pain from his wounds shrank into the background and his muscles responded to the fresh demands on them. His cracked armour shook as his boots hit the earth, but the severed breastplate just about held together.

The battle raged around him. Zealots fought hand-to-hand with beastmen and human cultists. The bloodshed was phenomenal – bodies, both human and mutant, were torn limb from limb in a welter of ferocity. Blood sprayed into the air in fountains, raining down on the combatants and drenching them. Lightning flickered between the five columns, throwing the melee into stark relief. Faces were frozen into grimaces of rage, or screams of pain, or looks of stark horror.

Eichmann's forces had made good headway on the initial charge, taking advantage of the leading slope and pace of the onslaught. Now they were getting bogged down, dragged into a mire of close combat that favoured the enemy. It was hard to tell which side had the greater numbers in the dark and the confusion, but the witch hunter's men were all mortal warriors and the dark forces clustered around the stone pillars possessed monsters and strange beasts out of nightmares.

Huss charged onwards, whispering old prayers and litanies as he went. He saw detachments of Eisenachers peel away from him, aiming to seize a piece of high ground at the base of one of the massive pillars. The tactics were sound, and Eichmann led them well, but it made no difference to him.

He was heading into the centre of it, right down into the beating heart of the horror. The longer the fighting dragged on, the more precarious their position would become, and so the only chance they had was to aim for the dark intelligence at the centre of the army.

Huss could already feel it. Just as at Weismund, so many years ago, he felt the shifting cloud of sorcery rising from the earth. He tasted the nauseating savour on the air, thick with motes of perversion and destruction. When he looked up, gazing at the towering columns of granite and seeing the purple lightning leap between them, he recognised the same hand at work.

Scripture speaks of another darkness, one from beyond the edge of creation, one that spills across the lands of living men.

Chaos.

The head of his warhammer glowed with the golden light of faith, just as it always did when placed amid spores of dark magic. Like a wound washed in alcohol, it flared up in a surge of pure illumination, gilding the outlines of the men around him in a faint lustre.

The zealots came with him. Unlike the regular troops they made no attempt to seize higher ground, nor did they measure their assault and retain formations. They did just as they had done since the siege of Eisenach and threw themselves at the enemy with wild abandon. They sang even as they whirled and danced into combat. They sang as they hacked at the faces of beast-men, and they sang as their weapons were knocked from their hands, and they sang as they were trampled into the mud. Even when downed, they still reached out with vengeful hands, clasping at tufts of hair or trailing cloaks and dragging their opponents back.

A vast, bloated creature wobbled into Huss's path then, surrounded by pink-fleshed and blinded beast-men. The surface of the creature's body warped and changed with every heartbeat – tentacles shot out, only to switch into arms, then shrink back into claws, then dissolve into a splatter of pus and fluid. Maws opened up, ringed with curved incisors and multiple flickering tongues. Quaking curtains of varicoloured flesh rolled across the earth, propelled by short-lived legs and several thrashing tails. A pair of deer's horns remained constant, perched across its shifting spine, perhaps the only remnant of the shape it had once worn.

The spawn of Chaos reared up in front of Huss, spitting a thick column of luminous bile at him from a mouth that had formed only seconds previously. Huss raised his warhammer high, intercepting the torrent of glowing mucus and sending it exploding around him in a rain of spinning, whirling droplets. The zealots, many of whom had kept on running to engage the beastmen, were caught in the torrent and fell to the ground, shrieking and tearing at their shredded skin.

The spawn reared up and eyes popped out from all over its flanks. Each one flashed with ill-focused insanity and hatred. Ebony spikes shot out from between parting membranes, the length of daggers and just as sharp.

Huss strode right into its embrace, lashing out with the warhammer. He flung it round two-handed, generating enormous force with each blow. The metal tore through the cloaks of skin and blubber, ripping it away in a thicket of tendons and lashing strands.

The spawn screamed, sending fresh flurries of vomit at him and stabbing out with its spikes. Where the bile hit Huss's armour it fizzed and boiled violently, eating through the metal like acid. Its spikes clanged from the plate, snapping and twisting as Huss maintained the furious onslaught.

He smashed into it, hammering it backwards and ripping huge chunks of translucent matter from its quivering torso. What remained quickly diminished into a weeping mound of bloody, pus-streaked fat. Its screams of rage became squeals of anguish, and it shrank back from the welter of terrible blows.

Huss gave it no respite. With a final, titanic lunge, he hammered his golden weapon down vertically, shearing the spawn into two halves down the middle. The remnants of the creature exploded in a hurricane of glassy flesh and half-formed horns, spikes and wattles.

A huge cheer rose up from the surviving zealots, most of whom had sprinted into combat with the blind beasts around it. Huss wiped his face free of the translucent blubber. It left red welts where it had touched his skin, but nothing worse. His whole visage seemed to glimmer with a protective halo of golden light, and the dribbles of corruption shrank back from it like oil sliding around a heated pan.

He strode onwards, kicking aside the last seeping fragments of the spawn's demise. The zealots followed him enthusiastically, even those who'd sustained terrible burns from the spawn-bile. The sound of chanting broke out again, as did the old Eisenacher cry of *Death! Death! Death!*

Huss ignored all of that. The only sound that passed his lips was the whispering of prayer. He scanned the battlefield warily as he murmured, his eyes passing over the press of murder and bloodletting that grew in intensity with every passing heartbeat and sword-thrust.

He could feel the presence of the one he'd come to fight. It had been growing in his mind for days, even though it still hadn't formed into a shape or a name yet. He remembered feeling its malice from high on the moors before he'd entered the Drakwald, and he knew its voice from the ghostly image of the child he'd killed amid the lesser standing stones.

It was close, and it was waiting for him. All the hosts of Chaos it had assembled around itself were merely the outskirts of its malice, the trappings of power it had accumulated in order to bring him into its presence.

With a sudden, terrible insight, Huss realised the truth of all that had happened. He had not been hunting the source of the corruption; the source had been hunting him. In a rush of clarity, Eichmann's words echoed once more in his mind.

All this is being done in your name.

Someone – something – had wanted him here from the beginning.

Ahead of Huss, the central pillar loomed up into the swirling cloudscape. It looked vast from close-up, like the tower of a mighty cathedral. The infernal energies lancing through the air met at that column and snaked across the stone, lashing and writhing like bodies in ecstasy.

Huss adjusted his grip on the warhammer, and picked up the pace. His zealots shouted and marched behind him, but he barely heard their clamour. His eyes, his mournful eyes that had always gazed so seriously and so impassively out over a world that never met his expectations, now glittered from the light of ruinous fires. His gaze locked on the base of the central pillar in a stare of such intensity that even the waiting rows of mutated beasts and mutilated heretics shrank back from it.

You may no longer fear the storm; for then, and in truth, you will be the storm.

With his face fixed into a snarl of fury, Huss strode onwards, his fanatical disciples in tow, his every step taking him closer to the pillar of stone and fire.

GARTNER BACKED AWAY, nearly tripping over the gutted corpse of a halberdier and feeling his nerve go at last. His sword dripped with the blood of gors, ungors, humans and undead, but already other creatures were approaching and the sight of them chilled him to the bone.

He'd seen the men around him cut down, one by one. One had been ripped apart by a whole host of chattering creatures – leaping sprites with wicked hooked noses and fingers like daggers. Much of his detachment had fallen trying to resist the charge of a drunken centigor – it had ridden straight through them, scattering men in every direction in a combination of kicking hooves and sweeping spear-blows before finally being brought down. Others had been killed by charges from groups of bellowing gors, or the silent stabs of undead warriors, or snaking blasts of crackling warpstone-energy from hooded shamans. Some of the adversaries hadn't even been recognisable, or were so horrific to look upon that men simply knelt down before them, weeping like children.

The Gallowberg was a living nightmare. The sound of the mutant creatures roaring and screaming made the earth tremble under his feet. Even some of the zealots had gone mad from that, throwing down their weapons or rampaging suicidally into the oncoming formations. Others fought on even when overwhelmed by the terrors around them, stoically resisting to the end.

From somewhere far off, Gartner thought he heard the report of Eichmann's pistol, but then everything was lost in the rush of combat. He'd warned the witch hunter. Despite everything, the man had insisted on pressing on, right into the heart of the forest, even when all hope for return had gone.

Gartner recalled their conversation after Vierturmeburg, and the memory of it was bitter. He should have left then. He'd had his chance, and now it was too late.

'Watch out!'

Gartner jerked his head back, just in time to see a broken-bladed cleaver whistle past him. The blade flew through the air, end over end, before lodging in the trunk of a tree just a few feet away.

Daecher rushed to his side. The man's sour face was bloodied and bruised, and he'd lost his crossbow. The knife he clutched in his left hand looked pitifully insufficient.

'So this is it,' said Gartner grimly, backing away as more gors emerged from the fiery gloom. Rows of red eyes locked on him, and the monsters started to grunt with satisfaction.

'Aye,' said Daecher, staying close and brandishing his knife. 'Damned witch hunters.'

Gartner tried to keep his sword up in a defensive posture as the beastmen circled, but knew it would do little good. It felt like the two of them were the only humans left alive, although the shrieks and screams of the zealots could still be heard from deeper down in the cauldron. The blade shook in front of him, and he was unable to still the tremors.

'I feel like I should say something,' said Gartner, and his voice trembled as much as his weapon did.

'Why?' asked Daecher, stony-faced. The gors broke into a run, nearly a dozen of them, jostling to be first in the line for the kill. 'All that's left is to die.'

Then the beastmen hammered into them, the cleavers came down, and fresh screams rang out into the fevered night.

EICHMANN WHIRLED AROUND, trying to see where Huss had gone. It felt like the warrior priest had only been in the melee for a few moments before disappearing.

Perhaps he'd been killed. If so, then the entire journey had been worse than a waste. After a strong start, the offensive against the mutants had ground into the sand, and his ramshackle army was at risk of disintegrating entirely. The Eisenachers couldn't cope with the febrile air of madness and agony, and most of their detachments had already broken.

They had no answer to the minotaurs and other huge monsters lurking amid the herds. Even when one of those massive creatures was felled at last, another horror, equally devastating, would take its place. Only the zealots still fought with their customary lack of fear, but they'd lost cohesion a long time ago and simply threw themselves at the enemy in scattered bands. Those attacks soaked up some of the enemy's attention, but the death-rate would finish them off soon.

'To me!' roared Eichmann, plunging his rapier into the throat of a beastman before turning to kick a wounded ungor away from him. 'Men of the Empire, to me!'

A determined mix of Eisenachers and Temple troops

still held their ground with him. They'd fought hard to reach the first of the huge stone columns, and now had their work cut out hanging on to the ground they'd won.

'This is hard graft,' grunted Udo, fighting close by in his usual brutal manner. Like all the cavalry troops, he'd long since lost his horse and had been forced back to where Eichmann had rallied the faltering assault. He swung the maul round viciously, taking the head of a grasping skeleton clean off. Behind it, more undead gathered, screaming silently at them. 'Damned hard graft.'

Those words worried Eichmann more than almost anything else. Udo enjoyed fighting even when the odds were long. If he was beginning to lose heart, then their hopes were slim indeed.

'Where'd the priest go?' shouted Eichmann, parrying a counter-thrust from a wounded gor and pressing home the attack.

'No idea,' replied Udo, crashing into the advancing group of undead and laying about him with his maul.

'We need him,' said Eichmann, still fighting hard. Despite its wounds, the gor was persistent and strong. 'Without him...'

Udo cried aloud as one of the undead got a blade through his defence. He fell back, clutching his arm. Two of the Temple men-at-arms rushed to his aid, beating the undead warriors back, but didn't push them very far.

With a dazzling flash of his blade, Eichmann finally dispatched his enemy. Feeling the burn of fatigue in his muscles, he drew back to where Udo leaned against the stone. The big man's face was pale. His jerkin was already soaked with blood.

'Can you fight on?' asked Eichmann. The tone of his

voice was more urgent than he'd meant it to be.

Udo grimaced at him, and nodded.

'Course I can. Just getting started.'

More screams rang out across the enclosed space of the cauldron. It felt as if they'd been hemmed into a bowl of utter hopelessness.

'We can't stay here,' said Eichmann, looking out at the massing ranks of creatures advancing on their position. Even as he watched, another one of his men was borne down by a whole pack of slavering ungors.

'We can't fall back,' said Udo, ripping strips from his shirt and preparing to bandage his wounded arm. 'They'll finish us.'

Eichmann nodded grimly.

'That they will. We're committed now, and only one thing will end it.'

He looked out towards the central pillar of stone, wreathed in boiling flames and lightning. The creatures massed around it were some of the most fearsome of all.

'Get that arm strapped, then muster all the men you can,' said Eichmann, wiping the gore from his rapier. 'We'll strike out for the centre. By the grace of Sigmar, that's now our only hope.'

CHAPTER TWENTY-ONE

THE COLUMN SOARED into the air, massive and dark. Lightning ran up its sides, dancing across the cracked stone. It reeked of beast-musk, blood and fear.

Huss fought his way towards it, sweeping all before him. Gors charged him and were knocked aside. Capering shamans sent bolts of writhing green fire hurtling towards him, but they blew apart harmlessly where they impacted. The golden aura around him had grown, and it shone in the darkness like the crowns of the old kings. Huss's hammerhead swept around, shining with flames of purity and brilliance, and the creatures of darkness withdrew from it in fear.

Huss felt reborn. He knew he'd sustained wounds during the combat, and that they were surely taking their toll on his already ravaged frame. He'd been marching or fighting for days with little rest and knew that he was hovering on the brink of exhaustion.

None of that mattered – the hammerhead whirled with terrifying precision, just as it always did when he was lost in the trance-like state of battle. He moved strongly and easily, defying the fatigue in his limbs. More mutants raced up to him, bellowing or cackling or shrieking with distorted human voices, and he rose to meet them with implacable, deadly silence. The column reared up ahead of him, mere yards away, dark and lightning-crowned.

Huss strode towards it, smashing his way through a whole band of shrieking ungors. As the scrawny bodies scattered away from the whirling warhammer, Huss followed them – and stepped into another realm.

It was like passing through the curtain of a waterfall. One moment, Huss was surrounded by the desperate cut and thrust of battle; the next, he was alone. He stumbled, before righting himself and looking around warily.

Behind him, glimpsed as if through frost on glass, he could see the close press of bodies in combat. The fighters were frozen, locked into the positions they'd adopted at the moment he'd stepped over the threshold. Huss could make out facial expressions of rage and terror, all mixed up together. Human faces were mingled among those of the beasts and the living dead, and it was hard to tell them apart through the glass-like screen.

His heart still thumping, Huss turned back. Inside the unnatural barrier, the world had been altered.

The stone pillar stood at the heart of a shallow bowl of grass. Lightning no longer licked its surfaces, and the stone was smooth and engraved with runes in sharp relief. Blasphemous scripts ran up the nearside face, written in tongues he didn't recognise.

Above the pillar the sky was dark but untroubled. The stars were out, and twinkled in a clear sable sky. Only one moon, the uncorrupted Mannslieb, sailed across the heavens, and its light was clear and vivid.

Huss looked down. The grass beneath his feet was lush and healthy, unspoiled by the tread of warriors or cultists. It was fragrant, like crushed herbs.

'Do you like this world, human?'

The voice came from in front of him, echoing on the warm night air.

Huss looked up. At the base of the stone pillar, hunched against it and leaning on the stone, was a bizarre figure.

Its long face was rattish and bestial. A narrow muzzle shot out from under a sloping brow. Tiny eyes glistened darkly, nestled amid folds of grey skin. Bags bulged under them, tight and shining and lined with black veins. Its hands hung down before it like an ape's, nearly grazing the earth before it. Its back was curved over in a steep arch, and robes of black and purple swayed down from them. It looked like a tattered heap of rags, piled on top of one another in a haphazard fashion.

Huss instantly remembered Weismund. The creature before him shared the same raw stench as the other one had. Just as the other beastman had done, this one carried a burden of dried human heads. They hung from the belt below its distended stomach, nearly touching the ground. As it moved, so did they, and their grey faces spun gently.

The creature leaned heavily on a long, twisted staff. The shaft of it was crested with a bronze bull's head, and it glowed dully in the moonlight. Flickers of balefire ran across its surface, ephemeral and fleeting.

The creature looked small; ruined, somehow. Its voice was strained and guttural, flecked with phlegm and congealed saliva. Apart from its eyes, which were bright and savage, it looked almost ready to expire.

'What are you?' asked Huss, drawing himself up to his full height. His warhammer still glowed with its golden sheen, though the light was dimmer than it had been. Just as at Weismund, the very earth exuded sickness.

The creature shuffled towards him, one step at a time. Movement seemed to pain it.

'I am the herald,' it said. 'What are you?'

Huss watched it carefully. Every nerve in his body screamed at him to move, to lurch forwards and smite the abomination, but his limbs were curiously heavy. The urge to discover more about the creature was strangely overwhelming.

'I am Luthor Huss, servant of Sigmar.'

'No, you're not.'

The beastman laughed, though the mirth was soon lost in racking coughs.

'I know what your name is, human,' it said. 'I know it better than you. I know where you came from, and what your destiny is.'

The deadening power on Huss's limbs grew more intense. He flexed his muscles, watching carefully as the creature drew closer. Two instincts – to lash out, and to find out more – struggled furiously within him.

'No man knows those things,' he said.

The creature stopped walking, halting just a few yards before Huss. At close range, Huss could see the sores across its furred skin. They swelled angrily, ripe to burst, as red as raspberries. Drool ran down from the creature's rattish mouth, thick and coloured with mucus. Its stench rolled out from under its ragged skirts – tart, faecal and repulsive.

'Do you not wish to know your origins, human?' it wheezed. 'They may surprise you. You may discover something about yourself that would trouble you. You may learn the truth of your placement in this decaying world, and those tidings might bring you much grief.'

Huss clutched the shaft of the warhammer more tightly. The motion helped his mind to clear a little.

'I would believe nothing you said.'

'No, you wouldn't,' the creature agreed. 'But words are like seeds: once planted, even in the driest soil, they will grow eventually. My words would torture you, human. They would return to you in the deep of the night, and you would heed them in the end.'

Huss tried to reply, and found that no words would leave his lips. A terrible sense of uncertainty suddenly gripped him. He frowned, trying to retain focus, and found that his limbs did not answer him. The golden light that bathed him flickered, guttering like a candle in a gust of cold night air.

'This place is deadly to you, mortal,' said the creature. It spoke slowly, confidently, careless of the proximity of the warhammer to its fragile skull. 'Strong magicks are woven here. None can help you within this place, for it is outside the laws of time and space. To break such laws requires much skill, much patience, and I have done it for you. Perhaps you should be proud of that.'

Huss felt a creeping coldness in his limbs, starting from the ground and working up. He fought against it, but the chill became stronger. He shivered, and tried to move. By then, even his fingers would not shift.

'You have been brought here because we wish you to serve us,' said the creature. 'A thousand lives have been sacrificed across the Empire in order to make these spells, to draw you to the Gallowberg where your true nature will be unleashed. You will achieve much for us. You will murder and destroy for us. You will be our champion.'

'No,' said Huss, and the effort of dragging a single syllable up from his throat felt massive. The last of the light faded from his warhammer, and the freezing paralysis extended further into his chest.

'That will be your punishment,' the creature said, 'and your vindication. You will learn what we have learned, and glory in it. This is what you will learn: faith is weak. Faith makes you hide behind fictions and legends. It makes you reject gods and invent shadows of them, and yet even shadows can be dangerous. You deceive many with your sermons and your example, and so the eyes of the world's custodians have turned to you. They can transform you, just as they have transformed me.'

Huss felt the muscles of his face begin to tighten. He struggled against the growing effect, straining with every inch of his body against the shroud of powerlessness, but still it grew.

He stared at the creature before him, running his eyes over the collection of charms and totems sewn into the pelts. A crow's head was there. Its collection of human heads clunked gently together as they spun.

'My... name,' he gasped, dragging up resistance from his innermost core, the one part of his body that hadn't been affected yet. 'This... done... in my name.'

The creature's eyes sparkled with malicious amusement.

'Your name?' it said. 'I don't think so. That's just another fiction given to you by that old man. Do you not recognise the name my disciples used? Do you really not know who I am?'

Huss looked into that shrewish face, deep into the animal eyes, and saw a vengeful expression that he knew from long ago.

Hylaeus.

The malice in those eyes was not the deep, unfathomable malice of the Dark Gods, but the raw, youthful malice of petty resentment.

Huss. Hush.

Jealously, arrogance, laziness, greed – they were human emotions of the basest kind, which kindled in every poverty-drained settlement of every corner of the Empire, tempting the weak-minded to atrocities and damnation.

Hirsch.

Huss stared at the monster, unable to look away, and recognised the heads of the old acolytes hanging at its belt. Even in their desiccated state, something of their facial expressions still lingered. He saw Kassel there, and Aldrich. In the centre, disfigured by burn-scars and missing half his jawline, was what remained of Theiss's face.

'You destroyed much the night you left me,' said Hirsch. 'But not everything – the old man couldn't hide it all from us. He tried to, in his shame and cowardice, but he failed. There were books in his chambers, books that I took from the flames that you unleashed. You didn't think I'd learned to read them? I had, mortal. I learned much while you and he lorded it over us, and I kept learning. Those books taught me where true power lies. Theiss knew it, and he surrendered to it in the end. I know it too, and, in time, so shall you.'

Huss stared down at the creature's mutated features in horror. As soon as the words left the beastman's mouth, he knew the truth of them. He could see reflections of Hirsch's old face there, hidden in the mutated folds of skin, the face that had tormented him in his youth. Something of the old, casual wickedness remained, mingled with a new strain of deeper sickness, one that had been gestating for decades.

'I followed his path,' said Hirsch, 'the one he failed to complete, and I kept my hatred of you warm, feeding it fuel during the long years of change and pain. And now I'm here, in the heart of my realm and at the birth of a

new power, one that will serve me in slavery until the
will of mankind to fight us is crushed at last.'

Huss tried to move. Too late, he tried to strike out.
His arms strained against their invisible bonds, but they
held him fast. He felt the veins stand out on his neck as
he struggled. Sweat ran down his forehead, seeping into
the scriptures tied there.

'Resist...' he gasped, speaking as much to himself as
to the debased creature that had once been Hirsch.

The beastman smiled, and the movement exposed
needle teeth and a pinkish rodent tongue.

'For a time, yes,' it said. 'But only for a time.'

SCHLECHT SAW THE Father disappear behind the screen
of ice, and roared with outrage. He lashed out wildly,
slashing out with the sword he'd taken. A human cult-
ist, covered in moving tattoos and with a bone mask
over his shrieking face, met the oncoming blade at the
neck. Schlecht's sword passed through, tearing sinew
free and slewing blood across the battlefield in a long
splatter.

Schlecht could still see the outline of the Father's
body. The stone column was enclosed in a translucent
dome around which the battle raged unhindered. A
clutch of arrows clattered down its smooth sides, and
fire refused to kindle on it. The figures trapped within
the dome appeared to be frozen. The Father was one
of them, but there was another presence there too – a
hunched monstrosity clutching a staff.

Schlecht ran at the dome. He collided with it while
running at full tilt, and bounced away painfully. His
tooth chipped, and he felt a fresh trickle of blood run
down his throat.

He screamed with frustration, hammering at the

unyielding surface with his free hand. The battle still thundering around him suddenly seemed unimportant. The sight of the Father – the man who'd given him everything and banished the horror of remembrance – drove what little restraint remained from him.

His movements became a blur of motion. He tore at his clothes, ripping them from his scar-ridden body. An ungor lurched into his path, reeling back from another zealot's frenzied attack and covered in blood. Schlecht let it go, consumed entirely with the frustration of being unable to reach the Father. He ran at the dome again, and staggered away from it, just as before. He didn't even make a dent.

He became dizzy from the impact, but the disorientation didn't slow him down. He ran at the dome a third time, whirling his borrowed sword in frantic circles.

The blade hit the barrier before he did. Just before the sword collided with it, he heard a strange, echoing sound. The metal trembled in his hands. A warm glow of gold swelled up from the hilt, and he had a fleeting vision of a woman's face again, though he didn't recognise it.

Then the sword plunged through, sinking into the dome's surface like an ingot being plunged into water. He lost his grip on it, and his hand thudded into the barrier.

The blade had gone, passing through the screen and out of reach. Schlecht watched it for a moment, stunned by what had happened. The sword was still visible, glimpsed as if through a misted window in winter, lying on the grass on the far side. It glowed softly, as golden as the Father's hammer had been. The sight of it was mesmerising.

From behind him, he heard the roar of an approaching

beastman. Schlecht turned to face it, barely registering the fact that he had no weapon left with which to hurt it.

A big gor powered towards him. Its shoulders were bunched, rippling with hide-bound muscle. Four horns jutted out from its lowered brow, each tipped with curving spikes of bone.

Schlecht knew then that his tortured life was over. The beast was massive, and there was no time to evade the charge even if he'd wanted to. He watched the animal's red eyes sweep towards him, and a curious elation surged through him.

Rather than attempt to protect himself, Schlecht spread his arms wide, welcoming the attack. As the gor crashed into him, pinning him against the curve of the dome, he felt all four of the horns pierce his chest. It was almost painless – certainly less than the pain he'd experienced when the comet-brand had been burned into his forehead. The sensation was numb, like being doused by a river of ice.

The beast roared in triumph, and tried to withdraw its horns. Schlecht smiled, and grabbed it by the back of the neck. He pulled viciously, hauling the gor's head closer to him in a bizarre parody of an affectionate embrace.

'Praise Sigmar,' he murmured, clinging on to the beastman and preventing it from tearing its horns free of his chest. It thrashed wildly, trying to shake him free and lifting him bodily from the ground.

'Praise the Father, who released me,' whispered Schlecht, feeling an enormous sense of peace descend over him, washing away the horrors of the past weeks and replacing it with a curious, benevolent calmness. He opened his mouth and stared down at the exposed nape of the gor's neck.

'Praise him.'

Then he bit down, hard and swift, ripping into the beast's spine and tearing through the sinews and joints like a man tucking into a hunk of cooked meat.

The gor screamed in agony, bucking and rearing in an attempt to throw Schlecht from its horns. What remained of the zealot's torso was torn up and cracked open by the spikes, but he kept his mouth clamped in place, gnawing away at the spinal cord until it was severed through.

When the two of them collapsed at last, locked together in death, the blood of both of them ran freely together. The two corpses slumped to the gore-soaked earth, intermingled and ravaged.

It was hard to tell where one began and the other ended. The beastman's face was buried in the gore and viscera of Schlecht's chest cavity, but the zealot's head had fallen back on hitting the ground. His eyes, vacant and unseeing, stared up into the lightning-streaked sky. His mouth, running still with a gurgling torrent of blood, was open. His brow, which had been puckered up around the terrible scars given to him by Huss, was smooth and free of care.

As Rickard Schlecht lay in death on the fields of the Gallowberg, alone and surrounded by the rampaging hordes of darkness, his face was cast up to the untrammelled stars wheeling high above the world. And as he had done long ago, back in the days of sunlight and plenty when the earth had seemed both bountiful and good, he faced the heavens, lying on the grass, his face stretched in a wide smile of perfect happiness.

Huss felt the coldness reach his face. His cheeks went taut and brittle, as if crystallising. The pain when it reached his eyes was sharp.

'Did you expect me to let you use your strength?' asked the Hirsch-creature. 'That would not be exactly fair. No, this contest will be for your mind.'

As the words left the creature's mouth, Huss suddenly felt a vast and pressing influx of mental images. He was seized with an overwhelming urge to listen, to absorb, to understand.

He tried to close his eyes, to move his head, to cry out loud – anything that would somehow relieve the terrible pressure. Instead it grew ever more crushing.

Just as before, when he'd stood on the heights of the open land and prayed for guidance, he felt the soul of the Drakwald open up to him. Visions crowded into his mind.

He saw himself at the head of Hirsch's army, striding out from the eaves of the woodland and into the sunlight of the open plains. That army grew with every step he took from the Gallowberg, until thousands upon thousands of beastmen followed in his wake. Their roars were enough to make the very trees bow before them. He led them out up into the highlands, and they destroyed everything they passed through. They laid the towns in waste, drinking the blood of the defenders in fresh orgies of celebration, before moving on to the next one and repeating the carnage.

Nothing stood against them until they came before the cold gates of Middenheim. By then, the number of fell creatures in the host was beyond counting, and they stained the land dark from horizon to horizon. The city's human defenders looked out from their walls, and despaired.

Huss stood at their head, massive and magnificent. His flesh had changed. His bald head had transformed into a lustrous mane of swaying hair. His human features had sunk down into the wide nostrils and heavy fore-head of a bull, and his feet had burst, cloven-hoofed, from his boots. In place of a warhammer, he carried a heavy double-headed axe, and runes of destruction had been painted over his naked chest.

At his side was Hirsch, whispering words of encour-agement and mockery. Together, they looked up at the Ulricsberg and saw the inevitability of their success. Nothing could stand against them. The walls would fall, driven in by the united fury of the wood, and the sacred flame inside would be doused forever.

This is what you can become – mighty beyond the dreams of mankind.

The words entered his mind, creeping through lay-ers of consciousness like curls of smoke. The voice was Hirsch's, though not as distorted as it was in the real world. Something of the old acolyte's mannerisms still remained in that voice – the petulance, the resentment, the spite.

This is what you will become.

Huss saw other visions rush in then, crowding out the picture of Middenheim with fresh impressions. They overlapped one another, blurring and shifting.

He saw Theiss's temple burning, and heard the old man crying out against the irresistible pull of death. He saw himself running from the conflagration, his hands dripping with blood.

Then he saw Hirsch, still in human form, crippled and weak, dragging himself back into the ruined chapel in search of the grimoires that had corrupted Theiss. He saw pages of the forbidden tomes being drawn from the fires, lined with blasphemous images and arcane scripts.

Then he saw Hirsch's long, slow process of transfor-mation. He saw swathes of fatty human tissue being replaced with the tougher hide of a beast, and ice-blue eyes becoming pink, then grey, then black. He felt the power growing within the acolyte's soul, and the grip of dark magic take hold of it at last.

This transition does not take long, once you have given in to the necessity of it. Think of the power!

The vision rippled into new forms. Huss saw a village he didn't recognise, high up in the bleak highlands of the north. He heard a woman crying out, locked in the agony of childbirth, before the view switched to a thick-bodied infant lying naked on a bed of dirty linen. It raged, red-faced and feverish, as puny and weak as any newborn.

Do you know where this is? Do you know the name of the child? I can tell you all of that. I can tell you who you are, mortal.

Huss felt his body begin to change then, and a lurch of panic welled up within him. The visions sheared away, leaving him back in the strange hinterland that lay in the shadow of the stone pillar.

The Hirsch-creature was still there, grinning at him. There was something eerily seductive about the mutant's smile.

'You have never been one with humans,' it said. 'They have never understood you, and you have never understood them. You have always longed to serve the cause of strength, not the cause of weakness. Now you can.'

Huss felt his toes begin to fuse together. He watched strands of hair protrude from the backs of his hands. He felt a terrible itching across his scalp, and knew then that horns were bulging up under the skin, ready to burst out.

'You fear it,' said Hirsch. 'Do not fear it. It will make you immortal. The beasts will serve you, for they know the soul of a warrior when they see one. Forget your shadow-faith. Here is *real* power.'

For a moment then, weakened by confusion and fatigue, Huss allowed himself to consider the gift he was being offered. Hirsch's words, laced with sorcery, penetrated his tortured mind, and they sounded sweet.

He was tired. His body was riven with wounds and his soul was pierced with grief. He had been fighting, alone, for too long. The Empire was frail, reeling after centuries of ceaseless war. Its citizens were corrupt and idle, ever-ready to indulge in petty heresies in exchange for the promise of gold, or safety, or pleasure.

They were not worthy of him. He deserved to serve a mightier cause, one that would reward his warrior's spirit.

'No,' he croaked, and the effort of forcing the words out made his frozen lips crack.

The Hirsch-creature shook its head, and tapped its staff on the ground. Fresh waves of paralysing magic surged up through Huss's body again, stronger than before. He felt like crying aloud from the pain, but his jaw would not open.

'Beware, mortal,' said Hirsch, its eyes glittering. 'Serve as the champion of the wood, or die here, unmourned and alone.'

It shuffled closer, wheezing as it came.

'You can be a servant of the gods, mightier than any before you. You can be Sigmar-in-Forest, as potent as the founder of your race. All shall fall before you on their knees, begging to be spared. All shall worship you.'

The mutant looked deeply into Huss's eyes, and smiled.

'For so long, you have had faith in mankind,' it croaked. 'Think of it – mankind shall have faith in you.'

Once more, the images rushed into his mind.

Once more, he felt his will to resist eroding. For so long, he'd been too weak to do what needed to be done. He'd been one man, alone, fighting against an infinite ocean of corruption.

He could give in. He could transform, just as Hirsch had done, and discover what his destiny had always been in the eyes of dreadful and eternal powers.

He could know, at last, what his real name was. He could know what had brought him to the temple on that storm-lashed night, and where he had come from before that.

For a second longer, he wavered.

'No.'

Speaking the word was even more painful than before. Huss felt blood bubble up in his mouth and spill down his chin. A dark throb broke out behind his eyes, nearly blinding him. Spikes of pain seared up and down his limbs, as potent and vivid as hot irons held against flesh.

'So you've chosen,' said the Hirsch-creature, sounding half-relieved, half-disappointed. Malice re-entered its voice, replacing the fleeting tone of persuasive sugges- tion it had adopted earlier. 'Death it is.'

It withdrew a few paces, breathing heavily as it shuf- fled away. Huss felt the pressure on his arms relax a little, and managed to shift his warhammer by a frac- tion. He pushed back against the dark magic holding him static, straining with every fibre of his being, and managed to take a single, agonised step forwards.

The Hirsch-creature turned and shook its staff. A cor- uscation of witchfire spun into being, spinning like ball lightning over the brass bull's head. The mutant flung the tip forwards, and the witchfire leapt from the staff and smashed directly into the warrior priest.

The frozen shell that had grown up around him shattered, falling to the ground like a rain of broken glass, and Huss was hurled backwards through the air. He landed heavily, ploughing a deep furrow in the earth before coming to rest. His warhammer flew from his hands, landing six feet away in the grass. Witchfire flooded across his body, kindling on his armour and roaring into life.

'Death, and pain,' mused the Hirsch-creature, firing another bolt.

More witchfire screamed across Huss's prone body, and it felt like his spine was being wrenched from his back. Agony flooded through him, burning and blazing with maddening intensity. Huss's back arched, his fists balled and his jaw clenched. The pain was so intense, so absolute, that he couldn't even unlock his mouth to cry out.

'You should have killed me when you could,' said Hirsch.

More bolts slammed into Huss, tearing up what was left of his armour and worming under the fractured plate. Huss felt blood-vessels burst behind his eyes. A rictus of staggering power locked him down, and he was unable even to lift a hand against it, let alone combat the dark magic that tore over him in searing waves. His vision became shaky, blotched with red where blood had got into his eyes. He heard a series of snaps, and only dimly realised the sound was his own ribs breaking. The stench of burning flesh coiled up in his nostrils, choking and intense.

'I was shown the fate of your soul, should you turn down this chance of greatness,' said the Hirsch-creature, flicking its tongue with contempt.

More orbs of witchlight leapt from the staff-tip, gouging out deep wounds and shredding through Huss's broken skin. He was shoved back along the ground by the force of the repeated impacts, right back to where the translucent dome of magic sealed him in from the rest of the world. With the last of his failing strength, Huss tried to push back against the dome, to find some way of rising to his feet, but his fingers slipped on the muddy ground and found no purchase. Something hot and wet burst within him, and a tide of blood exploded from his midriff. The world seemed to list heavily, and a wave of nausea rushed over him.

'It was not a pleasant fate,' said Hirsch, with relish.

Another barrage crashed into Huss's prostrate body, lacerating his now totally exposed chest and boring under his shattered ribcage. The pain became so overwhelming that the individual elements of damage merged into a unified wall of utterly consuming, utterly annihilating excruciation.

Huss's head fell back, and he cried out aloud at last. No defiance was in that cry, nor anger, nor lust for battle. All that remained was a pure cry of desperation, of a mortal soul adrift on a tempest of agony.

His arms fell flat on the ground, stretched out above his head, grasping for some handhold, some respite.

There was no way out, and Huss's fingers scraped along the inner curve of the dome. As his right hand fell to the ground again, limp and defeated, it landed on something solid lying on the ground. Out of instinct alone, he held fast on to it.

A flash of golden flame rippled out, running quickly across his body. Even in the midst of everything else, the touch of it felt strangely warm, strangely wholesome. His fingers closed tightly on what they'd stumbled across.

And then, just then, everything stopped.

CHAPTER TWENTY-TWO

'WHO DO YOU think I am?'

For a while, Huss didn't dare respond. He stayed where he was, listening to the sound of his breathing, and kept his eyes closed.

The pain had gone. Every sensation had gone, save for a nebulous feeling of warmth.

Slowly, warily, Huss opened his eyes.

He could barely see a thing. Everything around him burned with a brilliant golden light. It hurt his eyes, and he squinted through it, half-dazzled.

The source of the light was ahead of him. He couldn't look at it directly, and turned his face away.

'I do not know,' he said, and marvelled at the sound of his own voice.

The rasp he'd carried in his throat since the encounter with the bloodkine was gone. His wounds no longer ached, though he felt painfully raw all across his massive frame, like fresh skin under a lifted scab.

'Do you really not know?'

The voice was elusive. It might have been a man's or a woman's, though it was certainly human. Huss kept trying to look at the speaker, but the light's brilliance confounded him. He caught snatches of waving golden hair, of bone-white robes, but nothing more.

'I saw a soul like yours once,' he said, haltingly. 'In a village, besieged by the dead, alone.'

'And what did you do?'

'I tried to banish it. It wouldn't go away.'

Something like laughter echoed out from the source of the light.

'And then what?'

'It died,' he said, and the grief of memory stabbed at his heart. 'I wasn't strong enough.'

'Death is a transition. All boundaries can be crossed if one has the strength, and if one has the will.'

Huss tried to look at the speaker again, and failed. The light was far more potent than sunlight, and even to come close to it made his eyes weep uncontrollably.

'Who are you?' he asked.

Again, the laugh.

'You know who I was. You know what I am. You've always known, even when your mind overruled your soul and told you otherwise.'

Huss looked down and saw a battered sword in his hand. It was a badly-made weapon; the blade of a poor member of the Empire's armies. It bore the signs of much use, and the long cutting-edge was notched and blunted.

Unlike his own warhammer, there was nothing impressive about it. A thousand such swords were forged every day in village smithies, and each day their bearers were cut down as they wielded them in defence of their lands.

Despite all of that, he gripped it tight.

'Why are you here?' he asked.

The laughter died. When the angel spoke next, the voice was sombre.

'A man once said to you: *The world is a wide place.*

There are devils in it, and monsters, and spirits of the divine, and angels of mercy and grace among them. Those words were true. There are powers within the earth to defy the powers from outside it, such that the heroes of mankind are never truly alone.'

Huss felt the ambient warmth begin to fade. As if from a long way off, he heard the sound of the clash of arms.

'You passed the test, Luthor Huss,' said the angel. 'You were given a choice of destinies.'

'I was tempted.'

'Yes. Who would not have been?'

The golden light began to dissolve, and a chill air, bitter with the stench of burning, wafted over him.

'You resisted,' said the angel. 'That was enough.'

Shouts of men and beasts broke into the silence, and they sounded impossibly hoarse. A rushing noise, like that of a great wind racing across the mountains, began to churn and swirl about him. He felt like he was falling from a terrible height.

As the light faded, Huss found that he could look directly ahead of him. Everything was lost in a welter of rapidly diminishing gold, but he thought he caught a glimpse of two eyes, glinting at him with an earthy humour. Then they too were lost.

'Why?' he asked again.

The earlier answer had not been sufficient. He had no doubt that it was the truth, but it didn't feel like the whole story.

The angel laughed again, but this time from much further away. What remained of its golden aura drained into nothing, like the last rays of sunlight sinking into the fire-tinged darkness of dusk.

'Why did I come back for you, Luthor Huss?' said the angel, and the voice gave away something like exasperated, tolerant affection. 'Because once, in another world, you came back for me.'

EICHMANN RAN HARD, feeling the pain in his lungs grow as he sucked in the corrupted air. With every step he took, his dwindling band of fighters was ground down a little more. Less than a hundred of his men still lived, almost all of them huddled around him and Udo as they hacked their way towards the central stone pillar. The beasts attacked them with undiminished ferocity, knowing full well what they planned to do.

'What is that?' gasped Udo, clutching his wounded arm as he ran.

Eichmann looked up for a moment.

The standing stone loomed up into the night, but its base was lost in a glistening dome of ice-like crystal. The surface of the dome was frosted and translucent, and shapes of struggling figures could just be made out within. Eichmann thought he glimpsed a horrific, hunched rat-outline scuttling backwards, hands raised, followed quickly by the taller silhouette of a man.

'Blood of Sigmar,' he breathed, feeling the scale of dark magic radiating from it. 'I have no–'

He never finished the sentence. With a massive smash, like the crashing of an entire cathedral's stained glass exploding all at once, the dome broke open. Huge fragments of the magic-wound hemisphere flew into the air, flashing and sparkling as they soared upwards and then fell to earth.

All men and beasts in the vicinity threw themselves to the ground, covering their faces as the shards twisted through the air. Violent sparks of lightning snapped across the space between the stones. A rumbling tremor ran across the earth, cracking it open, and gouts of smoke roiled up from the chasms.

Eichmann fell prostrate like the rest of them, then scrabbled in the soil to retrieve his rapier. Something had hit him on the forehead, and he felt the thin trickle of blood running down his temple.

He looked up, feeling dizzy, trying to get his bearings.

Directly ahead of him, right where the dome had stood, two figures were locked in combat. One of them was Huss. His armour was broken open and hung from him, uselessly, in shattered plates. Every movement he made threw out drops of his own blood. He looked horribly wounded, though somehow he managed to stay on his feet.

His eyes were terrible to look at. They blazed from his battered face like two burning stars. In his hands he held two weapons – the massive warhammer he'd carried since Eisenach, and an old-looking sword with a notched blade. He was surrounded with a blazing aura of gold, and whip-curls of glistening power lashed out with every swipe of his huge arms.

Before him cowered a bizarre creature of fur and scraps. It held up a staff, using both hands to try to fend off the attacks on it. Witchfire flickered along the length of it, spitting with dark magic, but such sorcery paled in comparison to the golden fire wreathing the warrior priest.

All around Eichmann, men were beginning to recover themselves. Udo picked himself up gingerly, wincing as fresh bleeding broke out across his wounded arm. Like everyone else, the henchmen looked straight ahead, transfixed by the spectacle before him. Even the beastmen, many of whom had been injured by the rain of crystal fragments, seemed cowed by the display.

The warrior priest was awe-inspiring. Despite his horrific injuries, he wielded the warhammer with over-whelming speed and power. Blow after blow rained down on the cowering mutant-creature, crashing into its sorcerous defence and hurling it back step by step.

After absorbing such huge punishment for a little while longer, the beast's staff finally shattered, spiralling into a hundred pieces. With that, the last of the horrific creature's defences were gone. It tried to scuttle away from Huss, screaming in a mixture of human and animal voices.

Huss strode after it, drawing his warhammer back before releasing it in a devastating downward plunge. The metal crashed onto the retreating mutant's back, felling it in the single blow. Huss stood over its corpse, pounding it further with a series of staggering, earth-shaking strikes. The golden warhammer flew through the air, leaving trails of sparkling gold brilliance in the air behind it.

The screaming was swiftly ended, but still Huss laboured over the corpse of the stricken beast. His face was transfixed with both pain and anger, and the flesh of his exposed arms rippled with the effort of landing such strokes.

What was left of the creature dissolved into nothing more than a wet pool of blood, fur and bone. The earth around it was carved up and churned into a swamp of gore.

Only when the last morsels of solid flesh had been ground into a frothing pulp did Huss finally relent from the onslaught. He turned and faced the rest of the cauldron, and his eyes still raged with implacable fury.

'For the blood of Sigmar!' he roared, throwing his arms wide, and his mighty voice echoed from all corners of the cauldron. In that voice was pain, and vindication, and raging, awesome fury.

At the sound of that cry, even the hardened gors shrank back. The golden miasma swirling around Huss grew in intensity, flaring up in a corona of majesty.

Huss held the warhammer aloft, and the purple lightning that had crackled between the stones for so long suddenly snapped out of existence. Shamans all across the cauldron fell to the ground, clutching at their temples and screaming in sudden, blistering agony. A low, keening murmur passed through the ranks of the beastmen, one of trepidation and uncertainty.

Huss strode out from the ruins, his ruined armour still dripping with blood. Blazing light streamed from his forehead, flickering like the play of summer sun on clear water. The tattered bundle of scripture he'd always worn had unravelled from its wrappings and hung down about his neck like a garland.

Eichmann dragged himself to his feet as Huss approached him. Despite all his battle-hardened experience, the sight of a living saint in the full flow of holy wrath shook him to the core. Huss strode towards him, both weapons in hand, his face set in savage, righteous rage.

As Huss neared the remnants of Eichmann's forces, all of the fighters who had regained their feet, without needing any orders or example, fell to their knees.

Eichmann, having done the same, looked up humbly at Huss as he approached. The aura of gold nearly dazzled him.

'My lord,' he whispered.

Huss didn't look at him. His eyes were fixed on the ranks of creatures still in the Gallowberg. Though there were many of them, outnumbering the human survivors by many times, suddenly that seemed not to matter.

'Rise up!' roared Huss, his massive voice booming across the fiery space and speaking clearly to each one of the remaining mortal souls within that well of darkness. 'Rise up, and forget your despair! Rise up, and forget your sickness! Rise up, and become *great!*'

At that, the battered remains of Eichmann's command got to their feet once more, flocking to the golden figurehead in their midst. Though many carried terrible wounds and had worn fear on their faces like scars, they now thrust their weapons upwards in acclamation.

They had forgotten their fear. All they had left was hope, and it made them strong.

Huss swept onwards, charging into the wavering ranks of the beasts ahead of him. Once more the hammer swept round, crashing into the bodies of the gors and hurling them clear.

Eichmann watched the priest in action, and knew then that they could fight their way free. For the first time since witnessing the Gallowberg in all its horror, he truly believed that death would not find them that night.

'For Sigmar!' he roared, joining in the battle-cries of his men and racing after the warrior priest, his rapier poised and ready for the fighting to come.

And in his eyes, for the first time in years, was the true fire of faith.

CHAPTER TWENTY-THREE

'SO YOU'RE FEELING better?' asked Gorbach.

The old man leaned back in his chair, clasping his hands in front of him as he always did. The late winter sun glinted from the windows of his chambers, doing little to illuminate the space within. A fire crackled in the hearth, which at least provided a little warmth. In the months since Eichmann had returned to Middenheim, the bitter season of cold had begun in earnest.

'Much better, sir,' said the witch hunter. 'Thank you.'

Eichmann sat opposite Gorbach on the far side of the huge desk, just as he had done three months ago when asking permission to go after von Hessler. Most of his wounds had healed up, though he carried fresh scars over much of his body, some of which remained vivid and red.

'You look better,' said Gorbach. 'You've slept?'

'Some of the time.'

'Then tell me what happened.'

Eichmann frowned a little.

'You have my report, sir,' he said.

'I know. It's beautiful. I want to hear it from your own mouth.'

Eichmann collected himself, trying to decide how to start.

'I'm not sure I know myself,' he said. 'I'd begun to think we were all destined to die. We were down to the last of our men, and the forest was burning with magic. If I'd not seen it myself, I'd not have believed it.'

'Just the facts, please.'

'It was the warrior priest, Huss. He emerged from beyond some kind of sorcery, and I've never seen a man fight like it. He dragged us out of there, almost on his own. I don't know what had detained him for so long, but he had already been fighting something and it looked like whatever it was had damn near killed him.'

'He didn't say what it was?'

'He was evasive when I asked him.' Eichmann thought carefully, trying to recall exactly what he'd been told. 'To start with, when we'd just cleared the worst of it and were marching back through the Drakwald, he told me something about a divine presence and a corrupted priest. Then, later, he seemed to change his mind. He said the creature he'd killed had been a sorcerer, and he couldn't be sure that what he'd seen had been real. He didn't say anything about it after that – when I pressed him, he became angry, so I relented.'

'It was your duty to find out the truth,' said Gorbach.

'I know,' said Eichmann. 'Perhaps I should have tried harder, but at that stage we felt lucky just to have survived. In any case, I honestly think he didn't know what had happened. By the time I felt strong enough to raise the matter again, he'd gone.'

'Just like that?'

'Without any warning. From what little I know of the man, that's the way he lives. As soon as we'd drawn clear of the forest and were out of the worst danger, he left us. He took an old sword with him – one that he'd treated like a holy relic ever since the battle, though I have no idea why.'

Eichmann paused then, looking thoughtful.

'The last time I saw him was on the night before he left us,' he said. 'He was standing, alone, looking back at the forest we'd escaped from. I joined him, not really knowing what to say but feeling that I should say something. Despite pursuing him for so long, we'd hardly spoken to one another since our first meeting. I felt awkward about the way I'd treated him, especially after witnessing what he was capable of. In the end, I asked him what he planned to do once we'd returned to Middenheim.'

'What did he say?'

'For a while, he didn't say anything. He'd been badly wounded, and I could tell he was still in a lot of pain, so I didn't press the point. I was about to withdraw when he turned to me and gave a reply, of sorts.'

'Which was?'

Eichmann smiled, hearing the words in his mind again.

'He said that nothing had changed. He said that seeking witches was easy, but that seeking saints was hard, and that his task in that respect was not yet over. I knew then that he wouldn't come back with us, and could sense his desire to return to the wilderness once his strength had returned. The last thing he said to me was that I should remember where the soul of holiness lay – not in the deeds of noble men spoiled by learning, but in the lives of the simple, the ones for whom the Lord Sigmar had cared when alive. If the Empire was destined for salvation, he told me, then it would come from them. He spoke earnestly when he said that.'

Gorbach raised a sceptical eyebrow.

'I'd like to know more about this man,' he said. 'I'll ask the archivists for records of his training and ministry.'

'You can try, sir,' said Eichmann, 'though I've not

found anything on him since coming back. If he has a ministry, then it's of a unique kind.'

'So it seems.' Gorbach shook his head. 'The world is a strange place.'

He got up and walked over to a small side-table, on which rested a crystal decanter and two goblets.

'Drink?' he asked.

Eichmann declined, but Gorbach poured one for himself. He walked back over to the desk and leaned against the side of it.

'You should know that von Hessler is missing,' he said. 'He disappeared soon after you left for the Drakwald. Perhaps he was caught up in the cults you witnessed, or perhaps he feared the noose was closing on him.'

'I could look into that,' said Eichmann. 'If I had your leave, of course.'

Gorbach looked at him carefully.

'Are you sure, Lukas?' he said. 'I'd rather assumed...'

Gorbach trailed off, searching for the right words.

'You've looked tired for a long time,' he said, as kindly as he could. 'The life of a witch hunter is demanding. Perhaps you should think about–'

'I appreciate your concern,' said Eichmann, quietly but firmly, 'but that won't be necessary. I'm ready for duty again.'

Gorbach maintained his steady, inquisitorial look. His old eyes were intense.

'You do look healthier,' he admitted at last. 'The last time I saw you here, I was tempted to order you to rest. Indefinitely.'

'I feel much better. Even Udo has remarked on it.'

'Your henchman?' asked Gorbach, looking sour. 'I hoped he might have fallen by the wayside.'

'Not quite, sir, though I'll pass on those sentiments.'

Gorbach took a sip of wine, looking thoughtful.

'What is it, then?' he asked. 'You've witnessed scenes that would have sent many of my best men mad, and yet you've emerged looking better than I've ever seen you. What am I to think?'

Eichmann shrugged.

'I don't know,' he said, truthfully enough. 'There's much I don't understand. But, if you pressed me, I'd say that the warrior priest was the key. He had a way of stirring the hearts of those around him. Whenever he was fighting, I saw men forget their fear. Even after he'd left them, a little of that resolve remained. Perhaps he knew what power he had over them, or perhaps he didn't – he never seemed to remain long enough to witness the effect he had.'

'So do you feel as they do?'

'In some ways,' said Eichmann. He looked down at his hands. As he did so, the image of Huss entered his mind, vast and imposing, sweeping the enemies of the Empire before him in a storm of wrath and judgement. 'Something has certainly changed. At the least, I've witnessed the power of conviction again – the feats a man may accomplish when he has unshakeable faith.'

Gorbach gave him a shrewd look.

'And do you not have unshakeable faith, Lukas? That is what has always been demanded of a Templar of Sigmar.'

Eichmann looked up, holding the old man's gaze steadily. His lined face, laced with fresh scars across the cheeks, looked proud again, just as it had once done on that far-off day in Altdorf when the white towers had emerged over the horizon and the sun had shone on them.

'Perhaps it had diminished, for a while,' he said, still

seeing the vision of Huss in his mind's eye, his brow crowned with gold and his eyes glittering with fury. 'No longer, though. It is a good feeling, sir, to have it back.'

ABOUT THE AUTHOR

Chris Wraight is a writer of fantasy and science fiction, whose first novel was published in 2008. Since then, he's published books set in the Warhammer, Warhammer 40,000 and Stargate: Atlantis universes. He doesn't own a cat, dog, or augmented hamster (which technically disqualifies him from writing for Black Library), but would quite like to own a tortoise one day. He's based in a leafy bit of south-west England, and when not struggling to meet deadlines enjoys running through scenic parts of it. Read more about his upcoming projects at *www.chriswraight.wordpress.com*